Rachael Treasure lives in southern rural Tasmania with her two young children and an extended family of Kelpies, chooks, horses, cattle and a time-share Toy Poodle called Megatron. She is passionate about encouraging non-readers to read, as well as inspiring farmers to consider regenerative agricultural practices, and animal handlers to better understand their dogs and livestock. Rachael has been the proud patron of Agfest, Tasmania's world-class agricultural field day run by Rural Youth volunteers.

Rachael's first novel, *Jillaroo*, published in 2002, was a bestseller and has become one of Australia's iconic works of fiction, inspiring other country women to contribute to the genre of contemporary rural literature. She has gone on to write four other bestselling novels, two collections of short stories, an anthology of optimistic thinking, a TV drama and two country-rock songs with the Wolfe Brothers. She writes because she wants to inspire everyone about the sacredness of good food production and land care.

 rachaeltreasure.com

 Rachael Treasure

 @rachaeltreasure

Rachael Treasure

Cleanskin Cowgirls

HarperCollins*Publishers*

The newspaper article referred to on pages 344–5 was published in *The Land*, 7 February 2013.

HarperCollins*Publishers*

First published in Australia in 2014
by HarperCollins*Publishers* Australia Pty Limited
ABN 36 009 913 517
harpercollins.com.au

Copyright © Rachael Treasure 2014

The right of Rachael Treasure to be identified as the
author of this work has been asserted by her under
the *Copyright Amendment (Moral Rights) Act 2000*.

HarperCollins*Publishers*
Level 13, 201 Elizabeth Street, Sydney NSW 2000, Australia
Unit D1, 63 Apollo Drive, Rosedale, Auckland 0632, New Zealand
A 53, Sector 57, Noida, UP, India
77–85 Fulham Palace Road, London W6 8JB, United Kingdom
2 Bloor Street East, 20th floor, Toronto, Ontario M4W 1A8, Canada
195 Broadway, New York NY 10007, USA

National Library of Australia Cataloguing-in-Publication entry:

Treasure, Rachael, author.
  Cleanskin cowgirls / Rachael Treasure.
  ISBN: 978 0 7322 9902 6 (paperback)
  ISBN: 978 1 4607 0267 3 (ebook)
  Australian fiction.
A823.4

Cover design by Matt Stanton, HarperCollins Design Studio
Cover images: Girls in car by John P Kelly / The Image Bank / Getty Images;
all other images by shutterstock.com
Author photograph by Alastair Bett
Typesetting by Kirby Jones
Printed and bound in Australia by Griffin Press
The papers used by HarperCollins in the manufacture of this book are a natural, recyclable
product made from wood grown in sustainable plantation forests. The fibre source and
manufacturing processes meet recognised international environmental standards, and carry
certification.

For Claire 'Wooks' Headlam, my tribe

Before enlightenment, chop wood and carry water.

After enlightenment, chop wood and carry water.

Zen proverb, attributed to Hsin Hsin Ming

It is only a thought.

And thoughts can be changed.

Louise Hay

Part One

Prologue

Elsie Jones felt like Alice in Wonderland in a rodeo. She was bronc-riding her way out of life in a crazy brutal rush, getting bucked senseless and not finding any solid spot on the earth to land. Her being was thrown into stardust space, a place that swirled with nothingness. Far off she felt the hard smacks of the paramedics and from outside her body she saw them shining lights in her blank button-like eyes, searching her thin arms for track marks, pinching her cheeks with harsh gloved fingers and exploring her nose for powder. She hardly felt anything, yet she could hear and see *everything*. Not just in the world of now, but everything since time began. It was blissful, then terrifying, then blissful again, depending on where she cast her focus.

'EJ. EJ? What have you taken?' the medico demanded. 'EJ, stay with us.'

Her music manager, Jacinta Tylermore, was standing in her black minxy dress, looking down at EJ's lifeless body.

'Wake up for Christ's sake, EJ, *wake up*!' screamed Jacinta, her kohl-lined eyes wide with panic. 'You stupid bitch!'

She turned to the paramedic. 'Is she gonna die? We can't *afford* for her to die!' Her mouth opened in an Edvard Munch scream as she pressed her palms to her gaunt cheeks. Jacinta jabbed a tantrumous kick to the sole of Elsie's hand-tooled, turquoise-and-tan embellished cowgirl boot. EJ, watching from above, thought they were nice boots, those ones. Texan. Rawhide. In fact everything she saw about herself looked better than good, in her ragged Daisy Duke shorts and the gorgeous emerald-and-silver bustier, so perfectly fitted it plumped her breasts upwards, even lying down. She had never realised just how beautiful she was in physical form, barely able to see the teeny make-up-covered scar above her lip. She had also never realised how little Jacinta respected her, until now. Now, when it was too late.

'In the name of God, *do something*!' Jacinta wailed.

'You're not helping, ma'am,' the paramedic barked. 'What's she on?'

'I don't know. Possibly everything,' Jacinta snapped. 'Silly bitch seemed to be into *everything*, no matter what I said.'

Elsie knew Jacinta was right. She had been into and on *everything*. Every drug every US city had on the menu, along with every hard-dicked urban showbiz cowboy. All the designer clothes and every extravagance, from the purchase of the Nashville property she didn't want to the stupid soft-top pale pink sports car that made her feel like frigging Barbie sitting in a sorbet. Elsie had really wanted a red pick-up truck with an RM Williams sticker on the back declaring she was still an Aussie, but she knew she'd stopped listening to herself years ago. Elsie felt relief wash over her. Now the media and the public couldn't reach her; their savage judgements couldn't hurt her any more.

But just as she had these thoughts, EJ saw her own blackness: it was within her, and it had been the very thing that had attracted all the dark events that had led to this moment. It had consumed her whole being. She saw what the industry had turned her into over the past decade. It hadn't all been Jacinta's fault. She had played along. Elsie tried to reach for that place of knowingness and serenity again as she drifted above her body. She wanted to find, in her last moments of life, a positive stream of thought, so

she shut her mind down and felt the energetic swirl gently lift her
again.

It was a stream that took her to memories of her childhood
pony, Jasper, and her intense love for him. There he was in the
gnarled old orchard, the trees wearing the bare bones of winter,
the chilled wheat-belt wind losing its power on her as she pressed
herself against her pony's warmth and inhaled his baked-bread
smell. As she hugged him, she regathered the feeling of him. The
gift of him. The spark of him. She thought of how life had been
then, when she was a kid, in the purity of just her and Jasper. Of
what life had become. And of life, now, when it was no longer life.
Elsie Jones was drifting away.

'She looks too perfect to die,' came a voice in the chasm.

'Don't be fooled by perfection round these parts,' the paramedic
said blandly to the alchy-thin roadie who'd made the comment.
'Too often dolls in this game end up like this. Ain't no stuffin' in
the middle of most of 'em. Just all looks on the outside. They never
learn it's in the heart that it counts. Until it's too late. A person's
stuffin's in her heart. EJ? Can you hear me, sweetheart?'

Elsie tried to grasp the paramedic's words with her calloused
fingertips, still reddened from three hours of onstage strumming.

Stuffing? she wondered. She felt like saying to him, did he
know what it was like to live under such pressure? People wanting
to either *be* her or to tear her down. She'd had enough of people's
judgements. It was time to go. Now as Elsie floated further away
from the chaos, she noticed how her own pain and the pain
of humanity eased. She began to feel pure love. Without form,
without body, unconditional love was everywhere. It was blissful
and magnificent. At last in that drift she detected a faint glow
in the blackness: a pulsing green light that began to throb, with
red hues on its outer circle, the light's verdant green inner belly
growing steadily more pure and more white in its light.

'Tara,' Elsie heard herself think. Or say aloud? She couldn't be
sure. *Tara.* That was the name that kept coming. The name that
came with a tidal feeling of compassion and love. *Tara.*

Tara? Elsie wondered. Not primary-school-tubby Tara? Tara Green, who went mustering cleanskin cattle with her in the scrub of outback Queensland when Elsie'd bailed on school? The girl she had wounded so deeply so long ago? The one she had hurt so awfully?

Despite her confusion, Elsie wanted to drift towards the light that pulsed with the energy of Tara. It was a spaceless, space-filled, timeless universe of unconditional love. And so she let go. Elsie Jones, current number-one female country-rock music star of the world, simply let go.

When she did, she thought she would drift straight to the light. Onwards to heaven. At that moment of surrender, she never dreamed she would end up back in her hometown of Culvert, New South Wales, Australia.

Jesus, thought Elsie, surely not there? Surely not bloody Culvert? The world's biggest shithole.

One

'One day, I'm going to be famous,' Elsie Jones said to Tara, plucking at brittle wool on a pink moist skin that was slung over the killing-shed rail. It barely had a trace of blood on it, save for where the head used to be. An inside-out sheep, Elsie thought as she watched the last steam clouds of warm life evaporate in the air.

Tara Green dragged a thick chunk of bobbed red-brown hair behind her ear and raised her pasty balloon-shaped face to Elsie. Scraping a gum-tree stick through a river of blood that drained from under the corro wall of the killing shed, Tara began drawing pictures of stick men with giant bellies on the rough concrete. 'Famous? For what?' Tara asked, biting her bottom lip and scrunching her tiny freckled nose. She reminded Elsie of Tara's dumpy shaggy guinea pig, Trev, who was kept under the clothesline at the back of the abattoir house. The creature often shared Tara's diet of Barbecue Shapes, Allen's lollies, plastic-wrapped cheese slices and eighty-cent loaves of white bread, which were usually the only things on offer in the house at mealtimes.

Elsie shrugged her bony shoulders, then let them drop. 'I don't know. Just famous.'

Tara trundled on short legs to an old plasterer's bucket filled to the brim with offal, marking a zig-zaggy trail with her bloodied stick as she went. The offal too was still warm and glistened in the early-morning sun, steam skimming from it.

'If you are going to be famous, then I am going to be *fart-most.*'

'*Fart-most?* What's that?'

Tara giggled. 'The most famous farter in the world! A champion baked-beans eaterer and queen of doing magic poo tricks … and just magic in general, and that.'

'Poo tricks?'

'Wanna see my best magic poo trick?'

Elsie nodded, the blunt-cut ends of her white-blonde fringe dipping over her eyes.

Tara dived her hand into the bucket and sloshed around, searching. The guts were heavy and made sucking and puckering noises as trapped air escaped into the coolness of the day.

Fascinated, Elsie tiptoed in her ballet shoes, leaping lightly over the bloodied drain towards the bucket. She bent over, the bluebell dress clinging to her foal legs in the breeze. The secret inside-out bits that had just spilled from the sheep's carcass were gross and exciting all at once. Clutching her cardigan, Elsie swirled from the smell of the guts. The back of her throat gripped.

At home her parents rarely let her near the sheep yards when the men were working. It wasn't a place for women, according to Elsie's father. The occasional broken-necked wether that smashed against a fence or wobbly-legged pregnant ewe about to slump and die from toxaemia were not things Kelvin Jones believed his little girl should see. Nor should she hear the men's razor-rough words.

'Your father says workmen, stockyards and shearing sheds are not for young ladies,' her mother, Sarah Jones, had tutted with regularity every time Elsie, sitting pony-club-tall in her English riding saddle, had begun to steer Jasper down towards the action again.

'But …' Elsie would begin, knowing her battle was already lost. There would be no helping at shearing, no stock saddle for

Christmas or her birthday (which annoyingly fell on the same day), and no learning to camp draft or play polocrosse. Mixing with the locals in the town of Culvert was a no-no for Elsie, according to her mother. It was pony club, made up of the graziers' children, or nothing. As her mother frequently reminded her, her father held the esteemed dual position of Culvert councillor-mayor, so it was up to Elsie (or rather Eleanor — her Christened name — as her mother constantly reminded her) to behave in a way befitting the daughter of such a dignitary.

The elegant sandstone gateway to their property, Grassmore, was only five kilometres out of town, but aside from the weekdays spent at the Culvert State Primary School, Elsie wasn't ever allowed to visit her one friend, Tara. It felt to Elsie as if her mother was keeping her in prison until it was time for her to go to boarding school, seven hours' drive away in Sydney. In the meantime her mother barely tolerated Culvert Primary and the mothers who gathered for gossip at the gate.

It was a school of eighty kids, where most of the students were home-grown future good-for-nothing generational dole bludgers. There *was* a scattering of kids, like the Nicholsons, from families with little ambition beyond their town but a hefty dose of community martyrdom. They were the types who would take over the footy, bowls and cricket clubs, running them like their mums and dads had. Then there were the few kids like Elsie. Farm kids marking time until their squatter families shipped them off to boarding school to better themselves with a good education and a suitably classed marriage. For Elsie, Culvert Primary was hell, save for her friendship with Tara.

That's why that morning she had been inwardly so excited when her mother had said she was taking Elsie with her to collect the meat from Morton's Abattoir and Butchery. It had meant she might at least see Tara there.

Elsie thought of the sight of her father's ute the week before, the mesh crate on the back filled with six lambs, two-tooths, destined for their farm freezer. She had watched her father drive from the yards, past the back of the double-storey timber homestead with the bluestone extension that her mother called 'the conservatory', and through the black-soil plains sprouting tender green shoots of the coming summer's cereal crops.

'Don't you ride your bugger of a pony on my wheat crop,' Kelvin Jones had said hoitily to his daughter from the open window of his ute before revving away in a waft of diesel.

Elsie had felt suddenly sorry for the lambs and the way they jostled about and cast their noses to the now-moving floor of their confines. But she reasoned that chops were her favourite meal, and that was just how it was on the farm. You ate what you grew. Though not the tonnes of wheat that her dad trucked off in giant bins to the railway grain silos every summer. She could never understand why they bought bread from the local IGA. Elsie had clicked Jasper into a trot and smiled as she watched his winter-feathery hooves indenting trails through the fluffed-up soil that Grassmore's giant tractors had left bare. So what if she got another tongue-lashing? She'd be in trouble anyway. She always was.

Her father, Kelvin Jones, was known for his 'look down your nose' approach to people — even his own wife and kids. He was as hard on his men and dogs as he was on his soil and family. British habits still ingrained four generations on remained evident in him in the form of combed-over hair, moleskin slacks hoisted under a ballooning stomach, polished boots and an air of pomp, despite his sliding fortunes (his council salary was all that had kept the family afloat for years). Kelvin Jones wielded his position and power not just on the farm, but also around the entire community.

Some days Elsie wished he wasn't her father, but most of the time it didn't matter. He was there, but not there. He ignored her unless he was bossing her around. He was always in at the council, leaving instructions for the last remaining farmhands on notepaper lodged under an old branding iron on the machinery-shed bench. And on the nights he was at meetings he left Sarah and Elsie lists of things he wanted seen to in the house. Her father's presence made her cold and confused.

Today Elsie'd left her older brother, Simon, a clone of his father, in his too-short pyjamas on the couch, watching Saturday-morning TV, absently picking his hooked-over nose and scratching the crusty lids off his pimples, to trail her mother to the car.

'Stay,' growled her mother at Marbles. Elsie stroked the old dog's ears as she passed. Because the Morgans from Stradford Estate, the next farm out along the Eastern Highway, had got a Golden Retriever house dog years back, so too had her mother. And because the Morgans had got their daughter, Tilly, a pony and joined the Culvert Pony Club, so too had Elsie's mother.

Elsie sniggered to herself as she clambered into the back seat of the boxy Volvo. The Morgans had a Pajero. It wouldn't be long before they'd have one too.

At the sandstone pillars holding the gates, her mother took a right turn onto the bitumen and it wasn't long until they were passing the old faded signs advertising pies and coffee at the truck stop and servo.

'A new family's bought the roadhouse and the farm from Mr Reid,' Elsie's mother said absently.

Elsie nodded, but Sarah didn't look in the mirror to see if she'd responded.

'You'll have some new children at the school next term. I hope they're nice, but I doubt it.'

The roadhouse and service station lay just before the visitor welcome sign to the town, as if the place wasn't included in the bosom of Culvert's country hospitality. When Davey 'Chopper' Reid owned it, the servo had an air of 'Wild West' about it. It was yet to get a multi-national facelift from the corporate fuel giants, so Chopper, the mechanic cum deep-fryer/pie-warmer operator, had retained its rusty sheds, worn-out bowsers and oil slicks on bare dirt. Elsie'd heard her father saying the new people were mad buying such a dump, but that they'd got it for a song after Chopper Reid's heart had at last given out. Sarah had scoffed that he was a man who dipped into the bain-marie far too often, washing copious cheese-and-garlic deep-fried balls and wingdings down with mid-strength beer at midday, despite Dr Patak's warnings.

Because the Jones family had their own fuel bowsers on Grassmore and a mechanic at the ag machinery dealers at Rington, Elsie's parents had rarely gone to the place. Once or twice on days when the temperature topped forty degrees, Elsie's father had pulled in briefly for lemonade ice blocks to stopper their whingeing on the way home. (Ice creams were deemed 'too dear' by Councillor-Mayor Jones.)

Approaching the servo now, Elsie remembered Mr Reid and his black and gappy teeth and the way his belly pushed his oily overalls out further than Santa Claus's. She wondered if the new owners would be like him.

'I mean really, who would want a service station and what, six hundred acres of ordinary farmland that backs onto the town sewage plant and tip?' her mother mused. Elsie looked to the flat-plain horizon where the sewage ponds could only just be seen from the highway. When the wind blew in a certain direction, the waft blanketed the township in a pall of stench. Her father and his council had been trying for years to do something about it, but funds were always too limited. The outdated ponds and their misplacement had been a thorn in his side since he was first elected as mayor when Elsie was just a newborn.

Elsie's cheeks turned pink as her mother slowed the Volvo and blatantly stared at a beanpole of a man directing a truck laden with fresh bluestone into the yard. He had jet-black hair and broad shoulders beneath his brown flannelette shirt. A slim woman in bib-and-brace overalls was giving a hefty hoick to one of Chopper's old rubber-tyre swans as she threw it up and over into a big skip. She wore her thick golden hair in plaits and a red bandana over her head, and raised her work-gloved hand as they passed. Elsie looked about for children, but there was no sign. Timidly she raised her hand to the woman and the woman smiled.

Elsie slumped back in her seat.

'At least they seem to be cleaning the place up a bit,' Mrs Jones said, speeding up.

Elsie bit her bottom lip, wishing she'd seen the children. On they drove, past the pale brick wall and flagless flagpoles that welcomed visitors to Culvert. The wall bore a rusted collection of metal letters that read *Cul ert we comes yo* .

They passed the thick trunks of date palms that lined the war memorial stretch, then the sports pavilion and footy ground, and the old single-furrow plough mounted out the front of the showgrounds, before they pulled into Morton's Abattoir and Butchery.

Normally her parents only drove past the meatworks on their way to her father's bland red-brick council chambers and its tasteless pine-tree-stump sculpture of a man with a shovel. Elsie looked at the man every time Sarah drove her to school in the barely beating heart of the township; she thought he looked a lot like an alien from *Doctor Who*. Stopping instead at the abattoir felt really weird.

From behind the tank stand Tara was waving and beckoning wildly to Elsie with her round face all aglow. Elsie's mother made a beeline to the ramshackle office, so it was easy for Elsie to sneak away. She followed Tara, her skin prickling with excitement and fear. Tara was like that. She made you feel excited. And happy. Like anything, even scary stuff, was possible.

Now, watching Tara psyching herself up for her 'poo trick', Elsie was pretending not to be squeamish; she laughed nervously as Tara began to draw the guts up out of the bucket. They were pastel pink, like Elsie's shoes, with grey slithery bits. Other parts were a deep dark red, like the fading velvet curtains in the Grassmore ballroom. There were also dull beiges, like her mother's 'classic neutrals'. Elsie never knew there was so much colour inside a sheep. She wondered if her inside bits were the same.

Finally Tara found what she was looking for and, with a flourish, started to draw the intestines up and up, like silk ribbons from a magician's hat. Elsie giggled.

'Ta da!' Tara said, when at last the bowel end of the intestines arrived. 'We have struck it rich!'

Laying the bowel on the concrete, Tara began to manoeuvre the dark shapes that were encased within the intestines with her stick.

'What is it?' gasped Elsie, her cheeks red and her breath shallow.

'Poo sausages.' And with a squeegee action, Tara squelched what Elsie recognised as sheep pellets of dung through the translucent casing and out the soft pink puckered disc of skin at the end. Fascinated, Elsie sucked in a breath before pinching her nose.

'Isn't it amazing?' Tara said, her green eyes bright with joy.

'Tara!' boomed a savage voice.

In unison the little girls startled and spun around.

'You little shit! You bin playin' in the guts agin.'

Elsie looked up at the large shape of a man with arms as thick as tree trunks, his skin covered in an angry swirl of tattoos. His crimson jumper was small so his giant belly spilled out over a cracked black belt studded with silver like a pig-dog's collar. It was Tara's 'stepfather', Dwaine Morton. Next to him stood Elsie's mother, clutching her handbag close, her navy cardigan drawn tightly over her Liberty floral shirt, a frown on her face as she glanced from the strewn offal on the concrete to the girls and back again.

'Eleanor! What on earth? Look at your shoes!' She reached forwards and with long graceful fingers pincered Elsie's arm. 'Come along! Go sit in the car while Mr ... while the man loads our sides of lamb.'

Dwaine Morton smiled a grimace at Elsie as she passed. 'Oh, wait up,' he said. 'I think that little turd Tara has flicked your daughta with a bit of sheep shit, right there on her face.'

Before her mother could say anything, the man was reaching into his pockets with thick sausage fingers that had H-A-T-E tattooed on them. With a hanky that smelled of animal fat and old blood, Dwaine swiped at Elsie's face.

'Oh, sorry,' he said gruffly. He stooped closer when he realised the sheep shit wasn't moving: instead a large dark puckered mole sat above the right side of the kid's perfect lips. 'I didn't realise ...' His words drifted off into the morning air.

Elsie absorbed the sickening feeling of mortification and let her mother steer her away to the car.

'It was so much nicer when old Cartwright did the killing for us at home,' her mother muttered as she got into the car and slammed the door crossly. 'What rough people. I loathe having to come here. But your father said we can't spare the jackaroo any more to do the meat rations.' She sighed and turned the ignition.

In the back seat Elsie fingered the mole on her face: a rubbery stool, like the old leather pouf her father propped his socked feet up on when he read *The Land.* She imagined an ugly warty toad sitting on the mole. With her fingertips she combed her straight hair to cover it and avoided the reflection in the rear-vision mirror of her face and her mother's perfectly lipsticked, unsmiling lips. They never smiled.

For a moment Elsie wished the mole was a scar, caused by the flick of a stockwhip or a branch slashing her as she cantered on Jasper through the garden. A scar would be like a medal worn on her very own flesh. Like the diggers who visited the school for Anzac Day with their medals of war. They had told the class there was no such thing as winning in war. Nobody won. But the medals were important to the old men. It showed they wore scars of war, even if they hadn't had their bodies hurt. At the time Elsie hadn't understood, but now she thought she did. Yes, better if the mole was a scar. But the mole was a mole and it was ugly. Uglier than anything Elsie had ever seen.

Sometimes it grew thick hairs and it was painful to pull them out, as if they were rooted from deep within the bones of her upper jaw. Elsie swallowed the sickness the mole caused into her belly and let it settle there. She wished her mother would say something comforting, but her parents never mentioned the mole. Elsie knew she would be as pretty as a Disney princess without it. She knew her parents knew it too. Everywhere she went she let them down with the mole. Adults stared at it in shock, but said nothing. The kids at school teased her. That was why she and Tara were friends. To the other kids, Tara was the giant ugly toad and Elsie was the strange warty witch. She swivelled in her seat so she could see out the back of the car, over the cardboard boxes of meat now stacked in the back.

As they drove away from the killing shed, Elsie saw Dwaine dragging Tara by the hair to the old house. It was a house whose love seemed to leak from the holes in the walls and spill onto the dead lawn, crawling away to other families. Elsie was sorry Tara lived there. The last thing she saw before the car turned onto the main street was Tara's face, red and blotchy, crying, as her stepfather half dragged her up the steps. He raised his blood-smattered steel cap and kicked her fair on the backside before hurling her past the screen door Tara's mother held open with one gigantic outcast arm. Elsie felt a quiet distrust for the world settle in her core. Poor Tara. She had little chance of becoming fart-most. She had little chance of becoming anything with a life like that. And Elsie realised that she would never be famous either. Not with an ugly mole on her face, and parents like hers.

Two

In the back seat of the Volvo Elsie cupped her hand over her mouth and with her other hand grasped for the sheepskin seat cover in front of her.

'Stop! Stop the car!' she called urgently to her mother, gagging as she did.

The memory of the gut bucket, the smell of the raw fatty meat in the boxes behind her, the vision of Tara getting hauled by the hair and the lingering feeling of the grimy hanky on her face swelled in her stomach and came rolling upwards in a giant heave and in the form of Saturday-morning baked beans on toast.

Her mother glanced in the rear-vision mirror and hit the brakes in panic. If her pristine car interior was forever marred by the faint odour of vomit, lifts for Mrs Morgan could become a potential humiliation. Sarah Jones began screaming, 'Get out! Get out!'

Elsie tumbled from the Volvo, vomiting violently onto the grassy verge outside the roadhouse.

'Aw! Cool!' came the shrill voice of a boy, followed by another shriek of, 'Grab the tape! Let's measure how far she projected that!'

Elsie gave another splutter and up came the coarse edges of toast crusts. She glanced up, eyes watering. Was she seeing double? There before her were two stick boys. All bones and long limbs. They had identical shocks of black sticky-up curly hair and boots that looked five times too big for them and pants and jumpers that looked five times too small so their mismatching socks showed and their sleeves almost came to their elbows. She blinked again.

'Oh, wow! Amazing. Just amazing. The digestive system is extraordinary!' said one.

'What time did you eat breakfast?' demanded the other. 'Most of those beans are still *whole*! Don't you chew? Get the tape!'

The first boy ran to Elsie's grubby, now-vomit-stained ballet shoes. 'Here. Stand on this,' he said, inserting the tape under her toe and extending it out towards the last chunk of vomit seeping into the ground and causing great excitement for the meat ants in the roadside tufted grass. 'Wow. One point five metres. Spectacular. She's beaten your personal best, Zac.'

'Can you see any bile action on the beans?' asked the other.

Elsie gave another retch, thinking she would faint, then she felt her mother's hands on her shoulders.

'Eleanor, get in the car,' Sarah growled.

'Zac! Amos!' came a woman's light voice. 'Leave the poor girl alone! Can't you tell she isn't well?'

The woman, wearing gumboots with a bright purple singlet under her denim overalls, made her way over, dragging off her leather work gloves.

She extended a hand towards Elsie's mother. 'Guinevere Smith,' she said with a perfect smile, 'Gwinnie for short.'

'Sarah Jones, from Grassmore Estate,' Elsie's mother said, but without the smile. 'Just along the way.' She took the woman's hand as if it was germ-riddled.

'Is your little one OK?' Gwinnie tilted her head with genuine concern and sincere enquiry. She laid a hand on Elsie's forehead and made soothing sounds. 'Shall I get her some water?'

'No. Thank you. We're not far from home. She's fine.'

'Boys,' Gwinnie said, frowning a little, 'have some empathy! Stop making notes!' She stooped and addressed Elsie directly, her hand rubbing healing into her bony back. 'I'm sorry, darling. They are a pair! Mad professors from the day they were born. Just like their father.' She turned and glanced towards the beanpole man who was now inserting his index finger into his mouth then holding it up to the wind with a considered expression on his long lean face. She rolled her eyes and smiled. She felt kind to Elsie, the way a mother *should* feel.

'I didn't catch your name, dear?'

'Elsie,' she said quietly, trying to let her hair cover her face, looking down to the ground where the vomit pooled, misery churning within her.

'Actually it's Eleanor,' Sarah Jones corrected. Elsie stiffened. She hated her mother calling her that. Gwinnie ignored Sarah.

'I don't like my full name either. Elsie is a good choice. Such a pretty name. And such a pretty girl. Your mother is very lucky to have a beautiful daughter like you.'

Elsie felt rather than saw her mother's eyes roll at that. She hoped Sarah wouldn't be rude. Perhaps she should try and get back in the car now rather than make her mother impatient.

'Mum,' said one of the twins. 'Mum!' The boy was indicating his own face and vigorously miming wiping it.

'Shush, Zac,' Gwinnie said.

'But Mum, she has some spew on her lip. A bean.'

'Shush!' said Gwinnie, flushing with embarrassment. She leaned over to her son and whispered. The boy's face took on a look of fascination. He stepped towards Elsie, trying to peer through the blonde strands of hair that covered her face to the mole.

'Really?' the boy said, looking back at his mother. 'It's huge! Bigger than a baked bean! Like a broad bean, only black.'

Before Elsie or her mother could react, Mr Smith called out from the shadows of the car garage: 'Zac! Amos! Have you been trying to light your poo again in my workshop? Boys! Come here this instant!'

The two boys looked guiltily at each other before scampering away to their father, explanations already tumbling from their lips.

Gwinnie smiled and raised her eyebrows at Sarah Jones, who was clearly too flummoxed by this unconventional family to summon her usual ice.

'Those boys! Really!' Gwinnie said brightly. 'We encourage their creativity, but some days I wonder!'

'I'd best get Eleanor home. Nice to meet you, Mrs Smith,' Elsie's mother said formally.

'You too, Mrs Jones.' Then Gwinnie laughed a silver-tone laugh. 'Ha! Smith and Jones! How common and everyday we sound. How about you call me Gwinnie?' She stooped to Elsie again. 'I hope you feel better soon, Elsie. And one day you might like to come round and play with the boys. You are always very welcome here.'

'Common indeed,' said Elsie's mother as she slammed the door of the Volvo, clicked on her seatbelt and began to drive away. 'The sooner I get you out of this town and away to boarding school the better!'

Elsie hugged her arms about herself. Boarding school. She would rather be trapped in this smelly town than that. Better crappy Culvert where you could taste your own poo in the air, thought Elsie, than a horrible boarding school.

As they drove the few kilometres to Grassmore and turned onto the long drive, Elsie couldn't shake the image of the two stick boys out of her head. Had they really lit their own poo? she wondered, fascinated. She giggled. Somehow, despite the bleakness of her morning, Elsie felt relief that the strange boys were here. It was as if the stars had aligned over her hometown. Whether the folks of Culvert wanted it or not, the Smith twins had arrived.

Three

'But I'm in Grade Six now!' Rage flushed Elsie's cheeks as she stood in front of her mother, holding Jasper's reins. 'You said I could when I was in Grade Six!'

It was Saturday afternoon and the English-style country garden at Grassmore was vibrating gently with bees. Beyond the box hedge, the giant white weatherboard homestead seemed extra dozy in the summer sun, surrounded by an oasis of shady green and dabbed with vibrant flowers in neatly mulched beds. Elsie could never understand why the garden was so lush and the frazzled farm, criss-crossed by taut fences and dusty red tracks, was so dry. Lately she had begun thinking of the farm as 'Grassless' rather than 'Grassmore'. And on and on her father went about the overdraft. On and on he went about having to work three jobs as farmer, councillor and mayor just to pay for it all. On and on went the lunchtime ABC radio country hour about the slump in grain prices. And on and on everyone went about the drought.

Elsie swiped a fly from her face as Jasper took the bit in his mouth so he could snatch at the roses blooming a second time round in a swathe of blinding summertime white.

'Because,' Sarah Jones answered crossly, smacking the pony's nose, 'I changed my mind.'

Jasper laid his ears flat and tossed his head up and down in annoyance.

'But Muuuum?' Elsie let Jasper reach for another fat bloom.

Sarah Jones groaned and turned her back, making her way over to the compost bin beside the stone garage, tipping out the deadheads from her basket. 'Why do you always answer back? You wear me out.' Her mother thudded the compost bin lid on angrily. A sun-drenched Marbles lifted one ear slightly, then settled back to snoring on the mown grass.

'Why can't I?'

'Because I said, Eleanor. Because it's potentially dangerous. Because it makes us look like we can't afford to drive you. Because what would the other mothers think of me? We can't have the councillor-mayor's daughter out wandering the streets like that.'

'I wouldn't be wandering the streets!' Elsie protested, thinking the 'other mothers' were only Mrs Featherington and Mrs Morgan. 'I only want to ride to school! Now I'm twelve, I'm big enough. It's only a short way. Tara said she'll walk with me.'

'Tara,' her mother scoffed. 'Now that's small comfort. I suppose the walking might be good for her. Her mother ought to be ashamed of herself, letting a child get so fat.'

'But Mum —'

'I can't see why you won't keep the company of more appropriate girls. What's wrong with Scarlett Featherington? Or Tilly Morgan? You seemed to get along well at the last pony club meet. And they were good to you at the Wilsons' tennis picnic.'

Elsie scowled. Her mother had no idea. In the Culvert Gymkhana 'best hands and best seat' class, Tilly Morgan kept muttering the word 'mole' each time she passed Elsie in the show ring. Elsie had sat shame-faced on Jasper: she couldn't cover the mole due to her riding helmet and the ridiculous netting snood her mother had encased her long blonde hair in. Nor, at the tennis party, had her mother noticed Scarlett when she had plucked a date from her scone and squelched it onto her own face just above her lip and said, 'Who am I? Who am I?'

What was the point in explaining anything to her mother? She never spent time with her. She never listened. She never *saw*.

Elsie stomped after her as Sarah made for the next rose bush with her basket and pruning shears. Sarah glanced up, annoyed at the treetop clusters of galahs, engrossed with their own private conversation and busy with their bark-stripping. Jasper dipped his head again to grab whatever he could from the garden. He jerked up a pale pink gladiolus, roots, soil and all, and, after tasting it, tossed it to the ground disapprovingly. Next, with his big yellow teeth, he tore at the neat low box hedge that flanked the lawn, rendering a dent in its perfectly square form.

'Eleanor! Keep that awful pony away from my plants!' Elsie tugged half-heartedly again at Jasper's reins.

'Gwinnie said I could leave Jasper in the paddocks at their house, if you said no to riding on the highway from here,' Elsie continued. 'And I asked Mrs Guthridge when she was on recess duty too, and she said she'd ask Reverend Knopf if I can keep Jasper in the church paddock while I'm at school. There's an old bath for a trough and a tap. Tara and I made sure it works. So if Mrs Guthridge doesn't mind and Reverend Knopf doesn't mind and Gwinnie doesn't —'

'Gwinnie?' Her mother frowned, only half listening.

'You know, Mum. Mrs Smith. The twins' mum.' Elsie did not draw breath. 'If *Mrs Smith* doesn't mind, then it's OK. Elvis said … er … Mr Smith said he wants Jasper's manure anyway.'

Sarah Jones stopped trimming the dead rose heads for a moment. 'Manure? What does he want horse dung for? It's not as if they've done anything with the garden since they've been there. I find that family rather odd. And I find it odd you seem to want to spend so much time with them. They're not appropriate people for us. When you go to boarding school, life will change. And you won't be so … so … involved with them.'

Elsie felt molten lava bubbling up in her chest. The service station *had* changed since the Smiths' arrival. Within the first week Mrs Smith had hung pretty red-checked curtains in the windows of the truck-stop cafeteria. Always on the go, and always cheerfully busy, she'd taken down all Chopper Reid's pictures of big-breasted naked women, then freshly painted the walls a warm white and hung up artful photos she'd taken herself of natural beautiful things like flowers and spiderwebs and leaves.

And although the Smiths still sold the standard fare of pies and chips, chicken wingdings and dim-sims and threw together instant coffees to satisfy the tub-bellied truckies, Gwinnie now also offered cappuccinos and lattes from a proper Italian machine along with herbal teas in groovy teapots with colourful cosies she'd crocheted herself.

There were fresh eggs with orbs of sunshine that her two dozen chooks in their egg-mobile provided for all-day breakfasts for hungry travellers. The tourists often took snaps of the colourful chook caravan Mr Smith towed from paddock to paddock after the sheep had grazed there. And even though Mr Smith, or Elvis as he insisted on being called by Tara and Elsie, had been crook and was often away getting treatment in the city, he and the boys had overhauled the mechanics shop so that it looked clean and tidy, more like a car laboratory.

Sure, the Smiths pilfered a few things from the tip to use as decorations or bricks and timber for shelving or old wooden crates for seating and, yes, everything was second hand, but the Smiths had a way of infusing old things with new energy so they looked more than good. 'Retro' was the word Tara kept bandying around. And 'vintage' with a dash of 'shabby chic'. Tara was always coming up with terms like that, inspired from the magazines she pilfered from the doctor's surgery. Her mother, Nora, was in at the surgery at least three times a week, demanding a new 'description' from Dr Patak for either her suspected 'ammonia' that she'd contracted after a nasty cold or advice on her self-diagnosed 'early-stage old timer's'.

It wasn't just Nora who frequented Dr Patak's rooms. Sarah Jones often complained of a headache, or a sore back from gardening, or general fatigue. Never would she admit she was at the surgery almost as often as Nora, despite her more privileged life.

Unlike Tara's sedentary, depressed mother, who had already destroyed the springs in one rancid couch since living with Dwaine, Gwinnie was always on the go, painting things brightly in a palette of gloriously combined colours, or sewing a jazzy cushion cover, or potting a plant, or cooking a cake to put in the glass cabinet of the truck-stop cafeteria, or icing biscuits for the giant jars on the counter. And since Elvis's cancer, the twins' mother was often found chopping up raw food for the 'good health diet' that she'd put the family on to help with Elvis's recovery. She also cooked up fresh soups from the plentiful vegetables she grew in the old corrugated-iron tanks Mr Smith had cut in half for raised garden beds out the back of the house.

And at the kitchen table after school Tara often sat talking with Gwinnie about 'upcycling', with eyes as bulging as her guinea pig's in her admiration of the twins' mum.

Elsie noticed too that the family never used the words 'sick' or 'ill' or 'cancer'. They always referred to their dad's 'recovery' or his 'journey back to health', although judging by his thinning frame and papery grey skin and lack of hair, Mr Smith was a long way off that. Despite that, the roadhouse buzzed with love and activity. The girls gravitated there whenever they could after school.

Elsie's mum, on the other hand, couldn't bear recycling. She preferred shopping for 'designer new' on twice-annual trips to Sydney. She preferred to patronise the only other café in Culvert, Sylvia's Silverspoon Nursery Café, run by a grazier's wife trying to bring some class to the town.

'And what about Simon?' her mother asked now. 'Is he to walk to school with you and the pony? You know he'll never agree to that. He's already had to delay going to boarding school a year, waiting for you to catch up to him in high school. He's made enough sacrifices for you.'

'But Mum, what about you take him to the Silverspoon for a hot chocolate before school? You could have a coffee, and get some plants for the garden.'

Elsie saw her mother's body language soften a little. She might have been only twelve, but she knew her mum was glad of any excuse to get off the property and away from the endless jobs there, even if she said Culvert was a grubby backwater with no style.

'So? Can I keep Jasper at the Smiths'?'

Her mother let out a huff and, with a slender index finger encased in floral gardening gloves, hooked a loose strand of hair back into her perfect blonde bob. 'You know I don't like your little band of friends. The town is still talking about *that* incident. I can't believe you let the twins —'

'Mum! I've been good since. And it was part of an experiment. And the fire was only in a bathtub at the tip. And we waited for a rainy day, so it was safe.'

Her mother huffed again, placing some cut roses for the house into the basket, before scooping the other side of her bob behind her ear. 'Yes. The problem was what was *in* the bathtub.'

'It was only pig poo.'

'Eleanor!' her mother snapped. 'You know I don't like it. And I won't speak of it. So if I say yes to this riding to school, there are conditions.'

Elsie let out a breath and grimaced. She knew what was coming.

'Number one: you don't ride on the highway. We'll leave the pony at the Smiths'. And number two: if you ride to school each day, you are to go to classical-guitar lessons with Miss Beechcroft twice weekly.'

'But —!'

Her mother held up her gloved hand. Elsie knew the Morgans were sending Tilly to Miss Beechcroft so there'd be no worming out of it. 'Not another word, Eleanor. Not another word.'

Four

The deep blue sky above Culvert puffed with sluggish Monday-morning clouds when Elsie's mother dropped her at the roadhouse before school. Sarah cast Elsie a dark look when she saw Jasper's paddock. Little wire markers adorned with numbered triangular cardboard flags scattered the paddock, marking Jasper's dung piles. Elsie had stood with pink cheeks beside her mother, holding a string halter and lead rope in her tight little hand, knowing full well it was another of Zac and Amos's weird poo experiments. Sarah Jones had twitched a bit with annoyance, then given Elsie stern instructions not to muck around saddling-up. She drove away sedately, her nose in the air, a sullen Simon in the front passenger seat, jaded that he now had to get out of bed half an hour earlier for the sake of his sister's pony riding. Elsie watched as he fingered one of his pimples that had bulged into a sea anemone beneath his chin overnight.

As Elsie unhitched the gate, Jasper nickered, ambling over, ears pricked. Slipping his halter onto his speckled white face, she rubbed his forelock and ears and pressed her cheek to his for a moment.

She thought back to yesterday and the thrill of riding him to the Smiths'. They had set off after a Sunday roast lunch with the last of the mutton from the freezer. She had trit-trotted the short-legged pony along the grassy verge while her mother followed in the Volvo. Jasper's hooves clanked on empty beer cans and bottles that had been tossed from cars by local yobs. Elsie had looked down and wondered why, if it was so dry on the farm, there were still tinges of green grass stems buried in the thick yellow stalks on the roadside. Outside the Grassmore front gateway, Elsie'd had trouble hauling Jasper's head up from the tempting banquet of long native grasses that stretched all the way to Culvert. If what her father said about 'the drought' was true, then why was it only on the farm and not here on the roadside? Did they have too many sheep? Surely her father would know that if it was true — it was so simple, yet why did her father fail to see it?

Elsie had breathed in the hot wind that raced across the flat plains from the west and felt her spirits lift. She was on her pony. And when she was on her pony, the rest of the world and her worries melted away. Soon the roadhouse had come into view. She was beaming by the time Amos and Zac ran out to meet her, both boys' smiles matching her own at seeing the cute pony standing near the bowsers. Today the boys were wearing Hawaiian-print shorts, Zac's blue and Amos's green, teamed awkwardly with *Star Wars* T-shirts. Elsie had at last learned to tell the boys apart by the fact Zac had ever so slightly curlier hair.

'He's so totally divine and equine!' Amos said.

'And astronomically economical!' said Zac. 'Only one horsepower.' He had put his small lean hand on Jasper's already sweating neck. 'He won't need much petrol.' He took the pump from its cradle and waved it in Jasper's direction. 'Where do I fill him up, miss?' He grinned up at Elsie, the sun illuminating the light sprinkling of freckles that ran over his nose and cheeks. 'Did you know that animal methane is a sustainable closed carbon system, whereas the carbon emitted from fossil fuels is finite and very damaging to our ozone layer?'

'No. I did not,' said Elsie.

'Why, I ask you, are we, the Smiths, running a *petrol* station for cars when we ought to be servicing poo-nies who do poos for the birds and the bees and the air and the trees?'

Elsie smiled down at him and rolled her eyes. She was used to the twins' daggy humour now since they had moved to Culvert over a year earlier. Often their science jokes and comments went over her and Tara's heads, and the girls would look at the boys in bewilderment, but other times they couldn't breathe for laughing at their silly banter. They had never met anyone as clever as Zac and Amos, but they'd also never met anyone as dorky or daggy either. Even Culvert's Deputy Mayor Cuthbertson Rogerson's son, the pale, red-haired, skinny-limbed hyperactive Nathanial, was less weird and received less teasing than the twins. Some days, thought Elsie, it was embarrassing to be their friends, but at the same time, they were a refuge. The Culvert State Primary School was a battleground. Standing alongside Tara and the twins was better than standing alone and facing the wrath that Scarlett and Tilly could conjure with their peers when the teachers weren't about.

Elsie had jumped from Jasper's back and lifted the pony's tail. 'The nozzle goes in here, but I've lost the cap.'

As Zac pretended to fill the pony, Amos bent his long lean body over like a set square and began to wheeze laughter.

The sound of the Volvo's slamming door and Sarah Jones's voice evaporated their mood. 'Eleanor!' She wore her standard Sunday farm-day clothes of navy linen trousers and a floral over-shirt and pearls, looking extremely uncreased despite the heat of the afternoon.

Gwinnie Smith came banging through the screen door of the house and onto the verandah in a crumpled light blue sundress, her blonde hair sticking to her sweating brow. The freedom of the dress and her tanned lithe limbs echoed her youth in the eighties, pre-twins. She stepped into waiting thongs and almost floated down from the verandah towards them with a smile beaming on her face. 'Oh! Look! Your pony! He's so sweeeeet!'

She's always so cheerful, Elsie thought. So were the boys. It was as if they lived in a magic land. Even with Mr Smith's cancer, they were still always smiling. And joking and laughing.

'Sweet like you, Elsie my girl!' said Gwinnie as she gathered Elsie up in a warm hug and kissed her on the top of her head. 'Every time I see you, you make me long for a daughter. Dear girl. Once Mr Smith is well, I'll have to have a word with him! He needs to get back in the saddle and give me a baby girl!' She delivered a wide grin and a cheeky elbow nudge to Sarah Jones, who was flushing from simply being seen at the truck stop. Normally Sarah's Sunday afternoons were reserved for tennis with the Featheringtons, Miss Beechcroft or the Morgans, but this week was cancelled because the Featheringtons were away at their beach house. Not impressed by the blatant disclosure by Gwinnie Smith of her private bedroom status with her husband, and missing the routine of the weekend tennis, she hustled Elsie along.

'I must get back. Your father will be expecting me back to replay *Landline* for him on the video. Find a place for your saddle and bridle. I'm sure the twins will help.'

'I can't entice you in for a cup of tea?' offered Gwinnie, her summer-wheat-coloured hair lifting slightly in the warm afternoon breeze.

'No, you can't,' said Sarah matter-of-factly. Elsie's whole being cringed.

'Zac! Amos!' called Elvis from within the deep belly of the machinery shed. 'Have you boys been playing with the workshop toilet again?'

Both boys scurried towards their father's shed and Gwinnie gave Sarah a rueful look.

The slamming of the Volvo door and the aggressive rev of the engine told them what Sarah Jones thought about the situation.

Her mother had been no more civil this morning to the Smiths, driving off without even going into the roadhouse to see Gwinnie.

Elsie decided to push her thoughts of her mother aside. The important thing was Jasper was here and she was about to ride to school on him!

'Hello, boy,' she said happily. This was her dream come true. She led him out of the paddock and over to the mechanics shop, where she had left her saddle yesterday. Elsie passed the café window and Gwinnie waved enthusiastically from inside as she set down plates of breakfast in front of some travellers. The man and woman, clearly grey nomads given the caravan parked out front, were sitting prime position in the sunny window, obviously loving the warm Culvert welcome Gwinnie was dishing up along with free-range eggs, crispy bacon and creamy coffee.

Elsie was still smiling from the sight as she rolled the giant wooden door of the workshop back. It took some time for her eyes to adjust to the cool shady interior of the shed. There she saw Elvis Smith under the hoist, casting a bright light up into the guts of Miss Beechcroft's green VW and indicating to Zac what needed adjusting. Zac, a long curl of dark hair dropping over one eye, was biting his bottom lip with effort and hauling on a silver shifter as he stood on a milk crate. Amos was at the workbench taking a part out of a box, while on the CD player Johnny Cash was hearing a train a'comin.

Elsie smiled even wider. She loved this family. They were always up to something. The boys were never far from the shed, joyfully helping their father, who had his good days and then his not-so-good days.

'Hiya, Cowgirl Jane!' Mr Smith said when he saw Elsie. 'And hello to your trusty mustang.' Both boys grinned to see Elsie and the pony framed in the bright square of morning sun.

'Must be school time!' Elvis said, taking the shifter from Zac. 'Thanks, boy-o. Best get that grease off your hands, go kiss your mother and we'll fix Miss B's Beetle up after school.'

Elvis drew Zac into a hug and Elsie felt her heart tug a little as she watched her friend close his eyes, smile softly and hug his father back.

'Thanks again for your help,' he said, ruffling the boy's hair.

Amos put down the part on the workbench, ran to his dad and offered up a 'see-ya' hug too. Releasing both boys from his long arms, Elvis began to sing along to Johnny Cash shooting a man in Reno. Elsie turned the pony away and tried to remember the last time her father had hugged her. She couldn't. Had he even hugged her as a baby? She couldn't remember a single time.

With Jasper saddled, Elsie, holding a fresh warm cheese muffin provided by Gwinnie, posed awkwardly for the caravaners as they clicked a shot on their camera of the cute kid on the pony. Elsie made sure she turned her head away, as she did in all photos, so only the acceptable side of her face showed, though the position of the mole made it virtually impossible to hide.

'Look this way, sweetie!' called the man with the camera. 'Smile!' Her cheeks burned with self-consciousness, but soon to her relief the elderly couple were on their way and the twins were walking beside her in their rumpled hotchpotch second-hand uniforms stained with motor oil. Jasper moved forwards on lively little legs and Elsie relished the weight of her backpack bouncing on the curve of her saddle behind her. Her bare legs against the stirrup leathers and the thinness of her school uniform against the hot leather felt more than weird, but she chose to ignore it all. Her mother had tut-tutted her for wearing her school dress, suggesting she would be better off riding in her tracksuit, but Elsie had refused to change. The checked blue dress would be fine for the fifteen-minute trundle on the pony from the outskirts of town. Elsie sighed. She was in horse heaven. Especially with Amos and Zac beside her, and soon Tara. This was the best day of her life.

'How much do you reckon he eats?' Zac asked, squinting up at Elsie against the glare of the morning sun and laying a hand on the pony's neck. A magpie warbled from a straggly roadside gum as if to enquire too.

Elsie shrugged. 'I don't know. Lots. He's always eating.'

'We're attempting to establish how often he poos,' Amos said. 'And what his poo weighs, but we're having trouble calculating the input. Maybe we could put him in the sheep yards for a set period of time and record the weight of his tucker, then after he eats, how often he goes and how much his poo weighs? Then Dad's got some lab tests he wants to run.'

'Yeah!' said Zac, adjusting the strap of his canvas bag and tugging up his grey school trousers. 'Could we, Elsie? Just for a bit. He wouldn't be in the yard for long.'

'What do you want to do all this for?' Elsie asked.

'Oh, you know. Just as an experiment. It's something Dad and us are cooking up.'

Elsie smiled and looked down to the boys. 'Doesn't sound like it would taste too nice … whatever it is you're cooking.'

They both grinned back at her, each almost a carbon copy of the other.

'There's always something to cook up in life,' Amos said. 'No point sitting still. Mum says the world is full of infinite possibility if you believe it, and as we live in an expanding universe directed by the vibrational energy of human thought, anything truly is possible. Theoretically,' Amos said.

'Or realistically, depending on what you believe,' Zac added.

Elsie shrugged and wove her fingers through Jasper's mane as the pony pricked his ears towards the unusual smell of Morton's Abattoir and Butchery, now looming on their left.

'Sure. Anything's possible. The experiment sounds great. Whatever it is you are talking about. Infinite poo-sibilities! Measure his poo if you like,' Elsie said.

'Fantastic!' said Zac excitedly. 'We can set up the ex-poo-riment tonight!'

From her hazy cracked window, Tara felt the prick of tears when she saw Elsie riding along the roadside with Zac and Amos walking and laughing beside her.

'Oh, phew.' She was so grateful the day was beginning with her friends. She took in how pretty Jasper looked with his ears cast forwards and head raised. He carried his tail high and was swishing it in the golden morning sunlight. But Tara realised he wasn't prancing happily. He was acting up because of the abattoir sheds and the stench of death that reeked from the place. Elsie had to kick him on and reassure him at the same time. Tara breathed inwards sharply; the shame of her home settled within her bones like a cancer. She watched as Zac reached for the reins and helped lead Jasper up to the front lawn, if it could have been called that.

She saw Amos put two fingers in his mouth and let rip with a loud whistle. Even her brave friends were too scared to come knocking on the door.

She turned away from the window. The poor pony will get used to it, Tara thought. She had had to when her mother moved in with Dwaine. Tara knew you could get used to a lot of stuff if you made yourself think about other things.

She fought down her tears, walked from her bedroom, retrieved her scuffed school shoes from a dead pot plant and pulled them on, not retying the laces. Her aim was to get through the entire school term without ever untying the knots. They were her lucky knots, she had told herself, and they kept her safe on a pathway with angels. Shoes on, she stepped over the empty cans, bottles and food packets scattered on the grimy brown carpet in the lounge room. On her way past the cluttered kitchen table she reached for another handful of stale salt-and-vinegar chips and scooped some cold baked beans out of an already open tin and spooned them into her mouth, washing them down with a swig of Passiona, before grabbing up her school bag. She hastily looked inside to make sure Trev her guinea pig was still happily nestled in there with the fresh blades of grass she'd torn from the base of the abattoir tap earlier that morning. Tara was about to call out, 'See ya,' to her mother, but then she thought, what's the point?

It wasn't a kill day today so her mother and Dwaine were still snoring their heads off, smelling manky from all the Jim Beam they had drunk the night before. She hated nights before a non-kill day at the abattoir house. The gloom of no sleep, Dwaine's angry shouts at the Fox Sports coverage of the dish-lickers as another greyhound he backed failed to finish in a place. The fug of cigarette smoke crawling uninvited under her bedroom door. Her mother crunching her way through chips, then chocolate, then lollies. Washed down with Beam. Then later. When her mother was passed out from booze and sugar, the creak of the door and another uninvited visitor.

Dwaine's steps wavered and his weight was solid and ugly. The smell of animal fat, smokes, booze and urine. The press of one pudgy palm over her mouth while the other hand, which had each stubby sausage finger tattooed with the letters L-O-V-E on their back, stubbed into her. Tara would scrunch her eyes tight and pull her mind into a tiny pinprick of light. She would wait until she had controlled the hot panicked breath that flew rapidly in and out of her two small nostrils. When she roped in her panic so that her breath came slowly, she would then feel her body soften. She could float out and hover in the realm of angels she had danced with in her dreams.

All the while, the toad-like form of Dwaine pumped with his own hot breath in and out. When he spilled himself onto her, he would let out a quiet moan, like a drought-thirsty beast dying in a pool of its own muck. He would stumble off into the distasteful darkness of the house and climb into stained sheets beside Tara's mother.

When she heard him begin to snore, a fear-frozen Tara would roll over and hug her knees to her chest, reach under her pillow for the silvery wrapped chocolate she had placed there earlier for this exact moment and, sucking on the chocolate, she would cry herself softly to sleep, begging the angels and fairies to come and play with her in her dreams.

Now, with the sun raining down outside, Tara ran from the dimness of the stale house, slamming the door. She was a kid again, standing with her friends. The sunshine was too pure to let the craziness of the night cloak her any more.

'Wow! A real live unicorn on my lawn!' she said, jumping up and down in front of Jasper, who was rubbing the sweating line beneath his brow band on his outstretched leg. She felt the shadows of the house sliding off her skin up to the puffy white clouds that drifted by. She found a mint in her school uniform pocket and shoved it in her mouth.

'Unicorns are a mythical beast, Tara,' Amos said matter-of-factly.

'Ohnee if oo fink ay are,' Tara said as she chewed on the mint and swallowed. 'Jasper is definitely a unicorn. You just can't see his horn in the daylight. The moonlight makes it visible and on a full moon you can actually see his wings.'

'Really,' said Zac sceptically.

'Yes, really,' Tara said. 'It's true, isn't it, Elsie?'

From up on Jasper's back Elsie looked down at her friend, whose face was pleading up at her as if everything depended on her answer. Tara had a ring of baked-bean sauce around her lips and her hair wasn't brushed again this morning. Elsie frowned but also smiled at the same time.

'Yes,' Elsie said. 'It's true. Amos himself told me it was a world of infinite possibilities, which he then told me means that anything is possible. So yes, Jasper is, in fact, *very* possibly a unicorn.'

'Touché!' Zac said, shoving Amos. 'She gazumped you! She's right.'

Elsie saw Tara's body relax and then the four of them, along with the little white pony and Trev the guinea pig, made their way towards Culvert State Primary School. What would a life look like, Tara wondered, if anything really was possible? She unhitched her undies from her backside and swung her little legs out wider so her inner thighs didn't rub so much. For a start, in her world of imaginings she would leave Culvert and never come back.

'Today is going to be a great day!' she said. 'I can feel it!'

They were just walking past what they all called the Dolls' House, where the town's recluse, Mr Queen, lived, when, from over the high private fence around the beautiful leafy garden of his perfectly gorgeous storybook house, he turned the hose on them.

'Begone, varmints!' Mr Queen cried out in his shaky old-man voice. Jasper shied, Tara squealed and the twins laughed before they all hurried on their way.

Five

The shit ponds, as the local kids called them, lay adjacent to the Smiths' six-hundred-acre farm behind a high woven-link metal fence. As if the sturdy seven-foot fence wasn't enough of a pronouncement that human poo must be dangerous stuff, two strands of barb had also been strung across the top. Seven pink-bellied galahs perched there now, chattering above Dolly Parton's 'Coat of Many Colours', which was drifting from Elvis Smith's ute speakers. The raucous birds were also tilting their heads, keeping one eye on the human activity below.

Elvis and the twins were unloading timber lengths from the ute and stacking them inside a giant old weatherboard-and-corro farm shed. Over the years the huge shed had acquired a lean due to the steady push of the plains winds. Beside the shed a clump of ironbarks mimicked the shed's easterly stagger.

Tara, perched on the thick bullbar of the ute, Trev nestled on her lap, sucked on her cola Chupa Chup and looked up at the fence. 'Who would want to break into a sewage plant?'

Elsie followed her gaze to the raised beds of the sewage ponds and the brittle tufted grass that surrounded them. Further, beyond the ponds, were a large Colorbond shed, a cluster of higher tanks linked with large piping and a pathway to a small portable office, outside which a white Culvert Council vehicle was parked beneath the far-from-generous shade of an old contorted gum. Beyond that, behind yet another fence, a small rusted yellow Bobcat dawdled over the humps of the rubbish tip beneath a cloud of circling birds.

Scratching her calf beneath her school sock, Tara looked up at the twisted, jagged barbwire. The fence reminded her of the bleak war films Dwaine watched in the dead of night. The too-loud movie soundtracks would rip through the abattoir house, ricochet off the furniture and smatter up the walls, rattling Tara's fairy pictures on the other side and blasting flickering light under her door as she battled to sleep. Tara pulled the Chupa Chup out and twisted her mouth from side to side as she pondered how people-poo in a pond could invite break-ins. Elsie, who was sitting on Jasper, rubbing her reddened knees, was again reminded of Trev as Tara jutted her top teeth over her bottom lip and thought deeply.

'Kids, I suppose,' Elsie offered.

'Yeah, but we're kids and do we want to break into the shit ponds?'

'Well, we broke into the tip.'

'We didn't break in. The gate was open,' Tara reasoned.

'Yeah, but the shit ponds? I wouldn't want to get in there. If I did, Mum would kill me anyway. I dunno,' said Elsie, struggling with Jasper as he tried to rub his sweaty forelock on Tara. The warm afternoon breeze shifted its direction and thankfully took the waft of the ponds away to the east.

Elsie grinned. 'Maybe it's the poo that wants to break out,' she said, 'and rampage through Culvert.'

'Yes! That's it!' Tara's eyes were wide as she scratched Jasper behind the ears. 'Giant poo monsters that come alive on Wednesdays, trying to find the people who flushed them!' She held her hands out in front of her zombie-style and made slurping and groaning noises while crossing her eyes.

'Wednesdays? Why Wednesdays?' Elsie asked.

'Because it's a shitty day of the week. It's the furtherest from the weekend.'

Elsie giggled. 'You're nuts.'

'No. Not really. We're the only sane ones here in Culvert.'

'Really? How do you know?'

'An angel told me.'

'She did?'

'Yep. *He* did. We're the only ones in the town that the poo monsters won't touch because we are sane. We are completely sanely nuts-o.'

Elsie's smile broadened and she let a loud shriek of laughter escape. The sound lifted to the blue and even silenced the galahs for a moment.

It felt so good to be out there. For the first time in as long as Elsie could remember it had been an OK sort of day at school. Jasper's arrival in the morning closed the gap between the other girls and her and Tara. A few had broken from the pack and come to ask if they could pat Jasper as she settled him in the church paddock. Elsie had hastily unclipped her helmet, rummaged her hair forwards and combed it over her face with her fingers, answering, 'Of course.' She knew the novelty would soon wear off, but at least today the other girls had spoken to her, asking her questions.

Tilly and Scarlett, jealous, had of course kept away, muttering to each other behind cupped hands. The niceness would be short-lived. Elsie knew they would be plotting something, maybe spreading the word that if you touched Elsie Jones or her pony you would catch the mole-disease and soon your face would be covered in them. But for the moment, Jasper's mere presence had opened a once-closed-off door just a tiny chink.

Elsie's and Tara's day had got even better when Elsie's mother had left a message at the school that she had taken Simon home with gastro and could Elsie wait at the Smiths' after school? Elsie had quickly saddled Jasper and the four of them had headed out of the school gates. Passing Mr Queen's house, Tara peered through a crack in the high weatherboard fence. The back of the Dolls' House was even prettier from this angle with a secret garden of winding garden beds interspersed with neat green lawn, sheltered by well-spaced European trees. She could see a couple of Mr Queen's cats sunning themselves in a conservatory that was attached to the high-pitching pretty white house. The slanted roof was broken by several large attic windows. A stone fountain burbled at the centre of the scene, dribbling water over a winged cherub.

An overripe tomato landed on the trodden-dirt path beside her. Two more followed quickly and squelchily.

'Take your leave, vile intruders!' called Mr Queen.

Again Jasper shied, again Tara squealed and, as they scampered away, again the twins laughed, clutching each other as they ran.

When they'd arrived at the roadhouse, Gwinnie Smith had come out of the café to tell Elsie that her mother would be delayed. One of the Grassmore tractors had broken down and Sarah had to drive to Rington to pick up what must be an urgent and crucial part.

'If your mum's coming later, why not take the chance to ride Jasper out to the back of the farm?' Gwinnie suggested. And so she and Jasper had followed Mr Smith, with Tara and the boys piled on top of the timber in the back of the ute.

Now in the paddock, Jasper was happily nibbling on grass while the boys sweated, stacking the heavy lengths that would be used to reinforce the building. Elsie noticed how happy the boys were with their father; they were all excited that the defunct farm shed was about to get a facelift and they could expand their experiments out to the paddocks. Already in the shed were some second-hand machines and as Mr Smith, a former farm boy and mechanical engineer, had told the girls, they were about to convert them.

'We're going to trial no-till cropping and study the soil and native pasture regeneration that we hope will follow,' he said to the girls.

Not really understanding what Mr Smith was on about, Elsie still listened keenly to his excited spiel on doing away with ploughs and man-made synthetic fertilisers.

Even though he was chemo-thin, Elvis was brighter than life itself that day, standing tall in his cobalt-blue work shirt and denim jeans. He was talking fast and waving his hands excitedly.

'I don't have time to die,' he said over the compilation of country music that was, as always, blaring from the ute. It had rolled from Dolly Parton being an island in the stream with Kenny Rogers to Jimmy Buffett on his way to Margaritaville. 'Do I, boys? There's too much to be done. A whole world to change and inspire! When I saw this place advertised, I knew, just knew, it was my calling!'

Both boys grinned up at him from where they were stacking the last piece of timber. Elsie edged Jasper nearer and Tara came to sit in the tray of the now-empty ute.

'Sometimes what seems like the greatest crisis in life is the greatest gift. Y'know! I had to do away with the belief system that I was a victim. I was ousted from my own family farm cos I was the youngest, years back, but now with my love for agriculture and my engineering experience, this place is my nirvana! Life forced me to see that my health stems not so much from my inherited DNA, but my ingrained neural networking processes that were, I'm afraid to admit, looped on negative. But now, with the study I've been doing on human cells and vibrational energy and metaphysics, I've discovered I'm not a victim to cancer or the limits of my DNA! This is my chance to wake up! Through this, I'm being forced to truly live! And here I am in Culvert on this farm! Right, boys?'

Zac and Amos grinned while Elsie and Tara watched Elvis with fascination. Neither girl had ever heard so many words uttered from a man in one stretch. In Elsie's case, her father talked in sentences of no more than five words to her and it was always about the farm or the troubles he had on council. His talk was always about lack. Or trials and tribulations. Or what Elsie hadn't done, or couldn't or shouldn't do. And Tara never heard a man talk about his feelings if she didn't count rage expressed via frequent expulsions of the F-word.

'My aim here is to get away from this useless, limited, introduced pasture species,' Elvis continued, slinging his arm out to indicate the ground. 'It's time to get the red grass back, to let the wallaby and kangaroo grass take hold. Get both summer- and winter-growing perennials back. Feed the soil with what it wants, which is decomposing leaf litter and natural manure. Then, once we've modified the old seed drill, the annual plants can be sown right in. Then whammo! Soon the soils will start to function. A bit of fencing. A bit of water piped here and there. Some grazing to mimic the African plains and our little property will be an oasis in this farming desert. What do you think, boys?'

'Genius,' said Amos.

'We're with you, Dad,' said Zac.

As Elvis spoke, Elsie thought of the barren dusty expanse of Grassmore, of the roadsides on which she had ridden this morning, and she thought of her father. He would never use the word 'whammo'. Nor ask her for her opinion.

Zac and Amos looked to their father with equal admiration.

'That's the last of it,' Elvis said, wiping his hands after dragging the double door of the shed closed and locking it with a giant chain. 'Let's crank a bit of Hank for the drive home.' He climbed into the ute and pressed fast forward on the tape deck set in the dusty dash. 'Miss Beechcroft will be back for her Beetle any moment now. We'd best get her down off the hoist.'

At the mention of Miss Beechcroft's name, Elsie felt dread settle in her stomach. Guitar lessons were due to start on Wednesday. Surely after Miss Beechcroft'd finished teaching music at Culvert Primary she wouldn't want to go home and teach *more* music. By the way she yelled at students and stormed out of the room to hunt down the principal, Mrs Guthridge, with complaints, Myrna Beechcroft clearly didn't enjoy children. Suddenly Jasper gave a snort and reminded Elsie that she was on his back and she saw that for the moment she didn't have to worry about guitar lessons. Right now, she was on her pony, with her very best friends, and that was all that mattered. As Mr Smith started the ute, Tara, with Trev in her arms, dangled her legs off the back of the tray, while the boys climbed into the cab to ride beside their father.

Elsie urged Jasper on and began following.

'Look!' said Tara excitedly to Elsie as they bumped over the paddock. She pointed in the direction from where they'd come. 'Amazing! Seven galahs, seven trees and seven poo ponds. Seven, seven, seven,' she said, smiling. 'It's an angel-number sequence.'

'Huh?' Elsie asked.

'It's a sign. That there's going to be a miracle here.'

'At the poo ponds?'

Tara shrugged. 'That's what they reckon.'

'Funny place for a miracle.'

'You're not wrong,' Tara said, shrugging her shoulders, 'but I'm going with it! The great Poo Pond Prophecy! Bring it on!'

Six

'"Greensleeves"! She started you on *"Greensleeves"*?' Elvis Smith's dark eyebrows knitted together as he lay on the couch in the roadhouse, a coloured crocheted rug draped over his long legs and a steaming cup of Gwinnie's homemade nettle tea on the table beside him.

Elsie Jones matched his frown and nodded, holding onto the long narrow neck of the acoustic guitar, wishing she hadn't mentioned it to him. Tears pricked behind her eyes. The guitar upset her. Or was it Miss Beechcroft? She could see the beauty in the instrument, the way the warm tones of wood curved together, like a beautiful woman's waist. She liked the way the guitar sat snuggly on her lap, with her arm draped over it, as if the guitar wanted to be held like an old-fashioned movie star, but, after three months of lessons with Miss Beechcroft, the instrument remained an enemy. A frustrating mystery, like a pirate's treasure chest, found but locked. Elsie had no clue where to find its key.

Also locked away from Elsie was any kind of common ground with Miss Beechcroft. The music teacher remained unyielding and savage. During lessons she stood over her in a brown A-line skirt, thick tights and flat shoes, with her short chewed hair. She would look through her glasses with narrow eyes at Elsie's fragility as a musician, her disappointment jutting her square jaw out.

'Don't get me wrong,' said Elvis, just as the other one crooned 'Love Me Tender' from the roadhouse stereo, '"Greensleeves" is a terrific piece of music, but to engage a child like you with a musical instrument by teaching that *first*? She's got it wrong.'

Elsie wondered what he meant by 'a child like you'. She felt shame ripple through her. Did he think her as hopeless as her mother did? Did he too see how ugly she was with the mole? She knew it was the first thing anyone noticed about her. At school this week she'd discovered a new word. *Disfigured*. It had tumbled around in her head ever since. She was *disfigured* by the mole. She brushed her hair forwards.

'Show me what you've learned. Tars, will you turn the music down, love?'

Tara, who was quietly setting tables in the café to delay any mention of her going home to her mum and Dwaine, did.

Once the room was silent, Elvis wafted his hand at Elsie like a kindly king commanding a court musician to play.

Elsie twisted her lips nervously. 'I'm not very good,' she mumbled.

Mr Smith waved again as if to erase her concerns from the air. 'But, my darling kid, you have to start somewhere. Now play, my girl, *play!*'

Hesitantly Elsie sat on a chair, angling her body so the side of her face with the mole was turned away from Mr Smith. She drew the guitar to herself, bent her head intently and watched herself position her fingers over the strings at the correct fret, the way Miss Beechcroft had shown her. With trembling hands, she began to pluck the guitar so it twanged shakily, as if it was complaining to be played by someone like her. But before she had got even a few notes in, Elvis Smith was propping himself up and swinging his legs to the floor.

'Stop! Stop! Why classical? Why is she teaching you classical? You're not the classical type. Can't she sense that about you,

Elsie? Here! Give that thing to me! Can't she see the grit and guts inside you? You're not some flaky grazier's girl, Elsie. You are a full-blown cowgirl. And you need to learn to play like one! Like a buckjumper out the gate!'

Red-faced, Elsie stood and carried the guitar over to Mr Smith. He grabbed it, along with the pick. It became tiny in his hands as he swung it onto his leg and held it firmly, as if he was commanding a wilful dog to obey. Then, as if to settle it, he gently plucked a few strings and tuned it. He tapped the body of the guitar, counting a wooden lead-in beat, and launched into a powerful blues version of Creedence Clearwater's 'Proud Mary'. His voice carried deep and commandingly through the café, spilling out to the kitchen where Gwinnie was making tomorrow's soup of the day. The sound silenced the blasts of her blender and she joined in with a beautiful harmony, her singing drifting into the dining area, entwining perfectly into the arms of Mr Smith's melody.

Elsie's mouth dropped open. Tara, spellbound, stopped arranging the flowers on the tables and froze, holding a paper daisy aloft. Mr Smith was extracting a noise from the guitar like they'd never heard before. And his voice was a magic charm saturating the air, holding them all there in that moment.

'I wanna do that,' whispered Elsie. 'I wanna do that.' Her little feet thrummed excitedly on the floor.

Mr Smith continued rollin' through the song. He bent his head in a deep trance. The last of his hair, tenacious despite the chemo, flopped over his brow like the real Elvis's as he strummed and rocked his way to the end of the song. When he was done, a whoop emanated from the kitchen and Tara and Elsie began to clap with bright smiles on their faces.

'That's the kinda music she oughta start you off on. Easy chords and a beat you can relate to! You can't teach a person anything if they aren't turned on, lit up and in love with the idea of learning!'

Elvis patted the couch and Elsie moved over, self-consciousness burning on her cheeks. 'Look.' He positioned his fingers on the fret board of the guitar as he spoke. 'C, A, C, A, G, F, F, F.' He strummed slowly, exaggerating each chord and eliciting a rich sound from the instrument. After showing her a few more times, he passed Elsie the guitar, then swivelled around to place her fingers in position. Elsie felt the hard ridges of the strings indent her skin as Mr Smith pressed firmly on her nails.

'Guide the strings like you would Jasper's mind, via your energy and body position. You are a commanding rider. Treat the guitar like a horse. Now strum.' He drew her hand and the pick up and down over the nylon and metal strings. Elsie nodded nervously. He'd said she was a good rider! She had never heard a man praise her before. It felt terrifying and divine.

'It's not just about hearing the sound: it's about *feeling* it. Music is about vibration. Everything is about vibration. It's channelled through your very own soul. Didn't Miss Beechcroft teach you that?'

'Nope.' With Miss Beechcroft it was all about timing and precision and discipline and practice and perfection. Mr Smith shook his head. She could sense his nearness, but she didn't dare look at him. Beneath the illness that was ravaging his body, he was a strong and handsome man. Elsie thought about Zac and Amos at Mr Smith's age. She was struck by how nice the boys would be as men. Not like her own father, or sullen Simon, and certainly not like Dwaine Morton. Elvis Smith had a way about him that was giving and gentle. She was glad to be in his presence, getting all of his attention. The right kind of attention.

Not like Miss Beechcroft at guitar lessons. Whenever she made a mistake, Miss Beechcroft would smack Elsie's hands away from the guitar and huff. Then her cheeks would turn beetroot in sheer frustration, and the last straw would be her cat yowling to get out of the room away from the tension that tutor and pupil had generated in giant swirls of stubbornness.

'Do you want to learn? Or not?' Miss Beechcroft had asked several times over as the metronome ticked back and forth on the lace-trimmed mantelpiece. Elsie had sat in Miss Beechcroft's plum-toned lounge room and opened her mouth, speechless, not knowing what to say.

'Well? Answer me. Are you simple?' Miss Beechcroft asked, enunciating her words slowly in a BBC voice.

Elsie felt rage simmer. If she could smash the guitar on the fine-legged coffee table and even on Miss Beechcroft's head and the neurotic cat, she would. But instead she smothered her anger, became withdrawn, sitting in her own pool of misery, waiting for the hour and a half to go by so she could head home and focus on how nice it would be seeing Jasper in the morning before school.

But now as Mr Smith gently coached her to draw a warm honey sound from the guitar, she felt peacefulness settle upon her. Next he encouraged her to whip the guitar up into a gallop, draw it back to a canter with the timing of her strumming, then coach it to amble, like an old cowpoke pony who had done a hundred lazy miles. As the guitar answered her with rich deep sounds, Elsie felt the tension dissolve from her body, the way it did when she sat on Jasper. She felt excitement lift in her like birds on the plains thermals. She looked up to see Tara stepping from foot to foot, moving to the music, a smile igniting joy in her eyes. She was making Tara dance! She felt like kissing the high curve of the guitar's side as she drew the pick down and extracted the next full note and then made a chord change.

'Good! Good! Music is about feeling,' Mr Smith said, smiling and nodding, 'and using your energy and your pain and your passion to bring the instrument alive. You are a natural. You are a kick-arse cowgirl!'

Suddenly Mr Smith was up and disappearing out through the roadhouse kitchen swing doors and beyond to the family's living quarters. Elsie stopped strumming. Tara blinked and shrugged.

'What's he doing?' she whispered.

Elsie shrugged back, but euphoria encompassed her. *She was a kick-arse cowgirl!* Mr Smith had said it! At last she had a place on the map of her world. She and her pony and her guitar. She went on strumming the chords he had shown her, the words of 'Proud Mary' beginning to play within her mind. When Mr Smith came back, he was carrying a pile of tattered books. He moved the salt and pepper shakers and a sugar bowl out of the way on one of the coffee tables.

'Here. My boys are on other paths in life, so they don't want my old books. You can have them!' he said as he flung each book onto the surface of the table. 'A book of chords. The best of Johnny Cash. A Dolly songbook. And a mix of others — lyric writing, more sheet music, learn to play blues guitar, The Beatles complete, *Rock Guitar Songs for Dummies*, not that I'm saying you're a dummy. More like that bloody music teacher of yours is.'

'Two dollars!' said Gwinnie Smith as she entered through the swing doors of the kitchen, a blue gingham tea towel cast over her shoulder, her blonde hair loosely scrunched into a ponytail so the rest fell prettily around her face. She reached over to an old-style dresser decorated beautifully with assorted colourful china and picked up what the girls had come to know as 'the swear jar'. She removed the lid and waved the blue china canister in front of him. Coins within rattled.

'So far we have one hundred and seventy-eight dollars of Elvis's cussings.' Gwinnie grinned, looking at the girls. 'He's going to take me to Sydney to see Garth Brooks next time he tours. Right, honey?'

Elvis nodded, fishing in his pocket for some coins (which he kept on him for the express purpose of amusing his wife with the swear-jar concept).

'Bloody is hardly a swear word these days,' he pretended to grumble. 'Most kids your age drop the F-bomb daily! Wouldn't you say, girls?' Tara and Elsie giggled and shook their heads, knowing full well it was Nathanial Rogerson who was the world's worst, saying the F-word every five minutes when adults weren't in earshot.

'That's another two dollars. And I heard you say arse before,' Gwinnie said, 'so that's extra.'

'I did not!

'Did so!'

'You just said it yourself then.'

'I did not!'

'You did! You just said arse! Didn't she?' Mr Smith put on a comical face and pointed an accusing finger at his wife.

The girls giggled some more. Tara and Elsie could tell Gwinnie and Elvis were performing for them. They watched the pantomime with gratitude. The girls knew that the Smiths knew that they were an inconvenience to the adults at their own homes.

Elvis dropped a series of coins into the jar, then touched his wife on her hand. Suddenly his grin turned to a grimace. He cried out in pain and doubled over before slumping back on the couch, his knee jerking violently up and down with involuntary spasms of agony. Gwinnie was on her knees next to him, holding his hand, talking urgently but quietly to him.

'Darling? What can I get you? Shall I call Dr Patak?'

Elsie stood watching, fear heating her face.

It was Tara who was already scuttling away to the kitchen and quickly returning with a glass of water and the cluster of tablets that were kept beside the sink for Mr Smith. She passed them to Gwinnie.

Gwinnie popped a tablet and helped it to Mr Smith's mouth and offered him water. After he had downed the tablet and settled back down, Tara kneeled beside him.

'Too much rock and roll, right, Mr Smith?' she said gently. When Elvis managed a smile at Tara, relief swept over them all.

Through shortened breath, Elvis muttered, 'You can never have too much rock and roll, eh, girls?' Even in his pain he was being cheerful for their sake. He masked the depth of the sickness for all of them.

Elsie felt so much love and admiration for Mr Smith. A lovely, loving man, trying to give so much to his family and to the land. A man who might not live. Worse, she could see the panic on

Gwinnie's face at the sight of her husband, now deathly pale and with his thumb and index finger pressed to his eyes.

Elsie stood frozen, feeling it was her fault he'd collapsed. How come Tara knew what to do? She was now, with her small pudgy hand, gently stroking his arm, making soothing sounds and laying her other hand on his arm, and closing her eyes as if she was talking to her angel friends. Elsie watched Mr Smith's wiry body begin to ease a little and calm. A teary Gwinnie looked at Tara with such gratitude that for a moment Elsie felt a bolt of jealousy like a knife slicing her from her chest to her belly. Tara was like that. She seemed to have magic about her. And in that space Elsie felt useless.

Just then the service-station alarm bell dinged. A white Commodore drew up next to the bowsers, looking unusually clean and bright for a Culvert car, so much so it still managed to gleam beneath a dull autumn afternoon sun. Elsie groaned internally. It was her father. The little white petrol door on the side of the car popped open and Kelvin Jones started to get out.

Gwinnie glanced from her husband to the car, then reached for the two-way that was resting beside the couch. 'Zac? Amos? Do you copy? Customer. I'm with your dad.' The radio fuzzed and crackled.

'Got it, Mum,' came the reply, and from their mother's tone the boys understood their father had taken another turn. Through the big roadhouse window, Elsie saw one of the boys jogging from the machinery workshop to the bowser.

'Tara, sit with Elvis, please, darling. I'm just going to call the doctor,' Gwinnie said.

Mr Smith began to shake his head. 'No, no! It's just the chemo … a pain in my stomach. It's nothing. You know the doctor only believes in illness, not wellness. I'm going to make a miraculous recovery. I know it, but Dr Patak doesn't, so I don't want him here convincing me otherwise. Please.'

Tears welled in Elvis's eyes, the desperation of a man sentenced to death by the medical world. Gwinnie covered her face with her hands and drew in a jagged breath. Then she reached for the blanket that had fallen to the floor, lay down on the couch with her husband and put her arms around him.

Tara stood, arranged the blanket over both of them and looked at Elsie. There was no way they were going out to the councillor-mayor. She flicked her head in the direction of the kitchen door.

They left Elvis and Gwinnie in each other's arms, crying as life took them down a tunnel neither wanted to go.

Seven

Zac stood at the petrol pump. Culvert's autumn afternoon sunshine felt feeble and to Zac, life today felt flat.

'How much would you like?' he asked, looking up at the balding man he recognised as Elsie's father. Today Kelvin Jones wore a white button-strained shirt and a blue Culvert Council tie that draped over the contoured curve of his ballooning stomach. In the stomach's shade were tightly belted grey slacks with creases down the front, the cuffs sitting a little too long over RM Williams boots. As Zac reached for the fuel-pump nozzle, he wondered how on earth this man could be tiny, pretty Elsie's father. He wondered what he ate and drank to gain such a belly and would his methane production be lesser or greater than that of someone slim who ate a raw-food diet? He must remember to suggest it to Amos as an experiment.

Near the councillor-mayor's shiny boots was a puddle with a skin of oil that swirled like a dark rainbow in universal soup. Oil belonged in the ground, Elvis always said. Zac thought of his father and hoped he was OK. If anything happened to him, they would never realise their dreams. Dreams that had only just begun in the big shed out the back of the farm. The petrol pump moaned and the car's tank gurgled.

'Shouldn't I be doing that?' Kelvin asked pompously, looking down at Zac with cold blue eyes. He gestured to the nozzle. Although it wasn't a question. It was more of a command.

Zac frowned. 'No, it's fine. I can do it.' He held the pump and tried to ignore the fact Elsie's father was staring at him, shaking his head.

'I think you'll find I should be doing that. For you to do it is highly unethical and in breach of Occupational Health and Safety regulations,' Councillor-Mayor Jones said. 'How old are you?'

Zac glanced up at the bowser as the numbers spooled towards the fifties. *Surely Mr Jones knows I'm in Elsie's class?* wondered Zac.

'Um. Nearly twelve.'

'Look.' Councillor-Mayor Jones tapped his index finger on the bowser rules, signs that Zac himself had stuck up when they had overhauled old Chopper Reid's fuel pumps. *'Pumps not to be operated by children under the age of fifteen.* You're too young.'

Zac looked up. 'Well, that depends whether you are thinking within the boundaries set by our human experience of time as linear,' he said earnestly as the fuel continued along the hose and into the car, 'or thinking of the situation in universal measures of time, where everything that happened, is happening and is going to happen is in existence all at once, in which case I am already an adult so therefore, no, I would not be too young.'

Kelvin Jones looked slightly confused, then shook his head. The boy was being rude.

'Where is your father?'

'Inside. With Elsie.'

A cloud of irritation crossed the councillor-mayor's face. 'Hang that pump up at once. I need to speak to him.'

Zac paused. He knew this was serious. He set down the pump. 'He's ... he's not ...'

'He's not what? Speak up, boy!'

'He's not ...'

'Not home? Not sober? Not real?' asked the councillor-mayor with irritation. It was bad enough for Kelvin Jones that he'd been called away early by Sarah from council to get Elsie. He'd been hoping to stay longer at the offices, where the Year Ten work experience girl, Christine Sheen, was wearing a particularly clingy see-through top today. He'd now not only had to pick up Elsie from the roadhouse after school because Sarah had to get a part for the tractor in Rington, he also had to deal with this.

'Not well,' Zac at last finished.

As he entered the diner with the boy, it took Councillor-Mayor Jones a while to recognise that Elvis Smith was lying on the couch underneath a crocheted blanket with his wife. They appeared to be in comas. He was about to cough to make his presence felt when the dreadful chubby Green girl from the abattoir came out from the kitchen whispering that they were meditating, before asking him whether he'd like some soup. Following her like a lost puppy was Elsie. Was that thing on her face getting bigger? What *was* Sarah thinking, allowing their child to be with these people?

'Can we help you, Councillor … er, Mayor … er, Mr Kelvin. Er … Jones?' asked Gwinnie, propping herself upright, swiping tears from her face, while her husband remained on his back, his face as white as a sheet, his breathing shallow.

'It's about this,' Councillor-Mayor Jones said, indicating Zac beside him.

The bell of the roadhouse door chimed as Amos came in, worry on his face. Gwinnie detected the note of disdain in Elsie's father's voice and her inner Mama Bear fired. 'This? You mean my son?'

'Yes. He's a minor.'

'A minor? Well, he's certainly not a magpie,' she said with a touch of angry sarcasm in her voice.

Elsie's cheeks sizzled. She clutched her hands nervously.

'He is not of adequate age to operate a fuel pump. And I'd imagine your kitchen staff aren't of age either,' he said, glaring at Tara. 'Are they, Elsie?'

She opened her mouth, but no words came.

'From an OH&S perspective you are more than likely in breach of several fuel-service and hospitality regulations.'

He waited for a response.

Gwinnie's eyebrows lifted and then dropped. She glanced from Elvis to Kelvin standing above them. Was he serious?

Elsie felt like being swallowed up by the earth. She could see the looks of concern on Zac's and Amos's faces. She wished her father would just explode and splatter himself away into oblivion.

'Sir. Sir Mayor,' Gwinnie said in a tight voice, 'can you not see my husband is not entirely well? And we rely on the children to help at certain times. Would it not be so in your family too? If the situation were the same. They are bright children … Your daughter —'

Kelvin held up his hand. 'It's Councillor-Mayor and I can see from Mr Smith's condition that what you say is true, however I cannot ignore the fact you have minors illegally working in a business. In particular, my very own daughter. This is a grave situation.'

Gwinnie stood up, smoothed her hair as best she could and tugged her dress down so she felt less crumpled. 'And we are in a grave situation, *Councillor-Mayor*. Can you not see it's not a good time? And your daughter is not working here. In fact *Elvis* was helping *her* with her guitar before he —' Tears began to pool in Gwinnie's eyes. Kelvin Jones averted his gaze.

'Dad,' Elsie began timidly.

'Go get in the car, Eleanor,' he said, delivering her a look that could freeze lava.

She looked at him pleadingly, but could see his stern resolve. She grabbed up her school bag and guitar and scuttled out the door, passing Dr Patak who was just arriving in his old Mercedes. Gwinnie suddenly looked more pale than her husband.

'I told you not to call the doctor,' Elvis rasped, his hands covering his face.

'I did,' Tara said, indicating the phone in the kitchen. 'You need a doctor right now. If not for you, to help Gwinnie. It's up to you to show him how well you are. Not for him to tell you how sick you are.'

Gwinnie promptly burst into tears of relief. A doctor's advice would be so reassuring right now, she thought. She gathered up Tara in a hug.

'Oh, Tara, you dear girl,' Elvis said weakly, 'I believe you're right.'

Kelvin Jones, knowing he was about to be sprung by the doctor bullying the pathetic Smith family, clenched his mouth into a bitter straight line. 'This is by no means the end of it,' he said, reefing the door open so the bell chimed in hasty shock. He strode to the car, where he cast his daughter a glare, pasted on a wallpaper smile and delivered it with a friendly salute to Dr Patak before driving away without paying for his petrol.

Inside the roadhouse the Smiths, Tara and the twins stood in silence, each processing what had happened. What would the councillor-mayor do to them now? They couldn't afford staff: they couldn't run the roadhouse without the boys working there. He had them cornered.

Then Zac spoke. 'Did you see that, Mum? Did you see?'

Gwinnie looked to her son through a haze of tears. 'See what?'

'*Elsie's dad doesn't have a bum.* Councillor-Mayor Jones fully doesn't have a bottom! He was just a torso, with legs stuck on it.'

Amos nodded vigorously. 'Yeah, I saw!'

'How can he *sit* on council when he doesn't have a bum?' Zac asked, pulling a face.

By the time Dr Patak entered with his doctor's bag, the Smiths and Tara were already doubled over with laughter. On the couch Mr Smith was coughing, groaning and laughing and colour had bloomed once more on his cheeks.

'Councillor-Mayor No-Buttocks,' wheezed Elvis. 'Ah, my boys! My funny, funny boys!'

Eight

Judging from his red face and steamed-up glasses, Culvert science teacher Vernon Tremble looked like he was about to ignite in a loud *whoomph* like a Bunsen burner. He was not yet over the previous week's ordeal, when Nathanial Rogerson had left the burner's gas on too long before striking a match. The near-miss accident resulted in the loss of one of Nathanial's gingery eyebrows and sparked a day's stress leave for Mr Tremble. He returned to an official complaint from Nathanial's father, Deputy Mayor Cuthbertson Rogerson, who was livid about his son's 'potentially disfiguring accident'.

The Culvert Grade Six students in their final term had been allowed two lessons with the burners in the lead-up to high school next year. Now here they were again and Mr Tremble was taut with trepidation. He had nowhere to hide, as Miss Beechcroft was loitering for him in the staffroom, and he was still wondering if he was truly over his divorce and if the posting to a country town like Culvert was the right decision. He wished Zac Smith would just *shut up*. Zac had just pointed out to the entire class in a loud voice that Deputy Mayor Rogerson had failed to see his son was already disfigured.

'Let's face it. He was beaten over the head with the ugly stick from birth,' Zac quipped. At the back of the class, Nathanial was turning puce with anger, and the other children snickered nervously.

'It's clear also,' Zac said from his front-row command of the classroom, 'Nathanial could be considered permanently disfigured purely from his genetic make-up.'

'Zac,' growled Mr Tremble as another warning.

But Zac inclined his head with a know-it-all expression as if to tut-tut his teacher. 'Nathanial has obviously not become familiar with Dr Bruce Lipton's gene theories on the possibility of DNA changes via vibrational thought patterns,' he said matter-of-factly, half turning to his classmates, 'otherwise he'd be meditating flat-out during his impending puberty to alter his cell biology, so as to avoid resembling his family in any way.' This was met by a solo eruption of laughter from Amos while his classmates sat dumbly at their desks.

At the back of the lab, Tara and Elsie were poised on the edge of their seats, trying to will Zac to be quiet. They knew they were witnessing another science-class disaster in the making. This time it wasn't the flammable equipment but the volatile words and the flint minds of the twins that were about to spark an inferno of anger in Nathanial and most likely another day of stress leave for Mr Tremble. Elsie could understand Zac's uncharacteristic venom. She knew Nathanial's father and her dad had launched a targeted campaign against the Smiths' business soon after her father had seen Zac at the pump and she and Tara in the kitchen. She couldn't blame him. Zac was holding nothing back. She watched Mr Tremble get redder and redder and do just as his name suggested as Amos joined his brother.

'My esteemed twin has a point about Dr Lipton's recent work. We can no longer ignore the question, "Is science on the wrong track?"' Amos said, opening his palms to Mr Tremble as if giving a university speech to the great minds of the world. 'Newton's laws just don't seem to work in isolation and Darwin's theories are incomplete. Then there's current science saying that technology is the answer to our problems, and that through science alone we will conquer nature and the forces that are threatening our survival. Surely you won't be teaching us that stuff next year?'

Mr Tremble's eyes seemed to roll right to the back of his head before he cast his desperate gaze to the ceiling as if he wished he was anywhere but Culvert Primary teaching this particular bunch of kids, especially the Smith twins.

'Yes,' pushed Zac, 'these ideas are based on false beliefs derived from science that is not only incomplete but in some cases just plain *wrong*!'

'Enough!' Mr Tremble said a little too loudly. 'As I said before, this is not on the school curriculum. And I'm sure your classmates have heard enough, so could we all just turn to page fifty-two before lunch and we'll review the alternative energy options that you've covered in your projects.'

Nathanial scowled, his fists clenched: he was ready to tackle Zac to the ground, but he knew Amos would have his twin's back.

The other students didn't bother to reach for their books. They'd come to appreciate the distraction the twins always caused in science, even though Zac and Amos were total freaks who talked gobbledygook.

Mr Tremble gritted his teeth and rammed his glasses up. He looked down at the textbook on his desk.

Ignoring him, Zac half got out of his chair to speak. 'Even when our father was in primary school, he was taught about the earth's finite resources of fossil fuel. Yet here we are still running on those same systems. Why go round and round again teaching another generation the same stuff when we know it's big-oil business holding back the technology? Listed in our Grade Six text are solar power, coal power, wind power and water power, but that is so outdated! What about geothermal, infusion, wave power, or methane, or biofuel?'

Elsie and Tara felt Mr Tremble's fuse burn dangerously short.

'I mean you wouldn't even let us do an experiment in poo power?'

'Enough! Enough! Enough!' Mr Tremble said, stamping his Hush Puppy on the linoleum and hitching up his brown cords furiously. He looks not far off a heart attack, thought Tara. Maybe she should send him some healing.

'Mr Tremble, I don't mean to be rude,' Amos said, 'but this science you are teaching us is on the wrong track.' He looked at Mr Tremble with the open face of hope. The twins were just too smart for their own good. There were special schools for kids like them in the city, but not out here. Not in Culvert.

'Where is quantum physics in the curriculum so we can learn about the things science can't explain, like the tiny particles we are made up of and the forces underlying our physical world? And epigenetics?'

'Yes! Epigenetics!' echoed Zac.

'Are they in the texts?' Amos continued. 'Are you truly thinking the right way scientifically, Mr Tremble, and asking the right questions? You will be our high-school science teacher next year and these are areas all children need to know about!'

'Yes,' said Tara, 'I read something about vibrational energy and metaphysics and that. Can we study it next year?'

Mr Tremble flinched. Not Tara Green too? 'That's it!' he said, smashing a ruler onto his desk and pointing to the door with an outstretched arm. 'Out! Out! Zac and Amos Smith, out! Go straight to Mrs Guthridge's office. Not another word! You are both heading for detention, if not *suspension!*'

'Cool!' said the one-eyebrowed Nathanial Rogerson, nodding from the back row.

That afternoon, riding Jasper back to the Smiths', Elsie looked down sadly at the boys. Their suspension meant a suspension for her. She'd be back in her mother's Volvo being driven to school, with Surly Simon hurling nasty comments at her. Since he'd started at Culvert High he'd got worse. He already loathed the fact that his parents had held him off going to boarding school for a year until Elsie had caught up to his high-school years. For Elsie, there would be no more easy-going funny conversations about life, the universe and everything on their walks. No more hilarious banter that had her gasping for air and almost sliding off Jasper with hysterical laughter. Tara was in the same frame of mind. Without the sunshine of the walks that warmed her in all weather, her life would be covered by a cloud again. Jasper then lifted his tail right beside the Dolls' House and let a large pile of dung fall outside the locked front gate. The four of them stood looking at the pile.

'Oh, poop,' said Elsie, half turned in her saddle, looking down at the steaming dollops.

Next they saw Mr Queen running at them with a shovel, wearing a crimson skivvy, yellow hibiscus boardshorts and purple Crocs. Tara screamed and the boys began to bolt. By the time Elsie had gathered up the reins and kicked the reluctant Jasper on, Mr Queen was near her behind the gate. With mad ice-blue eyes glinting with humour, he smiled up at Elsie.

'Poo for my roses! Poo for my roses! Manna from heaven. Thank you, my dear,' he said, his small cragged face reminding Elsie of an elderly pixie. She understood now that he was just a lonely person and, like her and her friends, a bad fit for the rest of Culvert, and that he had most of the town fooled so he could keep to himself.

She smiled at him. 'Plenty more where that came from, Mr Queen. Sorry about that,' she said with a grin before riding off to catch up with her friends.

At the roadhouse yards, in the wake of the call from Principal Guthridge saying the boys were to be suspended from school for two weeks and banned from the Grade Six Leaver's formal, the four slumped about on the back patio lethargically, listening to the drum of bees busy in Gwinnie's garden.

'That's it,' Gwinnie said, setting down a tray of milkshakes and handing them out, 'home-schooling may be the only option for the rest of the year if that's how they're going to be.'

Elsie looked up at Gwinnie as she wrapped her lips around the straw and sucked. She had to think quick. Maybe if they were really good in the next two weeks, Gwinnie might change her mind. Hoping she could distract her, she asked, 'Gwinnie? As a way of the boys saying sorry to you, can we do a favour for someone? Before my mum gets here.'

Red-faced and a little flustered, Gwinnie glanced up at her while Tara and the twins looked at her, puzzled. 'What?'

'If the four of us bag up Jasper's dung, could you please help us by driving it down on the ute to Mr Queen's? He really needs some for his garden.'

Gwinnie sighed. Then at last smiled.

Half an hour later, the kids set out six chaff bags filled with fresh dung against the fence that sheltered Mr Queen from the madness of the world.

'There you go,' Elsie said, gazing up at the house. 'Manna from heaven for you, Mr Queen.'

'A good deed done,' Tara said. 'At least the angels are smiling.' And they turned, knowing that day was the last time they would share the journeys to school together.

Nine

On the night of the Grade Six formal, Elsie Jones gazed at her image in the bedroom mirror. Her reflection, bathed in late-afternoon light, showed a slim girl in a floaty lavender-blue dress with tiny white flowers embroidered on the bodice. Delicate straps lay on her bare shoulders and her small breasts could be seen budding beneath the fabric. She was still featherweight, but Elsie's limbs had grown long and slender. So much so that Jasper sometimes laid his ears back when she first sat on him, and her boots almost touched the ground. Her mother was refusing a bigger horse as boarding school loomed next year. Elsie felt a tug when she recalled her mother suggesting she pass Jasper on to a smaller child in the district.

'You won't have time to look after him once you have high-school studies,' Sarah said to her daughter. 'And you do know, as Simon knows too, you can only come home on long term-break holidays. The fees are expensive enough, so we won't be able to afford to bring you home mid-term just to see a pony you are now too big to ride.'

In her room she braced herself for Sarah's return. Elsie had let down the bun Sarah had so meticulously curled and put up. It took seconds for Elsie to unravel it and she rummaged her fingers through her hair before simply pinning a single blue paper cornflower onto her 'good side'. She thought the flower looked pretty, as did the dress, but all she could really see in the reflection was the giant mole standing out like a fat full stop in black permanent marker on her face. A full stop to any kind of life, she thought. Tonight she had painfully plucked a coarse black hair from it with her mother's tweezers. The tug on the hair and the sheer ugliness of it close up in the mirror caused tears to spring to her eyes.

Now, hoping her mother had forgotten the formal, she padded barefoot over to her bed, picked up her guitar, sat and began strumming 'Wild Thing' with about as much wildness as a tax-office clerk on anti-depressants. Voices were drifting up from below through the open window where her parents were entertaining in 'the best room' at the front of the homestead. It was the room that led to the old ballroom wing of the house.

'Of course it could do with some renovation,' Kelvin boomed to their guests, the Rogersons, after a house tour, 'but what with the fertiliser bill and the need for a new tractor, dear Sarah has to wait.'

Dear Sarah, Elsie thought. Her parents were really laying it on thick. Poor Marbles, who shed hair like a snowstorm and had a propensity for sniffing ladies' crotches, had even been banished to the working-dog runs.

'But the fundraising potential of having a functioning ballroom in the district delivers all kinds of opportunity for the community,' came a woman's voice. 'I had forgotten Grassmore's ballroom was so grand!'

Elsie knew that standing portly but barely reaching the mantelpiece would be Nathanial's father, Deputy Mayor Cuthbertson Rogerson, in his hideous grey suit, and seated before him would be his wife Zelda, her beehive black hair towering, her chins falling in wobbling sequence below. The inflated couple were there for a dinner party while their only child, Nathanial, 'enjoyed himself' at the formal.

Elsie knew Nathanial would already be at the Culvert Hall terrorising his classmates with his ADHD behaviour. Most likely popping balloons, or sucking helium into his lungs and talking like a Smurf. Or entwining Tilly and Scarlett in red and navy streamers while they ran screaming to dob him in to a teacher. Elsie sighed. She could hear her mother on the stairs. The door opened and her mother entered.

'You ungrateful girl! Why did you take your hair down? You look like a tramp now.'

Irritated, her mother fished under the bed for Elsie's recently kicked-off new shoes.

'It's so silly of the school to schedule events at this time of year, with harvest and shearing on for many people. And now your father, organising an important dinner to talk about council matters, like the upgrade of the sewage works. He expects so much of me! How can I be expected to drop you at the hall and serve the entrée?'

Elsie put down the guitar and silently pulled on her shoes, stood and turned her back to the mirror.

'I'm not sure you understand the sacrifices I make for you!'

In the flashing lights of the disco, Elsie first saw Mr Tremble going all out dancing to 'Nutbush City Limits', his glasses skewed on his face, his arms jerking as if he had some kind of neurological dysfunction.

Beside him, Miss Beechcroft, tipsy on a sneaky pre-formal glass or two of Riesling, mirrored him. She looked like a bird of prey, her black eyes gleaming behind her glasses, her sensible shoes stomping out a flat-footed rhythm, but all the while her beady focus was on the only single male at the event: Mr Tremble. Her wine-smeared goal was gaining access to the contents of his cord pants later that night.

Behind them Elsie could see Nathanial parodying the science and music teachers' every move, making faces and movements like a randy monkey. That was until Mrs Guthridge glided over and discreetly guided him away.

It would have been amusing to watch had the twins been there by her side, but Elsie stood in the doorway alone. She felt self-consciousness painting her face in a blush and totally vulnerable in her flimsy dress. Elsie knew Zac and Amos wouldn't be there tonight, thanks to their suspension. She scanned the room for Tara, but instead saw Tilly and Scarlett and their cluster of 'cool girls' standing near the drinks table. They spotted her and made their way over, like a posse of sharks, skirting around the edges of the hall, then leering at her from darkness shadowed more deeply by the flashing lights and spinning mirror ball.

'Doesn't your mother teach you anything about make-up?' asked Scarlett, standing before Elsie in her red dress, looking dramatic and older than her years.

Elsie just stood and blinked, the throb of the too-loud music and the blinding strobe of the lights assaulting her senses, the circle of girls pressing in on her, scrutinising everything about her.

'You could've put a bit of concealer on it, just for tonight, so we don't have to look at it.'

'Yeah,' chipped in Tilly. 'We've got a lot to teach you. But it's all good. Have you heard?'

Elsie looked at Tilly blankly.

'My mum's changed her mind on boarding schools. And she's told Scarlett's mum and it turns out we're now *all* going to Primrose Ladies' College next year, like you! So we've got plenty of time to become besties.'

Elsie swallowed the news like a stone. Surely they were teasing?

'How nice! We'll all be in the boarding house *together.*' Tilly looped her arm in Elsie's. 'But we're going to have to give you some beauty tips.'

'Come with us,' Scarlett said, scooping up Elsie's other arm and smiling. 'We'll help fix you up a bit.'

Before Elsie could protest, they had led her into the women's toilets. There the bright fluorescent lighting revealed the ugliness of the girls' intentions.

'Now!' Tilly shouted once they were in the concrete confines of the toilets.

Scarlett and the other girls violently pushed tiny Elsie forwards. The door of a toilet cubicle sounded like a shot as Tilly kicked it open. Fingers like claws clutched at Elsie's hair and thrust her to her knees. The stench of the Culvert Hall toilets made her retch: her classmates forced her head into the bowl. Then came the flush, the roar of the cistern and the scream of old pipes. Water splashed up into her mouth, over her face, blinding her eyes. The girls dragged her head back.

'It's not coming off! It's still on there. Better give it another go,' Scarlett said.

They forced Elsie forwards again. This time the flush was weaker, but still the stench of urine was strong. Misery washed through her. A sob escaped her mouth. It felt as if wire ran beneath her skin as she strained against the clawing pressure of the girls' hands. She was so much smaller than them. And mute to their fury, their jealousy. Elsie didn't realise it at the time, but their envy was a bushfire fanned by winds of resentment. If the mole wasn't there, she would be truly too beautiful for the girls to bear.

'Try this,' came one of the girls' voices. Toilet paper was spooled off the roll and roughly Tilly swiped it across Elsie's face, tweaking the mole painfully, yanking it. Blood seeped from its edges.

'It's huge!'

'Don't let it touch you!'

'Fucking moll,' said Scarlett and the other girls laughed. Elsie scrunched her eyes. She wished a teacher would come right now, but whenever she sucked up enough courage to say something about Tilly and Scarlett her words remained trapped in her chest. They were goody-two-shoes in front of the teachers. If her mother didn't believe her, who else would?

Elsie felt herself give in. Her hair trickled toilet water down her shoulders and stained her dress a deeper blue. Blood ran from the mole and Elsie tasted its bitterness on her tongue.

'Get off her!' came a voice behind them.

From where Elsie kneeled on the grimy tiled floor, she could see Tara's chubby feet, encased in reinforced-toe stockings and jammed into cracking silver op-shop sandals.

'Let her go!'

There was a quiet strength to Tara's voice.

'And what are you going to do about it?' Scarlett asked, her dark eyes glancing over to Tara.

For a moment Tara stood in silence, then she began to speak in a language Elsie had never heard before. It was partway Arabic, and perhaps partway Native American, but not, and it spilled from Tara's mouth in a cascade of power. The words were unintelligible, but the meaning behind them very clear.

Elsie looked up. Tara had hit puberty earlier than the rest of them and she was bursting out of a second-hand dark green satin dress, her rounded breasts smooshed flat, the seams straining at the waist, her bum made bigger by the giant eighties bow that had been tied with no care by her mother. Her legs ballooned out from the unflattering hem of the dress.

But still Tara stood there, fearlessly, undefeated, speaking curses in a language none of them had heard. The girls stood transfixed at the sight and the sound.

'You're fucking mad,' sneered Scarlett.

Tara's eyes flashed open. They were wide and emerald with flecks of gold in them, and it was as if they held a presence within them that none of them had encountered before. She just didn't seem like *Tara*.

'You were almost right, Scarlett,' Tara said. 'You thought it was Elsie, but I am in fact the witch. I've been saving the entrails from Dwaine's gut buckets and cooking them up in my cauldron all year, especially for you.' She pretended to stir a pot and then waved her fingertips at Scarlett's face for a more dramatic effect. 'And yes. I am mad. Dangerously mad. And I have just put a spell on all of you. It won't take effect today. Or tomorrow. But one day, when you think you've got away with this, your lives will all come crashing down. You yourself have sown the seeds of your own doom.'

'Yeah right. Nutter.' But the sting had gone from Scarlett's voice. Elsie felt the girls' grip release and soon they were stepping away from her, backing off, uneasy. Tara blocked their exit and ducked quickly into a cubicle. She grabbed up a toilet brush, dipped it in the toilet water and standing before them began to flick it through the air like a priest shaking holy water on her congregation. Again the strange language emanated from her lips, her voice deep and booming. At the feeling of the cold water splattering them, the girls all screamed, pushed past Tara and fled, banging the door behind them.

'Good riddance!' Tara said. She helped Elsie up, her chubby hands steadying her friend, her voice back to normal. 'Are you OK?'

Elsie caught her reflection in the mirror: lank hair, the cornflower flushed away to the Culvert sewers, blood oozing from the mole, her inner being crushed like a butterfly hitting a truck in a rainstorm. 'Yes. Thanks.'

'C'mon,' Tara said and she took Elsie by the hand and wrapped her other arm around her shoulder, 'let's blow this joint.'

As they walked away from the throbbing music and lights into the darkness towards the outskirts of town, Elsie turned to Tara. 'Were you for real back there? About the spell?'

'No!' said Tara, giggling. 'But yes. Sort of. If they ever have a crappy time, they'll think it's my spell. Genius.'

'And the language … What were you speaking?'

Tara shrugged. 'I've seen it on one of Dwaine's horror movies. Dunno. That's just what comes. Who knows what it means? It's been happening a lot lately.'

'Are *you* OK?' Elsie asked.

Tara shrugged again. 'I suppose. Yes. I've just gotta be.'

They trudged on in silence on the side of the road. Tonight it was hard to make sense of anything, but both girls knew exactly who would help them try.

Ten

The twins' faces were not only illuminated by the dancing flames of the bonfire, and the recent wonderful news that their father's test results had come back as 'clear', but their expressions were also lit up by the fact Tara and Elsie had arrived. Walking to them out of nowhere in the darkness, turning up without warning at the Smiths' giant machinery shed beside the shit-ponds fence.

Not only that, the girls were wearing *dresses*, and to the boys, in the swamping shadows of the night, they somehow looked magical beneath the sprinkle of stars above and the glow of the firelight.

'Friend or foe?' Amos had asked, peering into the darkness, a crooked grin on his freckled face.

'Jeez. What do you reckon?' replied Tara, trudging forwards, flicking yet another burr out from under the pantyhosed toes that poked like tongues from her sandals. 'These shoes are certainly not friends! I think my blisters have blisters.'

Zac rolled another two log stumps from the woodpile and patted their surfaces while Amos reached down to fill cups from a cooler containing Gwinnie's homemade lemonade and stood to pass them to the girls.

'Don't you know we're getting into fire season?' teased Elsie, who had pushed the toilet incident away as her hair dried on their walk. If Tara, who didn't have pretty clothes or a lovely room or a pony, could be OK — sort of — living in that horrible house with her horrible stepfather, who was Elsie to complain? She sat on one of the stumps, slipped off a ballet flat and began to rub her foot, determined to stay brave. 'We could see the flames all the way from the road. You're lucky Chunky Nicholson's DJing back at the hall tonight, or you'd have his fire crew onto you.'

The boys laughed sheepishly.

Gwinnie and Elvis had planned this night well in advance, knowing their boys felt shamed to be excluded from the formal. The Smiths were so incensed at the limited thinking of the people in the school system about their gifted boys that they had declared they would home-school Zac and Amos from now on. Their decision wasn't reactionary nor from a place of self-righteous parenting, and came with a lot of coaching for the boys about the behaviour and beliefs that had got them in trouble in the first place.

'Being extremely intelligent at maths, science and academics in general is one thing,' Gwinnie had said gently to the growing little men standing shame-faced before her in the wake of their suspension for 'defying' Mr Tremble. 'But emotional and social intelligence is often more important in life. As is learning to move through the world using your heart's brain, not your head's brain.' She laid the palm of her hand on her heart. 'What does your heart say about how you were with Mr Tremble? Were you considering his feelings and his views, or were you simply focused on getting your brain's clever points heard? On proving yourselves *right*. On putting Nathanial down? What will be the long-term effect of what you said to him? If you think you were justified because of how they have treated you, that's your mind's ego working. And when people let their egos get the upper hand, their life can have more bumps than it needs. Universal truths don't need proving, do they? So you shouldn't have to argue with anyone. Just being loving to all is proof.'

The boys had looked at each other.

'But he —' began Amos in a quiet voice.

Gwinnie pulled a face. 'No buts.'

Her sons, a mirror image of each other, shuffled their feet in unison, studying the toes of their scuffed work boots. Their mother's tone was rarely cross and the boys were chastened.

'You were a little persistent with Mr Tremble, weren't you? Wouldn't you say you kind of knew you were pushing him too far?'

The boys both nodded.

'Some people don't and won't think like you,' Gwinnie had said. 'You need to let some things go so as to get on with as many people as possible, even if they don't think or act like you. OK?'

'We understand, Mum. He's still a nong but.'

'Each to his own, Amos, each to his own,' Gwinnie said, shaking her head. 'Some people are slower to wake up. Especially adults and especially teachers who have been in systems for a long time,' she said. 'And yes, he is a nong but. But this is Culvert Primary we're dealing with, and the culture can even influence the smartest of boys but. Especially when it comes to speech but.' She laughed, then scruffled her fingertips through their curly black hair. 'Now go on. Git. Your father needs a hand … And he has a surprise for you.'

As the date for the formal neared, Elvis, using an old dozer he'd come by out of *Machinery Deals*, had lumbered out in a cloud of black diesel fumes to the shit-ponds shed. There, with the worn old blade, he had formed a perfect fire pit and, around it, laid the ground bare as a fire break for the boys' bonfire. Gwinnie and the twins set large stones from the paddock in a circle, making it look like some ancient ritual site. Then, using the old timber, burnable scraps cleaned out of the newly restored machinery shed and a few fallen old trees, the Smiths had built a small pyre that would burn calmly and evenly for most of the night.

The weather forecast showed the evening would be fine and still, so just on dusk, the boys had been allowed to drive themselves out in Elvis's ute, which was packed to bursting with swags, marshmallows, chops to throw on the ploughshare barbecue and even Mr Smith's guitar, should they want to have a strum. (Elvis lived in hope on that score when it came to his boys and music.) Also, for extra measure, a fire pump and water container had been set up on the back of the ute just in case of a stray spark. But after a flow of seasons under Smith management, and after a reasonable dose of spring rain, the roadhouse-property grasses were holding their greenness as the world turned slowly towards summer. It was only November and two and a half years of controlled-grazing one mob of sheep behind moveable electric fences and direct-drilling oats with modified machinery meant the place was not only finding its balance with moister, more fecund soils, it was also nowhere near tinder-dry like the other properties.

'So what happened?' Amos asked.

Elsie shut down and her hand involuntarily lifted to comb her hair down over her face. It had dried on the ends in seaweedy mermaid twirls from the toilet water and sat flat like a swimming cap on her scalp. The blood on her mole had crusted blackly. Her eyes slid away to stare at the dirt beneath her blue satin flats.

Tara twisted her mouth and wrinkled her nose. 'Boring. It was boring,' she said with a wave of her hand.

'Boring? Not a word needed here,' Zac said, clapping his hands. 'You've come to the right place. This is gonna be our night of nights! Right? Dad's test results came in today. He got the all-clear!'

'That's awesome!' Tara said joyfully.

'Oh, cool,' Elsie said.

At the grin on his face and glint in his eyes, the girls' spirits lifted.

'Here's to the Culvert Poo Crew!' They all stood to celebrate the news and pressed their cups together in a triumphant cluster, as if they were golden chalices belonging to victorious knights. They toasted themselves, Gwinnie and Elvis, the stars and the poo ponds. Then they all settled back and drank the homemade lemonade; Tara said it tasted of summer sunshine and Gwinnie's love.

'The shed looks good,' Elsie said, nodding towards the now-upright structure, illuminated by the fire. It had freshly oiled boards and a new corrugated roof complete with solar panels and clear skylights.

'Yeah!' said Amos. 'You should see inside!'

'Can we?' Elsie asked excitedly.

Amos shook his head. 'Dad's got her locked up good and proper.'

The girls glanced at the big double chain and lock that ran through the large corrugated sliding doors.

'Why?'

Amos poked at the fire with a stick. 'Let's just say he's got a lot of equipment and ideas in there that he doesn't want anyone to get their hands or peepers on.'

'Like what?' Tara asked, tilting her head. 'What sort of equipment? What ideas? Is it legal?' She was thinking of Dwaine's hydro-something 'crop' in the roof of the abattoir house, which had a skylight like the shed. The house was forever being visited by local coneheads. She would lie awake at night, hoping Dwaine wouldn't send them through her door, wishing she wasn't too scared to dob them all in to Constable Gilbert.

'What are you?' Zac asked sternly. 'The Culvert Police?' He cast Amos a dark look.

'Just asking,' said Tara defensively, tugging at her pantyhose.

'One day, when Dad's here with the key, we'll give you a look,' Amos said, not taking the hint from his brother. 'You're both gonna love what's in there!'

'What *is* in there? Tell us!' Elsie urged.

Zac shook his head. 'It's nothing interesting. Just machinery and stuff. Our usual sciencey stuff. So let's shut it, shall we, Amos?'

'Keep your undies on,' Elsie said.

'Got any more lemonade?' Tara asked, sensing the tension between the brothers.

'We got more than that!' said Amos as he leaped for the Esky.

Beneath the sweep of the sky, time slid by and soon the kids were giggling and chatting as they flamed marshmallows and sucked the melted insides from the blackened sugary casings. Amos wrapped his tongue around the end of his gum-tree stick for every last sweet taste.

When the packet was empty, Zac stood and went to the ute, where he carefully took out his father's old guitar case.

'Would you give us a tune, Elsie? All those lessons with Miss Beechcroft and we've never heard you play since that time with Dad.'

Elsie lowered her head and blushed. 'Don't reckon I've learned a thing from her. She says I can't master classical.'

'Course you can play!' Zac said. 'Your mother's always onto you about it. You haven't missed a single lesson.'

'Yeah,' Tara said. 'Go on. Play us some toons! We won't mind if you're crap. We're your friends. So even if you suck, we'll still give you a crap-clap.'

Elsie rolled her eyes. 'Thanks,' she said flatly.

Zac kneeled before her and unclipped the case, a look of pleading on his face as he handed her the guitar. As she checked her hands for stickiness, then took it meekly from him, Amos gave a small cheer and stood to throw a few more logs on the fire so that sparks danced into the night air.

After she'd tuned the guitar a little, Elsie began to play. She delicately plucked strings and strummed a chord sequence and the Elsie Jones they knew disappeared. The music she drew from the guitar was something otherworldly. The sound was etched with richness, depth and power. And then, adding to the music, she began to sing.

Zac's, Tara's and Amos's mouths hung open. It was the voice of an angel. A powerful angel. She looked like an angel too. Her singing brought together the darkness of the universe and the brightness of the stars and they radiated out of her. The vibration of her voice touched their skin and shivered goosebumps over their scalps, right through their bodies. She was singing Kasey Chambers's 'Not Pretty Enough', and channelled through her came all the pain and longing the song evoked.

Her friends sat staring, barely believing their friend was so transformed by music. She was bigger than herself, a part of the stars above and the earth below. As she lifted the song to its conclusion, all three of her friends were amazed by her grace, and one of them lost his heart to her.

Zac felt love for Elsie burst open inside himself like a firework. He was filled with the beauty of her soul that travelled to him on her music.

She faded the song into the night, opened her eyes and sat looking at them in silence. 'What?' she asked finally. 'Am I that bad? Bad enough to make you cry?'

All of them sat dumbfounded, the boys swiping away their emotion, but Tara letting her tears fall.

'Oh my God,' Zac said eventually, shaking his head. 'You're brilliant. Beyond brilliant! Beautiful.'

'Miss Beechcroft taught you that?' Tara asked, wrinkling her nose.

'Nup. She's still onto me to play the classics — this is bedroom guitaring. I just copy what's on the radio. And read stuff out of your dad's music books.'

'You copy what's on the *radio*?' asked Amos.

'Uh-huh.'

'Just like that?'

Elsie pulled a face and shrugged. 'S'pose it just comes to me.'

'What else from the radio do you copy?' Amos asked.

Elsie grinned and again pulled the guitar to her. With a percussion beat she tapped a rhythm, launching into the Dixie Chicks' 'Some Days You Gotta Dance'.

Soon Amos was up, stomping his boots in the dirt, grabbing Tara up by the hand, twirling her about so flames were mirrored in her satin dress. Zac hovered near Elsie, clapping his hands in time, shuffling his shoulders to her beat, a smile wide on his face.

Attitude flowed from her, her face contorting with soul-passion. Her little feet tapped in the dust and her head nodded in perfect time; her eyes were shut. When she finished with a roar in her throat and a twang in her voice, her friends let out a whoop.

Before they could catch their breath, she dished them up a rocking version of 'Proud Mary', a long way improved from the first shaky notes she'd played at the roadhouse six months or so earlier with Elvis. She whipped them to dancing frenzy again with a melody of Beatles and Johnny Cash songs memorised from Elvis's tatty old songbooks, a version of Garth Brooks's 'Wrapped Up In You', and eased them back with a simple and powerful version of Shania Twain's 'She's Not Just a Pretty Face'.

Again Tara, Zac and Amos were carried away by the pure essence of her voice and the far reach of the lyrics. Pride shimmered through all of them and suddenly Tara recalled the 'Poo Prophecy'. Here it was. The miracle of their friendship. The miracle of Elsie's voice. She would never forget this night.

When she was done, Elsie sat back, guitar on her lap, the fire slowing down to a slumber and her friends with their spirits on high and the warmth of her music making their hearts sing. Peace swamped her.

All of them suddenly tired, Zac and Amos went for the swags in the back of the ute, undid them and rolled them out on opposite sides of the fire.

'Well now the music show's over, it's time for a star show,' said Zac. 'Let's lie here and look at the constellations.'

'Look at the what?' Tara said. 'The constipations? At the poo ponds?' She giggled, then snorted, sending a ripple of humour through the gang.

'Your joke stinks, Tara,' Zac said.

'Yeah, it's really on the nose,' Amos said with a grin. It was as natural as honey flowing from a spoon, the way they came to lie down. Zac beside Elsie. Tara beside Amos. The twins so tall now their feet hung off the end of the green canvas of their well-used dust-beaten childhood swags. All four lay on their backs, the fire's sparks singing for a moment, then gone. The boys stretching their long arms up to the dome of black above, index fingers pointing to the stars, tracing the lines of the Southern Cross, the Iron Pot, the astrological formations, then the other more obscure constellations the girls had never known of.

They lay for a time in silence and each of them, boy and girl, and again, as natural as bees to a flower, began to hold hands. Amos and Tara. Zac and Elsie.

'You look really pretty tonight,' Zac said quietly, turning his head to Elsie so his deep brown eyes were fixed on her face.

Elsie felt a jolt of panic. The mole. Her hand flew to cover her mouth and she rolled her head away. She never thought about the mole when she was with the boys and Tara, but now, being so near to Zac and with him saying that, her body filled with tension.

Zac gently pulled her hand away. 'Why do you do that? I don't see it unless you cover it. You are a kick-arse cowgirl. Dad says so and I know so.' At the sound of his voice, Elsie felt herself relax. This was Zac. He was like a brother, only better than that. Simon was her brother and he sucked. Zac was better than a brother. He was Zac. She felt warmth tingling in her chest.

'Dad said in Grade Seven science Mr Tremble would try to teach us that the brain is where all the action is. But the brain is not the first organ in the body. It's actually the heart.' He rolled over, took Elsie's small hand and laid her palm on his chest. 'Feel it?'

She nodded.

'It's the heart that sends electrical signals to the brain and that's what triggers all the chemicals that guide the body. Our family's been studying it and trying to put it into practice.' His eyes shone in the firelight with relief and joy. 'Dad reckons the medical treatment he had combined with knowing that he had to keep his heart and his spirit happy all helped towards his healing. And even if he hadn't healed, he still said his heart would be happy because he loved us. But he did heal.' Zac's voice cracked. The strain of his dad's battle, now won, catching up with him.

Elsie felt tears of relief and empathy rise. 'That's so excellent,' she said, reaching out to gently squeeze his shoulder.

'He amazed the doctors. They're trying to work out how it happened as they said he was done for. But Dad learned that when we are sending the best signal from our hearts to our bodies, when we are feeling joy and peace and all those good things, that healing chemistry is optimised in our bodies. If he didn't heal his body, he intended to heal his spirit and die well anyway. So he kept teaching us that it would all turn out well either way no matter what the results showed. But he was able to optimise his healing chemistry … And it's all good now.'

'Optimise?'

'Yes, optimise. You heal fastest when you follow things that bliss you out.'

Zac stared into the fire, the flames of which were slowly consuming a gnarled tree limb.

'Being with you blisses me out, Elsie Jones.'

Elsie drew a sudden breath. She had heard the boys at Culvert Primary speak. They talked about cricket and footy. They talked about TV shows and PlayStation games. They talked in stilted short sentences. They never talked this way. Elsie knew Zac was smart. But that night he seemed so grown up.

'You are beautiful,' Zac said at last. 'Mum said for me to be brave enough to give a compliment to you. So there you go.'

Elsie felt as if she had stopped breathing. Could any boy say that of her? With her *disfigurement*? 'Are you for real?' she replied almost sarcastically.

They lay there in silence for a time, the awkwardness of their new feelings slowly choking the old flow of the friendship that had been so easy.

'Yes,' said Zac, a little quieter and less confidently.

Tara and Amos were lost in their own private conversation. Tara was giggling. Saying something about hearts and farts. Amos was chuckling back and poking her sides so that she squealed a little. Then for a time they all lay in silence.

'Shall we get it over with then?' Amos asked, propping himself on his elbow and looking over the last of the fire to Elsie and Zac.

'What?' asked Elsie, glancing across to Amos and Tara on the other swag, the embers lighting their faces so they both glowed.

'Our first kisses.'

'What?' said Elsie almost as a shriek.

Amos shrugged. 'Yes. Easier with mates like you and Tara than some girls from school who might laugh at us,' he said, tugging on Tara's nose. 'It's not as if Zac and I are catch of the day. We look like a couple of rubber bands that have been stretched too much!'

Tara batted his hand away, laughing. 'I suppose,' she said, wondering what it would be like to really like someone, fall in love with him. After the ugly nights with Dwaine, she didn't want to kiss any boy. But Amos wasn't a boy. He was *Amos*. He felt safe and funny, but above all kind. And he really did like her.

'Well, I know no one else would kiss me,' Amos said. 'And we should do it before high school, don't you reckon? Elsie? You in? You gonna give it a go with Zac?'

Elsie turned her head and looked at Zac's profile. 'No one would be brave enough to kiss me, what with …' Her voice trailed off and soon she could speak no words, because Elsie Jones was being kissed by Zac Smith.

First she felt his soft hesitant lips, then tasted his sweet marshmallow tongue. He reached for her hand and held it softly as they kissed. His brother too had rolled over and was kissing Tara. Her fists tightened as congealed and pungent memories of Dwaine flashed into her mind, but then Amos snickered.

'I think I dribbled,' he said, and Tara found herself laughing. The connection between this moment and Dwaine was suddenly banished like startled crows flapping away in the night. Again Tara recalled the Poo Prophecy. Here it was again. The miracle of their friendship, of the music. The miracle of their first kisses. She wanted to say that there would be more miracles to come at the poo ponds, but she was too busy feeling the weird zing that came from kissing Amos Smith.

It was short-lived. Headlights. The sound of an engine rumbling over the paddocks broke the moment. The slamming of a car door.

Stepping into the fire ring came Gwinnie Smith, her arms wrapped about herself, her eyes scanning the scene. She frowned at her sons lying on top of their swags with the girls in their arms.

'Do you know your teachers, Constable Gilbert and Elsie's parents are out looking for you girls?' she asked, shaking her head. 'You'd better come with me.'

Elsie and Tara stood up, the magic of the night blasted into history, the friendship with the twins feeling fractured and intruded upon by this adult presence. It was not specifically Gwinnie the kids were worried about. It was the judgement that came from a small town. From tonight, in the small, small-minded dying town of Culvert led by Kelvin Jones and his wife, there would be no going back for Elsie, Tara, Zac and Amos.

Part Two

Eleven

Four years later

'It is with great pride,' boomed Councillor-Mayor Jones on the microphone, 'that we announce the one point two million dollars in funding for Culvert's sewage waste system works upgrade.' The crowd of VIPs, politicians, the goody-two-shoes committee and grey-haired Life Members of the Culvert Agricultural Show society applauded. With great swagger, the navy-suit-clad councillor-mayor lolloped his large body across the small stage that had been set up in the corner of the CWA luncheon pavilion and pulled on a red tasselled cord. The small swarm of politicians who were frenzied with pre-election nerves clapped politely as a tacky artist's impression of the treatment plant was revealed from behind velvet curtains. From her vantage point in the CWA show kitchen, Tara noted they were the same curtains that had been used to unveil the new footy clubrooms ten years back. The mayor picked up his pointer and tapped on the diagram.

'Phase one of the project will be an audit of the existing treatment plant structure, then the construction of a state-of-the-art ...'

'State of the *fart*,' sniggered Tara as she swirled a ladle through pumpkin soup in a giant pot. She turned to the women in the kitchen. 'He loves his poo-pond pontifications so much they tell me he's going to proudly and profoundly pronounce Project Poo to the people *again* tonight at the Culvert Show Gala Ball! *Per*-leeze!' Tara rolled her eyes and grimaced. 'I'm not going to it. I don't want to hear this excrement again! How much hot air does that man need to blow out his backside? Everyone knows he's full of shit. They probably need to upgrade the town's plant because of the faecal content he alone speaks!'

'Tara!' cautioned Chunky Nicholson's wife, Barb, red in the face from cooking under the pressure of a luncheon deadline and worried the CWA ladies would again object to Tara's presence at the official function, even if she was only out the back in the kitchen. She had invited Tara to help because she was tired of seeing the girl wandering the streets of Culvert.

For the past year Tara had barely been considered a member of the Grade Ten student community of Culvert State High School. Instead she was classed as a town vagrant on the streets of Culvert, with her wildly curling long dark red hair and frumpy op-shop clothes. Shopping bag in hand, book in another, reading as she went, lollipop firmly inserted into one side of her gob, she ambled about with no apparent destination in mind. She'd nearly been hit by many a passing car, ute or tractor as she dawdled across the street, which was a difficult task in Culvert. These days, when it wasn't harvest time or school pick-up, you could fire a cannon down the main street at lunch hour and not hit a single soul.

For the past two years Tara had spent the bulk of her days at home nursing her mother. Nora Green had grown more and more obese. Tara had all but given up trying to get to classes to finish Grades Nine and Ten, but her appetite for learning was voracious. Her mother's care involved swiping a face washer in the crevices of her fat rolls, changing her nighties, so large that they resembled spinnakers after they were hoisted on the clothesline, and hauling her to the toilet. Then cleaning up the house after Dwaine. Cleaning, cleaning.

For years Dr Patak had warned Tara that her mother was becoming morbidly obese. These past six months Nora Green had not once left the house, moving only from the bedroom to the lounge and back again, Tara tending to her every need, Dr Patak making house calls with increasing frustration and resignation to the woman's commitment to self-destruction.

When her mother slept after lunch, Tara bothered the women at the local library almost daily. She arrived at the counter to order book after book on all manner of topics. Most of them the librarians deemed inappropriate for someone Tara's age, but knowing what sort of life she must live in that awful house, they'd ordered them for her anyway.

The books were on subjects like feng shui, extra-terrestrial activities, conspiracy theories, suppression of information on alien visitations, books on angels, books on fairies, books on astral travel, on self-help, on more self-help, on forgiveness, on sexual abuse, on love, on making money, on changing brain waves, on dreams, on beautifying the home and even ones on guinea-pig costumes and knitted clothes for dogs, though Tara Green didn't even have a dog. She was just plain weird, the Culvert Library staff decided, lovely and sweet, plus a little sarcastic, but *weird* nonetheless.

After her library visits she would stop by the IGA for four pies with sauce, which went directly out of the pie warmer into her mouth, then she wandered on to the bakery for an entire tray of vanilla custard slice, of which she would save the bulk for her and her mother when she got home. All the while in her head Tara would argue with herself, after reading a book on the dangers of too much sugar and fats, why, no matter how hard she tried, she simply could not stop eating junk. She knew the bottom line on the eating business was she just didn't like herself. In fact the word 'hate' barely covered her low self-opinion.

On the other side of puberty, Tara now stood at almost six foot and nearly a hundred kilos and, after hauling her mother about, she was as strong as a Mallee bull. The beer-gutted Dwaine had long since given up his visits to her bedroom. The appeal for him — her childhood — was gone, plus one night not long after the Grade Six formal Tara had almost busted Dwaine's skull with a fire poker before he could get on top of her. With blood falling in a veil down his face, and his screams as loud as the ones the pigs made when he slaughtered them, Dwaine had run from the room. Tara had, with a steely voice, dared him to call the cops. She had channelled the Archangel Michael for the task and she held the fire poker aloft in front of her like a sword, shaking within, but holding her outer self strong.

After that, Dwaine had retreated to a diet of internet porn and X-rated videos in the bedroom with her mother, leaving Tara be. Instead in the early hours of the morning Dwaine took to feeding Tara's mother giant bowls of fried food and chocolate and playing sex games with her, like hiding a Mars Bar in her fat crevices. Tara could hear most of it through the thin walls of the abattoir house and little by little she retreated within herself.

She also stopped going to the Smiths' roadhouse after the night of the formal. The happy family there reminded her too much of what she didn't have. What she would never have. She couldn't face the possibility that Amos would never kiss her again either. It was better to remain lonely. Poor Elsie had got in a lot of trouble for running away from the formal to 'be with the boys', and Elsie's mum had banned her from ever being in touch with Tara. Then the twins had started home-schooling, and the magic of that time was now in the past. The Culvert Poo Crew had disbanded. She never saw the twins now. She knew at some point Gwinnie had tried to intervene with Tara's home life after Constable Gilbert came knocking on the door with some lady from a government social service. The fallout from Dwaine was unbearable, and after a few interviews, Tara, filled with fear for her own life and her mother's, had bluffed them all. The home visits and psych tests had all come to nothing and eventually the 'government do-gooders', as Dwaine called them, had gone away. Now Gwinnie Smith and her family at the roadhouse were utterly blacklisted by Dwaine. Tara never walked that way: instead she wandered past the railway station, balancing on the tracks, reading, hoping she wouldn't hear the train come and it would smash her out of this world and this life, but unfortunately for Tara, like the cars, trains were infrequent at Culvert. Gwinnie, if she saw her, tried to stop and chat, but Tara always shut the conversation down. She just couldn't bring herself to open up to her. Shame fought within her body violently each time she looked in Gwinnie's kind eyes.

Now with the school year over, Tara knew the township folk would be less tolerant of her when they saw her in the streets. She also knew there was no way she was doing her HSC by correspondence with the other Culvert dropkicks. What they taught in school was crap anyway, she reckoned. Summer was rolling in and she was launching a career. She was about to earn her own money as a cleaner — she already had three clients interested in the business she had called 'Partners in Grime'. Tara was yet to get a cleaning partner, but it paid to think big. If she had read correctly the signs the angels were sending her, her whole life was about to turn. Her Doreen Virtue angel cards had shown her, and she'd feng shui'd the Morton house so much her luck *had* to change for the better. At least she had been convinced of that until the previous week, when the centre of her universe had imploded.

When she'd arrived home from the shops, Tara had made sure Dwaine was busy processing carcasses in the killing shed. She could hear the radio blaring eighties hits, and she knew his mind would be immersed in the issue of which horse to back on the TAB that night. Tara carried books in one hand and custard slice in the other into the house. The moment she stepped inside she knew the already dark energy of the house was altered to an even darker state. She had frowned, the hairs on her body standing up in dread.

'Mum?' she'd called out, setting her things down on the kitchen bench.

Nora Green didn't answer. She couldn't answer. She was slumped dead against the toilet wall. Her potato-sack-sized undies draped about her rolled-roast ankles, eyes glazed over, her skin deathly grey. Lank greasy hair sat flat on her flaking scalp where she'd sweated and strained at her bowels until her heart had given out.

Tara had stood in the doorway with her hand covering her mouth, tears welling in her eyes. 'Oh, Mum.' Her voice quavered.

She stepped forwards and laid a hand on her mother's. The coldness of the skin jolted her. Tara felt the sorrow of the ages swamp her. She had loved her mother, but hated her weakness at the same time. She'd hated the way she'd left her exposed all these years. To Dwaine. To poor diet. To a lack of care. To everything. All the reading Tara had done on becoming a better person, on healing, on the afterlife and the eternalness of love couldn't have prepared her for the rip of grief and shock that roared through her now. She knew she had to call the ambulance, Dr Patak or someone. But Tara first wanted to make her mother decent. She craned past her and flushed the loo, though the dreadful smell remained. Nora's tragic gigantic white legs were exposed almost to her bubbled upper thighs, the thick dark hair on them bristling like unscraped pork belly, her undies showing a dirty skidding stain. Tara was ashamed she hadn't helped her change them that morning.

She ran for fresh ones, then stooped to tear away the stained knickers and lift her mum's feet into the clean pair. She tried to hoist them up. Her mother was heavy in life, but now in death, she was like a mountain, unmoveable. Tara sobbed as she tried and tried again to pull the underpants up over her mother. Eventually she went back to the bedroom and grabbed a freshly washed coverlet she'd bought Nora from Manky's Department and Haberdashery Store one Mother's Day and draped it over her. She looked ridiculous in the floral quilt with her crusty mouth cast open and her jaw so slack her chin disappeared into her neck. Tara went to the bathroom for a hairbrush. She drifted back to her mother's body and, crying, she began to brush her mother's hair.

Dwaine had found Tara like that over an hour later. She had almost brushed one side of her mother's head bald. She brushed over and over, murmuring and crying, all the devastation of their ugly, wasted lives rippling through her.

'What the fuck are you doing?' screamed Dwaine when he took in the vision of the dead mother and the vacant daughter. She felt a hard backhand to her head. She cowered at her mother's feet, then, fearing his steel caps in her back, she had crawled past Dwaine, whimpering and knowing that she was now totally alone in this world.

Dwaine was shouting, 'Nora, Nora! Wake up, you silly bitch!' and shaking her.

Not wanting Dwaine to touch her mother any more, Tara at last dialled Emergency Services.

As it turned out, it had been no good getting an ambulance. They'd had to get Chunky Nicholson's fire crew in. Nora Green was so wedged in the dunny, it took five of Chunky's crew to crowbar and carry her out, even firing up the chainsaw for the door. The stench left behind made three of the men vomit. From the hallway, Tara had watched, blank. White. Cold. Humiliated. As the men had at last got her mother into the ambulance, Tara felt a comforting hand on her shoulder. She turned and smiled.

'Michael,' she said, 'I knew you would come.' There was no one there. No one at all. Then Tara Green had gone and lain down on her bed and pretended she wasn't there either.

As it was early summer, with already scorching temperatures, and their cool room was getting rather full from a run on elderly deaths, the Vanderbergs at Rington Funeral Service wanted to bury the fat woman quickly, so Nora Green's existence was all over within a few days. Dwaine insisted on a private funeral so not even the Smiths could come. It was just Tara, Dwaine and the half-cut Reverend Knopf. Done and dusted in an hour. Afterwards when Dwaine went out, getting blind at the pub, Tara sat on the sunken couch where her mother had sat. She wore her only dress, which strained against the fat rolls under her arms and over her back. Tara vowed she would get some money together and leave the abattoir house and this way of being.

As she did, she heard Gwinnie Smith knocking on the door, front and back, calling her name, but the shame of herself and of her mother kept Tara trapped on the couch like lead weight. Instead Barb Nicholson had stepped in later, banging bossily on the screen door, getting Chunky to force the lock. Chunky had recounted to his wife the horror-show story of getting the body out of the house, with the young daughter hovering and muttering like the girl from the movie *Nell*. The Nicholsons made everyone's business their business. Everyone in Culvert knew that without them the footy club would be stuffed, the cricket club buggered, the bowls twilight tournament dead in the water, and there would be no local show. The fire crew would also suffer, as no other bastard wanted to be on call twenty-four/seven — especially not to drag morbidly obese women out of dunnies. And so Barb made Tara her main 'project'; she had started by pressing the CWA to give her a role as a volunteer in the show kitchen. Which was why Tara was there that day wearing plastic gloves, a food-hygiene hair net and CWA apron, and listening to Elsie's wanky father. The councillor-mayor boomed on as she tumbled a pile of warm bread rolls into a basket.

'I'll take them, thanks, Tara,' Barb said now, grabbing the basket.

'Are you sure you don't want a hand?' Tara offered, wanting to get a closer look at the new improved shit-ponds picture. 'I can take Mr Poop's soup out to him if you like.'

Barb looked Tara up and down, taking in the clothes beneath her apron: Tara's pilling grey tracksuit bottoms, tatty runners and the red hoodie with stains on the front. It clashed with her hair horribly. Barb waggled her permed head and pursed her thin lips.

'Beverly won't have it. You know how she gets,' Barb said of the CWA president who was second in command to Barb on all things community and often tussled for leadership with her.

Tara knew Barb was trying to be kindly, but she was over being treated as either a charity case or a bogan loser. She shrugged. 'Suit yourself.'

She grabbed a roll, tore it open, slathered it with butter and scoffed it in two mouthfuls, chewing and smiling at the other two irritated CWA women who were now ferrying bowls of soup out to the show guests. The other reason she wanted a stickybeak was because she could see the back of Sarah Jones's neatly bobbed head as she sat at the front, sipping water. She wondered why Elsie wasn't at the luncheon. She had heard Elsie was back in town. That in itself made her nervous: she really didn't want Elsie to see what she'd allowed herself to become. When she was nervous, she was hungry.

She reached under a tea towel for a scone and shoved it in her mouth, surveying Sarah Jones as she chewed. She still looked like a prize snob, too far above the rest to help in a kitchen, preferring to organise posh pyramid-selling parties and luncheons with her upper-crust grazier ladies as fundraisers than to mix with Barb and Beverly and their type. As far as Tara was concerned, Elsie Jones must've gone the same way. Elsie hadn't been to see Tara once since she went to boarding school four years prior. Not once. And even though Tara knew she was back, Elsie hadn't even been in touch about her mother dying. Even if Sarah Jones may have forbidden her to call in, Elsie still should've at least tried to keep in contact. What kind of friend did that?

Twelve

Outside in the paddocks at Grassmore Estate, Elsie's brother, Simon, went another round in the combine harvester, severing the heads off uniformly short wheat soldiers, dwarfed and battle weary in tired dry soils. There was no point waiting for harvest time for this crop of pinched grain. It was stunted and stuffed. Simon and his father had decided to gather what they could early and store it in the giant bellies of their on-farm silos instead. It would only be a matter of weeks before the dams ran low and the grass dried up to dust, blowing away in the hot northwesterly that frazzled any hope of profits.

Then, from a rattling feeder, Simon and Kelvin would daily trail the gut-slicing hard-husked grain to sheep. Sheep that were already too weak to digest the pitiful crop, tottering on doddery hooves, punch-drunk from hunger, the acid of the grain burning their insides. Then the men, congratulating themselves on a job well done, would come inside, drink tea thirstily from cups, help themselves to Sarah's caramel slice, then sit and complain bitterly about the drought. About always being on the end of a grain auger, and the fact they had had to let all but one of the men go. Now it was basically just a father-and-son operation. Times were tough in farming, they constantly said. From her bedroom Elsie looked out at the depressing scene and the cloud of topsoil hovering in the air. What her father and brother did to Grassmore was, in her mind, a travesty.

Elsie'd chosen Social Science as a Grade Ten elective and had madly gone about Googling 'technological agriculture and its impact on humanity' as a project. At boarding school there was a zippy city internet connection and hours to spare during the sprawling lonely weekends. The more she discovered on the net about the damage caused by big corporations pushing synthetic fertilisers and chemicals on already struggling farmers, the disastrous consequences to soil health from ploughing and over-grazing land and poor farming practices in bare-soil irrigation, all backed by ignorant banking systems, the more she felt her insides turn with anger at the stubborn self-righteousness of her father and his protégé son. Their ignorance inflicted on the land. As a young woman, she could now see the way the men of her family were blinded by fancy catalogues and the flattering house calls the fertiliser reps made. The bigger the tractor, the bigger your balls, Elsie thought sarcastically.

Elsie was discovering that the ideal future of farming meant ignoring what the big companies and their paid scientists said, and recreating a farm that supported everyone on it, from kids through to grandparents. From her self-motivated studies, she knew that many farmers were already making the break away to no-till cropping and farming systems that embraced both old and new more balanced ways. She was learning the importance of building humus in the soil. Of direct selling to customers. Of honouring Mother Nature's cycles rather than trying to control them with science. The more she discovered, the more she saw her brother and father just talked crap about 'farming'. But what did it matter? Now she was back home the excitement of her learning had withered like the short-rooted plants in the dead soil on Grassmore. In this family she was a *girl*. She had no say. She was of no importance.

She was about to shove her iPod earphones in and crank up some Green Day when her mother broke her thoughts, striding back in from her luncheon at the showgrounds. She ordered her to the mirror. 'Hurry up, Eleanor! I still have to change too. Dad's campaign has started, and tonight is important! We can't be late. If he's re-elected, it comes with a salary raise.' Sarah Jones reached inside the wardrobe, her lips thinning crossly. 'I know Zelda Rogerson is pushing Cuthbertson to challenge your father as mayor. The hide — after all we've done for them.' She turned back to Elsie. 'So if you could just wear this dress when you perform tonight at the Show Gala Ball, and not say anything on the mic, just sing, that would be *wonderful*. Do this, Eleanor. For your father.'

Elsie looked at the green floral dress her mother held. Sarah had selected it from Laura Ashley in Bondi Junction. On the bed was a box that wore a ruff of white tissue paper. Inside were little matching flats. The same kind of shoes her mother had dressed her in when she was six. And again now, at *sixteen*. Elsie sighed. She knew she'd had enough.

It felt weird to be back. The house paddock where Jasper had lived was sadly empty. Her mother had sold him three years back to a girl in Rington who wanted a start in pony club. A girl 'from the right kind of family', her mother had said. Sarah Jones had spent the money from the pony on 'some nice new clothes' for Elsie that she'd posted to her in Sydney with the news.

When she lost Jasper, without even a chance to say goodbye, Elsie had cried for weeks. In fact she was still crying, sneaking out to the shed to inhale the scent of the few items her mother hadn't found to pass on to the right-family girl. An old saddle blanket. A few lingering hairs in a bent-bristled brush. It was an ache she just couldn't soothe. Even poor Marbles was so old and deaf now he barely wanted to come for a walk these days and lethargically remained on the verandah, Sarah Jones cursing him every time she had to step over his prostrate snoring body. Marbles would wake as he cowered away from Sarah's angry energy, flattening his ears in shame.

Elsie could relate to Marbles about her mother. Since boarding school her rare visits home were now torturously lonely. The state of the sheepdogs with their chain-mad expressions and ribby sides was just depressing. Her father's working dogs were so conditioned to fear a boot in the guts, they were well practised at not being seen and so weren't the sort to cuddle up to. They had little time for humans. No matter how many treats Elsie snuck out to them, they still whined and shrank in her presence.

Adding to her loneliness, after her escape from the Grade Six formal, now over four years earlier, her mother had forbidden Elsie to ever see the twins again, let alone Tara, who her mother believed to be the ringleader of the entire shebang. Poor Tara, Elsie thought. Sarah Jones, on their drive back from the train station, had recounted the gruesome story of Tara's mother being chainsawed out of the house. As she and her mother drove past the even more decrepit abattoir house, Elsie reasoned that it had been hard enough fitting in at boarding school, let alone staying in touch with a girl like Tara who all the other girls loathed.

Elsie thought of Tilly and Scarlett in the dorm at school and how they entertained the other girls with stories of Tara. They made fun of her obsession with poo jokes, her fat guinea pig that looked just like her, her weird angel stories and crazy-lady language, not forgetting the obese mother. The other girls always shrieked with laughter, egging them on, and during those times, Elsie felt relieved their focus was off her.

Then Scarlett and Tilly told tales of the loopy mad-scientist experimenting twins who had been kicked out of school. Elsie saw how the cruel girls divided the world into 'cool' people and 'daggy' ones, with no sense of how they fractured the world in doing so. Amos and Zac were top of Tilly and Scarlett's list of dorks, so to avoid trouble and being put up there with them, Elsie followed Tilly and Scarlett's lead. She knew she was being cowardly, but she chose to keep her head down and retreated into herself. She cultivated an icy 'I don't give a stuff' rock-chick image, spending the bulk of her time with her iPod earphones jammed in her ears, music becoming her only refuge. Defeated by both her mother and boarding school, she stuck to herself on visits home to Culvert and shoved any thoughts of her former childhood mates aside.

Alone in her bedroom, Elsie wondered if she should at least call Tara, but she felt she had left their friendship too long ago in the past. She also knew she had to lie low around her mother so that no suspicion was raised before tonight. She knew she'd so far been lucky not to be busted on her secret nocturnal activities in Sydney. She'd been sneaking out to play with a pub band on weekends. The rush that came from getting attention from an audience was her ultimate thrill. She wanted to keep that buzz with the band, and tonight she would claim that right. Still she felt utterly guilty for not contacting Tara, but what could she do? Her mother had made it all too hard since the night of the formal.

Elsie still recalled with a flush of shame her mother's painstakingly vague questions about that night. Gwinnie had told Sarah that she'd found 'the kids' singing and eating marshmallows around a bonfire. But Sarah would hear nothing of the truth. Nor would she accept that Elsie had been bullied by the girls at the formal. 'The Morgans and Featheringtons would never raise daughters who flushed other girls' heads in toilets!' Sarah Jones had exclaimed, shocked.

After that night Sarah looked at Elsie as if she was in some way even more tainted than the mole made her. Never would she ask Elsie outright about the boys. No way could Sarah ever just talk straight about sex.

Elsie'd overheard her father raging about 'having those young perverts charged', but Sarah had said that even if they did take action, the publicity would be bad for his political career. So they'd let it go.

Elsie now looked at her own sad face in the mirror. Tonight was the night to end this misery, she resolved. Her mother saw where she was gazing.

'That's better, isn't it?' Sarah Jones asked as she gathered Elsie's long sheen of blonde hair and draped it back over her shoulder. Elsie was taller than her now. 'The surgeon did a good job.'

When her daughter didn't respond, Sarah Jones went on, 'It's only the teeniest of scars, really. It'll be all healed by the time you head back to boarding school next year for Grade Eleven. Make-up will conceal it for tonight.'

Elsie looked blankly into the mirror, not recognising the girl there. She remembered how the operation had been arranged without any kind of discussion or warning. While inwardly she was relieved the mole was gone, the way her parents had organised it all had been the cruellest of cuts. Like the way they had simply sold Jasper without any discussion. They'd done the same with this and simply made the arrangement with not one word to her. Her parents were crap.

It had been a dozy sort of prep time after classes when the neat-as-a-pin unsmiling dorm mistress had come knocking on her door one Friday afternoon.

'Your mother is here,' she'd said, then sniffed with superiority.

Elsie had looked up with shocked surprise from the copy of *Horse Deals* hidden inside her biology textbook. She had been dreaming of one day owning a new horse and maybe even being allowed a tiny turn at farming just a postage-stamp corner of Grassmore, the way she'd been learning about on the internet.

'My mother?' she'd echoed in almost a whisper. Her mother *never* came to visit.

Sarah Jones had stood in the old hall beside the polished banister of the wide, grand stairs. Even though her mother was tiny, she looked just as imposing as the giant stern-faced clock behind her. In her neat outfit, perfect hair and make-up and freshly done nails, Sarah looked more like a kept corporate wife with too much time on her hands than a struggling farmer's wife from the wheat belt out west.

'Mum?' said Elsie, frowning at the top of the stairs.

'Hello, dear,' her mother had said. Elsie noticed her own overnight bag on the floor beside her mother's neat court shoes, and a waiting taxi outside.

'Ready?'

Elsie tilted her head. 'For what?'

In the taxi her mother explained that she and her father had booked Elsie into a leading Sydney cosmetic and reconstructive surgeon, and that by tomorrow 'that *dreadful* mole will be removed forever'.

It was the first time ever her mother had mentioned the mole, and surgery. The word 'dreadful' swarmed in Elsie's head. She felt nausea swamp her.

'He's very good,' Sarah had reassured her. 'Discreet.' She patted her daughter's knee.

Arriving at the hospital in the taxi, Elsie felt vomit rise, along with shame, and then she hurled the remains of her lunch onto her school shoes and the floor of the taxi. The emotional upset of the news that her parents truly hated her face as much as she'd always thought had tripped her up inside. Her mother had let out a frustrated cry and exited the taxi as fast as she could, thrusting an extra fifty dollars, with barely disguised fury, to the taxi driver, who was shouting in Mandarin and gesturing wildly to the spew all over the floor of his cab. Briskly her mother had taken Elsie's elbow and steered her into the hospital to meet the surgeon.

The black-haired doctor was freakishly perfect-looking, as if he had operated on his own face, with its smooth skin, Superman chin and slick of black hair.

'I'm Dr Day,' he said as if he was a radio announcer. He looked directly at her mole. On hearing his name, all Elsie could do was roll the tune of 'Camptown Races' around in her head, with 'do-dah-day' running on loop.

'So this is the culprit,' he said to her mother after he'd stood to more closely inspect the mole. Sarah Jones had nodded and smiled, looking up at him as if she was in awe. 'It's straightforward,' Dr Day said, cupping Elsie's chin. 'I work with the most complex of reconstructive surgeries following severe burns and with the most tricky of cosmetic procedures. This one will be a cinch.' His breath smelled of mango. He sat back at his desk and grinned like a Botoxed hyena. 'We'll operate on her first thing in the morning.'

Elsie had woken up groggy after the operation, uncertain who she was. Now three months later, she was even more unsure. The mole, she realised, had been part of her. Hate it though she did, it was at least a form of rebellion against her parents. Now she had become their *ideal* daughter and had had it removed just in time for her father's mayoral campaign, launched via a family portrait in the *Culvert Newsletter.* As Elsie stood before the mirror, she wondered what the awful surgeon had done with the mole. Did they keep such things in tiny glass vials to show medical students? Or did they just burn them in hospital incinerators? The humiliation of her youth might have disappeared up a chimney stack and be floating as ash over the ugly cityscape. She decided if her youth had gone, it was time to claim her adulthood, and tonight she would show her family and Culvert just what she was made of. The pub crowds of inner-city Sydney didn't just see her as little Eleanor Jones, daughter of the mayor. It was time Culvert saw her true self and it was time her parents learned she did not *belong* to them.

'Mum?' Elsie said to her reflection.

'Yes, dear,' Sarah said, pleased her daughter was at last speaking.

'Can I practise driving tonight, please, to the ball? It's not far and I'd like to give driving at night a go on the way home.'

'Why yes, of course, dear,' Sarah said with relief that her daughter was showing an interest in *something.* Although the thought of Elsie driving the Pajero did jolt Sarah Jones a little, it was a small concession given her daughter's *mood* — a mood that had seemed to last for years now.

'Thanks,' Elsie said quietly. 'I'll head down and put the L-plates on. Don't want to get dust on my dress doing it later.'

'Good idea,' said Sarah. Perhaps Elsie was learning something at that expensive school after all.

The Culvert Show Gala Ball was held as always down the less leaky end of the giant show pavilion shed. People were arriving in clusters in their best suits and dresses. The night belonged to the town's elite, so the sheep and wool producers were heading the charge to the pre-ball drinks. The local townspeople, the ones more inclined to go all out at footy finals, dragged their feet, seeing and understanding the unacknowledged class hierarchy and their place in it.

On the grass outside the shed, Kelvin Jones alighted from the front passenger seat puffed up and furious that his wife had agreed to let Elsie drive them. His daughter had motored along the highway at no faster than forty kilometres per hour the whole way, sitting straight-backed and peering through the windscreen, looking out for kangaroos, clutching the steering wheel and veering a little too far over towards the guide posts for Kelvin's liking.

'You can go a little faster,' he'd said angrily. He was used to telling her to slow down when she revved about on his paddocks, fishtailing the old rattler farm ute in the back end and spitting up dust doing circle work when she thought he wouldn't catch her. And here she was trundling along like she was driving Miss Daisy to a flower show. She was deliberately trying to antagonise him, Kelvin realised. He cast her a dark look and Elsie knew her father had caught on that she was stirring him.

In the back seat Sarah, perfect in a black Carla Zampatti dress, sat next to a freshly washed and neatly groomed moleskin-clad and RM-Williams-booted Simon. He was straightening his tie and slicking his hair over to one side, a mirror of his father's.

'She's just trying to make you late, Dad,' Simon said, 'and get your goat.'

'Am not, dick brain,' said Elsie, frowning at her brother in the rear-vision mirror. 'I'm not after anyone's goat. If I hit a roo in this wanker-mobile, I'm in shitter's ditch, so shut up, you bloody back-seat driver.'

'Eleanor!' her mother said.

Elsie pivoted around in the driver's seat. 'Oh, I do apologise, Mother,' she said in her best Queen's English, placing the palm of her hand on her chest. 'I forgot myself.'

Her father huffed. What an attitude, he thought. Now arriving at the ball, Kelvin Jones tugged his suit jacket over his belly and marched over towards the show pavilion, leaving his wife to make her own way. There he extended a hand to Deputy Mayor Rogerson, who was standing beside Zelda and Nathanial.

'Ah! The outgoing mayor,' Cuthbertson said through a gritted smile. 'Good to see you, old boy!'

'Very funny, Rogerson. Very funny,' said Kelvin, shaking his hand, but without a smile, glancing about for staff from the council offices to back him up.

Watching him through narrowed eyes, Elsie got out of the car and opened the door for her mother. I have to take it easy, she thought, even though she was ready to explode. 'OK?' she asked, forcing a smile at her mother.

Her mother nodded stiffly as she applied lipstick in the small round mirror of her make-up compact. Getting out of the car, she held her posture straight and smoothed down her clothes. There were strings of tension that ran in cords beneath the skin on either side of her long slender neck. She patted her hair back into its perfect blonde bob.

'You go on, Mum,' Elsie said. 'Dad needs his chief campaigner by his side. Thanks for letting me drive.'

'I'm watching you,' Sarah said coldly before walking towards her husband.

With relief Elsie saw Simon too had leaped from the car and was headed towards a cluster of young male farmers who were already standing about swigging on glasses of beer at the entrance to the pavilion. They met him with a collective of deep noises, like the baritone voices of rams.

Sarah glanced back at her demure-looking daughter, standing calmly in her pretty green dress with its blooms of tiny flowers. Her strange demeanour made Sarah feel uneasy. She walked back over to Elsie. 'I know you will do your father and me proud. You look so pretty now.'

Now? Elsie felt the knife. She waited until her mother was out of sight, disappearing inside the pavilion in the wake of her husband, then began to get the guitar case from the back of the Pajero. She flipped up the tartan picnic blanket Sarah Jones always took to tennis and instead of the acoustic guitar they had borrowed from Miss Beechcroft for the night, she emerged with her own electric guitar and amp. The one her mother didn't know she hauled around the pub gigs in Sydney. The one her mother forbade her to play.

Thirteen

The red-curtained display board of the planned sewage plant was now reset on a bigger stage in the show pavilion. The building was festooned with a woeful tangle of haphazardly hung balloons and streamers. On the stage stood the silent instruments of Rington's old-time waltz band, impossibly named Waltz Me Around Again Darlin'. In the wings, Christine Sheen, the mayor's assistant, swathed in a bold patterned purple dress with a plunging neckline, straightened Councillor-Mayor Jones's tie. She thrust her breasts out further just to see Kelvin's eyeballs roll when he saw her huge cleavage so close to his nose. He cleared his throat, tearing his eyes away, and looked down to his speech notes. The wickedly funny Christine smiled to herself. She got him every time. The councillor-mayor glanced at his watch.

'Where is that girl?' he said. Couldn't Sarah be more helpful in organising Elsie and getting her to the stage on time for his announcement? Kelvin could hear the swill of boozers who stood in front of the stage. He knew from the decades he'd been on council that the drunker the Culvert locals got, the less well received he was.

'She better be here. Where's Tammie? Can't she go find her?' asked Kelvin, looking around for his colleague.

Just then, Christine and Kelvin heard the corrugated door at the back of the stage open and close. From behind the stage curtain came the voice of a breathless Elsie: 'Sorry I'm late. I'm here. You go on. I'm right behind you.'

Councillor-Mayor Jones rolled his eyes at his daughter before hauling himself up the steps onto the stage. What on earth was the girl wearing? A dressing gown?

The microphone whined. The stage spotlight lazily roamed this way and that until it at last found him.

'You'd miss Skippy every time with that kinda spotlightin', Blue!' cat-called one of Chunky Nicholson's sons to Bluey Bourke, who ran the bi-annual amateur theatre group and always got roped in to doing the lighting for the ball.

When the councillor-mayor took position centre stage, another lowly local from the edge of the bar called out, 'The things you see when you haven't got a gun!'

Ignoring them, Councillor-Mayor Jones looked out blindly, trying to see the audience beyond the screech of the light, but the crowd was unseeable. All he could feel was just a vast blackness of hostile locals. Like most people, they were simple. What they needed was strong leadership. It was up to him to soldier on and guide them.

'Tonight, ladies and gentlemen,' the councillor-mayor said, steeling himself, 'we have an exciting announcement to make. One that will put the town of Culvert on the map and paint the town with a bright new future.'

'Instead of being painted in shit like it is now!' called out a clown from the bar. A murmur of laughter rumbled through the audience.

Kelvin persisted: 'Then after our formal proceedings we have some wonderful music planned from the ... er ... the Whirl Me About Dearest Dancing, er ... Dearest Old Time Whiz music band.'

'It's Waltz Me Around Again Darlin'!' yelled out old Funky Baker, the drummer. He was in the wings, swigging straight whisky from a flask kept in the pocket of his baggy cord trousers. He'd just returned to the band after his second hip replacement and the drunker he got from his hip flask, the more repetitious his hip-replacement jokes became.

Councillor-Mayor Jones cleared his throat. He could feel himself losing his grip on the tough audience and he knew Cuthbertson Rogerson would be watching very closely.

'But before much more ado about anything,' he said bombastically, 'we have a special treat for you. One of our very own talented local lasses has come back especially for us to sing the national anthem. Please be upstanding,' he said to the already standing crowd, 'and welcome my daughter, Eleanor Jones, fresh home from Primrose Ladies' College to our proud town of Culvert.'

Councillor-Mayor Jones extended one of his arms stage left, and the audience applauded and whistled loudly, not because Elsie was coming to the stage but because they were pleased Kelvin Jones was getting off it. When Kelvin turned, he first noticed the shocked face of his fellow councillor Tammie and the raised eyebrows of his assistant Christine, but it was too late. Elsie Jones was already on the stage, stomping past him in cowgirl boots and the tiniest of ripped denim miniskirts. Her legs were as long as a giraffe's; her skimpy top slung as low as a deep valley in the Swiss Alps. Her hair was tousled as if she had just gone several rounds with a testosterone-infused cowboy.

When she set her amp down with a thump and bent to plug it into the old timers' powerboard, the men around the bar erupted into wolf-whistles and hound-dog howls. Cool as a cat, Elsie positioned her slick silver-and-black electric guitar in front of her and shrugged a shimmering diamante-bedazzled shoulder strap onto bare skin. Bluey Bourke cut the lights to one bold spot. Elsie's father retreated to the shadows. If he dragged her off, there'd be a riot. He couldn't watch.

Beside the stage, old Funky Baker muttered into his hip flask, 'Hell yeah.'

At the back of the pavilion, Sarah Jones reached for Simon's arm to steady herself. 'Eleanor?' she whispered, her face draining to the same white pallor as a bag of flour.

On stage, shining like a diva, Elsie set her legs wide apart and stood strong. She reached behind her ear, pulled out a smoke and put it to her scarlet lips. Through narrowed eyes ringed black with make-up, she fished a cigarette lighter from the back pocket of her denim skirt and turned her head profile to the audience to light the cigarette. She sucked deep, tossed the lighter to the boys at the bar, then blew smoke rings into the air. More whistles followed.

Into the microphone she spoke. 'How are ya doin' tonight, fine citizens of Culvert?' There was a loud collective whoop from the crowd. 'I'm Elsie Jones. I may have been born and bred in this town, but I sure as hell *am not your type.*'

The grazier set stood transfixed, not sure how to react. The less constrained locals let out more raucous cries and enthusiastic clapping. The young men in the crowd shuffled forwards, hoping to see right up Elsie's skirt, and Sarah Jones had to be found a seat before she fainted.

Elsie dragged again on the smoke, then jammed it in the tuners of her guitar's headstock.

'Here's a little song I wrote back at Primrose for y'all. At least for some of you.' Elsie set about plucking the devilish instrument at a fast trot, like a pony in a hurry to get home. The deep throb of her guitar filled the show pavilion with a rhythmic beat. The sound carried aggression, attitude and a touch of heat. She turned to the microphone and let loose a sexy sigh. Then she began to sing with a twang that was tainted with an American southern drawl.

'I butchered my skin with a cheap and nasty tattoo.
I banged the team till I told 'em all to stop.
Pissed down the drain a whole bottle of good whisky.
No memory what I did then, all I know is it hasn't stopped.'

The catcalls from the audience intensified as the younger people of Culvert clustered forwards with excitement. Some were making sure this actually *was* little Elsie Jones from primary school. Where had the scared mouse gone? Where was the mole?

Elsie wielded the guitar with conviction, as if it was a wand casting a spell on them. Johnny Cash, Elvis Presley, Colorado Buck and all the other bad boys and gals of country music seemed to channel through her, busting open the tiny minds of the Culvert show crowd. It was infectious. It was like a shot of something new. Soon Funky Baker was up on his doddery feet, grabbing his drumsticks from the pocket of his tweed jacket, which he dramatically ripped off, revealing a white T-shirt and a faded sagging tiger tattoo that grinned at the crowd. He rolled up his sleeves and attacked the drums with the air of someone who had jammed blues with the best. He backed Elsie up with the same hard-hoof pony-on-the-road beat.

Elsie cast him a siren's smile as she strummed harder on her guitar and upped the tempo. There was now no reason to shield herself behind her hair from these people. Her *disfigurement* was gone and she was liberated. Not just from the mole. But from her whole family and their crappy farm and this entire shitty town and the people in it. She sought out Tilly and Scarlett in the audience: they stood in their demure dresses beside their mothers, open mouths of disbelief, and she winked at them as she sang.

'*Girls grabbed their phones and they started texting.*
Can hear Mama now sayin' she just can't take it.
Don't show them how you feel, only follow ya etiquette book.'

Elsie aimed her bile at her mother for getting rid of Jasper. She aimed it at the girls who had badgered her daily since kindergarten. Her father too, for his pompous self-importance. And at Culvert itself, for the way people had treated her, the twins and Tara.

'*It's time for me to leave your stupid old traditions.*
Time for me to say it how it really is.
Won't play the rules of all you crusty arseholes.
Ain't gonna act like that lady that you made me.'

Her voice got stronger and stronger and Funky kept on following her trajectory. He was reliving the days when he was a man who could thrash a kit to submission and bring an audience to their knees.

'*Don't you know we're all a little crazy?*

Just you're not brave enough.
And a little bit lazy.
Not gutsy enough. Not fucked enough.
Culvert 'n' all you can go and get stuffed.'

She strummed the guitar so that it distorted like an angry scream as she rose to the final peak of the song. She nodded to Funky, who thumped the drums in a giant finale so his sticks flew and his face shone with life. Half the audience clapped and cheered; the others stood silently as if they had all just been slapped. Funky joined Elsie centre stage and reached his gnarled old hand out for hers so they could take a bow together.

Elsie smiled thinly and looked out to the audience, searching for Tara. But she was nowhere to be found. That had been the plan, to do this for Tara. To show her she was back and still worthy of the Poo Crew. That she was sorry for not being in touch over the years. That she was through with her mother and the boarding-house girls. But Tara wasn't there. Elsie Jones's heart sank.

Up the back, in his coat and tie, hiding in the shadows, Nathanial Rogerson stood, his red face blotched with severe psoriasis.

'Cool,' he said as he watched Elsie jam the cigarette between her lips, unplug her amp and haul her guitar and gear from the stage as if she'd been doing it for a Rolling Stone's lifetime. The screams from the crowd of Culvert youngsters took a full five minutes to silence so that Councillor-Mayor Kelvin Jones could get a word in on Culvert's new poo plant. His heart beat hard like a drum, stress over what his daughter had just done crash-tackling his body.

Fourteen

In a rumple of sheets, Sarah Jones rolled over, fighting the hangover of memories that pounded in her head. Sharp images of her daughter spotlit on the stage looking like a Kings Cross hooker scrunched Sarah's brain into a migraine. Her daughter's tacky teenage rebellion had happened in front of the *entire Culvert community*! She groaned and shoved her head under the pillow.

Outside her bedroom, the homestead was in mourning for all the grand grazier dreams. The hallways were empty. The kitchen still. The place was saturated in regrets and poor decisions. Especially disappointments about not raising an agreeable daughter and leading an idyllic farmer's-wife life, Sarah thought. It seemed impossible that Grassmore could feel any more subdued than usual, but it did.

The Jones men were gone at dawn, Kelvin tugging his boots on furiously at the back door. Elsie's actions had sunk like a stone in the opinions of the show committee. For the rest of the evening, he had received the cold shoulder from the Who's Who. Without saying it outright, the Culvert silverspoons had made it clear to Kelvin that his campaign to be re-elected had not been enhanced by his daughter's performance. Kelvin had also been forced to receive one too many congratulatory back slaps from less well-bred locals, saying his daughter was *'more than a bit of all right!'*.

To top it all off, it still hadn't rained, and the bank was on his case, what with Sarah's new Pajero, Elsie's surgery, Simon's dental work, the need to put more super on his paddocks, where nothing grew. And then there was Sarah, bedridden with her migraines, *again*.

Simon had been shoved off home early by his parents just when he was about to get a grope of Tilly Morgan behind the Culvert Showgrounds toilet block, so he and Kelvin had stomped off to the ute in matching moods.

In her bedroom, Elsie hugged her knees to her chest, mascara from the night before still haunting her eyes. She had no idea what to do. She kept remembering what it felt like under the blinding heat of the stage lights, with the crowd gaping in shock and her guitar cast out in front of her like a weapon sending sonic shock waves of retribution through the crowd. She let the rebellion of her actions lift her, then, just when she felt herself in a place of strength, she would plummet again like a tiny doll falling from a cliff.

How could she have done that to her parents? They had sacrificed so much for her education, even with the farm going bad and the drought. They had paid for her operation.

But then the unruly she-monster would scream again that what they wanted for her and her life was completely different from what *she* wanted. And that the 'drought' that kept her parents' mood pinched and angry was her father's fault anyway, as was their focus on a perpetual lack of money and rain, and their constant worrying about what others thought. Plus she realised now she missed the twins, Gwinnie and Elvis, and Tara. They were 'normal' compared to her family and the tossers she'd met in Sydney, both at school and in the band scene in Darcy Kennedy's garage, with his collection of too-cool-for-school young musos.

She'd met Darcy when buying a packet of chewing gum at the servo near the boarding school. He was carrying a guitar and a chip on his shoulder about mainstream music and private-school girls. After that day, Elsie had found herself fronting the fledgling pub band The Fat Fannies, made up of a mishmash of Sydney wannabes. She had also found herself in love with the stage and a rowdy crowd, and discovered that with the mole gone, she was totally attractive to boys, but uninterested in any of them. Music was her love.

She stood and pulled on some ragged jeans she'd hidden in the back of her wardrobe. They were the ones she used to ride Jasper in and had rips in the backside and on the knees. She swivelled before the mirror to watch as she hitched a thick leather belt through the keepers and reefed it closed. She dragged on one of Simon's bluey shearer's singlets that she'd pinched out of the laundry and knotted it. From beneath her bed, she searched out the old cowgirl boots she'd bought in a Paddington second-hand market and pulled them on over a pair of dirty socks. She loved those boots. They symbolised freedom. In Sydney, traipsing along the concrete pavements, they had been her one defiant link to the country, while the other girls had tottered in their trendy high-heel shoes.

All dressed down, but with nowhere to go, Elsie sat and listened to a fly beat itself senseless against a windowpane. After a time, in almost a trance, not from boredom, but from a sense of imprisonment within her own life, she grabbed one of Jasper's old stirrup leathers also stashed in the wardrobe, and began to finger it and cry. She missed that pony, and the Culvert Poo Crew.

She gathered up some scissors from the wicker sewing kit her mother had given her. She began to fashion a wristband from the leather and thread it with a piece of leather thonging. For an hour, stooped over at her dressing table, she carved and cut so eventually the cuff fit perfectly around her slim arm. Her strumming arm. It'll look cool, she thought. Then after delicately indenting it with intricate patterns using some nail scissors and a school compass, she ran to the kitchen for some oil and began to polish the thirsty bit of leather in a rhythmic soothing action. Over time, she worked it into a beautiful rustic piece of jewellery carved with stars, barbwire, hearts and horseshoes.

'Kick-arse cowgirl,' she said as she knotted the leather band around her wrist, cinching it tight with her teeth and holding her arm out to admire it.

Just then someone clanged the old metal doorbell.

They rarely had visitors to the house. Most daytime visitors searched out her father in the yards or machinery shed. Elsie stomped down the stairs, making sure her boots were extra loud — a reminder to her mother that nothing had changed from the night before. She was on a rampage to freedom, even if she was trapped in her bedroom. Trapped on Grassmore. Trapped in Culvert.

Marbles used to bark when people arrived, but these days Elsie knew he would just flop his feathery tail from where he lay on the doormat. Whoever it was was being impatient. The doorbell clanged insistently again.

'*Coming!*' Elsie swung the giant front door open and gasped. 'Tara?'

'Yup. Cool wristband,' Tara said, waving the mop she held at Elsie. Then she stooped and picked up a blue bucket filled with rags.

'Thanks,' said Elsie as she tried to comprehend how *big* Tara had got. She still had a pretty tumble of beautiful dark red-brown hair that was lovely and long now, and the most amazing green-flecked eyes and full pretty lips, but they were swamped by her body, small against the fullness of her face and roundness of her shoulders. Elsie could barely believe the giant girl standing before her was the same person she had trundled to school with. She had boobs now that spilled up into a giant pillowed cleavage, and the Elmo T-shirt she wore was stretched and threadbare. Her tracksuit was pilled and sagging.

'I thought your dog had died,' she said, looking down at Marbles, 'but he opened his eyes, farted and wagged his tail so he could share it with me. Nice dog.'

Elsie laughed. Tara. Still funny. Still talking about farts. It made a nice change from the up-themselves girls at boarding school. Suddenly Elsie realised she too had become an up-herself girl from boarding school, deliberately shutting Tara out to save her own skin these past few years. She pushed away regret, frowning guiltily at Tara.

'Speaking of dying,' Tara continued, 'Mum did. She died.' She twisted her mouth and looked away, biting her lip.

Elsie's eyes widened. 'I know. I'm sorry.'

The silence went for too long. It was filled with pain for Tara, guilt for Elsie.

'The girls at school can be bitches …' Elsie's voice trailed off, the comment aimed mostly at herself. She gave Tara a look of deep apology. 'It was a bit hard … you know?'

'I think I do know,' Tara said, the hurt in her voice highlighting the gap between them.

'I'm sorry,' Elsie said, meaning it. She saw that her compromise to herself just to be accepted into the 'in' crowd had been a betrayal to both Tara and herself. She looked hopefully at Tara, knowing that the tussle in herself was over.

Tara, once again, twisted her lips back and forth. 'I understand.' She looked down at herself. 'I completely understand. Look at me. I'm shit.'

'Oh, Tars,' Elsie said, stepping forwards to set her things down and hug her. As she folded Tara in her arms, she felt the outer softness of body, yet the strength within her muscled frame. Elsie felt Tara shudder once, crying, then she quickly sucked in a get-it-together breath. She stepped back.

'I'm all good now,' Tara said, swiping the heel of her hand across her face.

'And I am all good for you now too,' Elsie said, more apology written in her expression.

Tara nodded and for a moment there was a quiet knowing that the cracks in their friendship had already begun to repair.

'You look great, by the way. Beyond bloody beautiful,' Tara said, tapping above her own lip.

Elsie's fingertips flew to her face and fingered the puckered scar where the mole used to be. She blushed. 'Mum,' she said. 'Guess she couldn't stand looking at me … it … any more.' She hastily changed the subject. 'You look great too.'

Tara gave a high clear laugh. 'Liar! I look like hell. It's lucky they haven't brought McDonald's and KFC to Culvert. I'd explode. No matter what I do, I'm addicted to crap food.' She rubbed her hand over her belly.

'But Tara —'

'Oh, shush, Elsie. Let's start over. Even though I may look like hell, I can make your house look like heaven.' She raised the mop and bucket and gave Elsie a shopping-channel smile, complete with theatrical wink. 'Your mum rang and left a message after she saw my flyer in Sylvia's window.'

'Mum asked you here?'

Tara's cheeks flamed a little. 'She doesn't actually know it's me. I put on a German accent. She thinks it's a professional mob set up in Culvert. I'm pretty good on the computer so the flyers look profesh. Ja, madam. Vee ken cleanz your 'ouse!'

Elsie laughed, pleased her mother was about to get another shock, and delighted that here was Tara. *Tara*. She could feel it deep within her now. Here was her *true* friend. 'You'd better come in then. I could do with a dose of heaven.'

'OK,' Tara said, brushing back hair that trapped golden sunlight in its red curls, 'and while I clean you can tell me how you rocked Culvert to its core last night. Word is on the street, Elsie Jones! You are a legend, a rebel and totally small-town famous! *Totally!* I want to hear all, pray tell.'

Laughing, Elsie took the bucket from Tara, linked arms with her and steered her inside. 'Let's rock this joint,' she said gleefully. 'You clean, I'll play. Amp you up from room to room.'

'Perfect! At last!' Tara said. 'I'm back with my partner in grime!'

They started in the kitchen, Tara dusting, scrubbing, wiping, shining, while Elsie started off with Miss Beechcroft's borrowed acoustic, playing 'Sadie, the Cleaning Lady', changing the words to 'Tara, the Master Farter'. They talked and sang and laughed. Then talked some more. About the twins and the demise of the Culvert Poo Crew. About small-minded locals. About awful girls in boarding school and how Elsie had tried to be like them, but had always been on the outer. About the books Tara had read. About the books Elsie had read. The music she *loved*. About their families, if Tara could call hers one. About Jasper being sold. About the farm dying. About what hadn't changed in Culvert. By the time they had got to the lounge room to clean, Elsie had retrieved her amp and electric guitar from the back of the Pajero. She began serenading Tara as she polished the antique sideboard, with a beautiful Charity Buck song.

'Far out, Elsie,' Tara said when she was finished playing, 'you are good. I mean really, *really* good.'

'And so are you!' Elsie looked around the room. Tara had moved like a river flowing through the space, shifting a chair here, a table there, lifting up items, dusting them, but setting them back in a new arrangement. Within fifteen minutes, the Grassmore homestead dining room looked ready for the royal family.

'Get real. Good at cleaning?'

'Yeah! Look at this place!'

'Well,' said Tara, dropping her gloved hands by her curved rounded hips, 'there is an art to it. Remember that folder I found on the tip?'

Elsie nodded, recalling the day the four of them had set out on yet another adventure.

'Since then I've been studying feng shui. Wind. Water. Balance. I figured if *I* couldn't be beautiful and serene, then I could at least make my surroundings beautiful and serene and that in turn might change me. As much as you can create beautiful and serene in Culvert, with the poo blowing through it. And in an abattoir house.'

At the mention of Tara's house, the room turned cold.

'Is he still there?' Elsie asked.

Tara looked at Elsie for a moment and then nodded.

'Fark,' said Elsie. 'You've gotta get out.'

'I know,' Tara said quietly, staring at the imported Turkish rug on which she stood. 'I've given myself three months to get the money together.'

'Then where?'

Tara shrugged.

Elsie shook her head and tears welled in her eyes.

'What about you? Your father's pretty bloody ordinary, in another kind of way.'

'At least I have a mother and father,' Elsie said sadly. The thought of Tara packing up and leaving Culvert on her own sent a shudder through her. Then she thought of her own dark future: more years of boarding school and the pressure to do well in the HSC, then university or a suitable husband. All she wanted to do was play music, and, if she allowed the truth, to farm Grassmore the right way. But neither of those things would happen despite her stance last night at the Culvert Show Gala Ball. Bugger them.

Elsie let loose with a loud strum of her electric guitar, the leather cuff urging her on. The sound rifled around the room and bounced off the fine china vases and sideboard dishes, scuttling under chairs and diving behind heavy formal floral drapes.

'Let's mop and rock!' Elsie said, but then stopped and leaned over her guitar from where she stood. She reefed open the sideboard, grabbed from it her father's precious aged Scotch, dragged the lid off with her teeth and spat it on the floor. She took a deep slug and passed Tara the bottle. Then she began at full throttle to bash out AC/DC's 'Jailbreak' and Tara began to whip the vacuum cleaner into a frenzy. Spinning, turning, singing, shouting and jiving as the motor whirred and the electric guitar distorted and fired machine-gun bullets of sound throughout the homestead, even shifting the dust in the old ballroom through sheer force of the vibration.

The girls had got almost a full way through the bottle of Scotch when behind them, in the doorway, appeared Elsie's mother.

'Excuse me?' Sarah Jones shouted. 'What is going on here?' Elsie and Tara looked at her, standing in her floral dressing gown, her eyes haunted and vulnerable but her hair perfect.

Elsie's guitar fell silent; Tara turned off the vacuum cleaner and set the almost empty Scotch bottle on the sideboard, quickly fumbling a coaster under it.

'Tara Green?' Elsie's mother asked.

Tara curtseyed. 'Yes, madam.' Then she giggled, but her giggle evolved into a suppressed snort of laughter. Elsie joined her and together they wheezed.

Sarah Jones looked at the bottle of Scotch. The tangle of cords between the guitar and the vacuum cleaner.

'I ordered a cleaner from Partners in Grime,' she said. 'There was an advertisement in Sylvia's Silverspoon.'

The girls went off in another spiral of laughter and snorts.

'Ja,' Tara managed, 'I am zee partner in grime. And she's my other grimy partner.' She pointed at Elsie.

Elsie scrunched her eyes, the Scotch tearing holes in the lining of her stomach yet fuelling her laughter, and lost it in a heave of belly-aching splutters. Even though the laughter felt real, it was hollow and defiant too.

'Eleanor Jones!' her mother said, her voice raised. 'Stop laughing. There is nothing to laugh about.'

Elsie drew her lips in and pressed them together tightly.

'I have just got off the phone from Primrose. After last night, I've been asking a lot of questions. Mrs Morgan was kind enough to tell me what Tilly told her, and your dorm mistress has asked your other classmates, who have corroborated the story. You've been lying about your volunteering. Telling the staff at the old people's home that you're sick. Then, as we have discovered, you have been going to a residential house to practise in a garage with a band. Then on the weekends you've been sneaking out at night and playing in the band in bars. A *band*? In *bars*? At *sixteen*?'

'Yes. The Fat Fannies. So?'

Tara stifled a giggle.

'I don't care about your band. You're a fat liar, Eleanor Jones.'

'And bloody Tilly and Scarlett are fat dobbers. They didn't tell you everything, did they? Once I had the surgery, I could suddenly be their friend. Not before though, Mother. No, before that they flushed my head in the toilets. But you didn't believe they'd do that, did you? Anyway, just so they'd be nicer to me, I snuck them out as well. Scarlett's banging the drummer and Tilly practically dry-humps the bass guitarist even though she's supposed to be going out with your precious Simon and shagging him.'

Sarah's eyes widened.

'I'm the only one in the dorm still a virgin, Mum. You oughta be proud of me. That boarding school you brag about is not all it's cracked up to be.'

Sarah Jones's cheeks flamed red. 'Proud of you? *Proud of you?*' Her voice was like the engine of a plane — it had both a low grumbling sound to it and a high-pitched whine. 'You ungrateful little bitch! You, miss, are gated.'

'So?' She scowled. 'I've been grounded all my life.'

Mother and daughter stood glaring at each other. The years of tension holding them locked in a stream of distrust and dislike.

'And for the last time,' Elsie seethed, 'stop calling me Eleanor. I hate that name.'

'Mrs Jones,' breathed Tara, trying to turn on her energetic capacity to calm people. She'd read a book about it once. But fuelled with Scotch herself, standing before the lady of the house, it just didn't seem to be working.

Sarah Jones turned on Tara. 'This is all your fault. Right from the start you've been dragging my daughter down. You lowlife! How dare you? Now get out. Get out! I want you out of my house. You, you … fat … fat … *abattoir girl.*'

Sarah Jones's thin neck was alive with angry veins. Her voice was like icy knives.

'If she goes, Mum,' growled Elsie, 'I go.'

'You?' Sarah shouted with fury. 'Go? Go where? Where on earth to, Eleanor? You're just a selfish, ungrateful, spoiled little girl. You've got nowhere to go.'

'Fine,' said Elsie, grabbing up her guitar and amp. 'Fine. C'mon, Tara, I'll show you out. And I'll show myself out while I'm at it.'

Fifteen

The paddocks of the roadhouse farm were almost unrecognisable to Elsie as she drove the battered old Grassmore Estate ute through the side gate to the Smiths' property, Tara and old Marbles the dog riding shotgun. The cab stank of Marbles's excitement at the sudden action after his sedentary years on the Grassmore verandah.

When the Smiths took over, the roadhouse farm was a tufted, dry, overgrazed landscape of rocks and bare soil, much like Elsie's own farm, but now before her lay an Australian grassland paradise. It was beauty beyond description. She had only ever seen such grasses in photos during her boarding-school internet roaming, an exploration that took her into an alternative virtual rural world.

Forms of new-age agriculture she'd never known as a child were now within her reach. She could find reasons for her family's dysfunction and the malaise of Grassmore and the district generally. Elsie had discovered websites showing beautiful natural grass species that had once covered the entire region. They were the very same grasses her grandfather and father had ploughed out and replaced with weak European varieties. Plants that withered at the first sign of heat and no rain and needed annual shots of superphosphate to keep growing. But now here before her, wallaby, kangaroo and weeping grasses wavered in the afternoon breeze. Poas saluted her with tall wisping yellow-and-green shoots, while a sprinkling of woody-stemmed shrubs brought a depth of olive green to the pale yellow summer landscape. Amid the grasses and shrubs were wildflowers as well: pretty daisies in bright white, violet and yellow fairy-clusters.

In the next paddock content woolly Merino sheep and dozing Brahman cows with hides like polished brass chewed lazily on their cud in the deep shade beneath restored self-sown clusters of young gums. In the paddock behind them chickens free-ranged around their colourful caravan. Young trees reached their leafy arms up to a blue sky as if in celebration of what the family here had done to the land. A family simply allowing the plants to live and to grow, to die and to breathe again in soil that was breathing and living, dying and cycling too.

Collectively, the plants gave the farm life that Elsie had never felt before in this landscape. She'd read *The Biggest Estate on Earth* and learned how Indigenous Australians had made and managed the continent, creating a paradise of rich grassy parkland just like the one in front of her. Grassmore could be like this. She just knew it.

'It's beautiful,' she said.

Tara nodded. 'They sure are something, those Smiths. Most folk say they're nuts. Creating a fire hazard with all the long grass. Chunky Nicholson is onto them all the time to burn off. They've dodged the council that many times about the long growth next to the neighbour's wheat crops. It was even in the Rington paper. Elvis Smith said it's regenerative holistic agriculture and time-controlled grazing, but the locals call it a mess and madness. Whatever it is, though, it's working. Can you *feel* the place? There are that many land devas and forest fairies flitting about, and it's teeming with sprites. The angels sure are singing about this.' Tara was looking out across the paddock, swimming her hand dolphin-like through the warm air.

Elsie looked over and smiled. Her friend was still into that weird stuff. For the most part, her whacky childhood friend with her crazy beliefs remained intact, buried beneath the weight and the hurt of her upbringing.

Elsie let her hand drop down outside the door of the ute as she drove on, her fingers brushing the seed heads of grasses, noting the green tinge beneath the long yellow stems, where a summer fire would have trouble taking hold. This was how she imagined the lost continent to look. The Australia that existed prior to 1788. She wished Mr Williams could see it.

'My history teacher, Mr Williams, says there was a Grass Rush long before the Gold Rush,' Elsie said to Tara. 'The Aborigines and their grasslands gave the newcomer white fellas all the riches they needed in the form of tucker, fresh water and abundance.' She cast her head down before looking again to the landscape. 'When you see the land like this, it makes me realise how much we've buggered the rest of it. Not to mention what the Aborigines went through and are still going through, of course. And to think I'm part of that white fella dynasty!'

She squinted against the late-afternoon glare of the sun as it sank behind them and reflected back at her in the grimy mirrors of the ute. She 'got it' at sixteen, about overgrazing and the introduced grass species, so why couldn't her father?

From the shed the twins heard the deep throbbing of what sounded like a chaff-cutter's engine and came out into the fading light, each shading his eyes with a long thin hand. A ute with more dings in it than a wrecker-bound car was thumping down the infrequently used side track towards them. The ute's once-white body was now blotched with rusting drizzles on its metal creases and its bullbar, bent and slightly crooked, listed downwards on a slant over the number plate as if the vehicle itself was drunk.

'Who the hell is that?' Zac asked. He glanced at Amos nervously and looked behind him to the recently carved and then covered trench that was only just starting to settle and seed over and shush its secret back in the long grasses of the paddock.

Amos shrugged. 'Whoever it is, they can't drive too well. And they shouldn't be coming that way. No one comes that way.'

The boys waited, standing outside the big shed until the ute halted. Their looks of concern surged into smiles when they saw Tara and Elsie get out, followed by an ancient Golden Retriever who nose-ploughed into the dirt as he tried to alight from the cab. Snuffing a little and shaking his head, the old dog padded over to the boys, a doggy smile on his aged face and his tail sweeping a greeting at them. The boys patted the dog, sniffed the putrid scent they now had on their hands and looked at the grinning pair of girls before them.

It took the friends just a glance to see how all of them had changed. And it took just a breath to see that everything still remained the same between them. The Culvert Poo Crew was back.

The twins had remained lean, but had shot up so that their feet and hands were even bigger, and seemed to dangle from the ends of their very long limbs. They each had a galaxy of reddened acne across their fine high-boned faces and the darkness of their hair and thick eyebrows was striking above the round brown eyes. Both twins were wearing the same checked farm shirts and faded jeans, so Elsie was reminded suddenly of two Woodys from *Toy Story*. She knew which was which, and reckoned Tara did too. Zac standing to the right of Amos. A double vision of boys in boots, each carrying different energies within.

The boys too were surveying the girls. Elsie was dressed like she'd come out of the shearing shed in a bluey and ripped old jeans. Her blonde hair was ruffled and the leather cuff on her wrist looked cool, but they didn't register her as 'hot' like most boys did. She was grown up, of course, and totally beautiful, but she was Elsie. She was, to them, more than her body and face. She was their mate from when they were little. They hadn't seen her around as they had Tara, whose spirit shone past her bad clothes and weight gain. With that mole gone, Elsie seemed weirdly damaged and vulnerable. And judging from the smell of alcohol and their slightly ragged gaits, both girls were sorely in need of friendship.

'Howdy,' said Elsie, suddenly realising just how drunk she still was.

'Good afternoon, fellow Poo Crew members.' Tara gave a comical curtsey.

'Howdy,' said the boys in unison.

'That crap-mobile sounds like it could use a tune-up,' Zac said.

Amos was already rolling the big double door of the shed back. 'You'd better bring her in and we'll give her a going-over.'

'Yeah? You sure? Have you got time?' In Elsie's world, it was rude to impose on people.

Zac tilted his head and grinned at her. 'Got nothin' to do and all day to do it. I could be saving the world, but,' he paused, looking over to the shit ponds before he waved as if swatting away a fly, 'meh ... I'll get round to it.'

Elsie laughed.

'Besides, it'll be faster than having you break down on the way home and us having to tow you.'

'OK.' Elsie looked properly at Zac for the first time. He was cute, despite his teenage goofiness. Girl-boy-crush kind of cute, she thought. Although he looked like Amos, he was different. A little more distant somehow. A little cooler in his disposition. He reminded her a little of herself. She liked that he was like her.

'We're not planning on going anywhere for a while.' She hiccupped, then felt a wave of grog-induced nausea. She retched, spun about and vomited suddenly, surprising herself more than the others.

'Woah!' Zac said. 'You OK?'

Elsie nodded, swiping the back of her hand over her mouth. She knew it wasn't just the alcohol her body was rejecting.

Amos was soon by her side with a bottle of water. He passed it to her.

'Aren't you going to measure that?' she asked, grinning up at him.

'Still reckon you don't chew enough,' he said.

Soon, like pups in a tumble of play, the friends were skylarking in the rich paddocks of the farm, Tara with the boys in a headlock swinging them around, laughter rising up from them all, as Elsie leap-frogged onto their backs.

A while later Zac was leaning banana-like under the bonnet of the Grassmore paddock basher, tinkering with the engine.

'It's kind of obvious you girls have left us behind on the sexual development front. Amos and I just keep growing like bean plants upwards. But you, well … Look at you both!'

From where they sat on the workbench, Elsie and Tara glanced at each other. Marbles at their feet let out a sigh as if exasperated too.

'Are you always this frank talking to women?' Tara asked.

Zac grinned. 'Women? Is that what you are now? Or are you girls in women's bodies? Me and Amos, we're just boys in what are becoming men's bodies, but we're still boys. It's such a weird time of life, isn't it? I can see you are nearly fully formed women physically, but I can also see you are still the kids we knocked about with. Surreal.'

'Do you always have to overthink and analyse everything? Even puberty?' Elsie asked.

'Yep,' Zac said, laying down a shifter on the side of the ute. 'You know our parents. They're upfront and out there when it comes to educating us on all things — especially sex! You should have seen our curriculum!'

'Or more likely, you *shouldn't* have seen it,' Amos chipped in as he cleaned the air-filter. 'It included sexual philosophies and theories most humans don't even need to know of. The books they've put under our noses are enough to curl your pubic hair! Mum even gave us projects on pornography and the social truth of the havoc it creates. Especially with boys and girls our age. Or boys and *women* as the case may be.'

Tara began to chuckle. She had forgotten how intense and interesting the twins were … not to mention funny. She had missed this. All the boys at Culvert High were base and gross compared to Zac and Amos. She wondered, not for the first time, why she hadn't allowed herself to hang out with the twins and particularly Gwinnie and Elvis during the past few years. But deep down she knew. She had no self-worth. All her lost and lonely years of high school sat inside her like boulders of sadness. She was so ashamed of that predator lurking in her bedroom. The memory sat in her belly and festered. Dwaine and his stiff little penis and gigantic blobbing belly.

To survive, Tara just couldn't be around the happiness the Smith family exuded. She had known their life wasn't perfect, but the children in that home were sacred, protected, given freedom to be themselves, and above all celebrated. It was too hard to be near it but not a part of it.

'I just wish I'd stop growing,' Tara said. 'I'm like a jumping castle that keeps inflating.'

'A jumping castle is better than one of those hot-air clowns they put outside vacuum-cleaner shops,' Amos said. 'You know the ones full of pressurised air that flick their long skinny arms about.' He parodied the movement. 'Zac and I are like that in a high wind.'

They all laughed.

Elsie rolled her eyes and dragged her hair back behind her ears. 'Growing up has done my head in too. I've gone from being a baby doll with a mole to a Barbie in the space of a year,' Elsie said, looking down. 'It sucks. Once I got these,' she said, cupping her breasts, 'and lost that,' she added, pointing to her scar, 'the high-school boys in Sydney started giving me hell. They drive me insane. They are so gross.'

'Yeah, it must be hell to look like you, Elsie,' Tara said flatly.

Elsie looked a little wounded as she glanced at Tara. In their younger days it was unlike Tara to host any kind of envy.

'Elsie will have to work harder than all of us to have her inner intelligence seen by others. She's going to have a line-up of the wrong type of men wanting her for all the wrong reasons. Aren't you, Elsie?' said Zac.

Elsie looked at him incredulously. He got it. He actually understood. When Zac noticed how she was looking at him, he inclined his head.

'Mum. She explained that to us about you once we heard you'd had an operation. As you know, she was a stunner too when she was younger. Little blonde thing like you, as the truckers who come by our place would say. She had all the men after her, but it was daggy old Dad who won her. He is such a nerd, he didn't really take much notice of the exterior of her. All he could see was her inner energy. He became her best friend first. Our gran warned Mum youth and beauty fade and a superficial man wanting her for her looks would dump her for a younger woman later. Gran told Mum that Dad could already see her, aged and wise, but still beautiful, years on. And the rest is history.'

'Gawd,' Tara said, still bitter. 'That sounds like a fairytale.'

The three others sat in silence, looking at Tara while her hurt roamed the shed.

'Well,' Elsie piped up, 'I'm just not interested in boys, or marriage anyway. I just wanna play music.'

'But boys can't help but be interested, particularly in someone like you,' Amos said as he poured oil carefully into the ute engine. 'The hormones are overpowering. It's quite fascinating to watch it from outside one's self. For example, I can't stop having erections lately. They just won't stop coming. If you know what I mean.'

Tara grabbed a rag and threw it at Amos, hitting him in the side of the head. 'Oh, please! Too much information,' she said. Great. So Elsie's looks turned him on. Tara felt deflated.

Amos picked up the rag and shrugged. 'It's just how it is. What's wrong with talking about it? Mum said if women don't learn to self-orgasm at your stage of development, they can miss out on a whole world of pleasure further down the track. There's nothing to be ashamed or guilty about, if you are healthy in your thoughts about it.'

Elsie's cheeks flamed. No way was she going to talk about masturbation, even with these guys. 'Amos!'

'He's right. I read a book about it once,' said Tara.

'Time for conversation subject change!' called Zac. 'Honestly, Amos, Mum may have been working on our social and emotional intelligence for years now, but you, my boy, are falling way behind!' He gave his brother a friendly whack on the back of the head.

'Thanks, Zac,' Tara said. 'You can start by telling me what on earth you are doing in here.' She gazed about the shed. On one side was a line-up of three tractors. They looked like the three bears: big, bigger, biggest. All had been painted meticulously in bright green and blue by the boys and even with Tara's limited machinery knowledge she could see they had been modified: they had space-age tubing and cylindrical drums mounted to them. There was a seed drill parked next to them, painted the same colours. At the other end of the shed were workbenches, and tools hanging perfectly ordered on shadow boards. There were large pipes from the wall with red and green stop valves jutting from them and beside that were red PVC tanks in the same three-bears row.

'Top secret,' Zac said.

'Do tell?' Tara urged, lifting one eyebrow.

Amos and Zac glanced at each other.

'Moonshine.'

'What? Big tanks like that? Bullshit.'

Zac made a clicking noise with his tongue. 'I'm afraid we've been sprung, bro,' he said, setting down his tools and slamming the bonnet. 'Start her up, Amos. See how she runs now. And after that, we'd better treat the girls to a sample.'

'A sample?' Tara asked.

Amos grinned, turned the old diesel over and glowed the starter before revving it to life.

'Beautiful!' he said at the sound of the engine. 'You girls! You're in for a treat! Cleanskins, here we come!'

Sixteen

Van Morrison's 'Brown-Eyed Girl' blared from the speakers of an old paint-smattered stereo as Tara and Amos danced, arms slung about each other, plastic picnic tumblers held aloft, home-brew of hundred-proof rye swirling within, the colour of honey and the consistency of rocket fuel. The music, the smooth moonshine and the mood within the shed were intoxicating, as was the wildness of the weather outside. The big double door was wide open to the vista where the full moon and a strong gusty breeze were spinning some kind of magic: the grasses and tussocks shivvied wildly in a crazy hula dance. The sheen of the moonlight reflected like spinning coins on the rumpled surface of the treatment ponds next door.

'That is *so* romantic!' Tara breathed, pausing momentarily to take in the view of the sewage works. 'Dancing by the light of the moon on the poo ponds.'

She bent over double in a cackle, Amos sniggering with her until the music swept them up again and they turned to each other's warm bodies. Zac and Elsie danced too, encased in the same magic bubble. A mesh-covered lamp that was mostly used to explore the undercarriages and inner workings of farm machinery had been strung from a hook and chain pulley. The light cast a beacon onto the party of four and created deep shadows in the corners and rafters of the giant shed. A sagging Marbles had long ago retreated to the bench seat of the Grassmore ute to doze in old-dog dreams while the music blared and the teenagers roared with laughter at the improbability of the night.

'I don't for a second believe those big tanks are filled with moonshine,' Tara said, waggling her finger at Amos. 'You're telling me porkies!'

He tapped the side of his nose. 'Shush. Just dance with me, Tars.'

'You and your Smith secrets. Come on! Come clean!' Tara said. 'What's really going on in here, you mad professors?'

'I swear,' Amos said, placing both hands on her shoulders and shouting above the music, 'we're bootleggers. We haul the cleanskins out via the rigs that pull into the roadhouse. They glide into the other shed by the bowsers for a bit of a service and we load 'em up. We have clientele all the way to the west. How else did you think we paid for Dad's extra alternative treatments and all these new machinery toys and this state-of-the-art lab?' He looked at her. 'Could we do it from pumping gas and tonging hot chips into waxed cardboard cups?'

Elsie dropped her arms from around Zac's waist and reached to turn the stereo down. 'Boys,' she said firmly. 'The truth.'

The twins appeared to be having some kind of telepathic debate.

'Shall we tell them?' Amos asked.

Zac shoved his hands in his pockets and shrugged.

Amos sighed. 'OK. Yes. The moonshine is a herring front.'

'I knew it,' Tara said. 'So what's in the tanks?'

Amos grimaced. 'Shit.'

'Whaaaat?' Tara replied.

'For real?' Elsie asked.

'Well, it explains the freshly dug pipeline,' Tara said. 'So what do you want tanks of shit for?'

Zac rolled his eyes at his brother. Amos looked down to his boots and rubbed the back of his head.

'Where do we start on explaining this?' He let out a big breath. 'One thing is, if we tell you, you simply can't tell a soul. Especially anyone from council. We're harvesting the sewage illegally and experimenting with it as a fuel source in modified engines.'

'Harvesting?' Tara said. 'You're stealing shit.' She laughed.

'You're stealing *Culvert* shit?' Elsie echoed.

Zac turned on his brother. 'And don't tell anyone from council, you say? You've just told the mayor's daughter! Dad is going to kill us!'

'Councillor-mayor,' corrected Amos.

'Don't bring that dick slash mayor slash councillor head into it. I have nothing to do with my father,' said Elsie. 'Bugger Councillor-Mayor Jones. Tara and I are your friends, Zac. For life. Your secret is safe with us. Right, Tara? So come on. Spill the beans.'

Later, at the far end of the shed where the light crept low, Zac unrolled a swag out beside the giant dark shape of a tractor.

'Won't your mum and dad be waiting up for you?' Elsie asked.

Zac shook his head. 'We always camp over here on a Friday night when we're working on something. Mum keeps the fridge stocked in here for us and it gives her a night alone with Dad. She still hasn't given up on a last-minute baby sister for us. So we leave them to it. Are you hungry?'

'Yes,' Elsie said. She took both his hands and with her blue eyes looked into his dark ones. 'But not for food.'

She slowly stepped backwards to the swag and pulled him down. Instantly Elsie loved the weight of him. The leanness of him. She inhaled his wilderness-country-boy scent: the smell of living grassroots and earth, not like the synthetic scent of the fancy-pants city boys who had crushed near her in the pubs after her gigs. Elsie felt Zac's hardness beneath the fabric of his jeans and the press of his erection so near her inner thigh that her blood pulsed through her body. Desire fluttered like a moth against glass in the deep place between her legs.

'Zac,' she breathed.

'Elsie,' he answered, his breath hot on her neck, the fuel of the whisky warming across their skin. Their lips met with a steady tenderness; they slipped out of their clothes. There was no need for words. They were being guided by the ages. When Elsie felt the tip of Zac's penis nudging close to her, he drew back.

'Condom,' he said, his voice husky. He was gone and she watched as he rummaged in a first-aid kit. What was he doing? Going to use disposable gloves for a condom? He tossed something shiny and small at Amos.

'That hit me in the head, bro,' Elsie heard Amos say, then a giggle from Tara.

Next Zac was back.

'So you just happened to have that stashed in your shed?' Her voice had a touch of accusation within it and she felt her heart sink a little. What else did the twins get up to out here on Friday nights with their cleanskin grog and with whom?

Zac laughed. 'I know what you're thinking, but it's my first time too. Mum. She … well, you know what she's like. She stashes them everywhere in case. Her safe-sex lessons are *intense.*'

Elsie smiled. 'Your mother's amazing.'

'I don't really intend to think about her right now if that's OK.' Zac began to kiss her gently again, tenderly, laying her back down.

Her hands shook from the swamping of hormones through her system. She wanted him on her, in her, all over her. Zac tore at the condom packet with his teeth. The wrapper glinted. A Bruce Springsteen song blasted. Sax moaning. Zac passed the rubber sheath to her.

'Me?' She fumbled. 'I don't …' He helped her. Next he was lying on top of her. Then it happened. She felt the tear within. The tiny rip of pain. Zac's eyes never left her face, his large hands continuously stroking her hair. When he saw desire return again to her eyes after the pinch of pain, he began to move in slow delicious movements.

'Elsie.' He said her name as if he had dreamed of her for aeons.

On the other side of the tractor, Tara was in fits of giggles in Amos's swag.

'I hope Zac hasn't put pinpricks in this so he can become an early uncle,' Amos joked. He looked into Tara's eyes. 'Tell me. Did you and Elsie have it all planned? Get drunk. Accost two naive boys. Are Zac and I your experiment in journeying to womanhood?'

'Ha! As if,' Tara said. 'This is all your idea.'

'Is it now?'

Tara looked at him doubtfully from where she lay under the rumpled sheets of his swag. Her body seemed huge to her, even lying down. 'As if I've ever been interested in sex,' she said. 'I'm offering myself to you in the name of science. To further your theories on human behaviours.'

'Oh, that's flattering!'

'The science aspect would turn you on more than I ever could,' Tara said.

Amos looked sympathetically at her. 'Shush. I want you, not the science. And anyway, how can I have a theory right now?' He pointed at the bulge in his pants. 'It's been biologically proven that there's not enough blood in the human system to sustain an erection and optimal brain function in males at the same time. You're either going to have to settle for Einstein *or* Casanova.'

'Great! I thought I was getting my special brainiac boy, but instead I'm just getting an ordinary hormone bomb deflowering me by the shit ponds.' She began to giggle again so that her bare breasts shook.

Amos buried his face in her neck. 'There's nothing ordinary about tonight, Tara.' He brushed her long curling hair from her bare shoulder and kissed her gently. She looked to his cheek, his acne failing to dim the way she saw him. As a perfect boy. A perfect man in the making. She pushed his hand away from her stomach. She hated it. Then she tried to push the deep emotion that stirred within her.

She began to sing, to the tune of Madonna's 'Like a Virgin', substituting the words for 'By the Shit Ponds'. But Amos did not follow her mood.

'Shush, Tara,' he said gently. 'We don't need jokes right now. I mean, I get it. At least I think I do … What you went through as a kid. Am I right?' His voice trailed off as he felt her body stiffen beneath him, tension tugging her muscles taut. Technically Tara knew this wasn't 'her first time' and that knowledge twisted a knot of devastation deep within her.

She lay in silence, tears spilling uncontrollably down her cheeks, wetting the thin pillow on the swag. She laid a hand across her face, ashamed.

'We can stop,' Amos said.

Tara's face scrunched with emotion. 'No.'

She tried to hide her ugly expression from him, turning her head. She heard the gentle murmurs from Elsie and Zac drift under the belly of the tractor, the hushed rustle of sheets, swag canvas, of skin on skin.

'Why me, Amos? I mean look at me. Your brother gets *her*. And you get me.'

'Lucky me, I say!' Amos said, drawing her into a hug with his long arms. 'C'mon. You know it's always been you and me. You know it.'

Tara's eyes searched the blackness above her in the rafters as 'Dancing in the Dark' blared through the shed.

'OK, have it your way, stubborn mule,' Amos said, rolling his eyes. 'Whatever it takes.' He straddled her and looked down at her face. 'Tonight, Dr Amos Smith,' he said in a Maxwell Smart voice, 'is going to introduce you to sexual function one-oh-one. Currently, I only have theoretical principles, so in this session we are going to explore the practical aspects of the topic. Step one, stimulate the woman with foreplay by touching, particularly her breasts.' Like a robot, Amos reached out and began to palpitate Tara's breasts.

A giggle erupted in her. The feeling of safety with Amos restoring itself within her.

'How does that feel?'

'Like a doctor's examination.'

'Ha! Give me some credit! Step two, caress the woman's clit-or-is.'

The way he said 'clitoris' caused another splutter from Tara and she couldn't stop giggling when his exceptionally long fingers slipped under the band of her tracksuit bottoms and into her knickers.

'Step three, maintain eye contact where possible and kiss her frequently. How on earth do you do that?' Amos asked, trying to kiss her and look at her at the same time.

Tara squealed. 'You idiot!'

'You're doing wonders for my ego,' Amos said. 'At least I won't come in my pants. I am a detached scientist. Now are you ready for step four?'

But Tara couldn't answer: she could feel Amos's fingers working into her moist body, sliding gently in and out. She could feel his nearness, his leanness and above all the kindness of his human touch. There was integrity and intensity in his kisses and caring. She moaned. And soon, they were both in the river. Heart to heart. Skin to skin. Over quickly, but a lifetime of memory. The percussion beat of the drums echoing in the machinery shed along with their heartbeats. The proud presence of the giant tractor in her vision. The way she simply let this boy fall into her. Like all the angels had willed it, despite the odds. Despite the ugly odds that Dwaine and her tragic mother had cast against her. Tara was flying in the stars, under the well-researched touch of Amos.

The next morning, at dawn, the girls sat in the ute at a crossroad, both transformed. The engine idled like a purring kitten. The cleanskin bottles the boys had given them nestled upright behind their seats like children out for a Sunday drive. The secret of the shed was tucked deep within them along with the night they'd spent there. Marbles dozed with his head on Tara's lap.

'Left or right?' Tara asked, looking up and down the highway.

Elsie clicked the indicator on to go left, to take Tara back to the abattoir house. Then she shook her head. She clicked the indicator right. That way would take Elsie back to Grassmore. She could drop Tara off later. The light on the dash ticked on and off like a question and an answer.

'That's the wrong way too,' Tara said.

Both girls looked at each other. They clasped each other's hands over the warm sleeping body of Marbles.

'I'm with you,' Tara said. She nodded in front of them, squinting ahead to the road that travelled west into nothingness. 'Just gun it! Let's just *go!*'

Seventeen

Saltbush dotted the landscape and drifts of red soil climbed the bases of slumping fence posts, gathered by outback winds. There was not a sheep in sight. Just the messages left by their deeply etched tracks between straggling trees. Lingering was the vision of their ghosts — thirsty sheep traipsing to old concrete troughs lined with cockatoos strung like fluttering white flags around their edges. The girls whirred over grids on a dead-straight road of single bitumen, occasionally veering two wheels on the dirt when a grey-nomad caravan shimmered into sight and passed by with no wave. Big road trains appeared mirage-like in the distance, then loomed and passed, rumbling dust and spraying gravel, roaring like jets. The sun was high, the dog was panting, the girls' backs were soaked with sweat. The long and dusty miles fuelled their uncertainty.

'Can we have the air con on just for a bit?' Tara asked, the hot wind that blasted from the open window whipping red curls from pink sun-shocked shoulders. Elsie glanced at her friend apologetically. She sat straight-backed and tall in the driver's seat, hovering on an even one hundred clicks. The roads here were so long and unrelenting, and her hangover so pressing, that she was having a hard time pushing concern away.

'Sorry, Tars. Can't spare the fuel.'

Tara tugged at the neck of her T-shirt to fan some air to her sweating breasts and looked at the pitiful cluster of cash and coins that lay in the grimy console of the ute.

Earlier that day, just a few Ks out of Culvert, the girls had tallied their money, looked at the state of the fuel gauge, and waited for a fleeting roadside sign of just a letter and a number, indicating the impossible distance to the next town. When they had realised they had not enough cash, hardly enough fuel and barely enough courage, both girls burst out laughing. Elsie had twenty bucks in her wallet, and all that was left of her train-travel money. And Tara had fifty from the first cleaning job she'd done yesterday before heading to Grassmore Estate.

'Seventy-four dollars and eighty-five cents. We didn't plan this too good,' Tara had said. She turned her head around. The chipped old wooden tray of the ute contained just a pair of fence strainers and a drum of tractor lube. It seemed ridiculous that her mop was lying next to a spare tyre, with her blue cleaning bucket clipped onto a rusted chain like a working dog. From the bucket the rags waved at her, the cracked red lid of Mr Sheen only just hanging in there after the last blast of wind from a road train, a bottle of Windex looking entirely out of context in this brittle, dusty landscape.

'Don't you reckon Mr Sheen looks like John Howard? I've always thought that,' Tara said.

'You're crazy,' Elsie said. 'Who would think that?'

'*This* is crazy,' Tara said. The girls looked through wiper-arcs in the dust on the windscreen out to the hot flat country and the giant, weighty blue sky.

'You sure you wanna do this?' Elsie asked, looking over to her friend.

Tara raised her eyebrows and breathed in deeply. 'Are you kidding? This is the best thing that's ever happened to me! I'm not sure what is happening, but I know it's good and there's not much else I'd rather be doing!'

Elsie's heart sank. She was half hoping Tara would say, 'Let's be sensible. Let's just turn around and go home.'

But where was home? Where in this vast landscape? The adrenaline of the fight with her mother, the magical night with the boys, the false bravado the booze had given her had dissipated. Elsie was beginning to feel not just sick, but unhinged. Lost. Panicked.

'Last night I lost my virginity' played on loop in her head. Elsie was mildly surprised every loop when another voice inserted 'to Zac Smith'. She had always thought it would have been one day with some wild and wonderful grungy muso in Sydney. Many had chased her during the secret band rehearsals and gigs, but she mostly felt disdain for them. Without her mole she knew they were just after her for her looks. She'd not felt safe around them. With Zac she had. Skinny weird Zac. She sighed. Should she turn the ute around? If she kept on this road, she would lose her life as she knew it. Cut loose into freedoms that were more frightening than fun. She swallowed down a lump in her throat.

'Hey,' soothed Tara, sensing Elsie's change of heart. 'We can turn back. If you want.'

Elsie glanced over to her friend, grateful. She was about to slow the ute when she saw in the periphery of her vision, tucked behind the seat, her guitar and small amp. She recalled the feeling she'd had on the Culvert Show Gala Ball stage as she sang. Powerful, in control, admired. Free. None of the things she felt in her family.

She gritted her teeth and set her eyes on the road. 'No way. Let's just keep going.' She suddenly realised she had always been exiled from her family. Always. Like the universe had somehow dropped her into the wrong house. And Tara had always been a refuge from them. Plus now she'd blown her own cover as a 'good daughter' at the Culvert Ball, she couldn't simply head back to boarding school and continue to battle with her mum. In Elsie's fractured mind that came from feeling so unloved and misunderstood by her family, she suddenly found immense comfort with Tara by her side, along with her guitar. She decided with both as her best allies, she could do anything. Anything!

'No. I have all I need. I have my gui-tara,' she said. 'Get it? With you, Tara, and my gui-tara, we can rock the world. Let's keep on going!'

'Very funny.' Tara grinned, reaching behind the seat and searching through the crap stored there, happily discovering Simon's pale old work Akubra. She jammed it on her head. 'I guess that means we're at large! Or at least I am; you're just running away.' She looked down and patted her stomach.

'Stop with the bad fat jokes,' Elsie said.

'You're the one who started with the bad jokes! Gui-tara … that's really lame.'

'Yes, but stop putting yourself down. Each time you put yourself down, I'm going to hit you. OK?'

'You are?'

'Like this.' Elsie delivered a swift punch to her friend's substantial upper arm, the ute swerving a little as she did. She was more used to paddock bashing than roads.

'Ow! Couldn't you just give me an affirmation or something?'

'Sure, but it needs physical reinforcement. Remember how Gwinnie Smith and Elvis kept on with their affirmations all through his illness? And how he had that rubber band on his wrist and he tweaked it each time he thought something that was not helpful to his healing. He's cured now, right? There must be something in it. Could you try a rubber band?'

'More like I need to try a lap band.'

'Get real,' Elsie said.

Both girls fell silent at the thought of the Smith family. Memories of the night before, with the boys. It took one glance at each other for them to be grinning, halfway mad with crazy-girl hormonal rushes.

'Do you feel different?' Tara asked.

'You mean in the fanny?'

Tara spluttered up laughter. 'No! Dick!' she said. 'I mean … in your heart.'

Elsie felt the wind lift her blonde hair from her tanned shoulders and smiled. 'Yes,' she said simply. 'Yes, I do.'

'I wonder what the twins are doing right now,' Tara said.

In the roadhouse kitchen Gwinnie was busy secretly beading silver drops of rescue remedy into a teapot for the benefit of Sarah Jones. She glanced out the swing doors to the profile of Constable Gilbert, who stood, looking much like a koala with his short limbs and round face and body, in the café. She hoped he wouldn't think the remedy was an illicit substance. Gwinnie cringed when she heard Amos talking to the adults.

'We used condoms,' Amos said in a loud factual voice. 'And we didn't partner swap, if that's what you're thinking.'

Sarah Jones let out a small cry. There was a cough from Kelvin Jones. Then came the sound of a thump, and 'Ouch!'

Gwinnie assumed it was Zac whacking his brother on the arm to shut up. Rolling her eyes, she grabbed the teapot and made a dash for the room.

'Jesus, Amos,' Zac said. 'Where's your emotional intelligence? As if Elsie's mum wants to hear her daughter's been … been … *deflowered* … even with a condom.'

'Deflowered?' Amos said to his brother. 'That's an interesting term for it.'

'Cup of tea, anyone?' Gwinnie asked, her voice high and as tense as wire.

Elvis sat opposite his boys, fingering sugar sachets end to end, a mild look of amusement barely hidden on his face.

'The girls have only been missing a couple of hours, Mrs Jones,' Constable Gilbert said, his black police belt slung tightly under his broad belly. He sighed. He hated this posting and this shitheap of a town. This morning he'd simply come in to get a cup of coffee at the roadhouse and had inadvertently walked into a storm.

Normally punishment for Constable Gilbert's habit of off-duty drink driving had been working for a long stint in the dull-as-dog-shit radio control room at Rington. But eventually his boss had drawn the line: he'd been caught shagging the 'very married' Wendy from Rington Ringlets hairdressing. The local fallout had been substantial, so his boss had sentenced Constable Gilbert to Culvert. It was only supposed to be a twelve-month posting. But here he was twelve years on, with no sign of a transfer back to Rington. He looked at the mayor and his uptight wife and thought his boss was an utter bastard.

'My daughter's been missing since yesterday, Constable,' Mrs Jones said, the frost settling in her voice.

'But they weren't missing, technically,' Amos said. 'They slept in our swags.'

Zac thumped his brother again.

'Ow!' complained Amos. 'Stop doing that.'

'Stop being insensitive.'

'Tara didn't think I was insensitive. And Elsie seemed to like your sensitivity, judging from the noises she was …' His voice trailed off when Mrs Jones let out a sound like a cat being run over.

Constable Gilbert told Amos to shut his smart-arse little mouth.

'Mrs Jones,' he continued, 'this won't become a police matter until they remain unlocated for a period of forty-eight hours. And as all parties are over the age of sixteen, there is no transgression of the law. The only issue is the Green girl is technically a ward of the state unless her stepfather steps in.'

'That would be a backward step,' Amos said, teasing the policeman for his ungainly choice of words. 'Dwaine's not Tara's father! We are simply teenagers exploring our sexuality with a couple of other teenagers doing the same. Where's the crime in that? And so what if they've gone for a raz in the old farm ute. They won't get far in it anyway. Once their endorphins decrease, they'll probably be back for more sex.'

At that point, Sarah Jones, whose red-tipped nose looked like it had been nipped by the same severe frost that was contained in her voice, burst into tears, sobbing like a dog stung by an electric fence.

'See,' Zac said, exasperated, looking to his parents for help. 'Can we try those flash cards on him again to improve his social skills? He's a walking faux pas.'

Elvis and Gwinnie cast Zac a cautionary glance.

'None of you seem to realise my daughter has *disappeared*!' wailed Sarah Jones.

Zac tried to seek out eye contact with her. 'She's probably just taking some time out with Tara. And for the record, I love your daughter,' he said earnestly. Sarah let out another cry and Gwinnie Smith spilled the tea.

Elvis Smith patted his son's back proudly, while Elsie's frozen father suddenly became animated and grew larger, like a rooster fluffing up his feathers, and blurted out, 'They ought to be whipped! Your boys ought to be whipped!'

'For what?' Elvis asked, turning calmly to him. 'It's a natural progression into adulthood.'

'It's a disgrace! Your boys are disgusting!'

Elvis stood suddenly. Since the illness had left his body Elvis Smith was once again a man who commanded respect. He was tall, tanned, sculpted well by physical work on the farm and in the mechanics shop and above all centred in himself. Here was a man who had faced a death sentence, healed and was now soul-strong. Here was a man not to be messed with.

'Do you whip your son, Mr Jones?'

Kelvin Jones purpled. 'Of course I don't.'

'Are you sure? I know you punish the soils and plants on your farm and treat your animals harshly. So maybe you stunt your son and daughter in the same way — put fear into them the same way. Your farming habits and mindsets are criminal. Controlling your dear daughter for the sake of ancient social beliefs. Making your poor son a carbon copy of you for your own ego. Limiting this town with your egotistical, narrow-minded politics. You're a megalomaniac!'

The words landed like acid rain on Kelvin Jones. His mouth flinched violently and he stepped closer to Elvis. 'How dare you, you grease-monkey upstart?' Both men stood before one another, their chests puffed out like angry chimps. Zac and Amos stared incredulously at their father. They had never seen him like this.

'Stop projecting your warped sexual values onto my young sons,' he said. 'I don't want my kids' first experience with women tainted by your limited judgements. Zac and Amos respect those girls and care for their wellbeing. Which is more than you do!'

'Why you!' Kelvin began dancing on his toes and raised one fist in the air as if to swing it. Sarah Jones let out yet another feeble cry, calling her husband's name.

'Now, gentlemen,' Constable Gilbert soothed, holding off on his intervention for as long as possible to maximise the entertainment he was gaining from the scene. 'You will soon make this a police matter if you don't tone it down.' He stepped between the men and flexed his chest out, hoicking up his heavy gun belt.

Eighteen

Elsie stomped out of the truck-stop door and made her way in the shimmer-heat to Tara, who was slumped at a picnic table, her head resting on her folded arms, blowing flies off her skin.

'I just spent every bloody cent on diesel.'

'What?' Tara exclaimed, sitting bolt upright and laying her palms flat on the tabletop.

'I had to! The next big town is way up in whoop whoop. The lady said we wouldn't make it with half a tank. Now my guts are rumbling. We have a dollar seventy-five, which won't even buy us each a dim-sim.'

'Oh, well,' shrugged Tara, 'it's not like I'm going to fade away in a hurry. You get a dimmie. I'll sniff it and then I can watch you eat it.' To combat the heat she had rolled up her tracksuit bottom legs and the grimy sleeves of her lank Elmo T-shirt. Elsie looked at her with a frown. Tara's legs were good, but she really had to do something about her clothes. They made her look bigger than she was. And if they were going to travel together, Elsie wasn't sure if she could put up with looking at her like that much longer. Not to mention the smell of her. Being that big in a hot climate, no matter how hygienic Tara was, was not easy. At first Elsie felt she was being judgemental like her mother in thinking those things about Tara, but then it occurred to her the ever-cheerful Tara had actually been depressed since long before her mother had died. She needed help.

Tara wrinkled her nose as Elsie moved closer and punched her.

'Ow! What was that for?' Tara frowned, cupping her upper arm. 'Do you really think hitting me is helping me?'

'It's cognitive reprogramming therapy,' Elsie said.

'Give me Elvis's rubber band any day then,' Tara said, pouting.

'You don't even notice you do it, do you?' Elsie pushed.

'Notice what?'

'The way you put yourself down like that about your weight.'

'Thanks, Miss Psychoanalyst and Thump Therapist,' Tara said grumpily. 'I wouldn't delve into my internal narrative, if I were you. It feels like I've been alone with my head, for like, ever. I read something about it once. About negative thought patterns on loop. So, yes, I probably have a few habits of the sort in my mindset. Thanks for the coaching.' Tara sat rubbing her arm, a scowl on her face, looking out to the vast saltbush plains beyond the roadhouse.

'I'm truly just trying to help,' Elsie offered glumly.

'I know you are,' Tara said, her voice far away.

A convoy of road trains had begun rumbling into the expansive gravel parking area. It was a roadhouse plonked in the middle of a vastness too expansive to comprehend. The whitewashed stones ringing the car park seemed pathetic against the flat never-ending landscape.

'Where are they all coming from?' Tara asked, watching the trucks roll to a stop, air brakes shushing loudly, hot motors ticking with heat. The smell of near-cooked rubber rose from black enormous tyres. The pungent scent of sheep and cattle dung oozed from between the rails of giant boxy stock trailers. Other huge trailers remained sealed up, their goods safely insulated from the intense heat of the day and the desert cool of the night.

'Must be peak hour,' Elsie said as she watched the assorted truckies unfolding themselves from their driver's seats. Men of all shapes and sizes leaped down from their cabs for showers, meals, snoozes and ablutions before they again took to the roads and the roos and the monotony. What would the men think about on their drives? Tara wondered. Of home? Football? Women, or engines, or the Sky Racing, like Dwaine? Or would they be thinking of nothing much at all? She didn't like the look of them.

'I reckon it's time for us to leave,' Tara said. 'Too many menfolk here for me. Next town's six hours away. We could drive all night … or we could camp in the back of the ute. What do ya reckon?'

'Camp! On the side of the road? Are you serious?' Elsie asked. 'With what? We don't have swags.'

'Do we need 'em? We could use Marbles as a stinky pillow,' Tara said, looking at the ute parked in front of them. Marbles sat in the passenger seat looking like a little old blonde woman waiting for her husband to drive her home from the shops.

'Remember I'm only on my L-plates, even if they are hidden in the glovebox,' Elsie said. 'I've driven to Culvert and back once! It wouldn't be safe for us to drive at night.'

'Oh, come on, Thelma! No guts, no glory.'

'Guts is what we'll get if we drive now. Roo guts! I'm not going.'

'Well, we can't stay here in the ute cab all night,' Tara said, glancing about.

'Maybe one of the truckies will let us use his cab for a snooze?'

'Yeah? And we get raped or murdered? Taken away as sex slaves?'

'Don't be stupid. They're good guys. Workers.'

Tara flashed her a look. 'Yeah? And how do you know?'

The image of Dwaine jumped to Elsie's mind and she fell silent.

Both girls let out an exhausted sigh at the same time as they looked at the battered old farm ute.

'Fuck, Tara. We have no money. We have no clothes. We have no phone.'

'And we ain't got no virginity no more,' Tara said with a snigger and both girls laughed, leaning their heads against each other.

'We sure as hell ain't got that. We can't get it back. We ain't got nothin',' Elsie said in a Yankee accent. 'We're up the crick, with an old smelly dawg.'

Tara sat looking at her holey sandshoes, thinking. 'We are not necessarily without a paddle, though,' she said, lifting her index finger, her face lighting with excitement. 'Your guitar!'

'Huh?'

'Get your guitar, Else. Just get it. Go!'

Before Elsie knew it, she was standing outside the truck-stop doorway in the glow of the outback sun, singing Cold Chisel's 'Flame Trees' with the hauntingly beautiful soul-sound of her voice calling across a desert sea to the trucker sailors. Zac and Amos's home-brew and very little sleep the night before had roughed up her throat so there was a huskiness to her voice that made it sound more mature, more weathered. Or was it the becoming of a woman that deepened her sound?

Memories, flashes of moments with Zac, skin to skin, dashed in and out of her mind. The images helped her find the full bloom of her song in this unlikely place. She felt sure-footed in her rough-hearted cowgirl boots, making her feel planted not just *on* the earth but *within it.* The guitar and amp too were alive with adventure, plugged into a shared socket with a drinks machine. The instrument conjured Elsie into a woman who looked older than her girlhood years, standing in the shorty-short remains of her now-cut-off denim jeans. The truckies paused, then stopped, drawn in by music that sounded so much more enveloping, more comforting and whole than a CD in a truck stereo. The long legs of the pretty kid making the music didn't hurt either.

Elsie mustered as much Jimmy Barnes music as she could recall and looked to the carved wristband as she strummed. The remnants of Jasper's memory captured in the leather gave her confidence, so she took command, with a gift that came to her as naturally as breath. Soon the staff and all the long-haul drivers were gathered at the picnic table and had dragged over more plastic chairs, enjoying the mini concert. At Elsie's feet lay Marbles, sleeping, curled around the guitar case. Also propped against the case base was an old cardboard carton on which Tara had written with an ear-tagging pen she'd found in the glovebox: *Our almost dead dog is hungry. Please help us feed him.* Beside Elsie, Tara moved her body with an in-built mystic rhythm as she sounded out a beat, tapping her cleaning bucket with the plastic handle of her pink feather duster and tinging her Mr Sheen can.

The long-haul men watched the blow-in country girls with fascination: the stunning blonde in the ragged cut-off jeans and the curvy one like an ancient beauty from another era with her red hair … and her bucket and duster. They were rare ones, that was for sure. It was nothing for the men to drop ten- and twenty-dollar notes into the guitar case and stand enthralled and in awe of this unlikely treat in the middle of nowhere on a regular hot-as-hell day. More and more coins spilled from pockets like rain, Elsie nodding and smiling, Tara mouthing 'thank you'.

As Elsie strummed the final chord on Alan Jackson's 'Little Bitty' and the men and women whistled and clapped, one listener called out, 'Who are youse?'

Tara and Elsie looked at each other in a moment of panic. Tara glanced over to the ute — their getaway vehicle — and thought of the cleanskin bottles stashed within. We're fugitives, she thought. We're underage drinkers. We're underage drivers. We're runaways. She knew Elsie's parents would be on their trail, and there was no way Tara wanted to go back now. So, no real names. She had to think quick. She looked down from her duster to Elsie's boots.

'We're the … the … ah … Cleanskin, er … Cowgirl Boots,' Tara said.

'The who?' the woman asked again, her Ocker voice veering sideways, like a band saw cutting through wood.

'Er. The Cleanskin Cowgirls,' Tara said.

Elsie gave Tara a big grin. 'Yeah, we're the Cleanskin Cowgirls!' she called out, and with her guitar strumming she rolled like a road train, singing Paul Kelly's 'To Her Door', a smile as big as the sky above.

Nineteen

Gwinnie heard the café shop bell ring just as she was finishing making up the sandwiches for the day. She tore off her disposable gloves and rummaged her fingertips through her hair, breathing deeply three times to calm herself before going out to greet the customer. The previous day's confrontation with the Joneses and the still-missing girls were very much on her mind. No matter how many times she tried to steer her thoughts to a place of calm gratitude, she just couldn't stop anger rumbling through her over the way Elsie's parents behaved towards her sons. And the way they seemed not at all concerned for poor Tara Green. All they seemed to care about was saving face and getting Elsie back where they thought she belonged. As she pushed her way through the swing doors, she only just stopped herself swearing out loud when she saw Councillor-Mayor Jones standing in her café.

As if things could get any worse! she thought. She pasted on a smile and looked at Kelvin and the posse of shiny-bum men with him, none of whom she'd ever seen in Culvert before. They were carrying folders and laptops and an air of 'stand aside, this is important men's business'. She gestured to the best table by the window that looked out over the roadhouse farm pasture.

'What can I get you, gentlemen?'

Councillor-Mayor Jones barely glanced at her. 'Sylvia's was closed,' he almost grunted at her.

'Any word from Elsie and Tara?' she asked gently.

He cast her a glance as if to kill, then his eyes darted to the men in his presence. Gwinnie's eyes narrowed. Of course, she thought, as if he would let his business associates know his personal troubles. He'd be pretending there was nothing amiss in his life.

'Shall I start by getting you some coffees then?' Gwinnie asked with forced brightness.

Kelvin Jones simply grunted a yes and the men gave their orders.

After taking care to make the coffees just right, Gwinnie set down the cups slowly, peering at the diagrams before the men. They barely noticed her presence — they were used to being served. Gwinnie quickly gleaned that their topic of discussion was the waste-treatment plant. She stood beside them, notebook in hand as if waiting for an order, but for the time being, they failed to acknowledge her. She had even more time to analyse just who these men were.

They looked citified, with grey faces, hollow eyes, sloppy bottoms that seemed to spread over the chairs, pot guts, and arms and hands infrequently used for any kind of physical work. Their glasses spoke of seriousness and their stooped postures told Gwinnie computers, mobiles and sitting on commuter trains or in gridlocked traffic consumed most of their lives. Like a giant walrus, Councillor-Mayor Jones sat at the round table with them, scratching his balding head and frowning. For the umpteenth time, Gwinnie wondered how on earth he had fathered such a beauty as Elsie.

'So are you saying that our townspeople produce thirty-six per cent *less* sewage than the national average?' he asked. 'How can that be? Do they literally … you know … evacuate less?'

The men glanced at each other. One cleared his throat. 'At this point, we can't accurately answer that question.'

The slightly thinner man pushed his glasses up the bridge of his nose. 'Does Culvert have a particular cultural group within the wider community that consumes a certain type of unusual diet that may explain this anomaly?'

Kelvin Jones glanced over to the Smiths' selection of fried foods and stands of chips and lollies set up for the locals. He shook his head. 'Not as far as I'm aware.'

Gwinnie was filled with dread. If these men were here to investigate what she thought, she and her family could be in big trouble with what they were doing over in the shed. She needed more information to pass on to Elvis. She thought about the money they'd already spent on the pipeline, the tanks and now the engineering equipment needed for the modification of the tractor engines. The last thing they needed was for these men to be peering through the high mesh fence of the sewage plant, connecting the dots between it and the far-flung farm shed and what the boys and Elvis were doing there.

'It's a mystery,' said one of the sewage experts, looking at the output stats and scratching his head.

Gwinnie cleared her throat. 'Anything to eat, gents? I have a fresh sticky date.'

The men turned to look at her as if she had just arrived in a space ship. Gwinnie looked at Kelvin as if he too was an alien form. Did the man not care at all that his daughter was missing?

Twenty

At dawn the girls got away early, fresh, confident, restored, breathing in the crisp coldness of the clear outback air. On the horizon the rising sun caused the sky to glow blue-gold, and momentarily Tara's and Elsie's gazes were drawn away from the dark road north and taken in by the eastern beauty of a new day. Both had been trying to watch keenly for kangaroos in the early-morning dimness on the side of the single-lane strip of bitumen. The roos seemed even bigger than the ones in Culvert. Barrel-chested skippies looking fit and savage, like they were heading to a boxing title fight. The wonky steel bullbar of the rust-bucket ute would be no match for one of those, thought Elsie as she nudged the old ute up to sixty kilometres per hour. She didn't dare go any faster until the sun was fully up and the roos had headed for shade in the saltbush and gidgee scrub.

Last night the girls had made enough money to hire a donga out the back of the roadhouse and share a double bed with clean sheets and AC. They had taken their meals of schnitzels, chips and gravy to their room, making up a bullshit story to the roadhouse staff about getting an early night because they were heading north for a gig and had to meet their fly-in band manager in Bourke. It was a roadhouse, after all, the girls reasoned, and the roadhouse folk there might well know the roadhouse folk — the Smiths — back in Culvert.

With hired scratchy towels hung over their shoulders, the girls had headed for the shower block, beetles crunching under their feet, moths fluttering in their hair under fluorescent lights. Ripe stenchy bore water reddened their tired sunburned skin as they stood beneath spluttering jets and soaped themselves clean with small circular freebie soaps that smelled like toilet cleaner. They rinsed their knickers and hung them in their room, and giggled for most of the process.

Now, silent in the paddock-basher ute, Elsie kept her foot on the accelerator and her hands clasped firmly on the big steering wheel. She adjusted the cap the roadhouse staff had given her to 'wear on tour'. Visions of her mother flashed into her head. Her mother in bed, distraught with a migraine. Not because Elsie was missing, but mostly because she would be worrying about what people would *think*. Tara too saw the movie of her life rolling in her mind. The awful home, the rottenness of Dwaine, the way she hated and loved her mother, and missed her but was so utterly glad she was no longer here. Guilt surged in and out like waves for both girls. In their silence, they grappled to find peace with the choice they had just made to run away. Sometimes it felt childish. Stupid. Other times, scary. To be so young and alone in this vastness.

As the day grew hotter, the girls tired. The miles wore them down. Marbles too shuffled and panted and sighed. It was as if the road was too long, the destination too unknown. It all seemed too hard, but neither Elsie nor Tara would voice it. Emus dotted the landscape in clusters like a collection of sculptures in a bizarre madman's garden. Feral goats wandered in herds far off on hillocks, their ears cast forwards in search of tucker. The girls' enthusiasm dwindled and died. Silently they passed bottled water back and forth. The radio didn't work. Nor did the air conditioning. And the ute rattled its metal bones as if in death throes. Tara drove for a while, as she'd learned a bit on the Smiths' farm, but her nerves got to her and Elsie had to take over again.

Just when Elsie was about to start to cry, Tara found an old cassette tape that had fallen down between the seats.

'Charity and Colorado Buck! It's our lucky day!' She jammed it into the dusty tape deck and out came the powerful, heart-throb voice of Colorado Buck. 'It's a sign!' she said gleefully, clapping her hands. With the music cranked to full volume they sang every word to the first song, 'Building Fences', and then when the duet came on with Colorado's wife, Charity, Tara squealed.

'I'll be Colorado,' she said. 'You sing Charity's bit!' And with joy they passed the miles crooning and country-rocking along the road. At last, having had enough of Colorado and Charity, Tara tried to eject the tape … but the button wouldn't budge. Next she twiddled the volume knob. That too was stuck.

'I can't switch it off,' she said over the top of Charity's crooning voice.

'Serious?' Elsie jabbed the buttons just as Colorado called Charity his honky-tonk baby. The girls glanced at each other and with renewed vigour began to sing again.

At last, after they'd heard the album another three times, a sign appeared, rising out of the landscape like an alien arrival. It was advertising a hotel thirty kilometres on. Then came a sign advertising Bernie's takeaway café. Then an ad for the RSL. And within twenty minutes, just before lunchtime, the girls rolled into Bourke, flanked by the brown-snake River Darling, 'Building Fences' blaring from the speakers as if they were trying to mimic a carload of doof-doof teenagers on a cruise through town.

The road took them into a frying-pan-hot concrete car park. Elsie cut the engine and at last Colorado and Charity were silenced. They set themselves up outside the air-conditioned cool of the IGA entrance, plonking Marbles next to the guitar case again. Their busking backdrop was a window slathered with notices advertising local babysitters, missing dogs and bowls tournaments. Their stage was a footpath beside a plastic horse that gave children wonky rides for two dollars, along with a plug-in point for their amp, and a row of what Tara described as 'mating shopping trolleys'.

It was a Tuesday; Elsie noticed a few mumsie types about, so after setting up their hungry-dog sign, she chose the songs she knew would tug at the passing women. She began calling up another era with her voice, evoking memories of girlhood in the women, before the men, the kids, the domestics had stolen their wild-souls away. Elsie had been to enough pub gigs in Sydney to see what music spoke to older women. She watched as an Aboriginal mum towing three kids ambled by, no life in her step. Another woman, rushed and red in the face, bustled past, her shopping bags hanging listlessly on the crook of her arm.

She hoisted her guitar in front of her and began to play from her soul. Soon a crowd had gathered. Just a few songs in, not only did Elsie and Tara have cash and coins lining the bottom of the guitar case, but Marbles also had earned bags of dog tucker and a few tins for just lying there in his old-man dead-dog pose. Tara had got a lot of comments about her bucket and duster drum kit and one fan even delivered to her a new metal bucket bought from the supermarket to expand it.

'You are really good. *I mean really good*, like you should be on *Australian Idol*, or somethin',' said one woman, leaning on her trolley, not wanting to go home. 'Play us another. Do you know any Slim Dusty?'

Elsie repositioned her pick and was about to coax the guitar to life again when she spotted a police car rolling towards them, sun blaring off the white bonnet.

'Ahh, sorry,' she said, casting a quick glance at Tara, 'we've gotta get back to our parents.'

Within seconds, the girls had tipped groceries into the buckets, slammed the guitar in the case along with the money and walked as calmly as possible away from the supermarket, urging a very dozy Marbles to hurry up. The old dog panted and padded his way behind them, his eyes dull, his tail drooping.

'Get yourself in that there ute before he stops,' muttered Tara.

Elsie looked down at her boots as she trotted around to the driver's side and began to snigger.

'What?' Tara asked, irritated, slamming the gear in the tray.

'You just said, *that there.*'

'What's so funny about that?'

'That there dog,' Elsie said in her best Nashville accent, pointing to Marbles. 'That there sheriff.'

'That there idiot,' Tara said, a smirk back on her face as they watched the cop pass without even really noticing them.

'C'mon, where's that there money?' Tara asked. 'Let's go get some takeaway.'

'Uh-uh. No way. No grease for you. We're getting healthy food. It's cheaper than takeaway anyway.'

Later, with a new Esky on the back of the ute filled with rice cakes, dried fruit, fresh fruit, nuts, celery, yoghurt drinks, honey and water, the girls drove on down the main street.

'Now what?' Tara asked. 'They reckon Bourke has one of the highest crime rates in the world, so you're not suggesting we camp down by the Darling with our vegan fare?'

'Nope. I have a plan. Follow me.'

'Follow you! I have to follow you. You're driving.'

Elsie drove back the way they had come and pulled up outside the large shopfront of Clarkson Rural Merchandise Store. The girls stepped inside and were met by an entire wall of colourful cowgirl and work boots. The sight of the boots stole Elsie's breath away. A short while later at the counter she sat two brand-new swags on the floor, along with an assortment of camp-cooking gear, a pair of white cowgirl hats, a pile of clothes and some new Ariats. From within the change room Tara called out, 'Else?'

Elsie put down the fishing rod she had been looking at and went over to the wooden louvred change-room doors. The assistant, busy on a phone call at the front counter, glanced up. Out stepped Tara in Wrangler big-girl jeans with a touch of bling and silver-and-white stitching swirling on the pockets and a pretty verdant green work shirt that set her deep red hair off beautifully.

'What do you think?' Tara asked.

The sales assistant gave her the thumbs-up and went on with her conversation, while Elsie's face opened in a smile.

'Perfect,' said Elsie. 'You look amazing. And try these?'

She handed her some work boots, a pair of thongs and some pretty blue horsey-girl boardshorts, along with a singlet top of navy blue.

'Just one small problem,' Tara whispered as she was about to try on the other clothes. 'How do we pay?'

Elsie winked. 'Watch this.' With her own collection of clothing, Elsie went to the counter and retrieved her wallet from the back pocket of her cut-offs. There she pulled out her Clarkson company card. It was the one she and her mother had charged all her father's rural products on whenever they were in Rington. There had been no need for it in Sydney, but now, the girls were shopping up big.

'Mum's sick,' Elsie said to the saleswoman, 'so she asked me to do the Christmas shopping this year. Dad and my brother are going to love their new swags. They are so into fishing trips,' she added, grabbing up the lines she had been looking at earlier and thrusting them forwards. The woman bipped the items with a handheld scanner.

'Nothing like getting it done all in one hit.'

Tara was standing behind her with an armful of clothes including work socks and Bonds underpants.

'Our sisters will love these too,' Tara said, thrusting the items on the counter, smiling angelically to the woman. 'And if you don't mind, I like these shorts so can I get them now and keep them on? Save having to change.' Tara swivelled and displayed her round denim-clad backside. 'Do you mind bipping my bottom?' The woman smiled and obliged. At the last moment Tara grabbed up an *OUTBACK* magazine and put it on the pile. It too was added to the bill.

The woman then took up Elsie's Clarkson card, scanned it, pressed a few buttons on her computer and within moments Elsie was signing an itemised account and thanking the shop assistant with her perfect private-school smile and demeanour. There was no trace of redneck runaway cowgirl in her now.

As they repacked the ute and settled Marbles down on a new hessian-covered dog bed, tag still attached, Tara looked doubtfully at Elsie. 'They'll know where we are when they get the bill,' she said.

Elsie shrugged as she opened some sunscreen and slathered it on her shoulders. 'Dad gets an end-of-month invoice. He's always behind on paying bills at Christmas time and even then, he hasn't time to do book work till after harvest so he won't look.'

Tara got in the ute, the seat feeling hot under her bare thighs, and started flicking through the magazine absently.

'And how will they know where we are if we don't even know where we're going?'

'Where are we going?'

Elsie shrugged. She started the engine. 'I have another plan. It'll put them off the scent,' Elsie said with sudden conviction.

She drove less than a hundred metres down the street and pulled over beside a bedraggled-looking phone box. Elsie picked up the sticky receiver and was surprised to hear a dial tone. She dropped coins in and punched the metal buttons.

She pictured the Grassmore Estate phone ringing in the vast hallway on the spindle-legged oak table. The twin phone ringing too in her father's farm office. Tears ambushed her as she heard her mother's voice on the answering machine, but only for a moment.

'Hi, Mum. It's Elsie. Just letting you know Tara and I are in Sydney. We're safe and well. We both have jobs. We're earning good summer-holiday money. I'll call you before school starts.' Then she hung up.

When she clambered in behind the steering wheel and hauled the door shut, she was shaking. She scanned the scene. The weedy street. The vandalised buildings. This was a far cry from her Sydney school in its leafy waterside suburb. So dark was her mood that it took her a while to notice Tara beside her bouncing up and down.

'Look!' Tara finally said, jabbing a finger at the magazine. 'Look! It's a *sign*.'

Elsie frowned and leaned over Marbles to see.

'There's an ad here for staff for Newlands Pastoral Company in the Territory. They're getting new crews together for the new year. In particular for a cleanskin muster on one of their stations.'

'A what?'

'Cleanskins. I read about it once. It's the unbranded cattle that they hunt out of the scrub and then muster up. With choppers and that. Y'know?'

'Where is it?'

'I dunno. Somewhere up in the Territory, out past Isa somewhere.'

Elsie grabbed the magazine from her. She took in the information, admiring the photo of a young man and woman in stockyard company shirts, holding horses outside a cattle yard. 'It says initial application by email. We don't have a computer.'

'We can find an online centre.'

Elsie looked doubtful.

'There's a number?' Tara pushed excitedly. 'Give them a ring now.'

'Why me?' Elsie asked. 'Why not you?'

Tara pursed her lips and folded her arms. 'Else, just face it, your boarding-school voice is better than my bogan tones.'

Elsie flashed her a look, grabbing for the ute door handle. 'Some day soon, Tara, you'll have to drop this inferiority complex.'

'What inferiority complex, oh great one?' she replied cheekily.

'You always joke your way through everything.'

'No, I don't. It's about floating over the top of life, so that nothing can get you down,' she lied.

But Elsie was already back in the phone booth, dialling the number. Her absence was short.

'Busy. Answering machine.' She got back into the driver's seat.

'Did you leave a message?'

'Nope. Let's just find an internet place. We'll send an application.'

'Na. Too sensible,' Tara said. 'Let's just call 'em when we get there.'

'Serious?'

Tara nodded. 'Have guitar, can pay for travel. Let's just drive! Cleanskin Cowgirls … we're on our way!'

'And the boys? Shall we call them now?'

'Oh, yes, good idea!'

They jumped out together and rang the roadhouse, praying one of the twins would answer. In the end no one did.

'They must be out in the paddock,' said Elsie, not sure if she was relieved or disappointed. She felt odd about Zac. She supposed it was her own fault. Sleeping with someone and immediately skipping town was definitely awkward.

When they were back in the ute, she turned to Tara, who looked downcast at having missed Amos. 'Which way?' she yelled over the music.

Tara glanced about. 'Signs … we need to follow the signs,' she said as Elsie inched along the road, waiting.

'Well? Have you received one yet?'

'Received what?'

'A sign.'

Tara began to smile. 'No, dummy! I mean we need to find an actual sign.'

'Oh! I thought you meant a funny-shaped cloud, or a feather, or a rainbow.'

Both girls fell about in fits of laughter, excitement building within them again with a sense of adventure. Now they had a destination, they also had an inner compass to guide them: there would be no going back.

Twenty-one

The clunking old ute limped into Mt Isa, spluttering past great mining stacks that rose into a wavering heat-vapoured sky. Giant yellow trucks trawled upwards on zig-zagging roads cut in the faces of huge shale hillocks. Colorado and Charity were still blaring, but the girls had learned to shut out their sound. Tara gazed up at the mine in wonder and looked at the tiny workers on the huge site. She saw humans as ants busily destroying planet earth to ironically build bigger and better homes.

On the other side of the road beneath the huffing chimneys in a haze of pollution were playgrounds and parks for the mine workers' children. It was weird that no one seemed to mind the kids playing in toxic pollution. Tara realised this mining game, for all families, was not just about money and carving out a life. It was also a culture that some loved — humans just did what they did without much thought. She wished her species would slow down. Would notice.

As they neared the town centre, she had to drag her thoughts to the here and now. Looking from her petrol-station map to the street signs, Tara began searching for the address of the Newlands Pastoral Company office. The girls both squealed when they found it. It was a large low white building tucked between a bakery and a dress shop. The signage on the front was clean and corporate compared to the homespun bakery. After a wonky park by Elsie, they got out, uncrumpled themselves as much as possible, tied Marbles to a post in the shade and stepped into the air-conditioned office. A neat woman behind the desk smiled at them.

'Be with you in a moment,' she said in a friendly but businesslike tone above the shrill ring of the phone. Her call gave the girls time to take in their surroundings. Even the lush pot plants seemed easy with their perfection, and the stunning aerial photos of the NP Co stations made the sheer size and grandness of this multi-million-dollar shareholder operation clear.

Tara picked up one of the brochures from a classy glass-top table. It showed NP Co's industry training programs. Elsie looked through a newsletter that reported staff stockhorse competitions, fishing competitions, get-togethers for fundraisers, Indigenous celebrations, social events and professional development. More photos of station crew in uniform shirts of blue with logos, big hats and glossy horses: young kids on a path to a rewarding life. Most of them even had ties on, along with big Akubra hats and polished boots. Elsie was getting excited. Some of the brochures were on the same regenerative agricultural techniques she'd been studying at boarding school. Tara too could feel the bright energy of the place.

Then the woman was off the phone and Elsie was tumbling out an awkward question about the job ad and waving the magazine at her. The woman pursed her lips.

'I'm sorry, girls. We don't take drop-ins,' she said, 'particularly ones with no résumés, no ID and no proof of age.' She had looked them up and down, not in a judgemental way; she had obviously seen all kinds and nothing surprised her. 'We have a formal screening process and the positions in that ad have been filled.'

Elsie's and Tara's bodies slumped when the woman said this. She looked at them again.

'Our ute was broken into at Bourke,' Elsie said, opening up the palms of her hands and widening her eyes in an expression of hopelessness and distress. 'All our gear, our wallets, our everything was stolen.'

'Even our working dogs,' Tara added, casting Elsie a quick glance.

'Kelpies,' said Elsie.

'Of course they didn't steal the old one.' Tara gestured to Marbles outside the glass window, who was lying on his side in his dead-dog pose.

'Mongrels,' Elsie said.

'The thieves,' Tara added. 'Not the dogs. They were excellent dogs.'

The woman sat looking at the girls, smelling a rat, but feeling for both of them. What an odd pair, she thought. One was all fairy princess in her brand-new Wranglers and the other, the pretty big one, was unreadable — she held a secret under all that weight. She sighed. Vera Cushing had seen 'em all. From the local applicants who thought they could ride a horse, until they were actually on the job and the skilled Aboriginal elder stockmen showed them otherwise, to the private-school city girls who had read a few outback romance novels and thought a stint in 'the bush' would be fun, having no idea that station work was skilled and complex. But Vera knew that within every person who walked through that door was potential. The company was a good one, and they relied on her to read people like books. And there was something about these two that touched her. She decided to string them out a bit. To test them.

'The stations are winding up for Christmas, so they're down to skeleton staff. The new intake isn't until the end of January.'

'We're happy to work right through Christmas,' Tara said quickly.

'Our families know we're on our gap year. They don't need us home or expect us for Christmas even,' Elsie added.

Vera looked at the extremely pretty girl's crystal-blue eyes and the pure face of the redhead. They were runaways. Casually Vera glanced at her watch.

'It's my lunch break now. Come to the takeaway with me. It's just across the road. You can both sit down and have a sandwich with me and then …' Vera inclined her head a little, like a slightly cross but kindly aunt, 'you can tell me the truth.'

'The truth?' Elsie repeated, her face growing red.

'Yes. The truth. Where you've run away from. Who I need to call. If I clear it with your parents, I have got a place for you. We've got a bit of a staff crisis happening on Goldsborough Downs. You can be taken on for a trial if you give me the honest truth.'

'The truth,' echoed Elsie again.

The woman got up from her desk. 'Wait here. I'm going out the back to get my bag. If you're not prepared to be honest, the company will not hire you and when I come back, you'll be gone. If you are in fact trustworthy, I'll help you in any way I can.'

Tara shrugged. She had no parents, and she knew a quick call to Barb Nicholson, whom the township and Constable Gilbert classed as her unofficial 'custodian', would support the idea, but she felt for Elsie, who had suddenly gone pale. They both knew talking the Joneses into this plan was going to be almost impossible.

Twenty-two

Elsie led the stockhorse out of the gooseneck trailer. The mare's hide was smooth to touch and her coat was white and peppered with dark flecks. Her black mane was hogged short like an upright fire brush and a long thin forelock fell between two kind, wise old eyes. The wispy ends of her tail flicked to keep the flies away and swished against her angled smoky black hocks. The colouring on her legs reminded Elsie of a watercolour of a cloudy sky.

'Wolfie will look after you,' said Gordon Fairweather as he laid a steady hand on the horse's rump. 'She's a veteran. We give her to all our newbies.'

Gordon was leading a chunky chestnut from the trailer behind Elsie and heading towards the other horses they had just unloaded and hitched to a rail. The gelding clumped down the ramp on giant-disced hooves, his bottom lip drooping, his blaze like melted ice cream down his big slab-boned face, his ears flopping sideways. He was clearly from lines of station horses selected for good practical breeding where temperament and vitality, not looks, were key.

'Elsie Jones, Elsie Jones, Elsie Jones,' sang Gordon. 'Sounds like a name for a girl who sings the twelve-bar blues. I seen you with the guitar. It's compulsory round here for you to play us a tune after knock-off. My missus, Elaine, she loves to dance me around to a bit of music.'

Elsie smiled, saying she'd be happy to.

Gordon reached for the forelock of the chestnut and smoothed it down. 'This big fella, Gazza, will do your mate.' Gordon put the back of his boxy roughened hand up to the side of his mouth and rasped a whisper, leaning towards Elsie. 'We put all the *big* girls on him. He's strong. He can carry a load. All day and into the night.'

Elsie glanced at the head stockman, a slight frown on her face.

'I'm not meaning to be rude, Elsie,' Gordon said in his roll-your-own smoky voice, 'but it's a sad fact that in the thirty years I've been working with the Newlands Pastoral Company, the kids comin' here for trainin' just keep gettin' bigger 'n' bigger from all that sugary shit and lolly-grog that's dished out to 'em. It's an epidemic from the city to the saltbush.' He shook his head as he hitched the lead rope in a perfect tie-up knot on the rail. 'They don't know the first thing about feedin' themselves proper, from a garden or nothin'. The world out there's just gone plain wrong.'

Elsie inclined her head, almost as if she was pleading with Gordon to go easy on Tara. 'She's lost five kilos already since … since … we began travelling up here.'

'And she'll lose a damn lot more with the work, and Mrs B's good cookin'. They all do.' Gordon chuckled.

Elsie smiled. Despite his forthright comments, she could feel the compassion in the man.

She looked out to the horizon, a broad sweep of sky and irrigated paddocks fringed by arid red dirt and tall sun-bleached grasses and low shrubs. It felt as if she was dreaming and not actually standing in the heart of a one-million-hectare property somewhere in the Northern Territory. Today her life looked so different, all thanks to Vera in Mt Isa. Vera and Elsie had teamed up together on speakerphone to talk to her mother, with Tara sworn to silence. Sarah Jones had hung on the other end of the line, her hands shaking with fury at her daughter and relief that she was safe — and heading for a 'gap year' on a well-run station, like many a grazier's child before her. And to be honest, on the inside, Sarah was greatly relieved they would save the thirty thousand dollars her school fees would have cost. Kelvin was not sleeping at night for the state of the farm books; and his mayoral salary had only just been kept from Cuthbertson Rogerson in the election. Who knew what might happen next time?

Elsie had said, 'I'll head back to school next year. I promise.' As she said it, she knew that promise was already broken. She was free.

Wolfie woke her up from her daydream, nudging her shoulder so Elsie had to balance herself out suddenly with a step.

'Don't let her do that,' Gordon said. 'Make her step out of your space. She can be a rude old girl when she first meets ya. She's testing ya. She knew your mind had wandered.'

Elsie twisted her lips tightly as she hitched the mare next to Gazza, self-conscious that her tie-up did not come easily, her brain addled with first-day nerves. Handling an NP Co station horse to go mustering nearly four thousand yearling Brahman heifers in the morning was a far cry from playing on little Jasper mobbing the sheep up when her parents weren't about. She watched as Gordon went back into the trailer to get his bay gelding, Bear, from the shaded cavern of the truck. Flies massed onto the dung pile the horse left as he ambled out, craning his neck and ears forwards, clearly glad he was home under the big blue sky of the station and in yards that smelled of safety, not like the fear-soaked scent of the yards at the rodeo ground where they'd held the draft.

'Just stick 'em here for a moment. I've gotta check their shoes before we let 'em go. I can see already Wolfie's pulled a nail,' Gordon said.

Elsie nodded, not sure what to say. Conversation was not her strong point as it had never been encouraged at home. At Grassmore, the workmen never chatted the way Gordon did. The Grassmore men just saw her father coming, ducked their heads and got on with it. Gordon kept on about a campdraft the crew had just come back from. The crew Elsie was still yet to meet and she couldn't wait.

Around two am the girls had woken to the clump of boots on the ringers' quarters verandah and the slamming of doors, the kick of the pump as the staff sought showers and a few hours' sleep before work began again. Then at dawn Gordon had come knocking on Elsie and Tara's door, asking for a hand to unload the horses he'd just driven in from the draft, travelling slower than the others with his precious load. Their day had begun before breakfast, but to Elsie now as she smoothed her hand over Wolfie, it felt as if her life had begun.

'Tara oughta have mixed their feed by now,' Gordon said. 'Then it's your turn for a feed. Mrs B will have a big breakfast cooked. She knows the crew are all knackered so she feeds 'em good.' He glanced over to the large shed where they had earlier left Tara busy in an enclosed area of the skillion. The shed had all kinds of mixes for the working horses in it, along with licks and supplements for the cattle. For a moment she had stood in the shed door, the rattle of the tin reminding her of Zac and Amos and the shed back home. Even though it had only been ten days since *that* night, Culvert seemed a whole world away. Still, Elsie clung to the memory of those moments with Zac.

'If we grab 'em some hay now,' Gordon said, interrupting her thoughts, 'they can camp in the yard cos we need 'em saddled before sun-up. It's gonna be a big day.'

'Not as big as what it'll be for us,' Elsie said.

Gordon chuckled. He watched, impressed, as Elsie, unbidden, reached for the shovel that was clipped to the gooseneck and began scraping up horse dung and carting it to a nearby bottle tree.

When she was done, she followed Gordon over to the hayshed, which was stacked almost to the rafters with big round hay bales. Gordon demonstrated how to start the tractor, to spear the spikes through the giant bales and to lift the forks up. The tractor responded, jerking the roundie up and down. Then he was off on the machine, inclining his head towards a steel yard gate where a circular metal feeder was placed in the centre of the rocky yard. Elsie, on foot, read his meaning. She crossed over the red dirt and swung the gate. After the bale was tipped in the feeder, Gordon unclipped a leather pouch on his belt, tossed his pocketknife to Elsie, nodded at the bale and proceeded to drive the tractor back to the shed. As Elsie began to hack away the outer netting of the bale, freeing the rich-smelling hay within, Tara came over with a barrow filled with the buckets of mixed chaff.

'All done,' she said, looking pretty in her cowgirl hat. She began to tip the feed into bins surrounded by tyres, the warmth of the morning sun already heating them so they gave off a faint odour of petrochemicals. The horses whickered from the rail. Gordon was already back with them, chaps on and farrier kit spread on the ground, bent beneath the belly of Gazza as he tacked in another nail with a small silver-headed hammer.

'He doesn't muck about,' Tara said, watching the way Gordon moved purposefully and with easy haste even after very little sleep and a night of truck driving. She was feeling the heat wrap around her, already causing her body to slump into lethargy.

'I get the feeling it's all systems go around here,' Elsie said as they made their way over to him.

He stood and stretched his back, then moved to pick up the hooves of the other station horses.

'After brekky you'll have a morning of induction with Gracie, our bean counter in the office. She'll sort your work clobber out.' He narrowed his eyes at Elsie's bluey. 'You'll need a proper shirt, EJ. You'll get burned to a crisp in that.'

Tara gave Elsie a wry smile. EJ.

'Yeah, *EJ*.' She grinned.

Elsie jammed her tongue under her bottom lip and pulled Tara a face. ''Tard,' she muttered.

'Lunch is at twelve-thirty, and hopefully your Boss Man Simmo, Michael Simpson, will be about and he can meet you. Then this arvo you'll have safety training and protocol with

Marcus Hinch, our company pilot and transport logistics guru. Y'know Hinchie who flew you in.'

Tara and Elsie nodded, recalling their trip yesterday in a plane that seemed to come out of a Biggles book.

'We just can't kill it!' Hinchie had yelled as he welcomed the girls aboard the Cessna that he told them had served the company for thirty years. Hinchie himself looked unkillable. He was a lean fit man who looked far too tall and broad in the shoulders with giant arms and hands to even fit behind the controls of the tiny plane. The single prop spun and sliced sunlight, and Elsie had felt a rush of excitement about where this adventure was headed. For even ballast Hinchie had sat Elsie in one seat with Marbles at her feet, her precious amp and guitar, and the treasured mop and bucket tucked behind her. Hinchie sat Tara opposite. Behind them were all manner of station stores. Marbles had been panting hot old-dog breath and Elsie drew him near to her as the plane taxied onto the runway for take-off.

'We've got some rangeland scientists coming off the station today,' Hinchie had yelled to them over his shoulder, 'so you girls timed your run perfectly!' He had strapped himself into his harness, reached for a Santa hat, dragged it onto his grey head along with his radio ear muffs, gave the girls the thumbs-up and off they had flown, towards an unknown red-dirt future at Goldsborough Downs as new employees for the Newlands Pastoral Company.

Now here they were the very next day holding horses for Gordon, who was still talking, even with the shoeing nails sticking from his mouth.

'Hinchie trains our rookies about how the stations operate and flies to each station on a regular run. But you're under my wing for the most part. The crew call me Crack … cos I get 'em up at the crack of dawn and get 'em cracking. And also on account of my pants.' He dropped the horse's hoof, stood, spun about and showed the girls his trousers from the rear. 'They drop a little on me as the day goes by.' He went back to work.

'Crack. OK. Sounds good,' Elsie said.

'My first round of advice for all newcomers to Goldsborough Downs is: There's a reason you've got two eyes, two ears and only one mouth. Look and listen more than you talk. You'll go a long way in life if you do.'

Elsie was slightly stunned. When she had envisaged turning up to a cattle station to find work, she'd imagined rough cigarette-smoking men of few words, slumpy station quarters and poor pay. Instead she could already feel the care the Newlands Pastoral Company put into training their crews and the place itself. It was so neat and tidy, everything was in order here. She could barely believe Tara and she had stumbled on a first-time job such as this. Of course, she knew the Primrose Ladies' College career adviser would be having a seizure by now. The women teachers at that school should know better what was 'out there' in rural industry for their country girls. For any girls who would never settle for uni and a 'sensible' job, this was where the career advisers should send them, Elsie thought.

In the yards, she and Tara undid the horses' rope halters. Once free, the animals dropped their heads to begin chewing. Even the NP Co horses were peaceful, Elsie observed.

After hanging the halters in an ordered tack room, the girls fell in step with Gordon Fairweather across the ochre-dust station yard towards a clump of trees, beneath which was the mess room. As they entered a Colorbond fence gateway, the smell of bacon and eggs drew them along a concrete path dividing a buffel-grass lawn.

Elsie wondered what Zac was doing right that minute. If he was thinking of her at all? The girls had sent postcards from each new town, and spoken to the twins twice, though the conversations were a bit awkward. They hadn't had time to decide what their relationships really were, after all. They'd only seen each other once in the last four years! But there was something between them, even if it was only the old Poo Crew bond that they just couldn't shake.

The girls had rung the previous night from Mt Isa, but had only reached Gwinnie. As they had hung up the phone, both had felt a little deflated. Elsie resolved to write a letter to Zac and even a song, and send it to him that week.

She walked into the mess room and there was the entire Goldsborough team, including the two bearded scientists finishing up their work on the station and flying out that afternoon with Hinchie. Moving about in the kitchen behind them was a jolly-looking cook and at the centre of the crowd at the table about a dozen people sat, amid them the most handsome young man Elsie had ever seen.

On his lap sat two red cattle-dog pups and on either side a pretty girl. The young man was laughing loudly with the rest of the people, the crew clearly at the end of a very funny story. When he looked up with his crystal-blue eyes and past Tara to see her, he flicked a fringe of sandy hair from his eyes and smiled widely.

Elsie glanced away shyly, but not before she had noticed his perfectly tanned skin and his sexy big silver belt buckle. An image of Zac flashed momentarily in her mind, of the sprinkle of acne. Then came an image of herself in the mirror with the giant mole on her face. The one that was no longer there.

Elsie barely took in the other names of the people in the room as Gordon introduced them. All she could hear was: 'This is Jake.'

Twenty-three

In the giant shed near the shit ponds Amos pulled his protective goggles over his eyes, dragged on some rubber gloves and began filling a beaker with brown sludge. 'What are we? Three weeks on with this stuff?' he asked deep in concentration as he jabbed a thermometer into the slurry and pulled a face from the stench. He wrinkled his nose and held the beaker at arm's length. 'Boy, this is really cooking with gas.'

Zac looked at the dial on the vat and shook his head. 'Too much gas if you ask me,' he said, tapping the gauge. 'I'm sure Dad got the calculation wrong.' He turned back to the computer and entered some more numbers.

'In another couple of months it'll be sweet,' Amos said. 'Sweet like my Tara.'

Zac hurled a rubber hose in his brother's direction so it bounced off Amos's back. He folded his arms across his Superman T-shirt. 'She's not *yours*. You can't own a person.'

'I'm going to marry her one day. I know it.'

'Well, I guess that's one way of kinda owning her. After all, marriage was set up by the church to control women and children as property.' With teenage swagger he spun himself on the revolving stool and fired an imaginary pistol at his brother, blowing smoke from his fingers.

'You're right,' Amos said. 'It is kinda outdated. Well, if I'm not gonna marry her, I'm gonna …' Amos searched for a word, 'I'm gonna *dedicate* myself to her.'

Zac pulled a doubtful face. '*Dedicate?* What the heck does that mean?'

Amos shrugged. 'Be committed to her for all of my life.'

'Humans are not by nature monogamous,' Zac said in his grown-up science-man voice. 'Society brainwashes us into thinking we are meant to partner for life. Biologically we are driven to mate with several others —'

'Biologically yes,' Amos said, drawing up his safety goggles and turning to his brother, 'but spiritually, most of us are all seeking *the one*. To make us feel whole. What if, just *what if*, the energetic of love for one person is enough to override the male biological function for his entire lifetime? It's been done. Many men have done it. And the way I feel about Tara —'

'The way you feel about Tara is in your underpants, caused by hormones,' Zac scoffed. '*The one?* I mean really? Mum said no other person can make you feel whole. That's up to you and your connection to universal intelligence.'

Amos shook his head, frowning. 'Don't you feel the same about Elsie, especially how she looks now after her operation?'

Amos saw a flicker of pain shadow Zac's expression and his jaw flinch.

'I liked her better before the operation,' Zac said flatly. 'Now she's something her mother wanted.'

Amos took in what his brother was saying. 'But she didn't like the mole. You know she didn't. You mean now she looks so perfect externally, you're not good enough for her.'

Zac's mouth twisted.

'I get it now,' Amos said. 'You're scared of not having a future with Elsie, so you bring it back to basics. The "men are supposed to be guided by their dicks" bullshit.'

'Whereas big imperfect Tara's good enough for you.'

Amos clenched his jaw. 'Tara is fat, sure, but so what? She's incredible. It's just you're not brave enough to fall in love and I am.'

'In love? Look, buddy, we're sixteen, OK?' Zac responded, his voice sharp. 'We don't know shit about life. We had sex for the first time with girls we've known since we were kids. So what? That doesn't mean we have to spend the rest of our lives with them. Anyway, they've gone. We've talked, like, a couple of times with them and got a few postcards. There's a lot of wet dreams to be had between now and when you see Tara again.'

'If I decide I can deal with that, then I can,' Amos said, his jaw jutting out defiantly.

They heard their father pull up outside in the tractor.

'He must be out of gas.' Amos put down the beaker and both boys went out into the bright summer sunshine.

Zac muttered, 'I just hope they're OK.'

Outside, Elvis stepped down from the tractor cab.

'Not bad,' he said to the twins. 'That was a three-hour run. The fuel conversion is improving, but if we can somehow extend it so I can do more runs, that would be ideal. I think if we adjust the pistons a little. Or maybe this batch is not quite there yet?' He dragged his cap back off his head and ran his fingers through his hair. 'Still, it's a miracle that it works so well.'

He looked at his two handsome growing sons, his face beaming. For most of his life he had dreamed of coming up with a solution to the global energy crisis. He'd accepted the fact his family farm would go to his older brother and set off to become a mechanical engineer with this aim. He and Gwinnie had planned and saved, and now here he and his boys were on the brink of a major engineering breakthrough.

Elvis knew around the world other experiments were being done converting human waste to natural gas. He and the boys had also been pleased human sewage was now considered a resource in third-world countries and that fermentation tanks had been installed in villages as a fuel source. The potential remained as yet unrealised in the western world, though. And here they were close to a solution on the engine conversions needed. Elvis reckoned Culvert could become a model town for the rest of the world, showcasing how the cheap, renewable resource of natural gas from human waste could revolutionise agriculture and how the carbon emissions could be recycled back into the soil with his farming methods and machinery.

His biggest hurdle would be the authorities. The boys shared his vision, but if it was to be fully realised in the corporate world, he needed them to be grown up. Not long now, he thought. Just a few more years and they would have a prototype and the boys would be ready. It was a shame they'd had to rely on stolen sewage for the project, but every application for research grants and access to waste had been knocked back by every council he and Gwinnie ever approached. Culvert had been the only fast track for him.

'How's it cutting?' Zac asked, moving to inspect the harvest implement on the back of the tractor; it included an air blower that collected the native grass seed.

'Terrific,' Elvis said. 'We've nearly filled an entire bin. If we bag it up for sale cleaned and supply it direct, we can get around eighty bucks a kilo for the kangaroo grass and up to two-fifty for the buffel. One fella told me channel millet cleaned is getting seven hundred and fifty dollars a kilo. Better than selling drought-pinched wheat to a bulk dealer at two hundred a *tonne*! Not to mention we'll be sowing the seeds of change,' Elvis said, guffawing at his own joke.

The boys looked out to the paddocks where Elvis had been harvesting the native grasses growing naturally in great swathes in the rested paddocks. Word was spreading about the amazing job the Smiths were doing. So much so, Elvis had to leave the boys to the mechanics workshop frequently while he dealt with more and more native-seed buyers.

Their costs for feed were zero and their animal health record was virtually flawless. Rural journalists were now knocking on their door for a story, such was the difference of the landscape from the surrounding sheep and wheat farms. He and his boys were the ones who had fat lambs when everyone else had sold theirs on as skinny. Their lambing percentages were well above the local average, and never once were they seen out with a grain feeder come the middle of summer. Their crops too reflected the same health, despite poor rainfall.

Of course the big cockies dismissed them as eccentric and 'small-time hobby farmers'. They muttered that it would never work on a bigger place. Who had time to move stock like that every few days in small paddocks, or who had sons who would want to be out shepherding mobs like they did in biblical times on the rougher unfenced country and along the roads? Yes, the other farmers reasoned, Elvis Smith and his sons were nutters. Nice people, but nutters nonetheless.

Even though Elvis's desire to spread his message was strong, the last thing he needed was journalists and other farmers poking their noses in and around the place. They were bound to ask questions about the shed. And he wasn't ready for that. He smiled as he watched Amos screwing a coupling onto a tank in the shed while Zac undid the fuel cap on the tractor and took up the end of the hose. He was so proud of them.

'Oh,' Elvis said, 'I stopped in at the house. While I was there Tara called for you again, Amos. Mum spoke to her.'

Both boys looked up.

'She and Elsie are about to set off mustering cleanskins. They said to say hi.'

Amos glanced over at his brother, feeling triumphant. Zac, who was known for his teenage poker face, gave little away, but Amos could tell he was smiling on the inside.

The dying light of the day filtered a red hue into the scattering of mottled cloud. Last-minute flies buzzed heavily by. Across the way the lights of the roadhouse flicked on. Elvis knew Gwinnie would be dishing up tucker for the truckies and setting their own dinner aside to share in the private section of the house when he and the boys returned. It's warm enough tonight to have a beer, he thought. Since his illness he'd not much cared for alcohol, but tonight, with the seed harvest in and the fuel-conversion prototype in the tractor working so perfectly, Elvis thought there was cause for celebration. He was about to haul himself back up into the cab and drive the tractor to the big shed when suddenly a blast shattered the peace of the world. The loud bang sent the cockies screaming from the gum trees, their wings flapping wildly. Then Elvis heard an agonised cry from one of his boys and screams from the other.

'Dad!' one son called from within the shed, terror carried in his voice. 'Dad! Please, *no!*'

Elvis leaped from the tractor and sprinted towards the doorway from where smoke now billowed.

Twenty-four

Elsie felt a shiver run through her despite the heat. From beneath the brim of her Roughrider, she looked at the blinding sun through her new station-supplied sunglasses. The blaring ball sat low in front of them, shrouded to softness occasionally by dust raised by the cloven hooves of three-thousand-plus head of cattle. They were almost at the yards after a full day in the saddle.

She felt another rush of vertigo and a cold prickle of sweat sweep over her; Wolfie was tall and she didn't want to faint off her, so she pulled up and leaned down over the mare's neck to compose herself. Was it heat stroke?

Zac flashed before her mind's eye, along with a rush and tug of longing and distress. The sense of him momentarily enveloped her and stole her breath, then came a steady flooding of her system of guilt. She knew after *that* night they were in no way 'boyfriend and girlfriend', but there was something otherworldly that held him in her heart and soul. But she was too young to fall in love like that. To be tied to one person. Plus she'd been fantasising about Jake *all day*.

Earlier this morning it had seemed natural for Jake and Elsie to take up position near each other at the rear of the even-paced ambling herd, leaving the other two female ringers, Giselle and Karen, disgruntled.

She couldn't believe she'd stolen his attention from the other girls. She still thought of herself as the 'before Elsie', the one with the mole who didn't stand a chance in the world of glamour-boys. Had Jake known the 'before Elsie', would he be giving her as much of a 'vibe' as he had been all day?

As she rode a little behind Jake, she couldn't help but compare the two boys. Zac's hands were long and skinny. While Jake's hands made her practically swoon. To her they were true man's hands. She imagined them brushing back her hair from her face, cupping her breasts, palms sliding down the back of her jeans, grasping her arse, then those same hands sliding into the front of her jeans. She didn't think of herself as a 'boy-mad' girl, but here she was drooling over a cowboy who wore trouble in his entire demeanour as easily as he wore his dusty work boots and big sweat-stained hat. Zac, spotty, earnest, goofy Zac, had started to feel like a figment from her small-town childhood.

She felt ill again.

Instinctively she looked for Tara, who was clumping along on Gazza a way off on the flank position of the herd. Despite Jake's attention, Elsie was a little jealous she'd been on the outer with the other girls, whereas Tara had been welcomed in like a bosom buddy. She breathed through her sickness and steadied herself, lifting the reins and making kissing sounds to move Wolfie on before anyone noticed her discomfort. It had been a long day of new experiences in this strange vast country. Gordon, with his crackling dry voice and gentle ways, smoothly commanded both the crew and the herd. The slow calm flow of human, beast and dog moved through an even more peaceful and vibrant living landscape. At Grassmore stock work was chaotic and stressful. Over the course of the day Elsie had come to see Gordon as the best of the best. Earlier, they'd learned from their fellow ringer Tyler that he'd waited three years to get a position under Gordon, such was his reputation in regenerative agriculture, stock handling and the grazing game. Tara's angels must have been working overtime on the girls' journey north to land them here.

When a beast made a cantankerous rush for freedom from the long walk of the herd, Gordon showed the crew how to guide it back, rather than hoon and chase. His big rangy Queensland-bred Border Collies were just as wise as their master and soon convinced the wayward beasts to walk quietly back with the herd. Crack managed the crew the same way, as often there were young-uns who were no different to the breakaway beast.

Earlier he'd delivered a little horseback lecture on the cattle's pruning of plants, manuring of soil and the way their hooves processed the leaf litter. 'The animals are managed so that they *improve* the land, not *destroy* the land. It puts a health and vitality into the soils, so that when dry times come, the land is resilient. A lot of folk on the other big cattle places mocked us at first. Said our stocking numbers and old-fashioned shepherding methods of moving big mobs across a landscape died out with the ark or was for African nomads. And yet when the dry hits, their stock health drops, and their feed bills go up, and they blame the drought and still don't change their ways.

'Me,' he continued, 'I'm one lucky bugger. The board of directors gives me scope for change. Those men who flew out the day you flew in — Dr Fred Provenza and Dr David Tongway — are both scientists, one in rangeland science and the other in restoration of landscape. David also does a lot of mine-site rehab. The company allows me to access men like that, and suddenly Goldsborough becomes a giant trial site for regenerative grazing work. And you young-uns are still blank enough in your habits and beliefs to be shaped into understanding the holistic nature of this game. I want to alter you into *animal empathisers* and *readers of landscape*. Lots of kids have gone out to new jobs, or back to their own places, and are making good changes there too. It's a ripple effect. And I'm a lucky, lucky bugger to be able to cast a tiny pebble in a pond.

'NP Co now know they can afford to use our staff to run the cattle the way we do. We've learned that the land can't support the big business the modern cattle world demands. If we let it go at the pace Mother Nature sets, over time the profits come. The shareholders are happy and the kids and the cattle turn out better in the finish.'

The new girls were listening well, but they worried him. They were no different from many who came through, but he got the sense their young roads had been harder than others. Sometimes parents just let you down, he thought. But he knew, from experience, that a person's hardship in childhood often became his or her greatest strength.

'I remember my first stint as a jackaroo in southwest Queensland,' he said, shifting a little in his stock saddle. 'We spent more time dragging the carcasses of beasts to a burial pit than we did selling the animals for meat. The boss just complained it was a lack of rain. More like a lack of brain. Always ask yourself what have you been taught to believe in that isn't true.'

'Like Santa Claus,' said Tara with a grin.

'He's not so bad to believe in,' Gordon said. 'At least Santa offers the hope of magic to folks. But what about the belief that you must stick by your family out of duty at Christmas even if they crucify you? When you follow your true path, you find your true family, your real tribe. Isn't that why you're here?'

He cast his blue eyes on them, and both Elsie and Tara felt he was reading them like books. Elsie thought of the choking presence of her parents and their old-world constraints, the coldness of her brother. Tara thought of her own dedication to her mother — a mother who hadn't cared enough to stop a monster consuming her own baby night after night.

Gordon swung his weight in the saddle and Bear swerved away into the dust, loping around the other side of the giant mob of peaceful steady walking heifers.

'He's magic, that man,' Tara said breathlessly, after he'd ridden away.

'Don't tell me you're getting older-man fantasies,' Elsie said.

'At least I'm not getting pin-up poster-boy obsessions,' Tara said, glancing over at Jake.

'What do you mean?' Elsie asked.

'That guy is up himself. He knows he's a stunner. And he uses it. Have you seen how Mrs B always gives him an extra serve of chips?'

Elsie smiled. 'He can't help how he looks.'

'He flirts with all the women.'

'There's no crime in that.'

'He's trouble and you know it.'

Elsie kept on riding, trying to ignore what Tara had said. She noticed one heifer looking slightly lame. She'd have to point it out to Gordon. Probably just a stone bruise, but she wanted to do a good job for him. And, part of her ego told her, she wanted to impress Jake.

The homecoming of the heifers and the crew was celebrated in Mrs B's kitchen with a big roast-beef dinner washed down with lemon cordial, followed by rum and beer. Marbles sat beneath the table, his nose twitching on the hunt for scraps. Tara rested her socked feet on the old dog and tried to ignore what was unfolding between Jake and Elsie.

Jake was passing Elsie every condiment that sat on the tabletop in a silly flirty game. Salt, pepper, tomato sauce, hot mustard, barbecue sauce, seeded mustard. Elsie played along, batting her eyelids and snickering, her head tilted a little. Tara felt herself prickle with irritation and she could tell the whole crew felt the same way. It was as if her clever, steady friend had momentarily lost her mind.

The staff phone rang in the games room, and reluctantly Tyler set down his fork and ambled, saddle sore, to the next room to pick it up. He returned and said to Elsie, 'It's for you.'

She sighed and reluctantly tore herself away from Jake's delicious side, which now smelled of fresh deodorant and shampoo. It'd be her mother. Tara watched her go, feeling something deep within her shift. She felt a rush of coldness, then got up and followed Elsie, unease swamping her. Elsie's face grew pale as she listened. Tara went to her side. Her friend's eyes were wide with shock.

She said, 'Goodbye, Mum,' in a whisper, then hung up.

'Elsie?' Tara asked gently.

'There's been a terrible accident. It's Zac.'

Twenty-five

The hospital corridors were lit by cold fluorescent tubes. Elvis reached for Gwinnie's hand and steeled himself. The family had become used to hospitals during Elvis's treatments, but this was different.

The Smith family followed their nurse escort to the ICU as if being towed behind her by an invisible thread of disbelief. They were not sure what they would find. Amos tried to block the feeling of fear that was drowning him. He saw hospitals as places that centralised the coming and going of human souls to and from the planet, from tiny babies entering the world, to old, sick or injured people shuffling out. He knew about his own energetic connection to the universal life so the intense energy of the place was unsettling.

He tried to quieten his mind now so he could feel the connection rise from the soles of his long skinny feet to the top of his shaggy head and out to the universal plane of everythingness. The experience of his father's cancer had taught him that faith and connection was the best path to choose when travelling through storms and outrageous joy. But right now, with his twin caught in a storm he couldn't have ever imagined, Amos struggled to find a place to tether his faith.

Was he the only boy in the world who thought as deeply about life? Apart from Zac. What if he lost him? If he had to go on twinless in the world?

He shuddered, thinking of the hot ignition of the blast just metres from where he'd been standing. The blinding flare of light. The roar of noise as metal warped and gas flamed. Zac screaming in the centre of an inferno. The stench of burning flesh and hair. The smell of his own brother burning. For a moment he'd thought he would vomit. Amos roped in his thoughts and consciously released the tension from his white-knuckled hands. He wished Tara was here.

'He's obviously sedated to manage the pain,' the nurse said briskly over her shoulder, 'and he's still coming out of the anaesthetic so you won't get much from him. Keep your visit short. It's just to let him know you're here.' She showed them into a room that stored all the surgical scrubs, gloves and disposable hair nets. 'Wash your hands thoroughly here. Then put these things on.' She handed them each a disposable outfit sealed in a plastic bag. 'Leave your belongings there.' She nodded towards a table that was set against the wall for such things. 'We can't risk infection, so be thorough. When you're prepared, the doctor will be out to brief you.'

Elvis turned on the long arm of a silver tap with his elbow and the nurse left the room.

On any other day, Elvis would be making jokes as they all stood in their disposable overalls, masks and hats, the way he'd done during his cancer treatment, but today, that inexhaustible repertoire of daggy jokes eluded him. He believed the explosion that saw his son so horrendously burned was his fault. He was certain there'd be an investigation of the shed and the family would be exposed. He had failed them. He had let his growing boys down, and his beautiful wife. All for scientific pride and glory. He berated himself for his arrogance! His son's bubbling still-burning skin. The sound of Amos screaming out, 'Dad! Help him!' The horror of Zac's guttural screams. The rush to the sink, the running water, the grapple to find his mobile phone, calling Gwinnie back at the roadhouse, not 000, such was his panic.

Gwinnie had reacted instantly. Swiftly. Local ambulance, flying doctor, even a bag packed for them all just before the staff hustled them to the Culvert airstrip. Elvis knew it wouldn't be until after Gwinnie had seen her boy alive that she would collapse. Only then would the woman of iron buckle and soften and crumple to the floor. If she let him, he would hold her like a broken bird. Then, he knew, after a shower, something to eat, some sleep, she would emerge the next day and carry on, bright as a button. He had seen her do it so many times before during his own treatment.

The doctor was coming soon, and soon they would be seeing their son.

When the doctor did appear, it was as if he had come straight from the set of a daytime TV soap. Dr Day was a walking cliché of tall and handsome, with flawless skin and neat-combed black hair. From that moment Amos thought of him as Dr Daytime TV.

'We've removed the intubation tube. His oral cavity is functioning fine, which is very lucky, otherwise he would be having difficulty breathing. He does, however, have severe burns to his neck and one side of his face. A section of his left forearm is exhibiting third-degree burns. Fortunately, as you know, he was wearing some protective clothing at the time, which saved his sight, but we can't determine if he has permanent hearing loss at this stage. Of course for now that's the least of our worries. It's too early to tell, but he may need grafting and reconstructive surgeries. Certainly on his arm, but possibly on his face as well.'

Dr Daytime TV glanced up and almost took a backward step: his patient was standing before him. Then he realised he was looking at a twin. He made a mental note to mention it to the psych. There would be severe guilt for the brother who hadn't suffered the burns. There may also be complications in the parents' mental wellbeing, accepting such changes to one of their boys while the other was whole. He sighed. This was just another day of human horrors. Always so many complications.

'We will also arrange counselling to help him with the psychological and social impairment that often follow facial burns. Are you ready to see him?' Dr Day swept his arm towards the door and clenched his jaw in a smile. 'Come this way.'

They shuffled forwards, entering the burns unit, trying beneath their masks to arrange expressions on their faces that conveyed to Zac comfort and hope, not horror.

Twenty-six

Culvert's Councillor-Mayor Jones alighted from his council car with the ease of a hippo squeezing through a cat flap. He held a blocking hand up to the journalists who were waiting to swarm him outside the roadhouse and glanced around for his police escort. The constable was nowhere to be found.

Where was that damned man? In the media pack was a pimpled cadet from the *Rington Gazette*, not much older than his own daughter, clearly terrified to be in the company of the older female journalists from the city. Since word of the explosion had reached the city, the high-heeled women and polyester-panted men had smelled local government excrement in the form of incompetency. They were on the hunt for the scoop — or the 'poo scoop', as one journalist put it.

The questions began to fire.

'Councillor, how could anyone not notice a pipeline being dug into a sewage-treatment plant?'

Kelvin thought momentarily of Elsie and fury enveloped him. She must've known about it, but had said nothing to him. She had *known* her friends' activities would bring him down and smear the township's good name (never mind the fact very few people had actually ever heard of Culvert until that morning).

'Reports have been leaked that the council was already investigating why Culvert had almost half the national average output of sewage compared to similar-sized towns. Why hadn't your team of experts, hired for thousands of dollars of taxpayer money, simply inspected the ponds and found the illegal pipe?'

'Would you say this has been a shitty day for the town of Culvert, Councillor?' one wag of a journalist asked.

'Get it right!' Kelvin barked, his face burning red. 'It's *Councillor-Mayor.*'

The journalists had discovered the story via a group email, where Nathanial Rogerson had sent his version to the media outlets — that a local loony father had blown up one of his sons with gas made from people poo. Poo that had been stolen from a sewage plant.

So it seemed public sewage theft was big news, and it would be Kelvin's head on the chopping block. He knew with the internet the first of the media reports would be making their way overseas right now. Kelvin wished Elvis Smith was here to take the full brunt of this.

Constable Gilbert was at last arriving in the police four-wheel drive, followed by the Deputy Mayor, Cuthbertson Rogerson, who sat so low in his driver's seat it looked like the vehicle was being piloted by a chimp.

Constable Gilbert got out, tucking in his shirt, his cheeks flushed, a grin on his round face. He winked a greeting at Cuthbertson.

'What took you?' muttered Kelvin to Constable Gilbert.

'Domestic situation to attend to,' the police officer said without losing his grin. He turned to the journalists, who were now firing questions at him. 'Are you ready, ladies and gents?' he enquired commandingly as he eyed a honey-pot blonde in a short skirt suit. 'I'll show you where raw sewage was being stolen right from under the council's nose, so to speak,' he said jovially. Kelvin flashed him a glance.

This case could be Constable Gilbert's ticket out of Culvert. He couldn't have dreamed up a better crime to put himself in the spotlight. He knew the Smiths were nutters. He knew the pain-in-the-arse mayor-councillor would be sunk. He opened the door of the police vehicle for Kelvin Jones and invited him in with a sweep of his hand. 'Track's a bit rugged for the council car in places, sir. Be my guest.'

He thought about the woman he had just been with. All she'd needed was a little compliment here, a little hand touching there and then he had her on a string. And on her back in a flash, he thought devilishly as he closed the car door, almost banging Kelvin's knee in the process.

He hitched up his gun belt and gestured to the journalists. 'Form an orderly convoy behind me and I'll answer all your questions when we've arrived.' To build excitement and tension, he added, 'And remember, no smoking near the accident site!'

Bright yellow police tape cordoned off the area. It flapped in the wind, humming eerily. At the arrival of even more people, the galahs went wheeling and screeching away over the high fence of the treatment plant towards the tip. Constable Gilbert nodded to a group of men as he got out of the vehicle, the media drawing up beside him, parking their Wagga Wagga hire cars in a row as if white city lines were printed in the paddock grass.

'All right, fellas?' Constable Gilbert asked the overall-clad men. 'Site secure?'

One nodded. They were bomb-squad experts, brought into Culvert to ensure there were no illegal weapons being manufactured in the shed. That rumour was again compliments of Nathanial. The power-company guys were there too, shutting off the supply to the shed, inspecting the rat-chewed wires that possibly caused the explosion. Some of the equipment in there looked so sophisticated it was hard to tell what its actual function was and that was making everyone nervous. Chunky's fire crew, including four of his sons, was there too. It had taken them fifteen minutes to put the gas fire out after the blast, but now the pipeline had been secured, they were merely hanging about for a gander of the whole shemozzle. Other men in orange high-visibility vests from the sewage plant were standing about in another cluster. They were watching a man in an excavator uncovering a buried pipe that ran from the shed all the way under the high mesh fence towards the nearest slurry pond of sewage.

As the media gathered up their cameras and recording devices, Constable Gilbert gestured for them to follow him into the dimness of the shed, where a large metal vat looked as if a giant bowling ball had ripped its way out of it with the force of a cannon. The smell of burned gas inside the shed was overpowering.

Again the journalists flicked on their lights for filming and the blood ran fast in their veins. Questions began to flow again. Pointed questions. Accusing questions. Like knives. All aimed at Councillor-Mayor Jones.

'Seems seducing virgin girls wasn't all this shed was used for,' Constable Gilbert muttered as he held up a bottle of cleanskin whisky. 'I think that Culvert's shit has hit the fan.'

Behind him Cuthbertson grinned while Kelvin grimaced.

'I'll see them pay for this if it's the last thing I do!' said the councillor-mayor.

Twenty-seven

When the Smith family entered the room, they saw Zac with his head turned away on the pillow. His young strong chest was bare and there was a structure like an igloo covering his left arm. He was attached to a drip and seemed to be sleeping. The room smelled of silver nitrate. Elvis glanced at Gwinnie and saw the scrunch of pain on her face. Amos had turned pale and his mouth had fallen slightly open, his big brown eyes staring at his brother.

'He's a little groggy,' Dr Day said, snapping them out of their silence. 'It's a case of wait and see over the next ten days. It's difficult to estimate the wound depths at this point. Because of the excellent blood supply to the human face and its high density of epithelial appendages, facial wounds heal rapidly. If after a couple of weeks he hasn't healed, though, he may develop hypertrophic scarring, so we will need to investigate excision and grafting. His arm, of course, will be slower to heal.'

The only word Gwinnie heard was 'heal'. She moved towards her son and shut out the rest of Dr Day's monologue. She collected herself with a deep breath, but it was all she could do to stifle a cry when she saw the hideous wounds on her son's face. She felt, for the first time in her life, fury towards Elvis. His overly ambitious (not to mention illegal) secret and his ludicrous dreams were not only dead in the shit-ponds water, now one of her sons was wearing the scars of those dreams on his face, arm and hands for life, and her other son was witness to his brother's suffering. She reached out and touched Zac lightly on his shoulder. He didn't move. Tears spilled from Gwinnie's eyes when she saw his beautiful face blackened around his left ear, his hair singed over the crown of his head. If his face looked bad, his arm and hands would surely look worse. Wound treatment cream smeared over the side of his face looked so thick it was as if he were about to swim the English Channel. The burn ran the length of his jawline and even through the cream Gwinnie could see weeping, blistered, cherry-red bubbles of skin and tissue that swathed down to his neck. She felt the rip of her heart again. This boy had arrived on the clean white sheet of the maternity ward sixteen minutes before his twin. It had been enough just to glance at that tiny mewing baby to know that his skin, his body, his heart and above all his soul were perfection to her. Seeing him so disfigured now, she felt the cruelty of life almost crush her. They had just dragged themselves through Elvis's survival only to be faced with this.

Gwinnie drew deeply from within herself. She reached for that place in her soul that sang to her with gratitude.

Your son is alive, she heard a voice in her head say. He is *alive*. And that is a great thing. Whatever else happens on his journey is now a blessing. Whatever way his face heals and re-forms itself is a blessing.

The voice inside her was insistent. It was the only way she could go on, instead of falling down now on the floor and howling out a guttural wail of misery and fury that her beautiful boy had been burned.

Elvis stood beside his wife, a broken man.

Amos looked at the mirror of himself lying on the bed. He felt Zac's pain and his heart tore too. He reached out and laid a hand on his brother's upper arm. 'Hello, other brother,' he said.

Just then the nurse returned with a young man decked out in hygiene gear. The nurse nodded at the doctor curtly and busied herself with checking the machines beside the beds. The young man stood at the doorway too. When the Smiths didn't react to the man's presence, she glanced at them. 'Your other son's here.'

'What?' Gwinnie asked.

But it was too late. The man had already lifted up a camera and was taking rapid-fire photos of Zac, then swinging the camera to capture images of the others.

'Get out,' Elvis said with force, stepping forwards.

The paparazzo backed away, a victorious gleam in his eyes. Then he was gone, bursting out the door, flying back through the corridors, down the exit stairs and out of the sliding doors, away from the mayhem of the city hospital.

Shock waves roamed around the room as the Smiths absorbed the knowledge that back at the roadhouse shed their illegal secret must have been exposed for all the world to see. Just how big would the story be? Now with the internet, unauthorised, prying pictures like the ones just taken would spread like wildfire and there would be no going back. Elvis suddenly realised how much trouble he and the boys were in.

He pulled up a chair beside Zac's bed, held his son's hand and rested his forehead on the crisp white sheet. He shut his eyes. 'I'm sorry,' he said hoarsely first to his son, then turning his heartbroken face to Gwinnie and Amos.

Gwinnie stepped forwards and rubbed her hand over his back. 'It's not your fault.'

He shook his head and scrunched his eyes shut tight. 'It is. We should've gone through the proper channels.'

'We tried,' Gwinnie forced herself to say. 'You know how important this is. It could revolutionise the world.'

'But look,' Elvis said, his voice choked. 'Look what I've done.'

Grief contorted Gwinnie's tired but pretty face. 'You didn't do it. It was an accident. Zac is just as passionate about changing the world as you are. We will recover from this. Zac will recover from this. We have a revolution to plan.'

Elvis smiled sadly up at his wife. 'Nice try, Gwinnie. I love you for saying that, but in truth our boy is scarred for life and I'm headed for gaol.'

Twenty-eight

Like a hard punishing whip to the skin, a letter from Sarah Jones arrived for Elsie about the Smiths' downfall. Elsie was at first excited to be getting mail as she watched Gracie walking from the direction of the station office towards her with a smile on her face. Gracie loved delivering the mail by hand.

Elsie's enthusiasm dimmed when she saw her mother's handwriting on the envelope and she almost passed it straight back. Instead she slumped down on the bench seat outside the mess room. Her feet felt hot in her boots, her toes sweating, the flies seeking moisture in the corners of her eyes. She swept them away crossly as she began to tear open the envelope. Her mother had barely written anything on the thick embossed stationery folded around a sheaf of newspaper clippings and website print-outs.

Dear Eleanor,

I hope you are well. FYI about your 'friends' and what was going on in the shed you spent so much time in. Your poor father is having to deal with it.

Love Mum xxx

Elsie could read between the lines. They were furious with her. They knew she knew all about the sewage pipe to the shed. The clippings started with a front page from the local Rington newspaper. Elsie looked at a photograph of her father putting his hand up to block the camera. She flicked to another article from a bigger regional paper with a picture of the Smith family's shed. The headline read *Town Bogged Down by Blast*. Then another from a city paper, then some global coverage. Another tacky article titled *Bog Hogs* from another magazine. Mother went all out, Elsie thought as she shuffled through clipping after clipping. Sarah Jones was keeping tally of just how angry she was with Elsie for the scandals she'd created with those boys.

The print before Elsie's eyes blurred. The explosion was news worldwide, not because a beautiful boy had been seriously injured, but because the sewage theft allowed subeditors to use their basest puns. *The Sh*t Hits the Fan in Small Town*, mocked one of the headlines in bold font.

There was even a quote from their former science teacher Vernon Tremble, saying the Smith twins were like local gangsters and deserved all they got. But the worst things were the photographs of Zac taken in hospital. The way his face was cast away so his blackened hair and red-raw skin screamed. His body limp on white sheets, his family standing around him. He was barely recognisable.

Suddenly she was transported back to *that* night. It felt like an age in the past, but it had only been this month! She thought of the light in the twins' eyes when they explained what was going on in the shed. She could hear the excitement in Zac's voice: 'The technology we're working on with Dad could revolutionise life for everyone. Few people think about it, but we have a superclass created by the world's dependency on fossil fuel for industry and transport. They control everything. If we get what we're doing in here right, the use of sewage as a power source could potentially overturn those world dominators as well as free up communities to access a reliable power source locally.'

'You're saying Culvert poo could save the world?' asked a drunken but interested Tara.

Amos grinned. 'Not alone, but if we can make it commonplace in the rural sector and in towns like Culvert, we would all be a bit more independent from the larger city fuel distribution hubs.'

Tara grinned. 'So you're taking on corrupt politicians, oil warlords, corporate car giants and conglomerate fuel companies! Woot!'

'Not so much taking them on,' Zac said. He had reached for Elsie's hand, and she recalled how a tingling warmth had spread over her entire body. 'More like showing Culvert people a better way. How they can regain their own economic power simply by using local waste for gas production for farm machinery.'

'Remember the Poo Pond Prophecy,' Tara said. 'Well, it's coming true. Another miracle on its way.'

'Oh, we've got a long way to go yet,' Zac said.

'But it's brilliant,' Elsie said, taking it all in and understanding the enormity of what was being created in here by these two bright boys and their parents. 'Especially with how the gas emissions are sequestered back into the soil quickly and cheaply using grasslands and managed grazing.'

She had squeezed Zac's hand back. Zac had beamed at her. In that moment the world had zinged with unseen stars flashing between them.

'I've been studying it in school,' she explained. Thrilled she 'got it', Zac had kissed her with zealous passion.

Her eyes blurred with tears. She'd scanned the text her mother had so spitefully sent and nowhere was there any mention of the vision and potential the Smiths' project had. They were just portrayed as weirdos stealing sewage to run their own tractors. Elsie's heart tugged as she looked again at Zac's photographs.

'Stealing *sewage*?' came the voice of Jake from behind as he peered over Elsie's shoulder. 'Wow! Friends of yours from back home? They must be some kinda guys! That's hilarious.'

She glanced up at him. He failed to see the strain on her face. 'Not really,' she said softly. Normally she would light up when he was within a five-metre radius. But not today. 'I'll catch you about later.' She got up and wandered slowly across to the machinery shed. Her head was spinning.

She knew she'd find Crack with Tyler and Dump on a ute service in the machinery workshop. Elsie stood in the bright sunshine, peering into the deep chasm of the shed for Crack. She spotted him in the jaws of an open-mouthed Toyota. 'Hey, Crack?'

'Yo!' he called, not looking up as he busied himself with cleaning a battery terminal.

'Mind if I take a sickie for the afternoon?'

Gordon frowned, withdrew himself from under the bonnet, wiped his hand on a rag and glanced at Elsie. Instead of telling her to 'take a teaspoon of concrete and harden up', he agreed, then watched her drift over to the quarters in a cloud of shock.

There, dragging open the screen door, stepping over a snoozing Marbles and kicking off her boots, Elsie took out her guitar, opened up the empty notebook she'd bought with the intention of writing to Zac regularly, and instead of a letter, began to pen her first song to him. With the air conditioner humming and drifting cool air about her tiny room, she let her voice carry the pain of seeing Zac that way in the photographs.

With time, the image of them together came to her. Them lying in their swags with a swathe of night-time sky above. Then on the bluest of days when she and Tara had rocked up before they had run away with the cleanskins. How they'd sat outside the shed in deck chairs around the deadened fire pit, laughing till their faces hurt, and then later, lying back in the jungle of grass, looking up at the clouds. She thought about what Zac had said to her. Words like welcome rain clouds gathered in her mind, bringing with them a mellow tune like a sun shower.

'*I got nothin' to do. All day to do it.*' Elsie could hear Zac saying it to her as if it was yesterday.

'*Could save the world. I'll get round to it.*'

Forget your troubles. I'm working through it.
Nothin' to do and all day to do it.
Nothin' to do and all day to do it, yeah yeah.'

Hot tears stung behind her eyes. The image of his burned face sizzled in her mind. She should have called him. Not just occasionally but every day. She should have written to him, longer letters expressing her inner feelings. But why would he want her writing that kind of stuff and calling constantly? A shallow, *silly* girl. A girl who had let a glamorous cowboy distract her.

Elsie looked about the tiny room. The stack of books by Tara's bed. One on the railway system, one on the war in the Pacific, a book on extra-sensory perception in animals, another on house design using straw bales. Then there was the energy of the room itself, so influenced by Tara's.

Tara had, in her term, 'feng'd' the room. She'd arranged bedding and cushions and hung cloth and folded colourful paper in the shape of birds and unicorns and strung them about. It was beautiful, and Tara was her own beautiful self — if anything, more relaxed and open since they'd got to Goldsborough, but Elsie had also felt her mate becoming more distant from her. She didn't want to think about why. She knew Tara had been listening whenever she talked to Zac. Tara knew the situation with Jake and was mad that Elsie wasn't being fully upfront with Zac. Elsie too could feel her own self drawing away from Tara. Around Tara, Elsie felt somehow … *less*, as if she wasn't as likeable or as funny or as kind as the seemingly more mature and empathetic Tara.

'It's not that I'm judging,' Tara had said, 'but I just don't want you to get hurt with Jake. You hardly know him. And then there's Zac … He cares about you. You have to make a decision.' Now with the accident she would become even more stern about Elsie's flirtations with Jake.

Tara had absorbed the news, then in her new coolness with Elsie shrugged it off, saying, 'It's terrible, yes, but these things are part of the master plan of the universe. It's Zac's journey; and anyway, what's it to do with you now? You can't be all over Jake and then act as though this tragic thing has happened to you and your boyfriend. As long as he's alive and not in pain once his skin heals, he'll still have a good life. It's just the way things go.'

Elsie had been cut by the dismissive comment. She was tied to a past she hated, and that, she decided, was Tara's and the twins' fault. They were no better than the rest of the people in Culvert. A feeling swelled in her that made her want to be reckless, heartless and even thoughtless towards the people of her past. She wanted the freedom to not give a shit about anyone or anything. If she rang Zac, like Tara had gently prompted, what would she say? The song was the best she could do.

'What else do I do?' Elsie asked Marbles, her pick hanging on her bottom lip, slouching over the guitar. She ran her bare foot over the bony back of the old dog as he sat like a giant bearskin rug between the beds.

She opened the bedside drawer, took up her lucky leather cuff and placed it on her wrist, breathed out a long breath and shut her eyes. Confused, she tried to shut Zac out, but then she began to remember his way with her. The sincerity of him. His vulnerability. She gathered up her guitar again. She was fearless when it came to her music. It was the one way she could communicate with him openly. Bit by bit a song began to shape itself, take form in the ethers and then flow into the physical, through her and from her. And even though she knew deep down she loved him, the message of her song would be … he was better off without her.

Twenty-nine

Tara arrived back at the ringers' quarters after her day with bore man, Ron. She was crumpled and smeared with dust and sweat from climbing windmills and had aching arms from turning big shifters on tight water valves. As she walked towards the long dozy verandah in the dying light of the day, her whole weary body was gathered up by the most beautiful sound, emanating from her bedroom. Tyler, Jake and the rest of the crew who had knocked off after a day in the yards were also traipsing in, floppy-limbed and silent along the path. They too were stopped in their tracks by the sound.

'There's a girl keeps calling,
but I'm gonna throw my phone away.
Cos I won't let her daytime dramas put a dampener on my damn good
day.
I got nothin' to do, all day to do it ...'

Tara recalled Zac saying those exact words at the shit-ponds shed when they'd first arrived, then later again as he sat on an old tip-rescued deck chair with them all in the paddock, drinking cleanskin whisky. Elsie sang on, completely unaware her team were standing in a semi-circle at the base of the verandah steps.

'Holes in a blue-jean sky.
I stop and wonder why, oh why.'

She tapped a rhythm on the wooden frame of her guitar and began the chorus again

'I got nothin' to do, all day to do it.
Could save the world, I'll get round to it.
Forget your troubles, I'm working through it.
Nothin' to do and all day to do it,
Nothin' to do and all day to do it … yes, sir.'

With a crescendo the song ended so that all that could be heard was the outback wind rushing through the verandah uprights and a far-off warble of a magpie in a heatstruck gum.

'Wow,' Jake said. The young ringers glanced around at each other, embarrassed by the emotion Elsie's singing had prompted. She was beyond talented. She was otherworldly.

'That's not poo-boy she's singing about, is it?' Jake asked.

'Shut up, Jake,' Tara said as she stomped up the steps, knowing full well Jake was pulling a fat face behind her to amuse the rest of the ringers. She knew his type. She raised her middle finger at him behind her back as she went into the quarters and slammed the door.

'That time of the month, is it, Tars?' Jake called after her.

Marbles had hauled himself to his feet at the sight of Tara and was huffing like a steam train and wagging his feathery tail against Elsie's legs in the small room. She reached for the clippings and thrust them at Tara, the large photo of Zac on top of the pile.

'What do I do? Do I write? Do I call?'

'I dunno. You've got someone else on the go up here, so maybe not.' Even after the music's spell, Tara was in no mood to let Elsie off so easily.

'On the go? You mean Jake? I have not. And Zac doesn't know that.'

Tara snorted and began to gather up her clothes and sponge bag for the shower block.

'You're not being fair, Tara. I need some advice here. I'm not good with boys.'

'Oh, I would disagree,' Tara said a little too harshly. If she was so heartbroken over Zac's injuries, enough to take the afternoon off work, then why was there any question on how to contact him? He was a friend, wasn't he? If Elsie felt he was more than that to her, then why tow Jake along on a string all day and all night? Elsie was changing. She was using her looks, now that the mole was gone, cashing in on pretty-girl privileges she was refusing to acknowledge.

There was a knock on the door.

'Yeah,' sang Tara, half expecting it to be Jake, loitering.

'Hello, Broad Bean.' Crack put his head around the door and grinned. He'd started by calling her Greenie, then Green Bean and now Broad Bean for obvious reasons. He was supportive of her as a worker and a mate, so she didn't feel hurt by the description. She liked her body more and more as it showed her what it could do. In any case, the hard work meant that weight was falling away from her — the jeans she and Elsie had bought in Bourke were now having to be hitched up by her belt, which was freshly hole-punched again for a third time by Grout in the tack shed using the metal punch they used on the saddlery.

Jake had become Peg because of the open secret that every time there was any kind of social event he was out to peg some girl. Tyler had become Grout as in bathroom tiles and Elsie was EJ Moody Blues, because she would sometimes go silent and as Crack put it, 'disappear up her own bum'. Tara, who had never encountered anyone like Crack, had begun to idolise the man.

'You feelin' better, Moody Blues?' Crack asked, running his eyes over Elsie. She nodded as he turned back to Tara.

'Good. Mrs Cloudhead is flying back tomorrow morning with Hinchie. So Boss Man wants someone to clean the house before she gets here. And you two are volunteering.'

Elsie and Tara looked at one another.

'We are?' Elsie asked.

'I know, I know,' he said, holding up his hand, 'just because you're women I shouldn't ask you ahead of the boys to clean. In fact Jake is neat as a pin with his gear, and Tyler knows which end of a vacuum sucks, but they're busy putting out stock licks tonight. And Kazza and Grindlewald are flying out tomorrow for Christmas break, so they're busy packing.'

Elsie's eyes narrowed. She was glad the other girls were leaving. Karen in particular had been very cold towards her. But she still couldn't see why she and Tara should be roped into cleaning.

'C'mon,' Crack pleaded as he leaned his big broad shoulder against the door jamb. 'Look, Mrs Cloudhead isn't happy about sending their sprog off to boarding school next year. NP Co can't afford to lose another manager, especially one like Simmo. So we're doing our all to keep her sweet.'

Crack was referring to their station manager, Michael Simpson, who was as brilliant on cattle logistics as he was on supporting Crack with staff issues and the general running of the property.

'OK,' Elsie said. 'But why do you call her Mrs Cloudhead?'

'Her first name's Skye,' explained Crack, 'and her head is always up there, out in the clouds. That's what happens when men marry for looks.' He glanced at Elsie. 'Sorry, Miss Universe, I know you can't help it,' he said, giving her a piss-take wink. She pulled a sarcastic face back at him.

'Cleaning is my speciality,' Tara said, not looking forward to sharing a job like that with Elsie in her current frame of mind.

'I got that feeling when you showed up here with your mop and bucket.' Gordon shook his head. 'You're a rare one, Broad Bean. That's a first for me. Some kids want to bring their bikes or their kites to the station, but never their buckets.'

She grinned. 'When do we start?'

Thirty

Goldsborough homestead's silver bullnose verandah gave it a more important tone than the less embellished buildings on the station. The dwelling was fringed by a large green lawn that fell away sheer to a winding but now-dry river. Some dark green water remained in a deep heart-shaped billabong that would soon be swallowed by the wet-season river. For now it was the favourite spot for the crew on a day off or if they had some energy left after work for a swim and a beer. By the homestead fences, trees offered shady patches around what was a plain but tidy garden, thanks to Fungus the station gardener, who, before he met Crack, had been called Fergus.

Elsie and Tara called a hello to him now, as they walked towards the house, bypassing the front door and going to the side sliding door, where a number of boots and thongs were scattered. Tara carried her old faithful cleaning mop and bucket, Marbles padding at their heels. The girls knocked once and slid the glass door open, Marbles settling on the mat for a grandpa snooze.

'Holy crap,' said Tara, standing in the kitchen. The garden and verandah were the best things about the house. Inside, the sickly yellow walls and plastic-fantastic kitchen, along with a thick scattering of family clutter, made the house far from welcoming.

Mrs B had filled the girls in on all the gossip about Mrs Cloudhead. With only one son, she had become increasingly unhappy on the station and started talking about moving nearer to Brisbane so as to be with Angus, instead of sending him boarding. Her husband, Michael, was at a loss. The station managers' wives on the other properties held fundraisers for local charities, setting out white marquees complete with bows on seats and fresh flowers like a wedding. They also ran business information days for rural women and rural health forums, and hosted the company men and international colleagues with grace and charm. Skye just did not fit the NP Co mould. And clearly she was not one for organisation, Tara thought as she looked about.

Just as Tara was about to search for the laundry and Elsie for the vacuum cleaner, they heard the door open. Before them stood Michael Simpson. They'd seen the businesslike but jovial boss out in the yards, but now here in his domestic chaos he seemed less assured. His future hinged on keeping his wife happy, and he didn't know how to do it.

'So can you fix it?'

Tara felt compassion for both Skye and her easygoing husband. She swept forwards, her pretty smile on her face. 'By the time my cleanskin colleague and I are done, this place will be fit for a *Vogue Living* photo shoot. Trust me!'

The relief that swept across the manager's face was tangible as he thanked them profusely, then strode to the door, equilibrium restored.

'Now,' Tara said. 'This lounge is all wrong with its back to the window. The family must face the sleeping dragon hillside over there, and the river. This armchair needs to face the east and over here we need a pot plant.' She was already dragging furniture about and tossing all the out-of-place items in her bucket. It was as if she had gone into her own zone of creativity, like Elsie with her singing. 'Else, go rummage around in a cupboard: see if you can find me a cloth. Anything with green on it.'

'You're fenging, aren't you?'

'You bet I am,' said Tara, taking down a painting of a barren-looking landscape and tucking it behind a cupboard where it could no longer be seen.

The next day, their life couldn't have looked more different. Instead of Tara mopping a pristine floor and Elsie arranging wildflowers in Skye's kitchen, they were on a cleanskin muster, their first proper one, bumping their way over a track, trawling through patches of bull dust and jolting over rocks, Tara wedged on the stock-truck seat, bracing herself with one hand on the roof. Elsie was relishing the fact that every time they hit a bump she was thrown against Jake, who was lodged against the passenger door, thoughts of Zac pushed to the fringes of her mind. Jake was *delicious*. Plus he kept half turning to her to deliver a crooked cute grin, as if she was the only person present.

Gordon shifted down a gear as they swayed in the semi-rigid truck through a dry riverbank. 'Only eighty kilometres to go!' he yelled over the roar of the engine. They had already been travelling two hours, first on good roads recently built by mining companies and now on what seemed like a goat track. Outside, the landscape sizzled.

'The country sure could do with a drop,' said Jake, gazing out to the haze of heat and the red dirt where plants seemed to barely survive as a brittle yellow or a pale listless green.

Luckily for them, the forecast showed there was no rain on the horizon. Rain would mean getting stuck out on the run over Christmas. The roads with as little as half an inch became so slippery in patches they were no place for a stock truck laden with wild cleanskins. With a good forecast, the team had decided to risk going out for the muster. It would be good to get the job stitched up before the new year.

Elsie knew Jake would be flying out with Hinchie on his second and final run for the week. She wished he wasn't. She pictured herself in her boardies and bikini top, bobbing in the middle of the deep billabong, with Jake swimming out towards her. The shimmering water on his muscled, tanned shoulders. His bare chest. His eyes locked on hers. Sitting this close to him, she could sense every fibre of her body wanted more …

Tara looked out the dusty window and frowned. The way Jake hooked Elsie in like a Barramundi on fresh bait made her sick. Of course, he'd been to the right schools; days ago Jake and Elsie had reeled off a few grazier-family names from their mutual circle. Tara had sat next to them in Mrs B's kitchen, feeling once more like the girl from the abattoir house. She had turned her attention to Gordon, and slowly she felt a girlish crush growing. She had recently begun to shut out romantic thoughts of Amos. He was too good for her. He was well educated. She was not. He was thin and good-looking. She was fat and flubber-faced. And she knew how men thought. She'd seen enough of Dwaine's girlie magazines lying about to know what they really wanted in a woman. One that looked like Elsie. Who'd want a dumb fat girl?

Crack broke into her thoughts. 'If it did rain, there'll be no beer and no bong swimming. We'll be stranded for Christmas with a collection of foul moods.'

'And not even Elsie's guitar to pass the time.' Jake pouted.

'What would be the point of Elsie's guitar?' Tara bit at Jake. 'There's no power out there for the amp, numbnuts.' He was going to ruin the surprise she had planned.

'I was just saying,' Jake snapped back. 'Wishful thinking.'

'Keep your wishful thinking to yourself.'

'Oi. Settle it,' Crack said, sensing the tension in the cab. He clutched the steering wheel and looked out to the long red stretch of track ahead of him. At least, he thought, the wild cattle tomorrow would replace some of the kids' rampaging sexual hormones with some pure adrenaline. That oughta shake them up a bit. He dropped back a gear and heard them all squeal when he gunned it up a creek crossing.

Thirty-one

'There's a letter,' Gwinnie called out as she came through the roadhouse door in a blue floral dress and cowgirl boots. She found Zac in the family's lounge, adjacent to the kitchen. There was no summer sunshine in here. Even with his bright beautiful mother standing before him, Zac remained in a cloud of gloom.

'The Ashes should be on telly by now,' Gwinnie said, glancing at the clock. She cringed. *Ashes*. 'The Test Cricket?' she added, pointing to the television.

He shook his head.

'Want one of Dad's or my books?'

He shrugged.

'Internet? There could be something new on that mechanical engineering blog you and Amos are always on about.'

He shot her an annoyed glance, then immediately felt guilty. She was only trying to help. He'd been home two days from the big city hospital and the whole world felt weird. Like it was moving in a slow, wonky vortex, spinning a little. He wondered if he had agoraphobia, such was his hesitancy to go outside into the sunlight, let alone to the farm shed again to see the extent of the damage there. The skin on his face pulled taut as it healed, and if it wasn't stinging, or burning with pain, it was itching and driving him mad. He'd been so surly at the hospital they had discharged him early, on the provision he went daily to the Culvert doctor's surgery for wound-dressing changes.

Zac glanced down at the letter addressed in Tara's unmistakeable hand. 'It's for Amos,' he said flatly.

Gwinnie frowned. She couldn't help but feel cross with the girls for skipping town on her boys. Then she remembered what it was like to be a teenage girl. She'd made some crazy choices in her time. She realised what had unfolded privately between her sons and the girls was none of her business, but looking at the state of her son now, she knew it would soon become her business. He was fast sliding into an unreachable place of depression. She knew the burns weren't the only pain Zac was enduring, and everyone was copping it. It just wasn't in his nature to be like this.

'Maybe there's a letter from Elsie folded inside too?'

Zac flashed her a dark look.

She set the letter up on the mantelpiece for when Amos came in later with Elvis, then spun back around to Zac with a smile on her face. 'Can I get you anything? Glass of water?'

It was hard to look at him. In hospital she had been able to focus on him healing and getting him home. Now that they were home, the difference not only in his appearance but also his demeanour shocked her. This would be for life. This dreadful scarring that ran up under his neck, along his jawline, past his ear and to his temple was forever. The twist of smooth skin on his forearm that was starting to heal to white would always be there, along with his hands, his palm lines erased as if his future was now uncertain. He had barely got through the awkward ugly-duckling stage of adolescence and hadn't had the chance to be a glorious young man in a perfect body.

And then there was Amos, growing more handsome by the day, though haunted by the fact his brother had changed, not only externally, but internally too. She firmly told herself to steer away from the negatives. Zac was alive.

As she walked away from him, she brightly called out, 'Sing out if you do need something.'

She could tell he was trying not to get irritated by her. It was unlike him to be anything other than relaxed and kind, but there was a bitter, angry tension that ran through him now and Gwinnie, being sensitive to all other people's energies, couldn't help but be thrown by it.

In the kitchen, she began to rinse some snow peas she had picked from her garden. She used to love preparing food for the family. Now their dinners together were weighted with worry. Elvis faced a full-blown enquiry with the council, the police and even the environmental protections board. His trial was three months away, but his lawyer said the best-case scenario would be three months' imprisonment, the worst, ten years. The future prison sentence, however long, sat like a vampire in their home, sucking away hope and plans.

Even though she was still furious with Elvis for putting her boys at such risk, she knew that all of them were utterly passionate about their work. She knew that what they created was something humanity desperately needed. But with the vampire it seemed there was no way to get the scheme back off the ground. Gwinnie Smith was not one to give up, but today, she sure as hell felt like it.

At the Smiths' shit-ponds shed, Councillor-Mayor Jones and Constable Gilbert watched smugly with their arms folded across their chests as young Amos Smith rolled the giant door of the shed closed and then Elvis Smith stepped forwards, lifted the chain and secured a heavy bolt and lock with a loud click. They turned and with a grim face Elvis dropped the keys into the outstretched palm of Councillor-Mayor Jones.

'Thank you, Mr Smith,' said the councillor-mayor, looking to Amos like a blubbery bumless red-and-white alien from *Doctor Who*. 'You have been very foolish and left this town and our local council with egg on our faces.'

'More like shit,' chuckled Constable Gilbert as he dived under the police tape that designated the area as a crime scene.

'Thank you, Constable,' Kelvin said coolly. 'That's more than enough commentary from you.' He turned back to Elvis. 'See what I mean? We're a laughing stock. Culvert was all set to become a sister city to the French rural village of Cullverte, but they have now withdrawn their commitment.' Kelvin thought longingly of the images he'd seen on the internet of the tiny French cottage he'd been offered free of charge to stay in once the document was signed.

'The Tidy Towns Committee has also been in contact and withdrawn its award for this year. And not only that, the funds for the wastewater-treatment plant have been diverted to Rington. Our outdated system is now to stay as it is for a further ten years thanks to your folly. You and your boys have brought disgrace to Culvert.'

'Yep, another ten years of us all smelling our own excrement,' Constable Gilbert added.

Elvis looked at the man standing before him. Kelvin Jones was not only obese in stature; he'd been pigging out on power too. Elvis felt a spark within him flare, but it could go nowhere. He could already hear the clickety-clack in his head of Johnny Cash's 'Folsom Prison Blues' running on loop. Not only his family, but the world would pay for his failure.

Gwinnie watched as the councillor-mayor's car pulled out of the farm gate and past the roadhouse, followed by Constable Gilbert's. She saw their smug faces as they drove away. She knew both men would be happy to put her husband in gaol, and when they did, they would be equally happy to saunter in to demand big servings of chips, potato cakes and chicken wingdings … on the house … due to the circumstances … and then the constable eyeballing her like she would be the prize now that Elvis was out of the way and Councillor-Mayor No-Buttocks feeling satisfied he was paying them back over Elsie.

She turned away from the departing cars and waited for Amos and Elvis to return. But when they did, then what? There was no more sitting around the table excitedly brainstorming pathways forwards for the fuel technology and supply chains they had hoped to create. Instead she knew Amos would go to his room to read his letter from Tara, Zac would read nothing but the clouds gathering outside the window and Elvis would excuse himself, going to the bedroom for a 'lie down', as if he was some kind of nana, not even taking over the household chores like he used to. 'You've worked all day and just as hard as me,' he'd say once he got his all-clear. 'Go and have a bath, darlin', and the boys will cook while I get the washing.' Those days were long gone, Gwinnie thought sadly.

Later at the table she made some attempt to bring them back to some kind of normality. 'Well? How are the girls?' Gwinnie asked. She was in no mood any more to shield Zac from the subject of Elsie and not hearing from her since the accident. He'd just have to deal with it. A bright smile lit Amos's face.

'It sounds so cool. They're on a one-point-two-million-hectare property that is part of the Newlands Pastoral Company cluster of seven stations dotted from Queensland to the Territory and even into the Kimberley. They do all kinds of training and extra courses like whip making, farrier training and even grazing studies. Tara said they're about to go muster unbranded cattle out of the scrub before Christmas. Cleanskins. It sounds awesome.'

'And Elsie?'

Amos glanced over at Zac, who was shovelling mashed potato into his mouth, his eyes downcast, thinking of the song lyrics she'd sent him about letting her go.

'She barely mentions her. Just says she's good. Still strumming a guitar.'

'Nothing else?' Gwinnie asked.

Amos shook his head. With a sudden push of his plate, Zac, steely-faced, stood abruptly and stormed from the room.

'Ouch,' Amos said.

'When will you leave it alone?' Elvis asked Gwinnie crossly, and he too stood and strode from the room.

Gwinnie sat, feeling the misery rise in her. She folded her hands in her lap.

'Nice try, Mum,' Amos said gently, and he patted her on the shoulder and went out into the darkness.

She pushed aside her dinner, folded her arms and let her head fall upon them. Her beautiful family, it seemed, had been utterly blown apart.

Thirty-two

It was the kind of surprise that overwhelmed. The campfire light illuminated Elsie's tears of gratitude. 'Oh my God. Oh my God. Thank you. *Thank you!*' she said over and over again to the crew, looking particularly at Tara, who she knew was at the centre of the plan.

No one had *ever* done anything as special for her. Being born on Christmas Day had meant a lifetime of birthdays buried under all the Jones family fuss, but this year, it was as if her childhood cloud had shifted. The brand-new acoustic guitar looked as rich as gold bullion in the firelight, its blond timber hues smooth and perfect. It was so exquisite, with its gentle curves and scrolled circular artwork around the sound hole, she couldn't stop gazing at it, and for the first time in days her focus was stolen from Jake.

It had been Tara who had done the whip-round among the crew in the lead-up to Christmas, sneaking into Gracie's office to use the internet to buy it. Hinchie had flown the guitar in from Mt Isa along with Mrs Cloudhead and her son, Angus, this morning, back from their Brisbane boarding-house tour. After the team had heard Elsie sing at the quarters, they'd all conspired to give her the present early so they could enjoy her talents around the northern boundary campfire.

Their campsite was surprisingly civilised, as the girls found out when they had rolled up in the stock truck just before lunch with Jake and Crack.

The 'kitchen' was a large bare red-earth patch, with a fire pit ringed with stones. In the middle of the as-yet-unlit fire was a swivel tripod with large hooks to hang giant steel stewing pots. The fire site flanked 'the quarters', which was a square concreted area under a steel frame slung with a corrugated-iron roof. There were metal stretcher beds in rows on which to cast a swag up off the ground away from ants and snakes, and a big brand-spanking-new composting dunny — Crack's pride and joy. He had been quick to point it out. Near it, a gum tree shielded by a few upright sheets of tin on another concrete slab served as 'the shower block' once a canvas bag of water with a hose and nozzle was slung there in the perfectly angled lower limbs of the tree. The shower bag, Crack explained, could be filled from the bore nearby and offered blissfully cool showers at the end of hot, dusty days. If you wanted a warm shower, you simply left the bag in full sun for the day, but, Crack warned, it'd scald you red.

As the sun now dipped below the scrubby horizon, horses, hobbled, munched on hay, while others tied to a night line strung between two trees dozed. Now the guitar was out, Grout threw a few more logs on the fire, illuminating the eager faces of the crew.

The giant barbecue plate that served as the stove to cook steaks on was now pushed aside and the crew were lounging back, waiting for Elsie to sing. Life could not get any better, she thought. Except for one thing: that hunger. The hunger for love. She decided tonight, even though most of the original songs she'd penned were for Zac, she'd sing them to Jake. He looked otherworldly in the firelight. He was just so *good-looking*. And he was keen on her! She pulled the guitar to her chest and began to tune it by ear.

It only took a few strums to tell her Tara had chosen perfectly. She gave her friend a grateful look across the tops of the flickering flames of the stone-ringed fire. Tara was amazing. Just when you thought she was off and away with the fairies or in one of her quiet insular states, she would gazump Elsie with a big gesture like this, or a problem-solving idea out of left field. Elsie felt a rush of guilt for her recent prickliness towards her friend. She wanted to think Tara had been jealous, but she knew that her mate was right to hear alarm bells. Jake was not to be indulged let alone trusted with a girl's heart. Elsie might have known that, but there was some gaping void within herself that kept her falling towards him, as if by being with him she would somehow fill up that missing part of herself. Every time she looked at him, she just couldn't help it.

'Well,' said Jake, holding out his hands to her, 'will you play us a tune?'

'Maybe just a couple,' Crack said. 'Early start, big day today, big day tomorrow.' The crew booed him but knew he was right. This afternoon they'd worked hard to set up the spear-trap fencing around water points in the area in the hope of corralling a few of the cattle over the next three days. Then there were the logistics of getting whatever wildish rogue animals to the loading yards and up into the truck. Elsie had noticed electric jiggers for the task. Even though Gordon Fairweather only used Low Stress Stockhandling methods, these unhandled cleanskins, particularly the cows with calves and the bulls, could be dangerous. With all hands on deck, ten staff in all, they'd also set up heavy steel porta-panels to create a yard, and a funnel of fencing lined with hessian so they could gather the animals and run them into the enclosure.

There were four-wheel bikes, and lasso ropes that belonged to the three guns-for-hire expert bull catchers, brothers, brought in from the Kimberley. All rodeo men, all clinging to their youth, all sporting old injuries, from bent knuckles to busted knees and broken ribs as a result of their constant craving for adrenaline rushes and adventures. Gordon knew the brothers well. It was not the first time they had run cleanskins in this part of the station. He called them Huey, Dewey and Louie, and all three were currently fixated on Elsie, and Elsie was glowing as a result. Tomorrow Dunk, the chopper pilot, named so because he always dunked his biscuits in his tea, one after the other, would be arriving not long after dawn to give them an idea of where the cleanskins were.

'I'll do a couple, Boss Crack, then play them a lullaby.' Elsie grinned as she ran the pick down over the strings and played the first few chords to Lee Kernaghan's 'Boys from the Bush'.

'There's just one more thing,' Jake said suddenly, standing up and reaching for his back pocket. He held an envelope out towards her. 'Happy early Christmas and birthday, Elsie,' he said, thrusting it at her. 'I heard you playing, told Vera about it, and she organised this for me. Sent it with Hinchie. So I guess Tara wasn't the only one thinking of you.' His tone was a bit spewy and one of the bull-catcher boys mimed putting his index finger down his throat.

Tara's expression shut down as she watched Elsie tear open the envelope. Tara knew Jake was buying his way into Elsie's pants, and into her psyche. He didn't care about her. He wanted her as his most golden prize. With his fifth-generation beef-breeder pedigree and big country estate and posh voice, not to mention his model looks, he could have any girl. And the other blokes were mostly won over by his easygoing chumminess and non-threatening ways. But, Tara thought, he was a man who did not come from a soul space. Tyler had already hinted Jake had some desperate society girl on the go in Sydney who hung in there for him, no matter what.

'Are you serious?' Elsie squealed as she looked at the paper. Jake stood above her beaming his perfect pin-up-boy smile.

'They're calling for auditions in January for their very first comp. This is bigger than *Ben Hur*. So there you have it. No excuses. A ticket to Brisbane. And I've already logged you in on the website and registered you. You're contestant number 496.'

'I didn't know there were that many country-music wannabes,' Crack said, peering at the music competition ad.

'You tryin' to get rid of me?' Elsie joked to Jake.

He grinned and reached again for his back pocket, this time producing two airline e-tickets. 'Not at all. Couldn't have you go by your lonesome, so I bought two tickets, if the boss'll give me leave for the week. You'll need me to help you, kinda like your security slash manager slash whatever else you want me to be.'

His tone was laden with meaning.

Elsie blushed.

'Vera's already put in for leave for you.'

Elsie looked down to the website print-outs Vera had stapled neatly together and sent with Hinchie from Isa. She looked again at the advertisement. It was calling for Australia's best new country-music artists. The prize would not only be announced by the famous Lee Kernaghan and the Wolfe Brothers at the Tamworth Country Music Festival, but it came with a record deal and a trip to Nashville to meet country-music legend Colorado Buck and his wife Charity.

'Colorado and Charity!' squealed Elsie, jiggling her knees up and down and leaping up to hug Jake with one arm, still holding her new guitar. 'It's a sign, Tara! A sign! *Colorado and Charity!*'

Jake tapped the fine print. 'It says here there's even the chance of a US deal with the Bucks' manager, should the winning contestant succeed in the Nashville section of the competition. I mean, look at Guy Sebastian on *Idol*. And what's-his-name who was runner-up. The world could be yours, Elsie!'

'I told Tara once that one day I was going to be famous. I had no idea how, but maybe this is it.'

'Be careful what you wish for,' Tara said. 'Fame is not an ambition any healthy person consciously feeds. I read it in a book once. Paulo Coelho.'

'Are you suggesting I'm an unhealthy person?'

Tara looked skywards. 'Not at all. If you want to give the gift of music to the world through your talent, that's fine. It's just fame itself won't necessarily bring you happiness or love.'

'Oh, and you would know?' Elsie's tone was cross. Tara was spoiling her big moment.

Tara looked down to the toes of her boots. 'No, Elsie. I would not know.' She stood up. 'I'm going to bed. I don't feel so flash.'

Crack glanced at both the girls. 'Settle, you two.'

They looked guiltily at each other. The rest of the crew had now switched off, turning their attention away from what seemed like a tiff between friends.

'Don't you see?' Elsie asked quietly, more gently, reaching out to touch Tara's arm, willing her to be excited too. 'It's a sign!' She turned back to Gordon and Jake. 'Tara's into signs.'

'Don't tell them that,' muttered Tara. 'I am happy for you. You got the guitar; Jake organised the competition. It's all meant to be, but I'm still going to bed.'

Elsie saw Gordon Fairweather smiling at her, but there was something beneath it. Like pity. Or sadness.

'I hope you enjoy it all,' Tara said. 'Good night.'

For the first time ever she did not enjoy her friend's singing and music as she played to the rest of the crew. She lay in her swag and pulled the pillow over her ears, searching for the true night sounds of this remote place. She could see a swathe of stars beyond the corro roof and she decided to focus on those. She wished on a thousand of them that Elsie Jones would be OK, but inside herself, she knew for now she had lost her friend on another pathway that could never be hers.

Thirty-three

When Tara rolled over in the morning gloom, she could just make out Elsie and Jake holding hands across the span of the stretcher beds. In the night they had nudged the beds closer, and moved away from the others. They were whispering, fingers gently entwining and letting go, entwining again, letting go, like snakes in a courting dance.

Tara rolled over and sat up with her back to them, swinging her legs out of bed. In her man's boxer shorts and a T-shirt, she reached for her jeans, underwear and station shirt on the foot of the bed and headed for the gum-tree shower just to get away for a moment. There was enough sunrise skimming over the horizon for her to see her way. In the shower she looked up to the gum and the blaze of light just peeking above the horizon. She inhaled deeply and let the almost-too-cold water wash her sadness about Elsie away. She wasn't going to let Elsie's decisions about Jake muck her day up. She breathed the perfume of the outback morning and told herself life was good.

By the time she was back, refreshed and ready to go, the bull-catcher boys were helping themselves to cereal, tinned fruit and UHT milk from a box in the Esky. Others in the crew were dragging on clothes, reviving the fire and lighting a gas stove for the billy.

'That's cheating,' Grout said, looking at Crack bending over the hissing blue flame.

Crack grinned. 'Caffeine needed fast,' he grunted, his hair still brushed vertical by the pillow.

Over breakfast Tara avoided watching Jake and Elsie carry on. She wondered if they'd slept together, somehow sneaking off when everyone else was asleep. Elsie sure did have a glow about her this morning. But in truth Tara really didn't want to know. She thought of Zac, who would still be enduring the most awful pain and trauma. To help herself feel less alone, she kept close to Crack, helping out as best she could as a newbie on her first station camp. As she dragged all the saddles out from the boxes under the truck and fetched the saddle blankets, Crack poked her in the ribs.

'I'm gonna have to rename you String Bean if you get any skinnier. You're becoming a fit young woman. I'm proud of ya.'

Tara felt a glow rise within her. It was as big as the outback sunrise that was now draping everything in gold. Praise from anyone, particularly a kind fatherly man, was so unfamiliar she felt as if she could cry. Her girlish crush on Gordon Fairweather deepened. She was sure he was just being a good mentor, but she wished it was something more. She wished he didn't have a gorgeous wife in Elaine, who lived back at the manager's quarters and who ran the cattle turn-off logistics with the other NP Co stations and helped Gracie out in the office during the end of the financial year or the quarterly GST return. She knew it was a classic teacher-crush and she wasn't planning on getting ahead of herself. But she was beginning to feel a longing for Gordon, and guilt for betraying Elaine.

A chopper came thumping in from the south. The moment of dreaming about Gordon was gone. Dunk was touching down with a roar, a whir and a stir of dust. He set down near some av-gas drums and, after filling in his paperwork, checking a few dials, dived beneath the rotors and came towards them with a beaming buck-toothed smile.

'Gonna bag us some cleanies today, boys and girls?' he asked.

Gordon shook his hand. 'Welcome to North Camp, Dunk.'

'Got the billy on? Any bikkies? Surely there's time for a cuppa before we set sail.'

Outback chopper pilots were renowned for their daredevil natures and extreme personalities. Dunk was a motor mouth. That was when he wasn't cramming it full and polishing off all the Arnott's Assorted Creams.

'Once I've done my run today, Simmo says I have to take your young girl home with me to the homestead.'

Crack frowned. 'Which one?'

'The one that does the cleaning.'

Tara's ears pricked up.

'The cleaning?' asked Crack.

Dunk nodded rapidly as he scanned the kitchen area, reached for the packet of Nice and began ripping it open. 'It's smoko time somewhere.' With a mouthful of bikkies and a gulp of tea he mumbled, 'Mrs Cloudhead was so stoked by what the cleaning girl did to her house, she wants her back there to help redecorate.'

'Redecorate? She wants to pull one of my crew out of my cleanskin camp to *redecorate*? Oh, be fair!' Gordon looked to the distance where the evening star was just hanging in there, shining brightly against an indigo morning sky.

Dunk shrugged. 'Boss Man Simmo said.'

Tara stepped forwards. 'It's OK, Boss Crack. I'll take one for the team. I'll still get one day in mustering and if they need me, they need me. Let's just cut her some slack. She's losing her baby to boarding school next year. A little lovin' from Tars is the ticket. I'm your girl.'

Crack shook his head. 'Honestly, String Bean, you are gold. Pure gold.'

Elsie, who was just rolling up her swag for the day (the bull-catching boys had told her stories about snakes who liked to slither their way inside the bedding), wished she had the capacity to impress Crack like that. And to be so generous. So cheerful. Tara, she decided, made her look utterly vain and selfish. It was good she was going. Here she was nicknamed Moody Blues. No wonder she was moody. Tara had been so negative about Jake and had been trying to sabotage the whole thing. After last night, Elsie knew he was a really, *really* nice guy. She stomped off to help Jake pack the saddlebags, trying to silence the voice deep within her that warned her not all was well.

Thirty-four

The first time the girls glimpsed the cattle crashing through the bush they felt adrenaline pump in their veins. Their horses felt it too. Gazza and Wolfie lifted their heads and pranced on the spot so the girls had to hold them steady. The two-ways strapped around their chests were alive with excited voices: Dunk shouting directions over the rev of the chopper; and Dewey sitting beside him in the cockpit with a shotgun, watching like a hawk in case his crew members got into a dangerous and deadly tangle on the ground with a big angry daddy bull. Somewhere off in the scrub the girls could hear the rev of the four-wheel bike manned by Huey. Also out of sight was the middle brother, Louie. He was driving the modified Landy with tyres strapped to its front for the purpose of nudging breakaways over to be lassoed, leg tied and later snigged onto Crack's truck.

On horses, Jake and Grout rode near Louie, ropes at the ready.

Suddenly through the bush there was a cry from Crack and they glimpsed him flying along on Bear beyond the steaming backs of tonguing, crazed wild cattle.

'EJ, ride *left, left, left*! String Bean, go right!' He was cantering through scrub beyond the hessian with his big rangy Border

Collies and gold-coated hangin' dog casting out in an arc, tossing an invisible net on the flank of the fast-flowing herd.

'Keep 'em blocked on that wing!' He was gesturing as he rode one-handed.

It all happened so fast. There must've been about thirty head. Cleanskins. Full of life. Full of fear. Full of fury at being trumped by humans. A further twenty head were contained at the water points and they too were bellowing their disgust. At the heart of the herd was a cluster of big-framed bulls, pimpled on their hides from insect bites, scarred from battles, their horns turning upwards in great wavering spears. They moved like lightning. For a moment Elsie and Tara thought they would run right past them. The horses, though, were locked onto them, their blood up, their instincts keen, leaping scrub, skimming through trees, pressuring, pressuring the invisible bubble of the mob. Will it be enough? Tara thought as she saw the rolled eye of one beast. She could see the old cow had made her mind up to break from the herd, taking her calf with her.

But Gordon and his dogs were onto them. A nip on the nose, a flurry of barking. The old girl turned. Bolting for the safety of the herd. The cattle cast their heads low at the hessian panels and for a moment baulked. But Gordon gave a roar and a well-timed stock-whip crack and the cattle galloped on. Huey, almost on two wheels, was making for the gate, also disguised in hessian, and rolled it shut on their tails.

Then everything settled to quiet save for the hefty in-out breath of the herd. The chopper choppered away back to camp and no doubt the biscuit tin. The bike and the Landy's engines cut to silence. The boys climbed the rail to get a count. It was the best muster in years. They'd have to send Gordon back with a load in the stock truck overnight to the homestead yards, because if they got any more big rogue bulls like the ones that were now in the yard, there would be no room on the truck.

Tara and Elsie dismounted and went to look at the cattle milling about, mouths open tonguing, steam rising from their backs, bunting one another in frustration.

'Wow,' Tara said. 'They're pumped.'

'I'm pumped,' Elsie said. 'Did you ever imagine us …?'

Tara beamed. 'It's the coolest.'

'I wish you could stay for more,' Elsie said, turning to her, brushing a fly from her sweating face. For a moment Tara felt a glimmer of hope, but behind Elsie Jake was striding over with a big grin on his face, his eyes, his energy, his intent locked on Elsie.

Tara's face fell. 'No, you don't,' she said, looking her in the eye. 'Three's a crowd.'

'Tars …' Elsie said, but Tara was already turning away, and Jake was already beside Elsie, flicking the brim of her hat.

'Howdy, cowgirl,' he said. 'Nice riding. You sure know how to swing a leg over.'

Naked, Elsie turned the nozzle of the shower and felt the bliss of cold water run over her sore, sunburned, dust-covered body. She began to wash quickly, knowing the water wouldn't last long. She turned her face up to the mottled leaves of the dozing afternoon gum and let the water splash over her face, absorbing just how wonderful this place was. A small squeal escaped her when she felt a hand reach around to cup her breast. Jake's burning hot naked body pressed against her as he scooped her in his arms and from behind began to kiss and bite her neck, his insistent erection nudging her hard between her soapy buttocks.

'Oh God, I've wanted you all day,' he said breathlessly into her ear. 'Last night … last night was amazing, but it's not enough, EJ, not enough.'

She was shocked to find him here and instantly her mind ran to panic — where were the others? Wouldn't they know? But her endorphins ran awash in her system. Her body softened and yielded to Jake's incredible touch. His hard hotness, the way he ran his hands up and over her soap-lathered skin. He was wet now too and inserting his finger into her from behind. His warm breath played on her neck as he spooned his taut body over her back. He reached for her hips, tilted his pelvis and with a suddenness that made her cry out again pushed into her. She sucked in a breath. It hurt. Fleetingly she thought she should insist on a condom, but after the pain eased it began to feel so good, and she just couldn't stop. She reached forwards for the solid trunk of the gum and closed her eyes as he thrust hard into her. She met him back, mouth falling open with pleasure and surprise.

The water fell on her back and she felt her nipples tingling with excitement. She could feel every cell of her body searing with electricity as Jake pumped faster and faster. His strong hands on her slim hips, his perfect legs and feet behind her. Somewhere a little distance away, the chopper was whirring to take-off speeds. As the engine roared faster, Jake pumped harder. He was about to come, but he was as smart as a fox and so withdrew at the right moment, turning Elsie around, grabbing her hand and shoving her palm around the shaft of his perfect pornstar penis. Elsie watched him watch as he guided her hand in a pump to orgasm. He shut his eyes, his chest wet and glistening. Elsie was breathless. The shower suddenly ran down to a single drizzle.

He gave her a white-toothed perfect grin, kissed her once on the lips, grabbed up his pile of clothes from the bush and made a runner into the scrub to dress himself, circle the camp and come in the other way as if he'd just gone to take a leak. Elsie, stunned, took a moment to compose herself. Her hands were shaking. It was the most exciting thing that had ever happened to her. She wanted to think that it was. In her heart she knew it was no good. He hadn't even tried to give her an orgasm. That mattered, didn't it? Some attempt, at least? Still she forced herself to smile. A man wanted her. A real-life, good-looking god like Jake actually wanted *her*. She turned her eyes to the sky. It was a miracle.

Tara sat beside Dunk in a bit of an emotional lather. She wanted to stay, but at the same time was excited by the prospect of a chopper ride home. Something had settled in her like a lead weight. Elsie worried her. As they lifted up, earphones blocking out the roar of the rotors, Tara glanced down. There behind the tin she saw two naked bodies. Jake driving himself from behind into her friend. She glanced at Dunk, but his focus was on steering the chopper up and south away from the treeline.

On the way home, she barely took in the beauty of the land from the air. The rocky red ridges, the deep channels carved by the wet, the swathes of outback scrub and the tiny marks of humanity in the form of fences, windmills, water troughs and roads. All she saw was the image of Elsie and Jake, until it was supplanted by the memory of Dwaine's red-raw ugly penis being shoved in her face when she was just a little girl.

Tara gulped back tears. Did Elsie really know what she was doing to herself? Tara knew that men who used women stole fragments of a girl's spirit, and she knew it would be a long journey through life before those fragments could be called back. Elsie had chosen the hard path.

Thirty-five

Tara stood in her bra and undies, looking in her cupboard for something to wear.

'Old Mother Hubbard. What to do?' she said, glancing down to Marbles, who lay farting and feathering the smell through the air with his happy tail, gazing up at her through opaque eyes. He was glad to be let out of the dog runs on Tara's return from the cleanskin camp and was making the most of the air conditioning. Tara looked back to the empty wire coat hangers. She couldn't go to see Mrs Cloudhead in her dusty, stinky, stand-up-by-themselves jeans. Her other 'good' pair were now so huge on her she looked like she had an elephant's arse, all saggy and baggy. Twitching her nose in thought, she opened up Elsie's narrow cupboard. Elsie and Gracie had done a little internet shopping last week, which had given Tara the idea for the guitar. Elsie's cupboard, after she'd used up her entire pay cheque, now had more clothes than it could handle.

'Too small, too small, too small,' Tara said as she flicked through the clothes on the hangers. Eventually she found a blue-and-white-striped singlet-style stretchy maxi dress. 'What the heck?' she said. She dragged the dress from the hanger and slipped it over her head, tugging it down over her curves. She giggled at herself in the mirror. On Elsie the stripes ran straight around her body. On Tara they wavered and curved up and over and around all her jiggly bits. The low-cut V revealed the long line between her breasts. She bent forwards in the mirror.

'Hello, ladies,' she said to her bosoms. She tugged the dress up, then brushed out her long deep red and golden curls, rummaging her fingers through them. She did a take-the-piss pout to herself. It would have to do. Then she slipped on her thongs, stepped onto the verandah, slamming the screen door of her bedroom, and breathed in the fragrance of the softening day. It was heaven out here this evening.

'Stay,' she said to Marbles and then giggled. He'd fallen asleep. Poor blind, deaf old dog. She skipped down the steps and made a beeline for the back gate of the big boss's homestead, out of bounds for ringers like her unless expressly invited.

Through the glass sliding door, Tara could see Skye Simpson sitting at the kitchen table, her head in her hands. She had hair like Sarah Jones — a neat conservative blonde bob — and she was wearing a burnt-orange linen dress and a short string of big chunky pearls around her neck, with a matching bracelet. When she glanced up on Tara's gentle knock, she revealed pink cheeks and bright blue eyes framed by lashings of mascara. In front of her were paint and fabric swatches and a scattering of home design magazines. Skye gestured to Tara to come in.

The house was heading back to its original state of chaos now she and Angus were home. Angus was on the couch, watching some god-awful violent cartoon that shattered the house with energetic turmoil. He was surrounded by chip packets and half-empty glasses of cordial along with his cricket bat and more tennis balls than the Australian Open warm-up. With a lovely smile and sliding over in her little black flats, Skye reached up to give Tara a hug.

'Oh, Tara! It is Tara, isn't it?' she asked.

Tara nodded.

'I can't thank you enough. The changes you made to the house while I was away were amazing. I'm so grateful. I was dreading coming home. But you. You made it easier.' She kept hold of Tara's hand. 'Angus, honey,' she yelled over her shoulder, 'turn it down! Turn it down and come meet Tara!'

'Is she another newbie?' the young boy asked, not glancing up from the television.

Tara looked at the boy. Something within her fired. A memory from her childhood seared through her system. Of the adults ignoring her because of that ugly violent betraying lying screen that flashed disturbing messages night and day into her home. Her mother had been transfixed by it. Some days Tara believed it was TV that had killed her and kept them poor. She walked over to the lounge area, picked up the remote from the floor, and turned off the TV. The silence and stillness enveloped the room and shocked the boy from his rudeness. He turned to look at Tara with his wide green eyes. She stared back at him.

'Hello, Angus. I'm Tara.'

'H-hello,' he stammered.

Tara winked at Skye. 'See this tub?' she asked, picking up a red toy bucket. 'I'm going to put it over here and you're going to see how many of your tennis balls you can get in it. I've been given the job of helping your mum get this house all nice for Christmas and for when you leave for boarding school. So part of my job is to give you a job. So quick sticks.'

'I'm not a little kid. I'm in Grade Seven next year.'

'I know. You're a young man. That's why you are starting to help your mighty fine mum. Because …' she picked up a tennis ball and lobbed it into the bucket '… you are so …' she lobbed another ball in the bucket '… grown …' another ball '… up. Tara three. Angus … nil.' She turned her back and smiled at Skye.

The boy was on his feet, grabbing up a ball. He threw and missed.

Tara swung about, cocked an eyebrow and passed him a ball. 'Here, have another go.'

'Yessss,' he said and pumped the air when the ball landed in its target. He continued.

She went over to Skye, who was standing in the kitchen looking as dumbfounded as if Nanny McPhee had just arrived in her house.

'How on earth did you learn to handle children like that?' Skye rasped in a whisper so Angus wouldn't hear.

'I read a book about it once,' Tara said. 'Now ... colours. Let's see.' She picked up the paint charts and tossed them away. 'You don't want them. Least not to start. Let's start with a clean slate of nice warm creams on your walls.'

It took Tara less than an hour to find out what Skye Simpson liked best of all. She liked: the colours blue, purple and green; soft cushions; horses; leafy plants; Mexican-style gardens and living areas; sweet potatoes; rocks; ice blocks with flowers in them; and Rod Stewart. As Skye spoke about wonderful things she hadn't even *thought* about in years, Tara had mapped out the entire house in terms of decorative colour schemes. She then wrote down all of the family's birthdays and worked out their ideal sleeping positions, guided by their feng shui energetics.

'Luckily for you, Mr Simpson is an earth sign too so you can both face east for sleep. It'll be easy to do in that space once we drag the bed around. You'll notice the change in your energy levels and sleep patterns right away. I promise you. Angus's health and behaviour will improve too. His bed position was way wrong!'

'Tara — you're amazing. Where on earth did you learn about feng shui so comprehensively? And what are you doing *here*?' She said *here*, as if Goldsborough was the ends of the earth.

Tara chose very early to be like Gwinnie Smith, and not her own mother ... always reading, always enquiring, always creating, always finding the best of a situation. Books had arrived in front of her like stepping stones. Each precious one had gradually and slowly extended her path forwards. Sometimes it would take a long time for the next stone of information to be discovered and laid, but as the months and years passed, Tara at last felt she was on her way — particularly at a moment such as this, when all her skills were coming together. She was enjoying seeing Mrs Simpson, who really was a nice woman, begin to find relief.

Tara smiled at her. 'Let's just say I had a lot of dark energy to dispel in my home,' she said. 'I studied feng shui night and day and made the house what I could so that my human luck would change.'

'And did it?' Skye asked.

'I think today it just did,' she said, smiling at Skye. 'Thank you so much for giving me this opportunity.'

After the initial cleaning and furniture moving, Skye invited Tara to stay for dinner. Mrs B had flown out that afternoon with Gracie so it was 'help yourself in the kitchen' anyway. Tara was glad to stay. Not only was the bedroom at the quarters lonely without Elsie, she also couldn't leave Marbles in for company as his farts stank as bad as Culvert when the wind blew a northeasterly.

At the homestead Tara and Skye had taken 'before photos' of Angus grinning with his swirl of mess around him. Then they had gone into each room to record the former chaos. Three hours later they had taken 'after shots' of the rooms once Tara had rearranged furniture, coordinated bedding and cushions, and placed ornaments. Skye was already uploading the transformation photos to the computer.

'Once it's painted, it'll look even better,' Skye said joyfully as she pressed send on an email to her cluster of friends. 'Michael will be happy too. There're only a few inexpensive items on the list to get.'

The table was set, a small vase at its centre filled with soft curving gum leaves and white blossoms that looked like ballerina skirts, when Mr Simpson kicked off his boots and came through the door.

'Wow!' he said when he surveyed the room. Before he could wash the dust from himself, Angus was dragging his dad by the arm for a house tour.

When they both came back into the family room, Michael Simpson was beaming.

'She's a genius, Michael,' Skye said, going over to him and kissing him on the cheek. 'Thank you for lending her to me. Can I keep her?'

'She's not a stray puppy,' he said, still smiling, 'but she is a genius. Tara, what you've done is amazing.'

'They don't call me a cleaning cowgirl for nothing,' she said with a grin. 'And to be honest, I am actually a bit of a stray. Just ask anyone in Culvert.'

'Let's open some champagne,' Skye said elatedly.

During dinner, Tara joined in on the conversation. At the abattoir house they'd never sat at a table for dinner, but she'd learned manners from books. She drew some lively and funny conversation out of Angus, which his parents could hardly believe, so that soon they were all laughing as they ate their simple but comforting meal of marinated station steak and salad. She felt so relaxed with the nice, if slightly uptight, couple and their spoiled only child that it was after ten before they cleared the dessert plates away.

'Gosh, Angus, it is way, way past your bedtime!'

'Muuum!'

'Yes!' Michael said. 'And I'm meant to be up again in the middle of the night to help Crack unload the cleanskins when he gets back to camp.'

Tara's eyes widened. She'd got so engrossed with 'fenging' the homestead that she'd forgotten the huge day she'd had.

'I'll get up! I'll help!' she said. 'In fact, why don't you stay in bed? I'll take the two-way to my room.'

'It's fine, Tara,' Simmo said.

Skye turned to her husband. 'Oh, stay in bed, darling. Tara wants us to try the new position.'

Michael looked at her, shocked. She sniggered.

'She's talking about the bed,' Tara said, giggling too.

Michael reached for his wife's hand. 'These are the wild cleanskins coming in,' he said. 'The cattle will be stirry, and it's a particularly dark night.' He pursed his lips.

'It's as simple as backing the truck up to the ramp, sliding the gate and letting them down into the yard,' Tara said. 'I'll be fine!' She wanted to mention she'd had experience with unloading stock many, many times for Dwaine at the abattoir house, but she didn't want to bring that part of her life into the conversation now. Today represented a whole new phase for her: at last, she felt free of Culvert and the misery of her childhood. Today was the start of a new chapter.

'OK, Tara,' Simmo said. 'Go for your life.'

Thirty-six

It felt as if Tara's head had barely hit the pillow when the two-way radio beside the bed crackled to life. She glanced at the clock. It was almost one o'clock in the morning.

'Goldsborough Base, you got a copy?' came the static sound of Gordon's voice.

'Yes, Crack,' Tara said into the receiver, 'Goldsborough Base receiving.'

Today on the muster it had been the first time she'd used a walkie-talkie and she felt like she was in a movie. She wanted to be silly with the thing, but she knew it was an important tool on the station and the staff used it with the utmost respect, except for the occasional amusing dig at someone. It took all her willpower not to muck about with Crack now. He'd be tired. The last thing he needed was a cheeky young ringer mucking about.

'String Bean? That you? Over.'

'Yes, sir. Boss Simmo said I'm your midnight ringer.' She paused, then added, 'Over,' grinning at herself for using radio lingo.

'I'm at the two-mile gate just getting onto Watson's track. I'll be there in fifteen minutes. These little beasties are doing a merry dance in the back. Think one might be down. Over.'

'OK. See you over at the yards. Over,' she said. For the first time in her life she felt she was truly on the path. She'd had plenty of experience unloading crazy dangerous animals at the abattoir house so it was another chance to show Gordon she was good at things. She straddled Marbles, who she'd felt too guilty moving so had left him sleeping between Elsie's and her beds, and hastily dressed, shoving her hair up in a ponytail. She thought of Amos briefly, wondering if he had got her letter. There'd been nothing back from him in the mail. Maybe he wasn't the type to move anything forwards with her, not without Zac and Elsie to make it a party of four. She flicked on the verandah light, went into the rec room to find a torch, then made her way to the yards. Maybe Elsie was right? Was she too young to be fixated on just one man?

The night was chilly and incredibly still. Tara could hear the rattle and the rumble of the stock truck and see the lights sweeping the landscape. Soon Crack was reversing the rig to the loading ramp, with Tara's guidance, standing in a place so he could see her in the side mirrors, making hand signals under the light of her torch.

Crack smiled at her skill. She'd obviously done that before. He'd had many a ringer just stand there, or flap their hands, not knowing how to guide a truck backwards or a vehicle onto a tow ball. Tara was an old hand, he could tell. He felt the gentle bump of the crate against the big rubber-coated loading ramp uprights, then he killed the engine.

He got out of the truck, bringing with him a length of poly pipe, and, bandy-legged, strode towards Tara with a grin on his face. She was shining the torch up under her eyes, saying, 'I come in peace,' in a spooky voice. 'Take me to your leader.'

He gave her a friendly shove. Tara had already set the yard gates up, and Michael had earlier put a bale in the feeder, so it was a simple matter of lifting the steel pin, drawing back the big sliding doors and waiting for one of the animals in the truck to step off, setting in motion a flow of cattle. The first cow came cautiously, snorting hot breath from her nose, staring blindly at the small dark gap between the ramp and the truck, then she stepped and rattled down the ramp, casting her head low, every sense in her on fire. The rest came rushing and clattering through the door, bumping and bunting, Crack doing his best to slow their push and speed by waving his poly pipe in front of their noses through gaps in the rail. Tara shone her torch through the lower railing of the truck; the smell of fresh dung was pungent. The bulls' impressive horns caught the light like clashing swords.

When all of the moving beasts had spilled from the truck, Tara could see one remained. A cow was down. She was in poor condition, and judging from the way she was covered in manure, lying on her side, heaving with breath but not making an effort to get up, she was a goner. Good for nothing but the dogs. Poor old girl.

For a moment Tara was transported back to the grimness of the abattoir, where animals not as fortunate as these had been handled all their lives by coarse rough men with no place in their hearts for their charges. Since she'd been on Goldsborough she'd seen how Crack came down like a tonne of bricks on anyone who didn't handle an animal with the utmost understanding and care. The wild cattle were different, of course, dangerous, but even so the crew had to be respectful and kind to them with Crack as a leader.

'There is one down, Crack,' she said.

'Thought she was too weak to truck, but I wanted to give her a chance. Sorry, darlin',' he said as he saw the black dull eye of the cow in the beam of Tara's torch. He rolled a gate shut on the rest of the herd, now safely in the yard, and hauled himself up into the cab, grabbing the rifle and filling the five-shot magazine.

'You OK with this? You don't mind holding a light for me?' he asked Tara.

'Seen it a thousand times. No one sheltered me from it when I was little. I just send them away with a blessing. It's all we can ever do.'

Crack looked at her in the darkness, her face illuminated only by a sliver of moonlight and the glow of the torch. There was something so deep about this girl, so old, worldly and wise that she took his breath away sometimes.

'I don't want you comin' in with me,' Crack said as he entered the loading ramp and went to the back of the truck. 'She could be faking it a bit and take to you, so climb up and shine the torch down, there's a good lass.'

Good lass. His praise rang in her ears and her young heart fluttered as she hauled herself up the side of the truck. Holding onto the cross railing, Tara shone the torch down on the head of the beast. She heard the safety switch click. Gordon muttered a few gentle words to the cow. She didn't move at all when he put the gun to her head and pulled the trigger. Three shots rang out in the night. Just to be sure.

The cattle in the yard started and crushed to the far railing, but settled quickly. The sound of the gun, the smell of the manure, the steel yards and truck, brought memories of the abattoir house rushing back like a kick to Tara's head. It wasn't just in her bedroom in the dead of the night that Dwaine had preyed on her. She suddenly remembered the chilling room, where, in the icy air, Dwaine, hot, fatty, sweaty, had cornered her and groped at her budding baby breasts and gripped at her crotch. He would then take up the rifle and put it under her jaw, telling her she'd be dead meat if she told. Like the tats on his fingers that had L-O-V-E and H-A-T-E, he would spell the word D-E-A-D. After he was done, he'd leave her in the chiller and go out and shoot the next beast waiting in the bloodied, shitty yard. Suddenly giddy, Tara tried to drag a breath in. Panic choked her. As she moved to get down off the truck, she dropped the torch. Grappling for the railing, her fingers missed, then she slipped and fell.

Her back hit hard on the rocky ground. Her breath was shocked from her. Gulping from a black-hole open mouth, Tara's eyes were wide with surprise. Pain shot from her lower back down one leg. She tried again to breathe but couldn't. She could hear the metal clang of the yards as Gordon ran to her, calling her name. Next he was kneeling beside her, concern on his face in the darkness.

She thought of the yoga breathing she had practised in her room on nights she couldn't sleep in the abattoir house. She began to still her mind and drift light throughout her body. The first breath came. Gulped in like a newborn baby. Then another and another until she was laughing.

'Far out, Tara, you scared the shit out of me!'

She began to sit up.

'Woah, take it slow, that's a high fall you just took. I'm surprised you're laughing. Why are you laughing?'

'Because it hurts like hell and if I don't laugh I'll cry.'

'And what's wrong with crying?' Gordon asked.

'Nothing.'

Tara's face scrunched with pain. Physical pain, and the pain of the past, which washed throughout her body as though a dam bank had given way. She began sobbing and, gathered up in Gordon's arms, released all the hurt, the shame and the guilt from her body, crying over those black-death times at the abattoir house.

He shushed her. 'What is it, girl? What is it?'

She felt him stroke the back of her head. 'I remembered something. Up on the truck. My, uh, stepfather. He was a bad man.' She swiped her tears from her face. They sat for a time. 'A real Barry Crocker.'

'I'm hearing you, girl. It's OK. You're away from it now. You're safe now.'

'But I'm not. It's with me every day. I try to read books. I try to be sunny and happy, but it's like a cloud. It sits there; it makes my world black.'

'Gawd, you poor darlin'. Don't worry, love,' Gordon said. 'After Christmas when Vera's back, she'll get you in to see someone in Mt Isa. Help you out about it. OK?'

'Sure, I'll go see someone, but at the moment,' Tara lifted her face and turned her large green eyes up to Crack's, 'I-I ...' she stammered, 'I just want to see you.'

She moved her face nearer to his, giving him every opportunity to kiss her, but he turned his head to the darkness. 'Sweetie,' he said, looking up to the stars, but did not release his hold of her. 'I can't, mate.'

There was a pause.

'Awkward,' said Tara, shuffling away from him with her sore bones.

Still Crack did not let her go. 'I'm married, mate, and that means something to me. I love my wife. You're the best girl that's landed here in my time, but you have to see you're feeling this way because you've found the first fella in your life who's been good to you. But I'm an old bloke who made a choice a long time ago to live with integrity. That comes with control. I'd hurt you. I'd hurt Elaine. I'd hurt myself. I can't do it.'

Tara smiled sadly. Of course, she thought, he's right. She would lose all admiration for him if he was led around by his desires like Jake was. And besides, she suddenly realised, he wasn't the first man to be good to her. It was Amos. *Amos.* Her heart sang his name.

'Well, I'm a little embarrassed then,' she said, pulling away from him.

'Don't be. You're not the first kid to get a crush on his or her boss. And you won't be the last. I understand, String Bean.' His voice was so kind. So gentle. His face so sad. He looked suddenly like an old man to her. A handsome man, but one far too old for her. What had she been *thinking*?

He took her hand and helped her up. She realised she couldn't read about these sorts of things in a book. She had to learn about her feelings herself. Life was excruciatingly painful, and ridiculous at times. But funny too. She swiped a grimy tear from her face, her hands still shaky.

'You sure you're OK?' Gordon pulled her to him gently and gave her a squeeze.

She stepped back and nodded. 'You're a good man, Gordon Fairweather. I wish more were like you. The world would turn gentler.'

He chuckled and she wrapped her arms about herself and watched him put the rifle back in the lockable box in the truck cab.

'C'mon, String Bean. Off to bed. A sleep-in and light duties for you in the morning. Gracie normally is our first-aid girl, but as she's away you'll have to be checked over by Mrs Simpson. Come with me and stop by the kitchen and we'll get you a packet of peas. You're going to be sorer than a buckjumper that's come off in the chute tomorrow.'

Feeling as though some kind of twisted knot inside her had let go, despite the pain from the fall, Tara followed Gordon, looking up at the stars and thanking the angels she had been sent one in dusty denim and a big stained hat to guide her here on earth.

Thirty-seven

Tara woke up the next morning, aching all over, unable to shake a vague feeling of unease. Something in the night had settled inside her like a dark cloud. Something misaligned. It wasn't over Gordon. She felt at peace with that.

She searched in her mind's eye, but got nothing. Sighing, she reached under her bed for her numerology chart, feeling a searing tug in the shoulder she had landed on. Next month she would turn seventeen. No matter how she played with the charts, the numbers looked good for her. Opportunities abounded. Maybe, she thought, as she got up from her bed, it's just the fall from the truck. Her jarred back and body were rigid and sore, so her chakras would have been jolted too. She lay back down and spent some time bringing light through her body like she'd taught herself from a book she'd read about 'energy centres'.

She looked through the gauze screen door at Marbles, who was sleeping in his usual nest of old hessian feedbags. He barely flopped a tail in greeting as Tara dressed and went outside to a low grey sky and heat that clung to her skin. Stooping to pat him, Tara looked up and wondered if it would rain. If it did, would the cleanskin stock-camp crew be stranded? Elsie stuck out there with Jake. She here, alone at the station. She dragged on her boots, wincing a little, and clumped down the steps. The old dog didn't even make a start to follow her to the kitchen.

'Not coming, Marbs?' Tara called over her shoulder. 'Is it because Mrs B's on holidays? No cook-up for you?'

The dog sighed and laid his head between splayed feathered paws. She trudged back to pat him again. The day was already muggy.

'Dear old boy,' she said, 'I'll sneak you some bacon later.'

Not long after, as Tara sat in the breakfast room eating cereal alone, she heard the gate swing open.

'How are you?' Skye asked, arriving in the kitchen, freshly showered in a cornflower-blue sundress and flats. 'Gordon said you had a fall.'

Tara's grin held a bit of a grimace. 'I'm all good. Just slipped.'

Skye looked at her with a questioning expression.

'I'm *fine*,' Tara said with conviction.

'I've still got to check you over, then if you're fit enough, would you be up for some more fenging around the station?'

'More fenging! Yes please!' Tara said excitedly, all sense of unease fading away.

She remembered one day after school when the Poo Crew had stolen through the shit-ponds fence and adventured beyond as far as the tip site. There on the rubbish piles they had found all manner of treasures. Elsie, an old cream can filled with cobwebs; Zac, a Holden wheel hub with a lion emblem; Amos, a perfectly good screwdriver with a pink handle; and Tara, a big folder containing Marie Diamond's notes and CDs on feng shui.

Tara had gazed at the folder with wonder, as if angels were handing it to her, and deep within her pre-teen body, she knew they had. This tatty *Diamond Feng Shui* was her jewel! She had taken the folder home, hidden behind her back as she scuttled past her mother, then later in her bedroom sponged off an oily substance that smelled a lot like tuna and delved into the rather sticky pages. She hid the book under her bed and at night drew charts and diagrams, then on her mum's old Discman listened to the CDs stored in plastic in the back of the folder.

She learned to escape what she now called 'her Dwaine Pain' through Marie's meditations. And then, so she could at least control some aspect of her life, she began to empower herself by changing her bedroom using feng shui techniques. With time she started to move things about and clean in the lounge, bathroom and kitchen. Dwaine of course cursed her, but Tara knew the book was the foundation for her survival. She knew she wasn't just cleaning for the sake of it. She could now see it was all part of an energetic flow. If she changed the energy of the house, she could some day soon escape. The world would propel her forwards to beautiful places she had only ever dreamed of.

Now, on Goldsborough, as she cleaned and decluttered in Gracie's office with Skye, Tara moved into a kind of flow. All morning the radio had crackled and buzzed with the excitement of another muster on the northern boundary. Voices came and went. She knew Gordon was making his way back out to the stock camp in the truck. On the radio, the bull-catcher boys and Dunk reported to Michael an estimate of how many more bulls had been spotted from the chopper and how many could be run in by that night.

Tara was glad to be away from Elsie and Jake and free of the delusional crush she'd had on Gordon. She could now admire him without the clutter of a love-sick hormonal teenage brain and here she was, getting paid to practise her calling. She didn't have to be on a horse to be a cleanskin cowgirl. She was still being one now. She flung open the door of the room that held many of the station files and was met by a blockbuster hit of stench. Tara wrinkled her nose as she entered, searched and at last retrieved a somewhat mummified mouse from behind one of Gracie's filing cabinets.

'You'd think a wildebeest had died in here. How do such little teeny creatures give off that much pong?'

Skye looked up from where she was rearranging the stationery supplies into a cupboard and laughed. 'Gracie will be so grateful you found it. It was driving her mad. She can't cope with them.'

Elusive dead mice were common on the station and during plague times bed legs had to be sat in ice-cream containers filled with water so that the tiny rodents didn't join sleepers overnight. Newbies soon became immune to the sight on waking of several drowned nightly visitors. Even Dorris, Gordon and Elaine's Jack Russell, got bored with diving on mice and flinging them with one chomp to their death. The incessant numbers and pestering of the mice during a plague meant a mouse could scuttle under her nose without her even opening an eye. The crew had got so immune to the smell of mice knocked over by bait that they often went for days enduring the pong before someone bothered to look behind a fridge or under a wardrobe. Goldsborough people learned not to breathe too deeply when in the vicinity of the tiny hidden corpse. But not Gracie. She would pincer her nose, squeal and complain until the office had been turned upside down. As she was away on holiday, dead-mouse search and rescues in the office were not so urgent. But this one, Tara thought, *has* to go.

Carrying the mouse by the tail, she dropped it in a garbage bag, then looked about the office. Things always seemed more chaotic before they began to improve in a clean-up like this, but with Gracie's desk now facing the door, she felt that things were set right. She knew the new energy of the furniture placement and the changes would bring prosperity to the airy office, which was the working hub of the station as much as the yards.

'I put your before-and-after photos of the house on the company blog last night,' Skye said, 'and everyone's gone nuts with comments. They all want you to help them with their own homes, Tara.'

'Me?' Tara asked as she hung a mirror on the back of one of the office hallway doors.

'Yes, you. You can't stay a ringer all your life. You're too smart and talented for that. What plans do you have after here?'

Tara shrugged.

'Well, I can help you. Will you let me help you?'

Tara looked at Skye. She remembered a book she'd read once by Louise Hay that said if you want your life to change, you have to clean out the mental rooms in your mind. The door so far had been locked on her self-esteem, being the girl from Dwaine Morton's abattoir house, but now, if she unlocked it and began to dust away the beliefs that no longer served her, Tara could see a path to a life she wanted.

'Of course,' she said, 'I'd love you to help me. Thank you.'

That night, at the Simpsons' homestead, with Tara again at the family table, the crackle of the radio sliced through the dinner conversation. Michael laid down his fork and wearily got up. He was not long back from checking the waters, as Ron had headed off in his van for his holiday fish. It had been a short water run as the herds were being grazed nearer the homestead for the Christmas break. While the staff were thin on the ground during holiday season, their practice of driving stock daily on outreach camps to fresh country had been put on hold for a month.

Tara set down her knife and fork to listen. It was Crack radioing in to say they'd gathered another twenty-six head.

'We got twelve ear-tagged and micro-chipped steers,' his distant voice said. 'A few old cows and the rest cleanskin mickey bulls. I'll truck them in tonight to the homestead, then snuggle up with the missus for a nanosecond of sleep, then head back out to pick up the horses and the crew first thing tomorrow. Over.'

'Roger that,' said Simmo. 'The mission's been a success then? Over.'

'Affirmative. Dunk couldn't see any more beasts from the air, though he said the wild donkeys and goats were getting up in numbers. Over.'

'Thought they might. We'll deal with that another day. Over.'

When Michael came back to the table, he looked at Tara. 'You up for cooking for the crew when they get in tomorrow night?'

She nodded and beamed. 'Absolutely.'

'I'll help,' Skye offered.

Michael glanced at his wife and then Tara, a faint expression of surprise on his face. This bright, friendly young lass had made such a change in both Angus and his wife. Angus had been surly, and Skye beyond depressed, about their impending separation. He knew neither of them was the type to make distance education work for Angus's high-school years. He'd been wracking his brain for a solution, and one seemed to have driven itself up from country New South Wales. If Tara kept tracking as well as she was, perhaps he could ask head office in Brisbane if she could stay on and oversee Angus's School of the Air high-school education, at least for the junior years, as well as step in as a general roustabout for the station? She knew her way around animals and the yards. He had witnessed it himself. She was gifted, this one.

That way, Simmo thought, Angus, who was not at all ready to leave home, could stay, and they could remain a family. Michael decided to keep the idea under his hat at risk of getting false hopes up in Skye. There was also the issue of whether Tara *wanted* to take on being a govvie and teacher to one boy. He'd have to ask her. She seemed to soak up the world around her — it'd be well worth having her about the place.

'Can I help cook too?' asked Angus. Michael had to stop himself running to call headquarters on the spot.

'The more the merrier, I say,' said Tara. 'As long as you don't make too much of a mess in Mrs B's kitchen, Angus.' She looked over at Skye. 'I'll get some chooks out of the freezer on the way back to bed tonight. I reckon the team'll be about sick of beef.'

'Brilliant, Tara, brilliant,' said Skye as she reached over to clasp her husband's hand.

The next evening the smell of roast chicken drew the weary but cleaned-up crew to the mess. Tara had been too busy in the kitchen to see them arrive and unload the horses and all the gear. Gear that would need a good clean and sort-out before everyone shut down for Christmas. Tara knew the job would be given to her, but she mentally shrugged her shoulders. She had a talent for cleaning and organising, so she might as well use it. And it seemed now, after following Mrs B's old CWA cookbook, she had a talent for roast dinners. The screen door banged and she glanced up as she hauled a giant baking dish sizzling with three golden chickens from the oven. Another three were waiting, along with two dishes of roast pumpkin and potato. On the stove, peas, corn and carrots simmered beside a giant pot of gravy that tasted even better than Mrs B's, although Michael, after dipping a piece of bread into it for a taste, said he would be swearing all of them to secrecy on that fact. Mrs B could be touchy. Skye and Angus were busily setting out plates and cutlery.

'Hello,' Skye called. Tara saw looks of surprise on the faces of the crew that the Boss Lady was in the kitchen with her boy helping out. They greeted her politely. Tara also saw Elsie arrive, looking tanned and beautiful in her crumpled clean jeans and pink Wrangler T-shirt. Tara could see she was travel weary — or most likely sleep deprived. She expected Jake to come in behind her, but he didn't.

'Smells brilliant,' Crack said. He helped himself to a plate and waited for Tara to carve the first of the chickens, steam rising as she offered him a drumstick. 'Elaine's cooked me some tucker, but just a little sample won't hurt.' He patted his stomach. 'You are a woman of many talents, Tara, my girl.' He gave her a friendly smile and a moment of understanding passed between them that all was not forgotten about the other night, but their care and admiration for one another had deepened to another place. To a place of lifelong friendship.

'How's your back?'

'Just fine, thanks,' she said as she kept carving.

'Better leave some aside for Loverboy Jake,' Crack said. 'He was following in the 4WD and I sent him to check the Stallion Springs waterhole. Michael said it was running dry and we'll have to move the spares if that's the case.' Crack was referring to a second mob of station horses that were having a spell from work. They cycled the horses in teams, and the next lot would be brought back in after Christmas when a full crew was back on board and the nomadic herding practice resumed.

'EJ's having a bit of time out,' ribbed Grout as he elbowed her a little. Elsie scowled at him and picked up a plate. Clearly her relationship with Jake on the stock camp was now public. Elsie glanced at Tara and gave her a smile of hello, but there was an edge to it.

'Wing? Leg?' Tara asked. 'Or *breast*?'

'I'll have the breast,' Grout said. 'Jake's been keeping all of 'em for himself lately.' He held out his plate and scrunched his face, his freckles folding together. Tara plonked the chicken breast on his plate and rolled her eyes at Elsie.

When they were all seated, Crack gave his customary brief to the staff before he made his way back to Elaine and his dog Dorris, who would be firmly planted in Gordon's chair, waiting for her master.

'Vera's just sent the itinerary in,' Crack said. He dragged out a piece of paper folded in his jeans pocket and slipped on reading glasses that he kept in the top pocket of his shirt. 'Hinchie is flying in at ten am. He's dropping in the last of the Santa supplies for our skeleton crew.'

'Is that Santa as in Santa Claus? Or Santa as in Santa Gertrudis?'

'Very funny bovine joke, Tara. Stick with your cooking. Hinchie'll then leave at midday back to Isa. Jake and Tyler are on the flight. Huey, Dewey, Louie, you're shipping out by road, taking the rest of our rusty ringers, OK?' The boys nodded. 'Then we're left with String Bean, Moody Blues, Boss Simmo and myself as station staff until the end of January. Mrs Skye and my Mrs Elaine too,' he said, glancing behind him, 'and of course Angus.' The boy beamed. It was rare his mother brought him to the mess room when all the crew were assembled. He decided he liked being there.

'So we clear?'

Everyone nodded. Elsie's heart jolted a little. She wasn't sure how she felt about Jake leaving so soon.

*

Back at the quarters, Elsie barely stopped to pat Marbles as she stomped up the stairs. She was exhausted. Not just from the rush of bringing in more cattle and the thrill of riding Wolfie so fast in and out of the scrub, but because her nights had been consumed by Jake. Or, more likely, *she* had been consumed by Jake. He certainly has an appetite, she thought, smiling but feeling a little sore, not just from horse riding. She was almost relieved he would be in later with the four-wheel drive. He was pretty intense. Now that he had her, he pestered her constantly for a kiss here, a grope there, when the crew weren't watching. And once night had fallen he was like a man possessed when it came to touching her, undressing her, sliding inside her. Again and again. She was giddy from it. It's lovely to be so wanted, Elsie thought dreamily. Never in her life had she felt so wanted. But there was something about the whole camp and behaving like that when working with the other men that left her feeling grubby. She was confused and annoyed and felt like crying. Plus, she noted, there was no letter from Zac waiting for her on the bedside table where Gracie normally left her mail. She was about to drift off to sleep when Tara, who had just cleaned up the kitchen, came in.

'I'm worried about Marbles,' she said. 'He's not himself.'

'Mmm,' was all Elsie could manage before she drifted away to dream of the horror of the hospital theatre and the doctor cutting and cutting until she had no face left.

There was a banging on the door.

The girls sat up. It was Crack. Tyler stood behind him, coats wrapped around them from the chill of the outback night.

'Jake's not in here?'

'No,' said Elsie groggily.

'Shit,' he said and they turned and left. Next thing, Elsie and Tara heard the diesel engine of a four-wheel drive fire, and saw the lights cast a low sinister beam across the buildings as Gordon Fairweather drove away into the night.

Thirty-eight

On the verandah of the staff quarters, Elsie and Tara sat on the bench seat under the gleam of a single bulb that was copping beatings from the hard-cased wings of flying bomber beetles. They tinked as they battered against the light. Joining them were flying ants and moths in a frenzy, while geckos, frogs and spiders on the walls ate their fill. From the window of the communal ringers' lounge the girls could listen for the two-way, though so far it had remained silent. On his bed at their feet, Marbles snored an uneasy rhythm. Side by side, waiting, they looked out into the night where stars swathed across the sky.

'He probably got a flat,' Elsie said, drawing her NP Co coat about her. She chewed her lip.

'Uh-huh.' But Tara sensed otherwise. She hoped her intuition was wrong, but reckoned that Elsie's world was about to tilt sideways and tip her onto another plane of living. This was what the inner feeling had been, the one haunting her for a couple of days.

'Or he pulled over for a rest and fell asleep. We were pretty tired.'

'Yeah, probably,' Tara said. 'Too much bonking.'

Suddenly Elsie was up on her feet, glaring at Tara. 'Will you just give me something? *Anything?* Some kind of reassurance? This is my *boyfriend* who's missing.'

Tara, shocked at the outburst, stared back at Elsie. In her head her mind flashed with anger at the word 'boyfriend'. Jake was not the boyfriend type. He was a ride-one, lead-one kind of guy and Tara knew Elsie was only as good for him for as long as he was actually with her. She knew from Tyler that when Jake went back to his big family farm and social circle of dynasty players over Christmas, he'd keep Elsie on ice but trawl the Sydney society girls. He needed a rich wife so his Mudgee family could keep on farming.

Tara knew the grazing sector was full of charmers like him, and for every one of him, there were a thousand city girls lined up for the prestige of property and the right to wear pearls every day, no matter how their husbands treated them or how little they had in common. Tara had seen Jake's values were founded on misogynistic, outdated views of how a woman *should* behave. She could see Elsie was blind to it.

Plus if Jake was Elsie's boyfriend, who was Zac to her? Tara recalled the flirty-girl voice she'd used on the phone with Zac before his accident, and the teary messages she had since left for him with Gwinnie, seeing as he didn't seem to want to speak to her any more. Tara began to bubble with anger. Who knew what he was going through post-accident? Amos had said he was a bit of a wreck, not just physically. Didn't Elsie understand it wasn't all about *her*? Poor Zac. *Elsie was riding one, leading one too!* She was being such a drama queen.

Tara thought of the now-folklore image of Elsie up there in the spotlight at the Culvert Show. Her inner cowgirl unleashed. Her energy flailing against the confines of her own sexist farming upbringing. If she stuck with Jake, she was selling herself out. *Again.* She would be sentenced to a life similar to, if not worse than, the one at Grassmore. Not only that, but Elsie was acting selfishly. To be leading Zac on like this while he was injured was wrong. Elsie's ego was getting way out of hand, Tara concluded.

But still, Tara felt compassion for her friend. She breathed into her belly and let out a slow breath. 'Everything will be fine. There's good reason he's late,' she said, but her inner core contorted within her as she did.

She slumped an arm around Elsie's shoulder.

'I'm sorry,' Elsie said.

Tara didn't reply. She knew what she was apologising for.

As they moved apart, the radio came alive. 'Goldsborough Base, you copy?' came Crack's urgent voice.

'Copy,' said Michael from the homestead. He'd been sitting by the radio paralysed with worry.

'We've found him.' There was a pause as the radio crackled.

'Oh, thank God,' said Elsie as a smile broke out upon her face. She opened her mouth and was about to sigh with relief and hug Tara when Crack's voice came over the two-way again.

'It's not good, boss.'

There was a long silence.

Eventually Crack's voice again: 'You'll need to call the RFDS. I'm very sorry, but we've got a body to fly out. Over.'

Elsie gave one quick cry of pain and she slumped forwards off the seat onto her knees. Head in her hands, she crouched on the verandah floorboards. Images of Jake's hands on her body, the flash of his face in her mind's eye. The way he'd winked at her from his horse. And now he was dead. *Dead?* It couldn't be possible.

'Elsie,' came Tara's voice from way off in the stratosphere. She felt Tara's hands on her shoulder. She shook them off angrily, made a determined growling noise through gritted teeth, got up and walked down the row of doors to Jake's room. She went in and slammed the door.

Tara hovered, then tapped lightly on the door with her cold knuckles. 'Elsie?'

'*Go away!*'

The next morning two planes were headed to Goldsborough. Hinchie's brand-new craft and the RFDS plane, its mission to take the body of a young man home to his family right before Christmas. His corpse was laid out in the cool room where they butchered the station rations, covered with a sheet. From what Gordon and Tyler could make out, Jake had hit a roo and lost it in bull dust.

'He would've been right had he been wearing a seatbelt,' Crack had reported on the two-way. The injuries to his body were minimal, but his head had hit the casing of the vehicle hard. Hard enough to kill him instantly. And, as Crack pointed out, like many young men his age, he had been going *too fast*.

Tara could hear the far-off drone of the planes, so she knocked on the door of Jake's room. 'Elsie. They'll be taking him soon. Did you want to see him? To say goodbye?' she asked gently.

Elsie was lying in Jake's bed, hugging one of his shirts. The plate of breakfast Tara had left for her earlier was untouched. 'No. *Go away.*'

Tara couldn't bring herself to also deliver the news that she'd found Marbles dead that morning. He'd gone in his sleep. Tara had hugged him and cried. Dear old Marbles, Tara thought fondly. Animals were angels. Gordon had already dug Marbles a grave and they had lowered him in. Tara had said a few words for the beautiful dog who had bolstered them during their drive from Culvert, who had been so glad to be loved. Then they had shovelled the red dirt quickly onto his limp blond body. It was too hot for corpses.

Tara stood on a sun-baked, rust-coloured airstrip and watched the planes approach. Despair hit her for Jake's parents whose whole world had been shattered. Maybe she had judged Jake too harshly? After all, he wasn't trust-funding it around the Gold Coast like some guys his age were and he'd been genuinely keen on learning how to look after the land and cattle out here on the station. Tara sent his parents a prayer. As she did, she felt more gut-wrenching grief over Jake's early death and then Marbles. She choked down a lump in her throat and thought of Marbles's deep foggy brown eyes. Animals had such pure souls, she thought. Not like many humans, who buried them under inflated egos or within greedy hearts. Perhaps her ugly but understandable hatred of men who preyed on women gave her the cold, detached feeling she'd had towards Jake. She tried to shake it away. Squinting into the blue, she watched as Hinchie lined up the runway.

She looked down to her dusty boots and reefed a tear away with the heel of her hand before the flies bothered her senseless. Under other circumstances it would have been a treat to see Hinchie landing in his brand-spanking-new NP Co Airvan OFI, and stepping out of the door under the wing with a big grin on his face and his trademark Santa hat — she knew he would be laden with seasonal parcels, tucker and mail — but all sense of festivity was gone. Nearby the ute was ready and waiting, Tara having done a run up and down the strip to clear it of any scrub turkeys that may have been dawdling about and could've been tangled in the wheels or splattered in the props. Puffs of dust rose as the back wheels touched down in a perfect landing, the nose wheel seconds later doing the same. The plane roared as it slowed and then taxied towards them, the propeller only visible as a shining blur. When Hinchie had cut the engine and climbed out of the plane, he waited until the Mt Isa police officer had safely made it down the steps. The policeman nodded at Tara.

She knew the cop had come to inspect the accident site, view the body and sign off for the coroner. After her mum dying, Tara knew death came with a lot of paperwork, but in Jake's case, it would be extreme. Hinchie nodded a greeting too. Normally she would've gushed in admiration of his new plane before helping him unload supplies for her first station Christmas, but the weight of Jake's sudden death was heavy in the atmosphere. Tara was about to head into the rear of the plane to help Hinchie when she saw two boots standing at the top of the steps.

Her eyes travelled up long legs and a sculpted lean torso to the face of a handsome young man with curling black hair that flopped over one eye.

'Amos?' she said incredulously.

He smiled at her. 'Surprise!'

Thirty-nine

In the kitchen, Amos dumped his bag at the door as Tara got some cordial out of the fridge, her cheeks still pink from the shock and excitement of seeing him. She was flustered and spilled the cordial before she'd even set it on the bench.

'I guess it wasn't fair to surprise you,' he said. 'I'd imagined you being more excited.'

Tara shrugged apologetically. 'I would be, but ...' She frowned and felt tears pulled upwards like the tide, so her eyes moistened.

Amos finished the sentence for her. 'But one of your boys has just been killed.'

Hinchie and Vera had briefed Amos in Mt Isa and he'd almost turned back home again. But his desire to see Tara was so strong that he'd just kept coming. Now he wasn't sure he'd made the right decision.

'He wasn't one of my boys,' Tara said warningly, 'more like Elsie's.'

Amos glanced to his bag, which contained a gift Zac had sent for Elsie. He knew that wrapped in the pretty rice paper was a box of really cool guitar picks Zac'd found online. And there was a card.

Tara shut her eyes. 'It's a mess. She's a mess. Plus Marbles died this morning. And I haven't told her yet.' Her voice choked.

'Really? Oh, Tars, I'm sorry. He was a legend, that ol' dog. I still remember his face plant at the shed that day ...'

Amos moved over to her. Even in the brief time since she had seen him, he had filled out. His skin was clearer now, his jaw starting to square and tinge with dark stubble. His arms and hands, shoulders and chest were more solid, and tapered to a trim waist. Tara sucked in a breath just looking at him. He was on his way to becoming gorgeous. And he seemed to be surveying all the changes in her in the same way.

He opened up his arms. 'Need a hug?'

Tara nodded as emotion folded her face into misery and relief at having him so suddenly *here* with her. *He was here!* She stepped towards him.

'Is this a hug as a friend? Or as a ...?'

'As a what?'

She looked up at him, desire firing, the mere presence of him making her feel all at once safe and happy, but also nervous and shy.

'You know ...'

'You mean as a boyfriend?'

Tara nodded.

Amos looked gently at her. 'That's entirely up to you. You can think of me anyway you like. If you want me as your friend, then that's that: I'll just have to cop it. But I think you know how I feel, so no matter what, I'm always going to be your friend and if you want, your boy.'

'More man than boy now. More like a man. You look good,' she said.

'So certainly do you! You look so fit and well. Station life suits you.'

They smiled at each other for a moment. Then she hit him lightly on the arm. 'What were you thinking, you big dag? Coming all this way to spend Christmas with me?'

He chuckled and pulled her into an embrace that felt like a familiar, safe homecoming. 'Why not come see my buddy? Zac's being a shithead and Mum and Dad said for me to get away.'

She smiled as she laid her head on his chest. She could feel the gentle beat of his heart against her cheek. She shut her eyes. She wanted to feel happy, but there was grief and confusion over Elsie, and poor Zac, left behind in Culvert with his long recovery still unfolding, and yes, poor Jake, gone so suddenly and so young. And Marbles. She felt the miles, the days, the drift of life pulling them in all directions. A fly batted itself against a window and outside in the home paddock one of the horses whinnied. Still Amos held her.

'I know I should've warned you, but I just couldn't stay at that bloody roadhouse any longer. Plus if I asked you, I was afraid you'd say —' He stopped.

'No?' she asked.

'We've got to stop finishing each other's sentences.'

'Yes, otherwise we will *know* we are connected by something greater than mere teenage infatuation. And that would be —'

'Serious,' Amos said, laughing.

'Yes, serious.' She laughed back. She liked the sound of his laughter. It was deeper and rich, and she could feel the infectious vibration of it through his broad chest. She had forgotten how much he made her laugh. She lifted her head and Amos was about to bend and kiss her when they heard someone coming, banging the screen door. Instinctively Tara took a step back, hoisted herself onto the bench and began to sip her cordial, trying to look as if she hadn't just been embracing her version of the most beautiful boy in the world.

'Tara,' Gordon said, coming purposefully into the room and glancing at Amos. 'Mrs Cloudhead needs ya. I'm sorry, but she wants you to be there when Simmo rings Jake's parents with the company's condolences, and then she wants ya to help write them a letter.'

Gordon extended his hand to Amos, shaking it warmly, introducing himself but with a grim expression on his face.

It had been the worst night of his life. He'd seen plenty of people busted up in station accidents, even lost a couple of older, boozy staff to heart attacks, but never a youngster in such a tragic way. He knew Jake would've been driving too fast, and he'd broken station policy by not wearing a seatbelt, but it was under his orders that the boy was on that water run.

Jake had completed two and a half years on Goldsborough and it wasn't as if he were some newbie who didn't know how to travel on a dirt road and look out for kangaroos on the verges. Gordon was angry with him for being careless with his life, and with Elsie, because together the two of them had behaved so unprofessionally and dangerously tired themselves out on camp. He gritted his teeth. He knew he was being too harsh, particularly regarding Elsie, who was so seemingly naive; she couldn't be expected to fully understand the station's unwritten rules about ringer relationships. They were young. So young.

The guy visiting Tara was equally as young, but as far as he could tell, was a good one. He'd better be. Self-aware or not, Tara was still vulnerable, and no surprise. He smiled apologetically at Amos.

'Under normal conditions, we'd be giving you a slap-up Christmas welcome to Goldsborough, but it's all gone pear-shaped, I'm afraid. Our worst of worst nightmares.'

Amos, with his open kindly face, smiled comfortingly. 'I understand completely. I'll help in any way I can.'

'Well, you can start by telling String Bean here to get her arse off Mrs B's kitchen bench. Mrs B goes nuts if she catches the ringers sitting up there.' He gave the young couple a wink. 'String Bean, maybe Amos would like to go sit with Moody Blues for a while. Just until your work is done. We got the copper heading out to the accident site, and Amos, I may need a hand to tow the vehicle back in, if it's not too gruesome for you, son.'

Amos nodded. 'I'll do whatever's asked. I'm just grateful the company allowed me here for Christmas.'

Tara at that point almost had to pinch herself. Her Poo Crew buddy, her lover, her friend was *here*, just to see *her*.

*

When they knocked on Jake's door, Elsie muttered a 'come in'. Tara turned the door handle and nudged Amos in front of her.

'Elsie?' he said, squinting into the gloom after the brightness of the day outside. The air conditioner was turned up and the room had a chill. The curtains were drawn and Elsie was curled up in a ball, still holding Jake's shirt.

She looked up in shock, then leaped at him, her arms outstretched. 'Zac! Oh, Zac!' She threw her arms around him, but Amos began prising her away from him.

'No, Elsie, it's Amos,' he said, searching her eyes.

She looked startled, like a deer in headlights, and chewed her lip, confused, dazed. 'No, no. You're Zac.' She frowned.

'Jeez, Else, what did those RFDS guys give you?' Tara asked. 'You're tripping. Zac's face. His burns. Remember? This is *Amos*.'

Elsie drew back and glanced at Tara, and beyond her out the door. 'Where is he?' she demanded.

'I'm sorry, Elsie,' Amos said. 'He still has to have wound dressings every few days.'

'But …' She shook her head as if trying to shake it on straight.

Tara thought people were supposed to grow as they became older, but in Elsie's case, now she was out in the world, she was only finding ways to shut herself in.

She wanted to say: 'Oh, so now you want Zac. Even though you're so heartbroken. Even though you barely knew Jake.' But instead she touched Amos on the arm, a spark running from his skin up her fingers. His body felt so firm. She turned her knowing green eyes up to his. 'I have to go to work now. Are you OK here?'

Amos nodded. 'You go on. I'll catch up with you.'

He put his hand on Elsie's shoulder and steered her out to the bench seat on the verandah. 'Let's sit here for a bit. Get you out in the light.'

Elsie drifted to the seat like a ghost. Just before Tara left, her small voice clutched at Tara's heart.

'Where's Marbles?'

Amos cast Tara a desperate look. She took a breath. 'He died, Elsie. I'm sorry. In his sleep.'

'What? When?' Elsie's voice was a shadow, her eyes back to staring blankly at the fog in her mind.

'In the early hours …' Tara began, but Elsie was already turning towards Amos, putting her slender arms around him and burying her face into the perfect hollow his shoulder made as he put his arms around her. He cast Tara an apologetic look, but Tara was already walking away again from Elsie Jones.

Forty

After lunch, the station was quiet. A hot gusty wind blasted from the north and rattled the gate chains in the yards. It stirred mini whirlwinds of dust through the work area, flinging tiny rocks up onto the tin sheds, veering off through fence lines and away across the parched home paddocks. The droving dogs dozed in stifling heat in the deep shadows of their kennels, getting coated in a film of dust, barely raising an ear to the willy-willies that passed by. The place felt abandoned, its remoteness suddenly feeling to all who remained there more a burden than a blessing.

Tara made her way to the office. Inside were Skye, the RFDS doctor and nurse and the Mt Isa police officer. Hinchie, looking older than he had ever done, was sitting in the corner on the big soft armchair Tara had placed near the window. His Santa hat rested on the arm of the chair. So much for the rearranged furniture inspiring good energy, Tara thought, deflated, looking at the grim faces. They were clustered around the computer, the constable typing a report on the accident, estimating the time of death, the cause, detailing the injuries in cold clinical terms. The board of directors, the coroner, the lawyers, the family, would need these things.

They glanced up at her and hesitated. She knew the people who were now part of this death-trail system really needed other things than paperwork and practicality to soothe them. Things like hugs, healing and an opening of their minds and hearts to the bigger view of life in this universe. But, as Tara had discovered when her mother had died, people had scuttled from the dark shadows of death that clung to the loved ones left living. People passing her in Culvert had resorted to clichés and uncomfortable looks, as if they wanted to deny that Nora's fate was their destiny too.

She wanted to tell them she had been around death all her life. She had seen in the abattoir the way a bullet could enter skin and bone and leave a perfect circular hole that barely bled red. The way a living thing would buckle at the knees and fold itself to the ground, the life-force energy that helped defy gravity and decay vaporising out to a place that somehow Tara innately knew. She had seen knives pierce skin and sever veins and watched the light fade from eyes. She had leaned closely over the sheep, calf or deer so as to hear, or feel or witness, that great moment when the giganticness of life was released from the meat bags that the creatures inhabited. She knew what death was. And she no longer feared it.

It wasn't death at all. She saw it was simply a transition of energy from one place to another. She could see the energy of the sheep, or the carrot grown by Gwinnie, or the wheat grown by Mr Jones turned into grain and then turned into bread, was all cycling around and around to feed other energies, like the people who ate them. Death was a gift of energy to another. Tara watched the world in that way.

But the older people in the office didn't know about her enlightenment, so Skye jumped awkwardly from the group and steered Tara to the tea room, asking her to help her make some cuppas as if guiding a child away from something shocking.

'You can tell me what's going on,' Tara said gently. 'I'm fine with it.'

Skye looked into Tara's steady green eyes and sighed. 'His parents and his girlfriend are flying to Mt Isa to meet his body. Then they will all fly back to Brisbane and then onto Sydney together. It means the RFDS will take him out tonight.'

Tara stopped filling the jug and turned to look at Skye's open, round face. 'Did you say his *girlfriend*?'

Skye nodded. She laid a sympathetic hand on Tara's forearm, both of them thinking of Elsie as they began to make tea for the men.

It took Skye and Tara an hour to get the words just right and even then they didn't know what *could* be right in a situation like this.

Dear Mr and Mrs Cleveland, the letter began.

Skye wrote the letter in her large classically looped hand three times so that there was not a single error on the page. They were about to put the letter in the envelope, but it just didn't seem enough. As Tara looked down at the forlorn folded page, she remembered Gracie hovering about the yards with a camera as they loaded the horses for the cleanskin muster. 'Photos,' she said suddenly. 'Let's make up a little album. Show Jake's parents what a ball he was having. That his life ended at a point where he was totally happy.'

Skye's face lit up. She knew Gracie loved to step out of the office, kick off her little black flats, pull on her boots and with the company's whiz-bang digital camera take hundreds of photos capturing life on the station. It was part of her job to provide pictures of the training days, the social events, fundraisers and the big work moments, like trucking cattle out for finishing, for the quarterly company newsletter. But Gracie's beautiful portraits of the staff were scattered throughout the computer files too.

'Oh, Tara, you are brilliant.' Skye looked up from the letter with a fresh flush of gratitude. 'I can't help thinking that if this were me, getting a letter like this about Angus … it would make me more angry than comforted. But photos, yes, they would give me comfort. That's what I would want the most. Pictures of my son.'

Skye clicked on the camera icon on Gracie's computer and up flashed thousands of images of the rich and rewarding life on Goldsborough. Peppered throughout the images of sunsets, barbecues at the billabong and dust-swirling cattle yards was Jake. Jake in all his beauty. Swinging from a rope in his boardies, riding out on his rangy horse towards a trough as the sun dipped low in the sky, in the smoko room face smeared with mince and sauce in a pie-eating competition, raising a beer with a blonde girl.

'Better leave that one out,' Skye said dryly. 'That was the last one. Before Elsie.'

'Oh, I see,' said Tara.

When they were done, they found photo paper, printed them and mounted them in a book, Tara writing funny captions.

'Shall we make an extra copy? For Elsie?' Skye asked.

'No. She needs to forget him.' Jake looked glorious in the photos. Too glorious on the outer to be real. But Tara knew the photos didn't show what was within him. Yes, as a young man he was charming and capable, but also as a young man, towards women, he was greedy and cruel.

'He even made a move on me once,' Skye said softly, almost wistfully, a dreamy expression momentarily drifting over her face as she remembered the moment, then she shut down again and shrugged. 'But us women, we know players like him. Can spot them a mile off, so I woke up. And besides, Michael is a good man.'

Tara looked from Skye to the photo of Jake. She's wrong, she thought. Some women, the ones like Elsie, who had a father as distant and untouchable as a satellite in the night sky, couldn't spot players like Jake. Women like Elsie turned their faces to whatever sunlight men offered them and often the men they turned to were ones who burned.

No one spoke as the RFDS pilot and nurse wheeled the trolley with Jake encased in a body bag towards the plane, the wheels catching on rocks and shuddering over the red-dirt runway. Tyler had plugged an iPod into the ute and was playing Jake's favourite

Colorado Buck song, 'Building Fences', as a send-off. Elsie stood with her arms wrapped about herself, flanked by Tara and Amos, something about the tension in her body language keeping them from touching her. She drifted near the trolley, putting her shaking hand to her mouth.

Gordon, Tyler, Michael, Skye and Angus all hovered as the RFDS staff folded the trolley legs up and, like pall bearers, Hinchie and the crew helped load it into the open side door of the plane, where the nurse waited to help lift it.

Amos stood a little way off, not wanting to intrude though desperate to hold Tara's hand, feeling sorry for everyone, including Zac back home.

As they began to shut the door, Elsie lurched forwards. 'I want to go with him,' she said.

'Elsie,' Gordon soothed, taking her by the shoulders.

'Please. I have to. I have to go with him.' Her voice was like a faraway scream from a cliff. It was high-pitched and heading towards hysteria.

Tara moved forwards. 'Else, you can't go.'

She turned to her friend, her blue eyes blazing wildly. 'Why? Why can't I?' she asked through gritted teeth.

'It's time to say goodbye now, Elsie,' Tara said. 'You simply can't go with him.'

'What's it to you? You're just jealous. You never liked him and you hated the fact we were together. Now you're gloating, Tara. Let me go.' She shook off Gordon and ran to the plane, reaching up so she could lay her hands on the shape within.

'Jake,' she whispered. She conjured the past few days of him. The feeling of him thrusting into her, alive with desire, hard with passion, the searing heat of his skin on hers, the grip of his beautiful hands on her thighs, her hips, her belly — it was all still so real. How could he be gone?

'Jake.'

Gordon took her by the shoulder and gently tried to steer her away.

'Let me go!'

It was Skye Simpson who stepped forwards.

'Elsie,' she said in a gentle but firm tone. 'You *can't* go.'

'Why?' Elsie asked coldly, disdainful of anyone who didn't understand the passion she and Jake had shared.

Skye matched Elsie's glacier tone. 'Because his girlfriend is flying in with his parents. Surely she and his family are going through enough?'

Tara could see the news blindsided Elsie, but Tara still couldn't excuse Elsie's behaviour; she knew their friendship was now strained to breaking point. All she wanted was the old Elsie back. Elsie Jones who was her friend. Her only girl friend. Surely she was in there somewhere, under the drama and self-involvement. She reached out to touch her arm, but Elsie spun from her, stumbling, sobbing, turning and sprinting back towards the homestead.

Forty-one

It was just before sundown when Amos tapped lightly on the door of Jake's old room, balancing a dinner tray on his arm.

'Elsie?' he called, reaching for the door handle and pushing it open.

The bed was empty, the sheets rumpled.

A note on the bedside table, in Elsie's scrawling hand, read: *Gone to the bong.*

Amos recalled the billabong to the west of the homestead that Hinchie'd pointed out as the best place for Christmas lunch as they circled for landing. The lushness of the riverside in the deep gorge from the air had stood out green and vibrant against the pale vegetation and red dirt of its arid surrounds. He turned with the tray that Tara had so carefully set and headed for the river.

The path down was well worn and previous NP Co staff had built beautiful steps out of solid timber in the steeper places. Amos was concentrating so much on his footing and not dropping the tray he didn't at first see Elsie. When he did glance up, she was in the centre of a deep green pool, cliffs of red stone rising up, a waterfall sliver dampening the rock from an upper pool just about exhausted from the summer dry. She duck-dived beneath the surface: she was naked. Her clothes were cast off on the banks of the billabong, draped on a giant stone. Amos turned back, but then coming to the surface, she spotted him and called his name. He grimaced but turned towards her.

When he made it to the bottom of the pathway, Elsie was out of the river. Like a siren she had settled herself on the rock, and with no shame about her nakedness had picked up her guitar and, with hair still dripping billabong water down her slender back, she began to play. Her voice rose up around the cliff faces and lifted to the paling sky as it faded into purple and orange and the sun sank in a big orange ball behind the clifftop scrub.

'Tara sent you some dinner,' he said, setting the tray down on a stump. She didn't answer, but smiled gently at him and kept on with a haunting version of Bruce Springsteen's 'The River'. Instantly Amos was transported back to the shed. He felt desire stir in his body and tried to pull in the feeling of Tara, but seeing Elsie there on the rock ... He told himself the science behind the reaction in his body. He thought of Zac at home, dealing with his healing. He took one more glimpse, then began to turn away, trying to shut out her incredible beauty there on that river's-edge rock. Her voice climbed the cliffs and raised the hair on the back of his neck.

Elsie finished the song.

'Amos,' she said in the saddest of voices. 'Please don't leave me alone. Don't go.'

Amos furrowed his brow and almost continued walking, but something in his heart cracked for her. She seemed such a lost soul. She was his friend.

'Please,' she demanded, the pain in her voice making it sharp. 'Please,' she added more sadly.

He turned to see her now standing on the grass beside the billabong. Naked, holding the guitar in front of her. She was shivering, although it wasn't cold. He stepped forwards. She set the guitar on the grass. He grabbed up her T-shirt, draped it across her wet gleaming body.

She clutched it to her and began to cry. 'Hold me, please,' she said in almost a whimper.

Amos encircled his arms around her, wincing his eyes shut tight.

She leaned into him, shuddering with tears. He held her. Every muscle fired with resistance as he thought of Tara, but he felt the lift of his cock beneath his shorts. His cheeks flushed red. The feel of her skin, the beauty of her there in this ancient magical place. But with it he could feel her desperation. He knew that fuelling Elsie's desire was the so-human fear of death and the unbalance of grief. Added to that was the fact he was a mirror image of Zac, the boy she left behind. As she pressed her breasts against Amos's chest, his conscience wrestled with his body's reaction — Tara would understand that Elsie needed him right now. Tara would know he would always be hers, despite this moment, and — and Zac need never know —

He bent his head as Elsie lifted her face.

At the ringers' quarters, Tara set down Elsie's note, turned and walked towards the path down to the swimming hole. It would be great for the three of them to go for a swim at sundown. To wash off the energies of death and the tainted friendship between them over Zac and Jake. It would break the ice between her and Amos too, away from the crush of the older people on the station. She knew he wanted her physically, but all today it hadn't seemed right to even kiss him, with Jake's body still in the cool room and Elsie so shaken. Now, though, with the awful day behind them, she could let herself be the girl she wanted to be with Amos. She pictured kissing him in the cool waters of the billabong and then later, holding him all night in her tiny single bed. She looked up at the beautiful sunset and thought of Jake and his girlfriend, now being reunited with him so sadly in Mt Isa. Poor girl. Poor Elsie, Tara thought as she walked. She picked such a cruel one, when all along she could've had a kind one in Zac.

From up on the clifftop, she stopped and looked down to the billabong. She saw them. Elsie naked on the grassy bank, Amos lying on top of her, his shorts half down. Both writhing in sexual union like serpents.

Tara's lip began to quiver. Her world folded into pinpricks of light. The air that had filled her lungs, the love that had filled her heart, now constricted in her body. She turned. She stumbled, she righted herself and she ran back towards her room.

From his verandah as he thought of the young lives that were scarred today, Gordon Fairweather saw Tara running past. He read her distress. He called to Elaine he'd be back soon as he stood up from his chair and went, not after Tara, but in the direction of the billabong.

The next morning, both Amos and Elsie stood silently as Hinchie dropped the plane steps for them. Gordon handed Amos his small backpack without so much of a glance. He then passed Elsie her bag and helped Hinchie store her guitars and the rest of the luggage in the hold. He waited for Amos to climb the steps up into the plane, then held Elsie there, his big square hand holding her forearm in a firm and honest grip.

'Elsie.' His outback eyes blazed at her.

'Yes?'

'Girls with looks like yours can become cruel and shallow. Don't become cruel and shallow. Don't break any more hearts.'

Back at the quarters, Tara pulled the pillow over her head to block the sound of the plane taking off, taking Amos and Elsie away.

Forty-two

The studio lights were hot and blinding and Elsie was finding it hard to centre herself. The past four days had been a whirlwind of media, makeovers and music sessions since her Tamworth competition win. She had so far liked being the centre of attention, posing for fashion magazines in front of Tamworth's Golden Guitar and snapping one-liners at scripted press conferences. She was back in Sydney now, fast learning that TV was her least favourite part of it all, especially *live* TV like this show.

The studio manager was barking at her. 'When the light comes on, the camera is on,' he said. 'Stand on this mark. Don't move. And for godsakes pull the mic away when you hit the stronger notes so you don't peak. I saw you do that on the *Australia at Night* show,' he cattily pointed out.

Elsie looked at him, hurt, but then something overtook her. *She* was the rising star. Not him. She looked at his stupid supposed-to-be-trendy 'Where's Wally' black-framed glasses and his orange sticky-up hair balanced at the other end by lime-green Converse sneakers that were like something a Muppet would wear. She lifted one eyebrow at him. She was, she thought, a kick-arse cowgirl after all and city dicks like him were wet dishcloths to her. Elsie channelled her best chilly Sarah Jones look.

The man's tone softened. 'When the side cameras' lights come on, look into them. Got it? You have a lot to learn, sweetheart, and I'm just trying to help. Just for now, imagine you're singing to one special person. And have fun.' He patted her on the arm.

One special person? Elsie thought bleakly. Who would that be now? Now she had hurt them all so horribly?

Elsie nodded and gave him an almost apologetic smile, feeling guilty and also slightly horrified she was now adopting her mother's expressions designed to slay people. She pushed away the self-loathing, guilty thoughts of what she had done to her friends and focused on her breath.

'Ready?'

She nodded again and clasped her microphone with sweating palms. She felt her heart knocking in her chest so loud she was surprised the hosts a little way off to her left couldn't hear it. Elsie watched as she was cued down from the count of ten from the ad break, then the camera light came on and Elsie Jones, first-ever winner of the Tamworth-to-Nashville Talent Search, gave it her all, letting the music fill her body. In her peripheral vision she could see the show hosts reviewing the rest of the morning's segments. Since she'd got there at six she had come to see what gruelling work morning television actually was. Everyone was propped up on coffee and seemed slightly arrogant compared to the people on the station or on auto-pilot. But now was her moment. Her chance to sing to all of Australia. To find a new path for herself, seeing as her old one with her old friends was totally road-blocked forever.

And sing Elsie did. Viewers in their homes, in airport lounges, on their commute, were all captivated by her voice and angelic looks. Her voice was made for a cover version of Charity Buck's hit 'Kiss Me with a Song'. When she reached the climax and conclusion of the song, all the studio crew gave her the thumbs-up before they cut to an ad break. The studio manager, realising the full glory of her talent, now gushed as he ushered her to an orange couch that looked like a jellybean. He settled her with a different mic beside the hosts, Jenni and Rog.

Off air, they greeted her, congratulated her, then looked more at their clipboards than her until the countdown cue began again from the ad break.

It was as if a switch flicked in Jenni and Rog. Suddenly they were effervescent, raving to her about her talent, and about her stellar performance at Tamworth, and about how she was on a plane out of here to Nashville in just a week's time to work with country-music legends Colorado and Charity Buck. 'And with the chance to win a record deal and tour package with their infamously famous manager, Jacinta Tylermore,' Jenni concluded. Then they fired her with pre-written questions and Elsie's head spun.

In the Smiths' roadhouse the rarely used TV had been turned on especially for the show. Everyone in Culvert knew that little runaway rebel Elsie Jones was going to be on the show that morning. Up flashed incredible images of the beautiful kid sitting small and fresh on the set of *Australian Mornings*. She was smiling as the hosts threw to a film package of her Tamworth win with her original composition, 'Nothin' to Do'. Golden confetti showering her, Lee Kernaghan and the Wolfe Brothers stepping forwards to congratulate her.

At the table, the Smith family watched. Amos, leaning against a wall, his arms folded. Gwinnie standing in the kitchen doorway, wishing Elvis was there to see it. She wondered if he was allowed to watch morning television in gaol. She was still adjusting to the fact her husband was hundreds of miles away. Thanks to the stack of charges the Culvert Council and police had cooked up, his sentence was five years unless he got parole. *Five years?* She couldn't help it. On days like this, watching her boys struggle, she felt as if her husband had let them all down with his big dreams on renewable energy. She knew she'd been swept away with his enthusiasm, never once thinking the piping of sewage from one place to another could have such hefty legal repercussions. She was sure the trial that had been held soon after New Year had been rigged from the start. The mayor had his contacts, and Constable Gilbert had given conveniently damning evidence.

Since the scandal, the Smiths were official outcasts in Culvert, relying more and more on passing traffic than locals, who had given their business a wide berth since the explosion. And with just the small farm and the workshop, the boys were working with a cloak of stress over their heads. She was toiling a gruelling seven days a week in the café and at the bowser to pay off the mortgage and the fines Elvis had been served with. They'd had a plan of affording employees by now to give themselves a rest, but there was no money for that either. The boys were surly with each other from dawn till dusk since Amos's return from his shortened trip to the Northern Territory. Even though they worked side by side each day, the chasm between them was wide. Amos had never said what had gone on up there on the cattle station with Tara and Elsie, at least not to her. But the girls had suddenly stopped calling and writing.

She looked at the impossibly beautiful Elsie on the TV screen and wondered what had happened. 'Oh, look at her! She looks so *young. Too* young!' She could only see the back of Zac's head as he sat gazing up at the screen. She turned her attention back to the host Rog, who was leaning towards Elsie.

In the studio Elsie steeled herself for another question.

'Word's out, Elsie, you're not just a talented musician: you are a bit of a cowgirl. Before your big break, you were up on an outback cattle station, weren't you?'

Elsie smiled and nodded. 'Yes, that's right.'

God, all this crap. Talking about herself when she just wanted to play music. To live and breathe music. It was where she felt safest. She loved an audience, but she didn't want to talk to them. On that couch without the shield of a guitar and a song, or the company of a band, she was raw and confronted. They were probably about to ask her stupid questions about rounding up cattle. She pasted on a smile, even though her heart was chugging like a steam train.

The male host looked at her directly. 'We understand it was your boyfriend and fellow ringer, Jake Cleveland, who registered you in the competition, but tragically Jake was killed in an accident on the station just before Christmas, right? How do you feel now?'

Elsie's mouth fell open. Pictures of Jake from the NP Co website, grinning beneath the brim of his sweat-stained Akubra, were being flashed up on the monitor screen in front of them and beamed out to the nation. His smile was perfection.

'Jake and I … We … I'm … not …' Tears roamed in her eyes. Panic sprinkled fireworks over her skin. She sweated. The camera operator invaded with a close-up. The studio manager gave the thumbs-up at the hosts and grinned. Good television.

Elsie licked her dry lips. 'I'm not really over that yet.'

Her female host dived in to showcase an act of compassion, as if rescuing her. 'So really, all of this, and everything you might achieve in the US, is thanks to the love you and Jake had for each other?'

Elsie was trying to draw tears gently away with her fingertips so she didn't ruin her stage make-up. She was nodding mutely, thinking only of Zac, imagining him and Jake's girlfriend watching. Guiltily picturing Amos at the billabong. Jake in the bush shower. Zac at home with his injuries, thinking she was his girl. She felt cold through to her core.

How did these people find this out? her mind screamed. Had Tara, Skye, Gracie or Gordon let that angle of the story leak out of anger towards her? It wouldn't be like them. But then she remembered Jake's story was the perfect 'story' for marketing purposes. Jacinta flashed in her mind. After her Tamworth win, she remembered Jacinta Tylermore had plied her with Scotch until the whole story had tumbled from her own lips.

Elsie had met the bizarre manager the night of the competition and the next night, in an upper-class Sydney hotel, had signed her life away to Jacinta Tylermore Music Management. If she was good enough for Colorado and Charity Buck, who was she to question her? Elsie had been ushered into the hotel bar by a PR rep from CMT USA. The young woman, who spoke like a slide guitar, drawled out, 'No doubting we'll find her in the oxygen room.'

Elsie had only just stopped herself from saying, 'What's an *oxygen* room?' Despite her days in Sydney at school and in the pubs, she was more hick than she had realised, and found it difficult to focus amid all that heavy gilding and marble in the hotel lobby. She was led towards a glassed-in area with a discreet sign above its entrance: *Smokers please*. A painted finger pointed to a doorway.

Inside the plant-filled room, drawing on a cigarette with her arms folded across a concave stomach, was a tall woman who was waving at them. From a distance she looked commanding and attractive due to her leanness, stylish black dress and height, made greater by the bright orange suede stilettos she wore and a beehive of black hair. But up close, Jacinta Tylermore was freakishly overdone, her features just past human, the hair polished like wood and the make-up thick and severe. Elsie found she couldn't stop staring.

As Jacinta gushed and praised and waved her hands about and repeatedly hugged her, Elsie was both drawn to and repelled by her. She talked like a truck revving too fast in the wrong gear, as if the wheels and the motor were out of sync. Elsie Jones didn't so much feel as if she had met Jacinta Tylermore as if she had collided with her. It felt freakish enough for Elsie to be standing in a room that piped oxygen into it for smokers. That in itself spoke of human madness, but to also have her senses assaulted by a towering, wildly gesturing, loud woman made Elsie feel as small and helpless as a mouse in a cosmetics laboratory. She had tried to focus on details about Jacinta's plans for Elsie's world tours with the Bucks, websites, social media and promo videos, along with new hit singles, but she was clearly in some freaky 'Hotel California': she had checked in but she could never leave.

From that first night, Jacinta seemed to invade every waking minute of Elsie's day, controlling when she woke, deciding what she ate, what she wore, who she saw, what she bought, so that soon it felt as if Jacinta had taken the place of Sarah Jones. It was like having a mother/manager on speed. (She probably was on speed.) Just when Elsie was about to explode, Jacinta would soothe, cajole and bribe her with the most manipulative behaviour. And who was Elsie to argue? She had no one else in her life. She remembered Jacinta saying that night at the hotel as she poured more straight Scotch, 'Honey, if I am going to represent you, I need to know it all! All the dirt. All the scandal. Every little bad thing you have done, so I can protect you. The media are monsters.'

But far from protecting her, Jacinta Tylermore had served her up. She had crafted the story to suit the marketing. Now, her past, her mistakes, were being broadcast for all of Australia to see.

And seeing it now was Zac, in front of his family. He stared at the images on the screen of the impossibly handsome, now-dead ringer who had apparently been Elsie's *boyfriend*. He turned to Amos and glared at him.

Amos was already heading out the door, though, his face red, his need to get away overwhelming. Images of him and Elsie at the billabong, of Tara's distraught face, were haunting him. He fled to the workshop.

'Zac,' came Gwinnie's gentle voice. But Zac was already on his feet, stalking to his bedroom, shutting the door, resting his forehead against the wall, trying to find breath for his winded soul. Next he found himself sitting on the bed, tearing up the letter and the song that Elsie had sent him, with all her love.

On the TV Jenni from *Australian Mornings* thanked Elsie and said, 'And now to the nation's weather ...'

Showers for Brisbane and Sydney and cloudy in Melbourne. Gwinnie switched off the TV and stood in the silent, empty roadhouse. 'Well, I guess that's it then,' she said to no one. 'It's all over.'

Forty-three

On the other side of the world Colorado Buck felt his phone buzz in his jeans pocket.

He fished it out. It was a text from Charity.

Jacinta wants a word about the new Australian talent.

He texted back an *OK*.

He swung towards the house, driving the electric golf cart right onto the lawn. Leaping from it, he strode up the grand front steps of the ranch house two at a time, passing the inviting aquamarine waters of the large pool, where he noticed his youngest daughter, Sunlight, had left another floater. There would be no swimming for him that evening after his song-writing session. He swore as he trod on a squeaky dog toy that belonged to their new Giant Poodle pup, Snuffles, and almost tripped on an inflatable ring. He wished Charity would get the staff to clean up after the kids and her a whole lot more. He'd have to call Jose Luis in the staff quarters or clean it up himself.

Swiping the white cowboy hat from his head, he sauntered in through a side door in his Cuban-heeled boots to the kitchen and promptly trod in puppy poop. He held back from cussing as he scooped off his boots and tossed them on the floor. He found

Charity and the kids whizzing up some fruit smoothies at the giant kitchen bench. The house was airy and cool from the air conditioning, but the smell of dog crap was lingering in Colorado's handsome, perfectly even nostrils.

In the kitchen, pool water puddled on the imported terracotta tiles from discarded swimmers, and mini lakes of fruit juice spread on the benchtop. Snuffles was creating a puddle of his own under the kitchen table. The blender roared and the kids and Charity barely glanced up when Colorado arrived, now with wet socks from another poodle puddle. Over the sound of the blender, with a high-pitched scream Sunlight wielded a stick of celery at her large dolly, battering it about its blonde curled head, shouting, 'Lipstick taser, lipstick taser!'

The boys, Vegas and South, were throwing baseballs with gusto at the thick royal-blue curtains shielding the northern side of the ranch house from the harsh Texan sun, calling out, 'Steeeer-rike!'

Colorado waited for Charity to shut off the blender. 'Any harder and you'll break a pane, boys,' he said slowly and calmly, dumping his hat onto the counter. 'Best quit it.'

He leaned over, kissed his wife and patted her on a backside highlighted nicely by the clingy soft fabric of the five-hundred-dollar sundress UPS had dropped off that morning.

'Hello, darlin',' he said in his delicious Texan drawl.

He knew Charity missed the shops and her friends when they were out on the ranch. She in turn knew her husband had to settle down and focus on writing a new album, otherwise they would be in financial strife. Between Charity and the kids, the Texan ranch, the Las Vegas flat and the Nashville homestead, the bills just kept coming. Because of a whole world of changes to the music industry, mostly due to the internet, Colorado was feeling pressured to move with the times or fade into music-history oblivion, and a significantly reduced income.

Even his record company of fifteen years was starting to make him feel like a has-been, with reduced advances and fewer scheduled concerts in smaller cities. Colorado's jaw twinged. The pressure was on. He really must get to the studio, but something kept him lingering near his wife. He inhaled the smell of her skin: the scent of pool water, Texan sunshine and Chanel. Wrapping his arms about her, he kissed Charity from behind on the nape of her neck, where her shoulder-length blonde hair met her honey-brown skin. His hand slid lower, cupping one cheek of her buttock. He hadn't quite got used to her new arse. It had cost him about twenty-five grand, not to mention new clothes to fit it, so he thought he might as well make the most of it. Charity seemed to like it. She smiled her cat-like smile and turned her large hazel eyes on him suggestively. He felt his body responding in his Ellen underpants.

'Dada!' roared Sunlight, as the three-year-old intercepted their intimacy. She always threw tantrums when Mama and Dada 'got kissie'. Even in the dark of night and in their marital bed, the little girl was like an Exocet missile, seeking out and destroying any kind of sexual activity between Colorado and Charity. There would be no new baby in the family on her watch.

'Hey, sweetheart,' Colorado said, putting his hand on the crown of Sunlight's head and releasing her mother from his grasp. 'Dada's just goin' to his studio.'

Sunlight lifted the celery stick and whacked her father on his leg. He caught her gently by the wrist and glanced with a slight look of annoyance at Charity. She may have a new arse to die for, but she really needed to focus more on controlling the kids. He'd been using the excuse that she was ten years his junior, so 'she was young and needed to learn about the world'. But that was ten years back and now he'd begun to see her continued immaturity as a kind of manipulation. His daughter did it too. It disturbed him. Charity seemed to sense his judgement and stooped to soothe the little girl, looking up crossly at him.

'Hey, bubba. Dada's here to work,' she said, scooping her up. 'Work, work, work. Y'know it's all Dada ever thinks about. C'mon, you wanna ride your pony? Sunlight wanna ride her pony?' She tickled the child on her belly. 'C'mon, boys, we're goin' horseback ridin',' she called out.

The boys groaned.

Colorado entered his soundproof recording studio feeling utterly grateful to be away from his family in a bubble of silence. He'd had the studio custom built when they'd first bought the ranch house with money from his first album, 'Building Fences'. The same-titled single from that album had bought the Nashville pad and the rest of the album royalties had got him his custom-built 'Ranshion', a property and homestead like he'd always dreamed about, ever since he was an oily, snotty-nosed kid growing up out the back of his daddy's Perryton mechanics shop.

The silence was soon shattered by his own doubtful thoughts. He looked at the mixing desk, intimidated by the creative mountain he had to climb. Colorado hadn't had a hit since 'Lead Me Round, Tie Me Down' and his band and team leaders were getting twitchy. He looked at the lifeless guitar beside the silent piano and sighed. He'd never had such blocks before in his musical career. He rubbed his tired eyes and did a few chin-ups on the gym equipment set up in one corner. Picking up a set of kettle-bell weights, he turned the computer on and flicked to Jacinta Tylermore's number on his cell.

The phone rang out and he hung up before he had to listen to her revving voice on the message service. He clicked the computer mouse and there was an email from her. He opened it.

Hi C,

Attached footage of the Australian winner, EJ. She's a knockout. Let me know what you think. Flying her out next week.

Seeya, J x

Colorado sighed. This strategy of bringing in a younger energy to mentor was Jacinta's idea. A way to stop the decline of his and Charity's career. With cynicism he clicked on the footage.

On the large computer screen came the Australian logo of Country Music Television backdropped against a spotlit stage.

There, the little blonde Tamworth and now Nashville winner of the American-CMT-sponsored award stood, her legs slightly apart, wearing a short-as-short skirt and a black bustier with some cowgirl boots that looked like they had seen the real deal in life. Normally when Colorado Buck saw such clips, he groaned internally. It would be yet another wannabe clamouring for the bright lights, fawning all over him and Charity in a quest for fame and stardom. Another cardboard-cut-out pretty girl mimicking all the musical styles others had tried before them. Colorado knew he had to watch the clip. This young miss would be his and Charity's protégée for the next twelve months, goddammit.

Then he heard her voice. He looked at the screen more closely. He turned the volume up. She was altogether something else. Behind her starlet face was some sort of depth and pain. She controlled the song like a veteran. She came with an edge. Colorado could see it. Charity, being a Montana girl, had had it, and now this lass, ten years Charity's junior, had it.

He hit a few buttons on the panel and her voice came over the sound system. The hair on the back of his neck stood up. He even felt an erection stirring in the undershorts Ellen had presented to him last time he was on her show. Within a few bars he was singing along.

'I got nothin' to do … all day to do it.'

Suddenly he became excited about next week's trip to Nashville to coach the girl on the new CMT reality-TV show, *Country Proud, Country Loud.* He adjusted the stallion bulge in his pants, turned the sound down on her really quite impressive song and, with her image playing on loop on the screen he parked his gym-toned Wrangler-butt on a stool with his guitar, began to pen his first new song in months.

Part Three

Forty-four

Ten years later

It didn't feel real to Tara, seeing Elsie on the TV like that. Styled to perfection with several thousand fans chanting, 'EJ, EJ, EJ!' under the lights of an LA stadium. Tara had been moving a cluster of remotes from a bedside table at a client's Sydney harbourside penthouse when she'd accidentally flicked the big screen on, revealing Elsie in such a random way. Tara knew the universe was an intelligent force, of course, and EJ appearing before her like that was not random at all. Something was about to shift. The past had been buried for too long and would now bubble to the surface in some way.

At first she'd fumbled with the remotes, trying to shut the thing off, swearing as she did. She couldn't stand television, especially the news or entertainment gossip. She'd told her clients that if they truly wanted peaceful energies to flow in their lives, they needed fewer electronic devices in their living space, particularly in their bedrooms. No one could gain centredness when they were addicted to news, entertainment gossip and electronic doohickeys.

Despite spending hundreds on Tara's feng shui consultation, the Sydney corporate couple who had hired her still had a remote for the blinds, a remote for the lights, a remote for the giant TV that took up one whole wall at the foot of the king-sized bed, a remote for the stereo and a remote for the alarm clock. The world had gone mad, and now, seeing Elsie up on the big screen, looking so styled and almost plastic, she knew it was worse than she'd thought. There was something about Elsie that told Tara all was not well with her, despite her polish.

Tara realised even though she worked daily on her business and herself, she too was like Elsie. Today, she resolved, was the day to step towards facing her unresolved past. She was just about through with city living and city people. She'd given it her best shot. She had tried so hard to bring a wider awareness to clients through her business, but in the end it was exhausting and she hankered for rural land again, and wide open spaces.

For the past ten years she'd built her business up from humble beginnings. During the time she worked as governess for Angus Simpson on Goldsborough station, she would moonlight after work on her fledgling business with the help of Skye and Gracie and encouragement from her Mt Isa counsellor. Once Tara had built a website through their friends and NP Co connections, she had set the foundations of her new career despite living in the outback. As more people heard word of Tara's talents, clients had started emailing photos of their nightmare rooms and clutter. Tara would then email advice and computer-generated diagrams, all for a small fee. As time passed, she devised a questionnaire for clients to fill out. With a follow-up phone call she would ask more questions; then she would assess each living space, use the birthdates of the inhabitants and Chinese feng shui energy wheels to work out their directions on the earth's magnetic compass and then give advice on colour, furniture position and individual symbols to enhance people's lives.

Marie Diamond was still her idol, the woman who had shown her the way via that oily folder found on the Culvert tip all those years back. Tara was grateful to her every day. Cleanslate Consulting was booming. Her testimonials had grown. Clients wrote to her of finding new lovers, of sick children recovering, of bankrupt businesses restored to good fortune, of people emerging from depression, all after Tara had advised them. She was never surprised. Only grateful. She knew her work was all about the physics of vibrational energy and there were no tricks or gimmicks to it.

Most of her clients thought it was about positioning pot plants and moving beds to make themselves feel better. She knew most of her clients weren't aware that astronomers had found the planet was moving to a lighter vibrational frequency and that the magnetics of the earth were shifting, thereby affecting everyone. As unaware as most of them were, she could see that people were now seeking ways to be more open-minded and live more in harmony with the natural world. It meant that there were more people knocking on her door than she could handle.

When Angus Simpson had finished his School of the Air lessons in Grade Ten and applied for an NP Co apprenticeship, guided by the effervescent Tara, Skye had encouraged Tara to expand Cleanslate Consulting and set up shop in the city. Tearfully the crew had farewelled her from Goldsborough, Gordon being the saddest to see her go.

At first Tara had gone to Brisbane, but her inner guides had told her to move to Sydney. She followed her intuition and, with her savings, had put a deposit on a skinny terrace house in an up-and-coming suburb. She proceeded to do it up, as well as build clientele. Not long after, she found herself training six other young 'intuitives' from three major capital cities to be associates in her web-based business. She also began to attract money in the bank, though abundant finances were merely a by-product that came from living her true calling. She was funnelling her money to charities, and helping an organisation that looked after pets that had belonged to elderly people who had passed or had to go into homes. She was happy and settled, if not a bit of a recluse.

The five-storey home had stairs running from the front hall, zig-zagging up from landing to landing to the attic. It was artfully filled with books and beautiful things. Each day at sunrise, Tara practised gratitude, affirmation and meditations and jogged the stairs to keep herself fit. Her thick beautiful red-brown hair cascaded around her heart-shaped face, settling in gentle curls on her softly rounded pale shoulders. Her large green eyes were alive with life and humour.

She was more beautiful, inside and out. Every day she calculated her colour charts and dressed accordingly in floaty, pretty clothes that celebrated her curves. She ran a successful business and was lovely to be around. Her conversations were founded on lively wit and ageless wisdom. But her bed was empty. When it came to men, Tara's heart was closed up and as unyielding as a rusted rabbit trap. She had tried therapy and reading, Nick Ortner's *The Tapping Solution*, praying and wishing, but nothing reprogrammed her cognitive patterning enough to help her on the issue of the opposite sex.

Even though people saw the sunshine in her, she knew there was a dark cloud still within. Her aloofness with men all tracked back to her past, back down the gurgling, ugly Dwaine Pipe. Back to Culvert in remote New South Wales. And to a boy she had once loved, who had turned away from her on a billabong bank by an outback river. A river that had dried up soon afterwards, like the friendships she'd had in her childhood.

Tara looked again at Elsie Jones on the giant screen, larger than life, looking devoid of any kind of flaws, the scars of her past hidden within. Tara's mind crowded with memories of Amos and her system churned with longing and hurt. Sordid flashes of the couple down by the outback river; sordid flashes of Dwaine in the toxic tangle of her abattoir-house sheets, which had pink flowers scattered on them like tiny sores. She felt it all hit her in her base chakras. As she looked out to the gleam of the harbour water and the white shapes of boats, she also felt a bunch of angel guides knocking on the door of her heart right now. Letting out a breath of defeat, she gazed up at Elsie again on the screen and knew it was time to unlock her heart. Time to truly surrender and let go.

But how? She didn't want to face the darkness of the abattoir house, the pain of Elsie and Amos's betrayal, her own life that some nights, with no one to hold, felt like a lie. She gritted her teeth and tried again to turn the television off, but the big screen kept blaring Elsie's music.

'*She's still learnin'. She's still yearnin' to love the skin she's livin' in,*' sang Elsie.

At last, Tara gave in. She knew the angels needed her to hear what the TV segment had to say. She stood before it, head tilted back, arms by her side, eyes wide as if she was mesmerised by an alien visitation via the big screen.

'In the States,' began the female reporter in a clipped cloned tone, 'she's a household name, the queen of country rock who's crossed the American country-music canyon to mainstream pop charts.' Footage of Elsie smiling flashed on the screen as the reporter spoke. She looked every bit the star, posing in photo shoots, in a gold dress at a red-carpet event, lighting up a stage with her silver guitar and powerful voice. 'Her career was boosted to stellar heights after she was caught in a love triangle with country-singing veterans Colorado and Charity Buck. Born as Eleanor Jones, she was as obscure as the tiny western New South Wales town of Culvert from where she came. A town briefly famous a decade ago for, of all things, a sewage theft scandal; a town that since then, thankfully for the locals, has found a sweeter claim to fame.' Tara watched footage, dug out from some old computer file, of the Smiths' shed taped off after the explosion, the sewage-treatment plant and Culvert's woefully designed council offices.

'The singer has not been back to Australia since leaving for Nashville ten years ago,' the reporter said, 'but now, fourteen number-one hit singles and six platinum albums later, it seems America is ready to lend EJ to the world, with a planned tour to twenty-five countries, culminating in her old home, Sydney, Australia. Country-music fans will be pleased to know that Elsie Jones is, after all this time, returning home.'

Tara at last flicked the television off with the first button she tried. *Home*, she thought. She felt energy shimmer through her. Home? Was that the nudge the angels were trying to give her? Surprised, she checked her feelings again and began to hear the word 'home' repeating over and over in her head. Culvert was *home*. Her mind rushed as she realised that's what was missing from her life. Belonging. She had felt it on the station, but not here in the city. She realised she could conduct her business from anywhere and anywhere could just as well be Culvert. If there was any place that could benefit from her healing talents and if there was ever a place able to shift her own deep healing within, Culvert was it. Goosebumps lit up her skin like party lights. She turned to one of the many computers her clients had lined up in their bedroom and nudged one to life with a bump of the space bar. With a curious smile on her face, Tara watched the flashing cursor in the Google search panel as she typed *culvert nsw real estate*.

Forty-five

A little drunk already, Elsie looked at her tired face in the mirror. Maybe it was time, she thought. Time to visit *home*.

Fifty concerts across however many states, staying no more than two nights in however many hotels. Airports and media and sound checks and marketing meetings and photographs and fans. The UK and Europe next, then east towards Japan, then south …

She groaned. She needed a break. Sure, her latest album was enjoying hit after hit and the cheques Jacinta was writing her were beyond comprehension, but she wasn't sure she could take it any more. Nor stand this ache inside. She still missed Colorado, and, if she was honest, she even missed Charity, the bitch, and those brat-pack kids. Touring and performing as a solo artist was *so much pressure*. Making music was her love, but they could keep the other crap that came with it. She looked at the lines of cocaine she'd carefully chopped out on the hotel table beside the in-room service menu. Clutching her robe around her, she stooped over the powder, hating herself as she did. As she inhaled abruptly, violently, bitterly, she wondered how on earth had she got here? But where was here? In which city? Which hotel?

She was filthy rich and filthy famous and all alone. Just her and her fix. As she drifted off on the ice-cold, stiffly made bed, she remembered the day in the dressing room years before and where it had all unravelled.

Charity Buck had slid the small package towards her, then pressed a perfectly manicured finger to her lips in a seductive 'shush'.

'*Don't*, whatever you do, tell Colorado.' She had given EJ a captivating wink in the dressing-room mirror. A photo of her three children and a beautifully bare-chested Colorado was tucked in the corner. Elsie looked at Charity, shocked at the sight of the plastic-wrapped cocaine tucked inside a zip-lock sandwich bag with Marge Simpson on it. But Charity, the wife and mother of three, and iconic country star to millions, simply shrugged.

'A girl's gotta do what a girl's gotta do.' She pursed her lips and turned to check her intricately braided long blonde hair extensions in the mirror. She wore an otherworldly custom-made deerskin dress, stitched with eagle feathers, beads and perfection; she also wore the highest heels Elsie had ever seen. In contrast to Charity's finery, Elsie wore a simple shimmering silver-and-black slip and tall patent-leather patterned Liberty cowgirl boots with diamantes on them. Her long blonde hair fell straight over her shoulders. She looked like a shapeless baby next to the towering, womanly Charity. And that's exactly how Charity had wardrobed it, after many fights with Jacinta.

Outside, Elsie could hear the roar of the fans in the stadium as they chanted for country music's golden couple to appear. Charity looked at her image in the mirror, stooping forwards, applying a little more lip gloss over her perfect lips the make-up artist had already painted, hauling her surgery-enhanced boobs up in a super-sexy creamy lace bra, smoothing out the thick elastic underwear worn beneath her dress to keep any hint of 'post-baby lumps' at bay. She then set her eyes on EJ again.

'At home, I mostly do it in the laundry so if I spill a little, he's gonna think it's washin' powder. What a man don't know, won't hurt him none. Not that I ever do no washing, but Colorado don't think like that. He's a little slow when it comes to noticing the little things about me.'

EJ hesitated. How could she break it to the queen of country rock that she really didn't want to do any drugs with her? Least of all drugs offered to her by the wife of her idol and her mentor, Colorado Buck. Especially not behind his back. And not before the first night of their LA concert launching The Colorado and Charity Love Revival Tour, featuring Down-Under Darling, EJ. She'd have to say no. But saying no to Charity was like saying no to Adolf Hitler.

'I ... I ...' Elsie had stammered.

'You haven't changed.' Charity grimaced coldly.

Charity was referring to the first time she'd met Elsie inside a Nashville recording studio. Fresh from the flight over from Australia, Elsie had been overcome with nerves, blown away not only by Charity Buck's expensive beauty but also the unarguable aura of her commanding presence. Elsie was temporarily rendered speechless, and Charity was merciless.

'Do. You. Speak. *English*. In. Auz-tray-li-ya?' Charity had said that first time. Elsie knew it was a power-play rather than mere teasing.

Charity had leaned close. Elsie remained a gaping-mouthed idiot, star-struck and mute. Even Charity's breath smelled perfume-sweet. How could Elsie ever measure up to these perfect people?

Beside her, back then, in the insulated crush of the soundproof studio, Elsie could also feel the too-close, too-invasive presence of her music idol Colorado, who, like an old-style painting, had seemed to follow her with his eyes everywhere she went from the moment she'd been thrust into the room with him. According to her brand-new manager, Jacinta Tylermore, he was a man to 'watch out for' and to 'avoid fucking at all costs'. Or her contract 'would only be good for wiping her arse'. Jacinta sure had a way with words.

Elsie got up from the hotel bed, the room a vortex, and drifted over to gaze down at the street below. It was daytime. She had a show that night. But where was she again? She widened her eyes, then scrunched them tightly shut. Then opened them. That's right! How could she not know? She was in Nashville. She *lived* in Nashville, but the paparazzi had been hounding her so badly that Jacinta had booked her into the Select just while the concerts were on so she was near the venue. Shocked that it had taken her that much thought to process where she actually was, she decided to lie back down. She must be more bombed than she'd thought. This was her last fix, she promised herself as her head hit the pillow.

She shut her eyes and began to hum a melody. She remembered that first night. That first night of the concert. A smile crossed Elsie's face and she relived the memory of the freight-train thrum of that first-ever huge crowd. She could see her new Maton now, propped up like a star itself on the stage. In the stage wings, Colorado had swept past, giving her a wink. Then he steered himself to his wife's side, burying his face in the nape of Charity's neck.

Elsie pushed aside her first flush of jealousy. Colorado was a father figure to her. *A mentor,* she tried to tell herself sternly.

'Fuck off,' Charity had spat at him. 'You smell like you've drowned in Southern ... and had your face buried in some brown-sugar back-up singer.'

Colorado, hurt and angry, looked away.

Elsie knew moments later on the stage, Colorado and Charity's marital love for one another would shine like the Northern Lights, swirling and dazzling the audience. Wives twenty-five years married would slide hopeful hands towards their husbands as Charity and Colorado sang their duet 'Valentine Divine'. Elsie watched as they plastered on winning smiles and claimed the stage, hand in hand. The royal couple of country rock. From the wings, Elsie looked to the guitar she would soon win the world with. She felt the stomp of thousands of fans shimmer through her heart. She wished she had someone here who loved her to see what was about to unfold. A face flashed into her mind. Zac, under a blue-jean sky, looking up to the clouds. She had hurt so many people that she didn't ever deserve a normal boyfriend, especially one as kind as Zac. Music would be her love instead. She heard her cue and with her own winning smile strode onto the stage.

In the hotel, the phone was ringing beside the bed. Elsie knew it would be Jacinta. She swore, lifted the receiver, then slammed it straight back down. She was enjoying her float down memory lane. Her body was feeling lighter than a feather, her mind in a shush of peace, like small waves sighing in and out on the shore. She remembered, after that first concert, a knock on her dressing-room door.

'Hang on,' Elsie had said, but before she could reach for her robe, the door had opened.

In came Colorado. The expression on his tanned face was strained and panicked. 'She's *that* wasted,' he said, his voice choked.

It took him some time to register Elsie was standing before him in just her bra and knickers, her stage make-up and hair still done, about to step into her jeans for any kind of after-party that might unfold.

Colorado hesitated for a moment, his eyes hungrily scanning her nubile body. He coughed a little, then averted his eyes. 'Jacinta cain't get no sense out of her neither. I really think she's on more than just migraine tablets and the pick-me-ups the doctor gives her. She's off her head.'

Elsie grabbed up her robe, drawing the oriental silk number over her spray-tanned shoulders. She reached out and laid her small delicate hand on his upper arm. 'I'm sure she's just overtired,' she lied.

Beneath her palm Elsie felt a rock-hard bicep. She felt a rush of longing. He looked so vulnerable right now and open to her. She loved it when he wore his stage jeans so tight. Her eyes slid to his big rodeo buckle and the flat weightlifting stomach that his white T-shirt clung to. For an old guy, he was scrumptious. Smelled good too. It made her blush and she too had to drag her eyes away. She unstuck her hand from the pulse of his rock-hard arm muscle.

How many times in the past few months had she felt this way in his presence when they were working closely in the studio? The buzz of song writing bonding them closer and closer together.

'Jacinta's even talking about pulling her off the tour, she's that bad,' Colorado said. 'It'd be just you and me. Could you do that for us, Elsie?'

Elsie's big blue eyes opened wider. 'Of course I could!'

His face lit up a little. 'Great! That's my girl.' But then his expression closed again with concern. 'It's not the show that's the problem, though,' he said, his voice for the first time thin with despair. 'It's her. She's been impossible lately. To me and to the kids. She's not even interested in them. Angry all the time. Yelling, pitching stuff at me. She oughta get a place on the Giants team, she's got that strong an arm.' The joke fell flat. He shook his head sadly and glanced up apologetically. 'I'm scared, Elsie. It feels like I'm losing her.'

Elsie took his hand in sympathy. 'No, you're not losing her. It's just the pressure of work. Once the tour's over, you can all go out to the ranch for a holiday. It'll be fine. She just needs a break. We all do.'

Colorado's dark eyes gleamed with gratitude and admiration. His gaze fell on her and stayed. 'You think?'

'Uh-huh,' Elsie lied.

'Oh, my sweet, sweet girl. You're the best. C'm'ere.' He pulled her to him and gave her the biggest of hugs. Elsie felt a rush of blood to her nipples as they pressed against his solid chest. She also felt his broad hands pressed against her back. They soothed up and down in a comforting way. She answered him by rubbing her hands up and down his long, firm back. But soon their touch morphed into something else.

The rubs of comfort became gliding hands of desire moving over the fabric of their clothing. Their skin on fire beneath. Breath came to them more quickly, shuddering deeply, longingly. Elsie shut her eyes and leaned her head on his chest. Then it had happened. Like air rushing through an airlock, like the tide rushing in to meet the river mouth. An unstoppable current of desire. It took a matter of moments for Colorado to tug open his big belt buckle, lift Elsie up by her tiny backside, sit her on the dressing-room bench, unwrap her robe, drag down her knickers and bang her solidly, her back against the mirror, lipstick and hairbrushes scattering. It lasted less than two minutes and when he was done Colorado, breathing hard, couldn't look himself in the eye in the mirror he was facing. Instead he buried his face in EJ's neck and let the sense of relief soothe him. Ever since he had seen her on the demo tape he had wanted her. She was, he thought, his greatest muse. Elsie, on the other hand, couldn't help but think, was that it?

Just then Jacinta had burst through the dressing-room door. 'There you are,' she barked, pretending she hadn't noticed the way Elsie and Colorado had pulled apart, their faces flushed with desire and now embarrassment, Colorado hoisting up his trousers, Elsie grappling to cover herself with the robe.

'I've had to call a doctor,' Jacinta said to Colorado. 'But don't worry, I've found a discreet one. She's asking for you. You've got two minutes, so you'd better spray yourself with something pretty, then go soothe her or fuck her or something. If you can get it up again. Just do anything to stop her doing whatever she's doing.' Jacinta, with her long red nails, laid a hand on Colorado's broad shoulders and practically shoved him out. Right before she left, she put her head back around the door and pointed from her own eyes to Elsie's with her long talons. She hissed at her, 'I'm watching you.' Elsie had swallowed and nodded.

Later, after Charity had been carted off to hospital, Elsie'd stood mute, watching as Colorado hurled a San Pellegrino bottle against the mirror so that shards of glass flew in an explosive smash.

'Damned if I do, damned if I don't!' Colorado yelled at Jacinta, the veins on his neck standing up with fury. 'She's a good musician; so what if I banged her? OK?'

Banged? Elsie's mind reeled.

'The world will know. Your wife will know.'

'How will they know? You're not cancelling the rest of the tour.

And we are writing an album together. It's the best stuff I've come up with in years. *Years.*'

Elsie waited for Jacinta's customary pause as Jacinta tugged a cigarette from a packet and lit it angrily.

'Don't the fuck smoke in here. You know I hate it,' Colorado had said, grabbing the smoke from her, sucking on it deeply himself before stubbing it out in a shallow plastic tray of eye shadow.

'Charity has to get her shit together is all. Then we're back on. What city we on in next?'

'You don't wanna know. Biggest bible-belt town around … infidelity round those parts goes down like lead bullets in your balls. They don't take to tramps neither,' Jacinta said coldly in Elsie's direction. 'So you'd better keep your dick in your pants, Elsie must keep her legs shut and Charity'd better get clean, otherwise the tour's cancelled. You can't go on stage alone with EJ. The world will go nuts about it.'

'Like I said, who's to know I've been near her? The once,' Colorado muttered at his boots. 'Not for want of wanting more,' he said, giving Elsie a private look, letting her know he was hooked.

'Keep it in your pants, is all you need to do.'

'What you think I bin doin'? I been playin' it straight since the last baby was born. It was you who brought her here and dangled her in front of me. C'mon, Jacinta. Have you had a look at her? She's gorgeous.' He took Elsie's face in his hands.

'Gorgeous and dangerous and she'll destroy your career and your marriage.'

'I am in the room you know,' Elsie said, taking his hands from her face.

Colorado looked at the scattering of mirror glass around him, the way his broken image reflected back up at them.

'I've about had it with you women,' he said through gritted teeth. 'Elsie excluded. And for your information, Jacinta, I'll fuck whoever I like and I'll fuck up whatever the fuck I like! I'm the one paying you. Got it?'

Colorado had glanced at Elsie. She had already been feeling

outside of this entire scene, and now she was even feeling severed from herself. Did Colorado really fuck whoever he liked? Elsie had thought she was somehow special to Colorado. Her talent with music surely made her special to him? More special than other girls? What was it with her and picking the wrong men? She saw Jake's face. Then the face of Amos down by the billabong. She shut her eyes, but it didn't help.

Next she had heard a knock on the dressing-room door …

But then the knocking got more insistent. There was banging on the door. Elsie barely opened her eyes. She was in Nashville now. Alone. Except not alone. There was someone at the door. Was it time to go to pre-show hair and make-up?

'Huh?' she said before she faded out again.

The hotel concierge swung the door open for Jacinta.

'Fuck me,' Jacinta said, shaking her head. 'EJ,' she said sternly, stepping into the room, 'get up.'

Forty-six

The sheep cast their heads low as they eagerly waded through long fresh grasses, browsing on seed heads. Amos sat on the four-wheel bike, Arnie, his Collie, panting behind him, wet from a quick dip in the dam, now soaking Amos's back. Both man and dog watched as Elvis hitched the last electrical tape to the top wire of the permanent fence and made his way back to Amos.

Amos didn't like coming out to this section of the farm. Each time he looked at the shed and the sewage ponds it was a reminder of the past. Those awful days of the accident and the local persecution that had followed. If things had tracked right, the technology they'd built in the shed could have helped the world's energy crisis. With global fossil-fuel supplies predicted to run out by 2088, Amos still felt such resistance to letting the project go. The small experiments they tinkered with at home were nothing compared to what they'd been doing in the larger shed. But maybe it was time to let it go? In Amos's opinion the gaol stint had been harder on his father than his brush with cancer. His father looked like an old man now. He was greying, stooped over and had lost the proud tall way he had walked through the world. As his lifetime dreams had withered from the scandal, so too had his spirit.

'He's made the seat wet,' Elvis complained, pointing to Arnie. The dog flopped a dripping tail and looked away guiltily.

Amos shrugged. 'Not much I can do about it. He likes a swim.'

'On cold days like this?'

'It's refreshing.' Amos grinned. Elvis smiled at his son. He was so proud of Amos. He always found a way through with humour for them. And he was so grateful he'd stayed to help Gwinnie during his time in gaol and was even still here, helping them claw their way back from the financial edge. Amos had leased more country and restored it in the way they had their own farm. They could now run more stock to pay off the legal debt; with more and more farmers walking off, Amos's land leases were accumulating. He spent long hours, until well after dark, in the mechanics shop to make sure the job was done right for the few customers they had left after the scandal. He was pleasant to people at the bowser, even the cruel and condescending Councillor-Mayor No-Buttocks. Elvis just wished he'd live a little. Go meet some girls. Go travelling. But Amos didn't seem to desire any of those things.

Elvis swung a leg over the bike, shuffling Arnie back. Amos glanced over to the sewage plant.

'What a waste,' he said. Not only had they lost access to a valuable fuel resource, but also to the fertiliser that had been a by-product from their biogas production trials. The nitrogen-rich natural fertiliser from the algae that bloomed in the wastewaters of the gas production process had helped bring the soils here back to life. But since the pipeline was cut the fertiliser was now no longer available for the lease properties either. So much potential locked away.

For a moment he thought jealously of Zac, who had upped and left. Amos thought about how he could've left too, but who would've taken care of Gwinnie, the farm and the business while his father was in gaol? He supposed he ought to be happy and grateful — few boys had the opportunity to run a farm the way they wanted — but the void in him felt like an entire black hole. His father followed his gaze to the ponds.

'You've just got to let it go,' Elvis said.

Amos shook his head and turned to the shed. He thought of the last time he'd been in there with Zac. They had severed the heavy chain with giant bolt cutters and stepped into the gloom. It was the same day Zac had packed up and gone for good.

Once inside, the boys had stood looking at the biodigester tank, the now-severed gas pipelines to the overflow tank, which was still ragged from the blast. Amos shivered.

'It was a stupid idea,' Zac had said.

'C'mon, man, it was not.'

'Yes, it was. Take a look at what others are coming up with … an engine powered by magnetics. You can't get cleaner energy. You know it's a better concept than ours.' He flung his arms out, indicating the large tractors in the shed. 'This technology is superseded already. Dead in the water. Shitty water at that.'

'I disagree. Every household has food and human waste. In India, all those sacred cows wandering about are producing up to ten kilos of dung a day each. All that garbage tipped in the streets that could be converted to gas too. The disease that could be reduced. The deforestation reduced. Water contamination reduced. Poverty alleviated. Cropping land lost to ethanol production could be reclaimed for food production. We all have to think big and yet create small energy centres locally. This is the future.' Amos angrily jabbed his pointed finger to the tanks. 'And you know it.'

'What I do know is it's not going to happen for us.'

'You're wrong.'

'It's not as saleable as magnetics. It's not *sexy*. Selling people's shit back to them is impossible in the developed world, and even if it wasn't, some big company would come along and bury the technology. The oil magnates and top dogs control everything. As if the shitty Smith family in shitville Culvert can take them on.'

'I disagree. Power comes from within. Tara once told me —'

Zac made a scoffing noise. 'Tara, Tara … Tara? You idiot. She's long gone. She had another fella when you went up there, didn't she? Like Elsie had. Both of them were lying to us.'

Amos clenched his jaw. The guilt over Tara finding him with Elsie at the billabong swamped him. 'No, she didn't have anyone else. Tara would never lie. She's an amazing person.'

Zac narrowed his eyes. 'Then why aren't you two keeping in touch? She was rooting someone else up there — like Elsie.'

The explosion hit Zac from the side. Months of pent-up anger flew from Amos as he leaped up and tackled his twin. Zac sprawled hard on the concrete floor and, when he came to from the shock, began to struggle in the furious white-knuckled grip of his brother.

'What is it with you?' Zac spat as Amos straddled him.

'What is it with *you*?' Amos had scruffed Zac by the shirt collar and rammed his back into the concrete. 'I can't stand your negativity any more. You're a bitter bastard. Blaming everyone else for your misery. Mum and Dad raised you to be a better man than this.'

'Man? What do you know of manhood? We're both still living with Mum and our dad's in gaol. Our lives are fucked.'

The base ugliness of Zac's words had fuelled more rage in Amos. He raised his fist and swung a punch. It collected with Zac's jaw. Teeth, sinew, skin took the impact of hard-boned knuckles. Blood emerged from Zac's mouth where his molars grazed the inside of his cheek. Zac spat blood and bitterness and looked at his brother with a fire in his eyes.

'What? Not game to hit the other side?' He turned the raw scar on his face towards his brother. 'Go on then, Mr Perfect. Finish me off.'

Amos looked down to his brother. 'Mr Perfect? Oh, I'm not Mr Perfect. You know why Tara doesn't speak to me? Huh?'

Amos waited for the moment to deliver the blow. He watched the questions run in his brother's eyes. 'It's because she caught Elsie with Mr Perfect up there on the station. That's why.'

Zac looked up at his brother in disbelief. Hurt engulfed him, followed by rage.

'You ...' He wrestled with Amos, both boys grunting with exertion. 'Bastard! So she wanted the good-looking brother, did she?' His voice was choked. 'The one without the scars. Fat Tara not good enough for you any more? Wanted the bombshell?'

With renewed fury Amos launched again at Zac. Then Zac swung, his knuckles collecting with Amos's cheek. Amos reeled back, then scrambled backwards away from Zac and stood.

'It was you who insisted we were too young to settle for the one girl. Besides, it's not the scar on your face or Elsie that's the issue, mate,' Amos said in disgust. 'It's the ugly scar in that heart of yours. 'Bout time you got over yourself or got out all together. Mum and I don't want you or need you here.' Amos tugged down his shirt, turned his back to his brother and walked away out of the shed and into a wind that cut cold through his clothes.

Now through the wet patch of dam water Arnie had left on Amos's shirt, he felt the cold Culvert wind cut through him again. It brought with it the powerful stench of sewage. He looked again to the shed.

'I can't, Dad. I can't let it go. This is too important to let go. I'm going to call Zac. I'm going to ask him to come home.'

Forty-seven

In the roadhouse Gwinnie Smith rummaged her fingers through her messy blonde hair and took off her computer glasses. She could hear Elvis and Amos coming on the four-wheeler. Her ears were tuned to the sound of engines these days. Without looking she could tell if it was the stock-carter's truck as he pulled in for diesel or Miss Beechcroft's ancient backfiring Beetle or the rumble of the Nicholson son's new Jeep. Then there were the dreaded purrs of the council and community-service fleet cars that could bring Councillor-Mayor Jones or one of his cronies to her bowser.

After all this time at the roadhouse Gwinnie Smith saw how very slowly things changed in Culvert, if at all. She wished she was somewhere else, back on the coast where she grew up, her ears tuned to waves again. If it was pumping from the south, offering up good left-handers, she'd be up and out of bed with the board under her arm before school. Or she could tell if it was offshore, causing the waves to lap gently at the sand, so she could lie in bed a little longer. She longed for waves these days. And no engines. Maybe, she thought, I've just got *old*.

Gwinnie watched sadly as Elvis and Amos parked the bike outside the workshop. She looked at the two men. They were so different these days. Life had become mundane for them. For her too. She glanced at the clock. They were cutting it fine with the car service. They hadn't even been in for lunch yet. She'd have to take them a sandwich or something, but the thought of going back into that kitchen made her feel depressed. Gwinnie wanted to do a meditation. In the past she'd used her meditations to gain more energy for living, or for a closer connection to her husband hundreds of miles away when he had been in gaol, but now, it seemed, she used meditation to escape from life.

As she submitted another bill payment online, Gwinnie wondered what had happened to her gorgeous little family. All the positive thinking and spirituality in the world hadn't managed to stop the erosion that had set in since Zac's accident and the family's exposure to the authorities. She pushed herself up from the table with the palms of her hands and ambled into the kitchen. There on the fridge was a postcard from the Caribbean. Zac had been gone seven years now. *Seven years.* She remembered the day he had suddenly left.

He'd come in through the back door from the farm shed on foot. There was blood on his shirt and his nose was still dripping. He grabbed up a tea towel, tore open the freezer door and angrily rummaged for a packet of frozen peas.

'What happened?'

'A whole lot more than you think,' he said angrily.

'Where's Amos?'

'Who cares where he is?' he replied before stomping to the lounge and gingerly pressing the peas to his already swelling cheek and nose.

Gwinnie followed him and opened her mouth to speak.

'Save it, Mum. I'm leaving.'

'But —'

'But what? Dad's in gaol? So I have to stay here?'

'No?'

He turned to her. There were tears in his eyes, blood crusting on his top lip. The scars on the other side of his face made it worse. He looked so pitiful and tortured that Gwinnie began to cry.

'I'm leaving, Mum. I have to. I can't be around him any more.'

She had nodded mutely and let the tears roll silently down her cheeks. Just when it had seemed as bad as it could possibly be, Zac had reached for the newspaper, and before she could stop him he saw the giant front-page article and photograph of Elsie and Colorado Buck, caught by the paparazzi on an island somewhere, Elsie topless, Colorado lying beside her. COUNTRY CHEATS, the headline blazed. He'd simply absorbed the image and headline in silence, then gone to his bedroom and packed his bags. After giving his mother a rough emotional hug without looking her in the eye, he had walked to the train station.

At first there'd been no word from Zac. Gwinnie had checked his savings account. All the money was gone. She had demanded the whole story from Amos, then fretted, then calmed herself, telling herself Zac was a grown man and she had to let her sons go at some point, then she fretted again. After weeks they had a call. He was in London. Next a postcard from Spain. Following that he'd Skyped from Korea. He'd looked well and happy as his cheeky backpacker mates dove in and out of view, saying hi to 'Mum in Culvert'. Then she and Amos didn't hear from him in months. She kept emailing a weekly letter, but her notes got shorter and shorter. There was never any news. Not here in Culvert. Not now Elvis was in gaol. She had started to get frantic at night, waking in a sweat. Wondering if she ought to call the authorities to find Zac. But she had soothed herself and sure enough a letter had at last arrived. Hastily she had ripped it open and read it. That letter had filled Gwinnie's heart with pride. It had given her the strength and hope that they could, as a family, carry on.

Dear Mum,

You were right. The Universe is a clever, clever thing. I finally found a place where my life's work can be fully appreciated. Our life's work. I've got myself a job with the charity arm of a

*corporation working to help restore Port-au-Prince in Haiti after
the earthquake. No time for self-pity over loss of poster-boy looks
here, Mum! It's a troubled, poor and sometimes dangerous place,
and there's only about four per cent of forest left on the place as
the people need wood for fuel, but guess what I'm doing?*

Zac had left the rest of the page blank with a PTO at the base. In
block letters on the next page he'd written:

*I AM IN CHARGE OF INSTALLING HAITI'S HUMAN-
WASTE BIODIGESTERS!!!! POO POWER FOR THE
PEOPLE! How cool is that? I love you, Mum. You taught me
well. Love to Dad, Zac xx*

She was so glad he was doing well, but he hadn't mentioned Amos
in his letter. She prayed he would come home safe, soon, so her
family could heal its fractured feeling and they could be together
again. She knew the tropical look of his latest card belied the
truth about Haiti. Zac was working in the roughest slums, where
sometimes gunfights broke out and lasted for days. It was diseased
and dangerous. She wished him home, but at the same time, what
was here for him? He was following his calling where he was. He,
at least, was keeping their family dream alive in a meaningful
way. She felt sorrier for Amos, who'd made the sacrifice to stay.

Gwinnie looked out the northern window of the roadhouse
to the paddocks beside the highway. The long grasses and shrubs
looked pretty in the bright sunlight with their seed heads reaching
up to the blue. She had at first loved seeing the land come alive,
but now she felt displaced from Culvert, and as though she had
wasted much of her life here.

When they'd first seen the farm and roadhouse business next
to the sewage works, they knew it had all they needed. A farm and
a sewage plant! Elvis had been recently flush with cash from his
brother's buyout of Elvis's rights to the family farm and Gwinnie
had felt in her bones it was the right move. But some days now

she felt like packing up and leaving and not even telling her sons and her husband where she had gone. She knew she loved them too much to do it, but she did think about it. Gwinnie went back to the computer and looked down at the bills and sighed. Maybe they should think about a sea change and put the roadhouse on the market? But who would buy out here? Things were extra slow in Culvert. Drought had dried up the activity of the surrounding farmers and people were slowly but surely leaving town, or dying.

Gwinnie'd already been to three funerals in three weeks. First old Funky Baker, leaving a big hole in Waltz Me Around Again Darlin'; and next Dwaine had died from blood poisoning from an infected wound, so their only local abattoir had closed, meaning any home-use animals needing processing had to be trucked to Rington. Gwinnie had made herself go to his funeral, in honour of Tara, to make sure Dwaine Morton was put in the ground, never to return. On the day of his death, Gwinnie'd left a phone message with NP Co and sent a letter to Tara at Goldsborough station, but she'd never heard back from her. She had a sinking feeling Tara was lost to her and to Culvert for good. And why should the poor girl ever come back here?

After Dwaine's death, rumours were circulating that Elsie's mother had cancer and had shut herself away in the big old Grassmore house to die.

Then Chunky Nicholson's wife, Barb, had suddenly dropped dead in her kitchen when she was dipping lamingtons in chocolate for the fire-brigade fundraiser; she had a brain aneurism. Now the town was in uproar — there was no one to run the canteen come footy season, and they were short a CWA secretary, a teacher's aide at the school and a flower lady at the church since her passing. The funeral had been extra upsetting as no one could waste water on flower gardens, so the only decent flowers on show as they carried her coffin past was a bunch of agapanthus (now listed as a noxious weed with council) and some summer daisies. Some said they could've trucked some blooms in from somewhere distant over the mountains, but Chunky was never one for giving his wife flowers.

Gwinnie had offered to help supply and arrange some kind of vegetation, thinking there were plenty of native grasses and plants that would bunch up beautifully, but the townsfolk simply told her there was no need, then less than tactfully turned their backs and went about their business. Despite how kind and smiley she was, Gwinnie knew no one wanted to associate with a woman whose husband had been gaoled for stealing public shit. No wonder the boys held a current of anger within them towards their father, or at least the situation created by their father.

The once-a-month visits all the way to Sydney to see Elvis in gaol became costly and depressing for them all. A few times, Amos refused to visit his father, using care of the stock as an excuse. On those trips, Gwinnie had pushed her large service-station sunglasses up her nose and cried quietly, alone on the train.

She felt more tears on the rise now as she began to open what she thought would be a bill from Clarkson Rural Merchandise Store. Instead with surprise and delight she discovered a big fat cheque for the heavy lambs they had sold the previous month. It was enough to meet several of the larger bills. The flash of good fortune made her smile. As Tara used to say, it was a sign that maybe things would turn around.

Gwinnie sat up proudly. They were getting the property management more than right. While every other farm was blowing to dust, theirs and their lease country was holding on strong and they were even turning off stock that, given the conditions, could be considered 'finished' for the butchers. Even though the sheep were only sold in small numbers compared to the bigger farms, at least they weren't hand-feeding half-starved corpses with hard grains like the other farmers. She felt a surge of admiration for Elvis and Amos. With the cheque in her hand and the view of the oasis out the window her optimism returned. Today, Gwinnie Smith decided she would book herself in for a haircut at Culvert Snip and Clip and tomorrow she would start wearing her pretty dresses again. What was the point in longing for the coast or her youth, when life could feel OK in the moments of now? C'mon, Gwinnie, you can do this, she said to herself.

As she did, the phone rang.

'Good afternoon, Culvert roadhouse, Gwinnie speaking.'

'Is that the beautiful Gwinnie Smith?' came the voice of a woman down the line.

Gwinnie spun about and pressed the receiver closer to her ear. 'Yes?' she said slowly.

'I hoped I'd get you. I *knew* I'd get you. Hello, Gwinnie. It's Tara Green.'

A smile beamed on Gwinnie's face like the sun emerging from behind a cloud.

'Oh!' Gwinnie pressed her palm to her chest. 'I was only just thinking about you. Tara, it's so beautiful to hear from you!' Suddenly for Gwinnie the world felt brighter.

'Gwinnie,' Tara said, a cheeky smile in her voice, 'can you keep a secret?'

Forty-eight

When Elsie came to, she first saw the digital display of the clock and a glass of water by the bed with two tablets and a note. She remembered vaguely Jacinta being there, and some uptight lady doctor who'd injected her with something. She sat up and squinted at the note from Jacinta instructing her to take the tablets when she woke. Her head felt like someone had stuffed it full of ceiling insulation and her guts felt like she'd guzzled Jif cleaner. It was late afternoon and she could hear the traffic thickening in the Nashville street below. There was also the sound of someone humming in the bathroom. Elsie unfolded her long legs and tugged her T-shirt down over her knickers, padding to the bathroom.

'Hello?' she called gingerly. She cringed, wondering if she had picked some bloke up again.

From around the bathroom door a middle-aged woman with flame-red dyed hair and curves bursting out of a white maid's uniform appeared with a mop and a bucket in hand.

'Oh, sorry, sorry,' she giggled in a high-pitched Hispanic accent. 'Did not know you there. Did not see in bed. Job new. I new job.'

Elsie frowned and rubbed her forehead. Could this day get any shittier? 'Would you mind coming back another time?'

The maid looked at her, eyes scrutinising. Narrowing. Then recognition dawned on her. She started flapping her hand holding a cleaning cloth and pointed at Elsie.

'Ah, you! *You!* You singer!' she called out loudly and excitedly.

'Yes,' said Elsie vacantly. She was about to turn her back and go lie down again, but the maid kept speaking.

'You make sex with that man! Big man! Tall!' She waved her hands in the air for extra effect. 'Hat. What his name? *Colorando?*'

Elsie pulled a face as if there was a bad smell in the room.

'He have lovely wife. Beautiful. And children.'

Elsie's mouth dropped open.

It had been years ago now, right before her career had skyrocketed, but still the scandal with Colorado was the only thing people focused on. Not her music. Not her talent. Not her hit songs.

There had been weeks of tacky entertainment channels devoting hours a day to their 'sex tape'. They had been caught backstage one night by someone with a camera having hasty sex on an amp behind a thick black stage curtain. It had been a stupid thing to do, but at the time, Elsie had thought she was in love. A YouTube frenzy followed, clocking up hits in the millions. The footage was grainy and shadowy, but there was no mistaking it was them.

Images of the 'lovers' were beamed into people's catalogue-furnished lounge rooms on huge flatscreen TVs. Shopping centres blared the news across entire walls. Big-haired, white-toothed journalists interviewed each other, speculating, accusing, gossiping, gossiping, gossiping. Ugly talk from beautiful people. Over and over they played footage of Elsie behind large dark glasses as she was caught 'leaving Colorado's hotel'. Behind her Colorado's outstretched hand did nothing to block the intrusion of the cameras and the crush.

For weeks after their first concert without Charity, everywhere they went, they were followed by greedy people with a hunger to spread gossip. The professionals' telephoto lenses were trained on their windows; television cameras whirled overhead in choppers. File photos of the three Buck children looking their cutest and Charity looking her worst were added to the mix. The story to start with was all about the 'cheating dirty old man' and 'that husband-stealing trollop EJ'.

Elsie remembered the storm of assistants and agents and executives confronting them in Jacinta's plush offices the day the story broke. 'You're both in serious breach of contract,' Jacinta growled at them. The hyena within licked its bloodied lips and gave a toothy grin. To her, in truth, this media storm was a boon. It was a sure-fire way to put Colorado in the place she wanted him, move the painful Charity aside, and put EJ right there where Jacinta wanted her — a frontrunner: a household name. Jacinta knew that with the right strategy EJ would come out of this looking squeaky clean. What young woman so far from home wouldn't fall for the older mentoring man? She had the media release compiled in her head already. Fans would turn on Colorado, but forgive him eventually. And Charity, now the drug secret was out, would bear the brunt. The mother-police would crucify her. EJ, Jacinta saw, was sitting in the box seat. Not that she'd let her know that now.

What Jacinta hadn't been telling them was that Elsie's newly released single 'The Skin She's Livin' In' had been downloaded across the globe a record eight billion times in an astonishing three weeks, and that wasn't counting full album sales, which had climbed to over the two million mark. Here was pure youth and beauty singing about a core facet of wisdom, and there before them stood Charity, who clearly couldn't bear the aged skin she was living in. Jacinta couldn't have scripted it better herself.

As the leather couch squelched under her jeans, Elsie had reached for Colorado's hand.

'I don't care if my career is gone, Jacinta. We are not just friends. Can't you see?'

'Can't *you* see this is bigger than just you?' Jacinta asked. 'You go, an entire crew goes. No jobs, no gigs, no money for their families. You got hundreds of people relying on you.'

Elsie wove her fingers into Colorado's. Now, above all, she needed him. For days he'd sheltered Elsie from the papers. They had spent their time tangled in hotel sheets, exploring the world of their new lover's body. For a time it was easy to forget the kids, the chaos of Charity's addiction, the constant calls from Jacinta. They had more concerts scheduled, but Jacinta had cancelled them, fearing a riot.

Elsie couldn't stop her eyes dragging back to the image of her own face printed in a magazine. Perfectly pretty, but the editors, having got the story of her mole from Nathanial Rogerson's Facebook, had airbrushed a giant one onto her face. As she looked at the photos, Elsie dragged her hair down the side of her face with her fingers and buried her head into Colorado's shoulder.

'Will you quit that! We're not in primary school now!' Jacinta yelled at her.

Even Colorado moved so that Elsie would have to sit up and let go of his hand. 'Babe,' he said in a husky voice, 'we really got to sort this.' He spoke to her as if he was addressing one of his children.

'Fuck off!' Elsie said, standing abruptly. Jacinta looked around the room at her stunned staff, then back to Elsie.

'Would you mind?' Jacinta asked Colorado. 'I'd like a word alone with her, if I may.'

Colorado shrugged. He stood up, tall in his Cuban heels. 'Sure,' he said. He didn't even look at Elsie as he sauntered out of the room.

Elsie felt as if she was back in her childhood, about to be berated by her mother, with her father gone to the barren paddocks or absent at the council offices.

'You lot too,' Jacinta said. The other marketing people seemed to sigh a little, then filed out of the office.

Jacinta leaned her tiny backside on her expansive desk, crossed her ankles and folded her arms. 'You know, dear girl, I'm on your side.'

Elsie breathed long out of her mouth. 'You sure about that?'

'Someone's gotta be. Cos you and I know he's goin' back to his wife.'

'Really? How do you know?'

'Because they all do, sweetheart. They all do.'

Elsie had swallowed hard. She nodded, bit her lip and the tears began to fall.

Now, as she saw her reflection caught in the bright lights of the hotel bathroom, behind the maid, Elsie felt like crying all over again. Couldn't people just leave her alone? Maybe if she explained to this woman what it was like, then she would in turn be kind. Elsie turned on her winning celeb smile. 'I used to do a bit of cleaning once,' she said. 'With a friend of mine.'

The maid jutted her chin out. 'You? Cleaner? No. I don't think so.' She set down her mop and bucket. 'You home-wrecker slut. I come back. Finish room later.'

The plush hotel door clicked shut and Elsie was left alone. There before her in the bathroom sat the mop and the bucket.

'It's a sign,' she whispered. 'It's a sign.'

Forty-nine

Tara's new silver Jeep was crammed full of her favourite possessions. The window was wound down, the wind in her hair. Behind her sat her stone Buddha, her Japanese blossom-print quilt, her maidenhair fern plant named 'Nana' and her fluffy green bathrobe. On the front seat was a box of her most precious books, Wayne Dyer sitting on top of the pile as if he too, in hardback form, was looking out to the ever-flattening plains of the west. She sang along to Elsie's latest album, thinking over the whirlwind of change sparked the day she saw Elsie on television. Once the epiphany shattered the opaque wall in her mind, there was no holding her back. She revved along the road eager to create new energy and new memories in Culvert. She turned and grinned at her Wayne Dyer book.

'Excuses begone!' she said.

Three months earlier, when she'd searched Culvert real estate on the internet, she'd been overjoyed to find Mr Queen's Dolls' House for sale. Her dream home. And the old abattoir house. Her nightmare home. While scrolling through the listings, she also saw Grassmore Estate flash up. Images of Elsie and her in the lounge room with Elsie's guitar and her mop came to her. Her past was suddenly in the here and now.

She had scanned the pictures of Grassmore. The photographer had tried to capture the appeal of the large farm homestead, complete with ballroom, but the years of rural decline and drought made the house and farmland look not just tired but abandoned and sad. Hopeless even. Tara knew the energetics of the place were also a reflection of the slow rusting of the Joneses' marriage and lives. Tara wondered what had become of Elsie's brother and parents and why they were selling up. Grassmore had been listed for three years and the price reduced several times.

As she sat in front of the computer, Tara had shut her eyes, breathed in three times and asked her angels if she in fact should relocate her business to the big rambling farm and homestead instead of Mr Queen's house. She could easily stretch her finances that far, but did she want all that farmland to start with? It was in a bad way and she knew it needed to be rejuvenated as the Smiths had encouraged their land to life, but something blocked her. It had been Elsie's dream to farm that way back when they were teenagers. Not hers.

She had looked away from her computer screen. Beside her on the desk was a photo of a dolls' house in a toy catalogue that had slipped out of the newspaper. Next to that was a twenty-cent coin, the silver image of the Queen right in front of her.

'OK,' Tara said with a smile drifting to her face. She was now sure that Grassmore's future lay elsewhere, and that Mr Queen's Dolls' House was the home for her.

One phone call to her lawyer, who contacted Rington Real Estate on her behalf, saw her snap it up for one hundred and twenty-seven thousand dollars; and for another thirty thousand dollars she had also bought back the abattoir house and block from Dwaine's family. Tara had some wrongs to right.

Within a matter of weeks of buying the places she had gathered her favourite crew of Sydney builders and shipped them out to Culvert, headed by her wonderful tradesman, Gizbo. She'd put him and his builder boys up in the Culvert Pub, all expenses paid, including beer, and sworn them to silence about her identity. The builders loved both working hard for Tara and stringing the locals on, putting them off the scent of their favourite employer.

'Steve Irwin's missus is planning on a wildlife refuge for stick insects,' said one of Tara's builders to a Nicholson boy.

'Olivia Newton-John's havin' it off with Russell Crowe and they want a love nest in an anonymous place,' said another to a perplexed local. 'Culvert's perfect for 'em.'

'Richard Branson's setting up the equivalent of a Playboy Mansion, only filling it with untouchable virgins instead of slutty bunnies. Kinda like an art gallery, where you can look but you can't touch. Sick I'd say. More money than sense,' said another to a waitress.

'It's Nicole and Keith,' said the plasterer. 'They want to breed Alpacas and run an Alpaca riding school for kids. Lady Gaga's wardrobe artist is designing the saddles.'

The publican had listened in to their ever-more-outlandish tales, grinning as he wiped up the bar and polished glasses, happy with the influx of lively, funny tradesmen. Suddenly because of this mystery real-estate purchaser, not only were his empty hotel rooms full, but more and more locals were stopping in for a meal or a drink to hear further rumours from the friendly boys who ate their evening counter meals in overalls splattered with the classy colours the new owner had selected.

Gizbo would report back to Tara on his mobile each night from the privacy of his room. He loved working with her. She was funny and clever. Never condescending as so many rich bitches could be, and so practised at planning and guiding him, even from photographs. She made his job easy and the house was, according to him, 'coming up a treat'.

'The woman from Rington Real Estate called round this arvo,' Gizbo had said. 'She was kicking herself she hadn't asked for more money for the joint. She reckons with the drought, falling grain prices and the youngsters leaving and the oldsters dying that commissions for Culvert and now even Rington real estate are at an all-time low. Won't be long, she said, until she shuts up shop too.'

Tara thought of the nosy agent, who had badgered her Sydney-based solicitor for details on his anonymous buyer. She felt sorry for her, and really for all of Culvert and the surrounding region. It was time to shake them up out of their own apathy.

'Now about this abattoir house,' Gizbo had said, 'what's your plan there?'

Tara knew exactly what to do. Seeing the house online after all those years had been confronting. The photographs showed blank window eyes and boards dropping unevenly down into long unmown grasses. The front door was boarded shut, as if the darkness inside should never be released again into the world. The killing shed was slowly being engulfed by Mother Nature as she pushed seedlings through the thick film of cement, cracking the concrete monstrosity to rubble over time.

After hanging up from Gizbo, an email whizzing through cyberspace soon gathered a demolition crew. They had joined the builder team at the pub and by the end of the week had begun to knock down every brick, chisel up every bit of concrete and tear off every board so that soon the house, the killing shed, the yards were all gone. It was a bare, blank patch on the earth. When the last truck rolled out towards Culvert tip, Tara's landscaping crew arrived. Sylvia's nursery was never busier as the landscapers ordered in topsoil, plants, advanced trees, potting mix and poly pipe. No one knew what was being created there, but Sylvia was making money for the first time in years.

Like the rest of the crew, the landscapers, who owed a great deal to Tara for their recent business success, were keeping their cards close to their chest.

'It's Jamie Durie,' said one of the customers. 'He must be moving to Culvert.'

'Or Jamie Oliver?' suggested another.

The landscape crew always simply smiled and said, 'Maybe.'

Her team of people were, as Tara described them, 'pure place people' and they would not be swayed from their mission to help her build her dream in Culvert.

Tara knew the sale of the properties and the activities would be sparking a tsunami of questions in Culvert so, at night, as she lay in her blissful bed in her Sydney house for the last few weeks, she closed her eyes and blessed the town. She conjured up the image of the Dolls' House and talked a little to Mr Queen's hovering soul in the thin silver film between the here and now and the passed souls of the planet. She promised him that when she got there, she would adopt back his precious cats who had been sent to the Rington Cattery along with a breathtakingly large donation after his death. Then she visualised herself hovering in the empty rooms as teams of angels cleansed and healed the space.

This night-drifting sustained her; it was something she'd done all her life. It was unconventional, but it was how she had survived her childhood. She imagined the bare block that had once been the site of her childhood home. She sent it love and healing. She sent her little child self love too. Then Tara would roll over, thanking the Archangel Michael for giving her new energy and the courage to do this. Then she would hug herself, knowing she was safe, but lonely. One day, still, she longed to be held. Held by a kind man who cared.

Amos came again and again to her mind, and she usually pushed him away, but now as she at last passed the fifty-K speed limit sign of Culvert, she felt a buzz of excitement. She would visit the Smith house that night because she was coming *home*. Home without fear. Without limits. She was utterly changed and ready to prove herself to herself. A big smile spread across her face.

From the southern end of town, Tara could see she may have changed, but Culvert had not, unless to grow tattier and closer to death than she had imagined. The signs advertising Sylvia's Silverspoon Café and the Smiths' roadhouse were faded, and the Golf Club billboard had a giant hole in it — like someone had driven golf balls at it. The paddocks that spread to the west were almost grey, so deathly low was their energy. She drove further into town, turning past the old school, finally pulling up outside the lovely leafy trees that spread their arms in welcome over the high fence around her new house.

She got out of the Jeep, stretched and walked through the wrought-iron front gate shining with a glossy new coat of emerald-green paint. She stood on the path and looked up.

The Dolls' House was everything Tara imagined it to be and more. She practically skipped like a child along the path and up the wide steps. Her key slid in the lock as if it was drawn by magnets. It turned as easily as the tide. The door swung open silently. She stood in wonder.

The stained-glass window above the door spread rainbows over new carpet in a wide airy hallway. To the right a broad staircase with a gentle gradient led her gaze upstairs to the light from big windows on a landing. She climbed the stairs, feeling Mr Queen at her side, happily escorting her up. In the largest room facing east the big windows were shielded by summery giant leafy old elms. The trees took her eye to views beyond the ordinary Culvert rooftops next door and out to the plains. Dry and overgrazed as it was, Tara saw beauty in the vastness. She sighed with relief. This was what she was missing. Space. Solitude. The country. Culvert reborn.

She was about to head downstairs to inspect the kitchen, which she knew opened onto a large north-facing deck, and the lounge room and its fireplace, when she heard a knock on the door. Tara frowned. Maybe it would be the real-estate agent come to welcome her? But how would *she* know she was here? Tara instructed herself not to be annoyed by this intrusion and instead to feel gratitude someone was dropping by. She trod down the carpeted stairs, her hand drifting on the polished banisters. The hairs on her skin stood up. That would be Mr Queen again. His happiness at her arrival must be flooding the house and her system. He must be glad someone had come to love his house to life and fill it with goodwill and love, plus soon his dear old cats.

Behind the door's stained-glass window stood the large form of a man. It must be one of the builders, perhaps Gizbo, come to welcome her and finalise anything that needed doing. She swung the door open, a big smile on her pretty face. Then she froze.

'Amos?'

He stood before her, tall, broad, grown utterly into manhood. His big square hands held a bunch of flowers, freshly picked from Gwinnie's garden. Tara recognised the blooms instantly.

'Welcome home, Tars,' he said with a grin.

Goosebumps prickled Tara's skin. She felt tears rise in her eyes, then she began to laugh. She raised a hand to her mouth and saw it was shaking. Her heart drummed loudly in her chest. 'Amos! How did you know I'd be here? Did Gwinnie tell you?'

He grinned even more, enticing dimples to his cheeks. 'Mum? No. How would she know?'

Tara gave an innocent shrug of her shoulders.

'Hey, you're not the only one with psychic powers round here,' he said as he stepped forwards and gave her a kiss on the cheek. 'Once the abattoir house was bulldozed, I knew. I just knew it. I also asked Gizbo when he came to get fuel for the drive back to Sydney. He gave nothing away, but I could tell from his expression my questions were on the right track.'

'I thought you had a no-gossip policy at the servo?'

Amos chuckled. 'You got me on that one. Time for a cuppa?'

'Got nothin' to do …' Tara began.

'And all day to do it.' Amos laughed outright.

A cloud of memory crossed the room as simultaneously they pictured that day at the Goldsborough billabong — and Elsie. They looked searchingly at each other, then Tara stepped aside and gestured to the kitchen. 'You can have a cuppa, if I can find a kettle and some tea.'

Amos fished around in his back pocket and handed her a cellophane package. 'Mum's homemade lemon and ginger. She said to say hi and dinner's at our place if you want.'

She looked at him incredulously. 'You sneaky peeps.'

'You were coming around to visit me anyway, weren't you?' Amos teased.

Tara took the flowers and the tea from Amos, smiling up at him, drinking in his perfection. The way his black hair flopped over his forehead. His kind dark eyes. The honest man's hands that still had oil in their fingerprints, even though Tara knew he would've spent a long time scrubbing them clean. Just for her.

'Wow,' Amos said, looking around the beautiful hallway singing with golden afternoon light before he moved towards the kitchen. 'This house is just how I imagined it. Only more beautiful. Mr Queen must've loved it here. No wonder he barely left it. It's so beautiful compared to the rest of Culvert.'

Tara smiled with gratitude. Amos wasn't making this some grand romantic reunion like she'd dreaded and dreamed about for years. He wasn't even commenting on how much weight she'd lost or how changed she was, like most people would around Culvert when they saw her. Instead he had simply stepped right into the moment of now and was here with her.

Tara beamed up at him. It was just how it ought to be.

'Now, speaking of Culvert and beautiful,' she began, 'I have a cunning plan you might be interested in ...'

Fifty

It was a sunny spring evening at the Culvert Council offices and in exactly one hour and eight minutes the staff were due to go home. The days were shortening and the sun was tipping lower in the sky, casting beautiful light on the ugly brickwork of the building. Many of the staff were thinking of what they might have for dinner, or watch on midweek television that night, but not Councillor-Mayor Kelvin Jones. He was watching his secretary-receptionist, Christine Sheen, who was bending to empty her wastepaper basket, in a skirt so short it almost showed her Bear Grylls. This simple sight was making Kelvin's heart race.

Suddenly Councillor-Mayor Jones's eyelids fluttered, he clutched his chest, and he keeled over, dead, right there and then on the new purple-and-yellow carpet, which had taken the council seven meetings to choose. In his podgy hand was the resubmission of the sewage-plant funding proposal and, as he fell, the paper scattered into disarray like runaway dreams.

Fellow councillor Tammie Donningham, coming out of her office, had the presence of mind to call the ambulance and police, while Christine stood there screaming, looking down at the giant body of her boss, his bodily fluids leaking out of him. On hearing the screaming, Deputy Mayor Cuthbertson Rogerson came out of his office, assessed the situation and scuttled off home around the block to find his wife, Zelda, who was a nurse. It would be quicker than waiting for the Nicholson boy, who was the Rington paramedic, or Dr Patak, who now moved almost as slowly as a corpse himself.

When Tammie had put down the phone to the ambulance service, she slapped Christine on the face to shut her up, then, with gritted teeth, rolled her sleeves and quelling her nausea, kneeled to begin CPR on what felt like a blue whale.

In a matter of minutes around the block, Constable Gilbert's pager was beeping urgently from trousers that lay on the floor of Deputy Mayor Rogerson's bedroom. Constable Gilbert frowned, trying to block out the incessant beeping as he rogered into Zelda Rogerson on the Deputy Mayor's king-sized waterbed. Zelda, on her back, grabbed the constable's buttocks harder. It took less than thirty seconds for Constable Gilbert to blow his load, roll off, slap Zelda on her sizeable rump and drag his undies back on.

'Police business, darlin',' he said. 'Gotta go.' Outside, his squad-car radio was alive with questions as to his whereabouts. The Rington radio room was demanding he get to the council offices toot-sweet. But he'd only got as far as the en suite when, half-mast-trousered, Constable Gilbert came face-to-face with the Deputy Mayor. Zelda drew up the sheets around her pink body and cried out in shock.

Following this chain of events, it took less than fifteen minutes for the news of Elsie's father's death to arrive to the outskirts of town where Tara was sitting at an outdoor table in the backyard of the Smiths' garden, enjoying the starters of what would be a wonderful meal with Gwinnie, Amos and Elvis. But there, before the news of the mayor's death made it to them, they were about to get another shock.

Normally the western-plains bus from Sydney, which for reasons lost in the mists of time included Culvert on its itinerary, stopped in the next town, as no one ever seemed to want to get off in Culvert, but tonight it pulled up. The Smiths and Tara heard the gush of air brakes and the rumble of the idling engine. They looked at each other, perplexed.

Next, around the side of the house came Zac, his backpack looped over one shoulder, his clothes crushed like Indiana Jones's, plaited cotton bands on one wrist, his hair, his everything looking dishevelled but still gloriously handsome, despite his scarred face.

Gwinnie cried out and cried; Elvis too. Amos beamed. Tara nodded, knowing it was all about to unfold as it should.

'Brother! Father! Mother! Friend!' he called out. Dropping his pack, Zac opened up his arms and enfolded them in a giant group hug.

'*My God!*' Gwinnie said, drawing back and cupping his face in both hands. 'Such a surprise! Why didn't you let us know?'

'Someone did know.' Zac grinned as he looked at his brother. 'Someone paid for my ticket.'

He slung his arm around Amos and deep laughter escaped both of them.

Then Zac's eyes travelled back to Tara. He lifted her up and twirled her around. She laughed, looking down at him.

'Hello, Tars!'

'You smell like goats, old shoes and saffron rice!' she said. 'Good adventures? I was just hearing about you in Haiti.'

He set her down. 'Well, I ain't in Haiti now.'

Then they all stood about, joy flooding them, all feeling the stars align once more over Culvert for them.

Before they could talk more, the bell of the service station chimed as a car pulled in. Amos excused himself, casting a gentle smile at Tara as he left and giving his brother a happy shove.

Gwinnie and Elvis stood, glowing, beaming, smiling at the sight of their son. He was here. After seven years, home!

Zac nodded at the barbecue meat that was set under a cloth. 'Got enough for me? I'm starving!'

'Yes!' Gwinnie said, snapping awake. 'Of course! I'll get the rest.' She hugged him again, then practically danced away, calling over her shoulder, 'Elvis, give me a hand in the kitchen, love. The boy needs feeding up.'

After another hug from Elvis, Zac plonked himself down under the blissful shade of a wisteria bursting with new green leaves, helped himself to the big jug of water and looked at Tara. 'It's so good to see you,' he said.

'You too!' She nodded at his face and touched her own. 'Is that it? It's not as bad as I imagined.'

Zac laughed mildly, holding out his hand and indicating the smooth red welt that ran along the back of it and up over his arm. The skin was white, taut and hairless compared to his other tanned arm. Then he touched his face. 'It's no big deal. Can only grow half a beard so I look like a half-skinned rabbit if I don't shave for a few days.'

Tara smiled. 'Does it hurt?'

'It used to. Then only my ego hurt. Haiti changed all that. The poverty there, Tara.' His eyes clouded with memories.

'Put it in perspective, did it?'

He nodded and looked down at Gwinnie's brightly patterned cloth table napkins. He shrugged one broad shoulder. 'I'm a lucky guy. Working for the Cleanagain biomethane company has restored my faith in humanity's future. And you, Tars? You look wonderful.'

'The external is merely a reflection of the internal,' Tara said. 'Most of me is healed. It only took me every day of my life to do it. And I still have to work on it every day. And even then I still have the scars on the inside. Sometimes, often in fact, at night when I'm on my own, which is all the time, they rip and tear a little.'

She said her words with a touch of flint. Zac's eyes narrowed in pity as he frowned.

'Dwaine?'

Tara nodded. A fly buzzed by.

'We were never sure. Should we have done more for you?' Zac asked quietly.

Tara dismissed his notion, shaking her head. 'What used to happen in that house isn't important any more ... it's past. It's up to me to not be a victim. It's up to me to heal myself. No one else. And I'm getting there. Still a loner, though.'

Zac grimaced. 'That's no good. You're a champion, Tara, and you don't deserve to be alone. You deserve a good bloke. And I think I know of one.' He indicated his head in the direction Amos had gone.

Tara shot him a glance. 'That's the past too.'

'Yes, it is. Maybe it's up to both of us to fully forgive some other people too so it can become the present and even the future in your case?' he suggested.

Tara looked at him enquiringly. 'You mean Amos and Elsie?'

Zac nodded. 'Did she ever tell you what really happened between them?' he asked.

'What do you mean? I saw. They were together. You couldn't get much more together.'

'Ah!' Zac said, lifting a finger. 'But they weren't. Amos stopped himself at the last minute. Told her he cared about you too much.'

Tara paused to absorb the news. She felt winded, like a punch to the stomach. To find out, after all these years, there had been no betrayal was a shock. 'Are you sure? You believe him?'

'He's my twin. I believe him. When he called me in Haiti and told me, I knew it was the truth.'

'Why didn't he tell you before? Why didn't he tell me?'

Zac shrugged. 'Said he'd hurt you too much and he'd been so mad with me for being surly and bailing out on him when Dad went to gaol that he'd withheld that part of the story from me.'

'And Elsie?'

'She agreed with him to stop. She said she was in love with me and cared too much about you. Fancy that! All this time we just thought they were selfish bastards.' He looked at her with a twinkle in his eye, but Tara was lost in thought. A door in her universal world had reopened.

'Elsie said that? Amos said that?'

'Yup.' He spread his palms on the table.

'You don't want to go find Elsie?'

'Nope. That part is history. History splattered all over the papers and the net for the poor girl! I had to go to a third-world country to escape reading about her love life. Imagine what it must be like for her.'

'Have you heard from her?'

He looked at Tara as if she was insane. 'No, man. As if. I mean God. She's a huge star. She's probably dating Johnny Depp by now.'

'She's probably miserable. You should get in touch.'

'Seriously? How would I get in touch? Facebook-stalk her management? No way!'

'Yes way.'

Zac flicked his handsome brown eyes at Tara. 'I got too much to do in life to be worrying about girlfriends, particularly old ones from years ago who are now famous and would have no interest in me. Plus I've got work to do. Me and the oldest born-again virgin in Culvert are teaming up again. It's time to get our dreams cranking again.'

'Awesome. You got room for one more old born-again virgin on your crew?' She laughed.

'Sure do! But for godsakes, Tara, you get back with my brother. This has gone on *waaay* too long.'

Tara's cheeks flushed with self-consiousness just as Gwinnie and Elvis arrived back with platters and bowls of enough food to feed a small village.

Fifty-one

Out at the bowser, Miss Beechcroft got out of her Beetle wanting fuel, but also busting to tell *someone* the gossip.

'I was at the IGA,' she said breathlessly to Amos, who was kindly checking the oil under the curved bonnet while the pump thrummed. It was hard to focus on her monologue. He was still on a high from not only having Tara back, but also Zac. Still, Miss Beechcroft kept on.

'I was standing at the checkout next to Chunky Nicholson's fourth son, who was buying a Powerade at the time, not that he needed a Powerade, because no one has seen him run since he quit on his dad's footy team in the under sixteens, and boy has he got *big*. I'm surprised the paramedics supply overalls that size. But anyway, his pager went off and he raced out to the ambulance, which is normally in Rington but just happened to be here as he was seeing how Chunky was getting on after Barb's death. Anyway, the doors of the IGA got stuck open again. You know how they do. Which is not good given that the breeze meant the smell of the ponds was all over town. Anyway, the doors stuck so that everyone could hear the radio from the ambulance blaring out that Councillor-Mayor Jones had just died. Just like that. Just then.' Miss Beechcroft barely drew breath as she blurted this all out to Amos, who now stood holding the pump as the fuel ticked over on the dial.

Kelvin Jones died? He absorbed the news, wondering how it would reach Elsie, who was somewhere in her rockstar princess tower on the other side of the world.

'And,' she continued, 'all this was happening after the girls at the IGA were telling me some hot young redhead had moved into Mr Queen's old house. A businesswoman from Sydney. What sort of business she's hoping to do here is anyone's guess.'

'Everything else OK?' Amos asked almost too cheerfully, given that he'd just been told of someone's death.

'Huh?'

He nodded towards the bonnet of the VW. 'Rest of the car running right?'

Miss Beechcroft scowled, irritated. She had forgotten how socially inept those Smith twins were. They never gossiped. Amos had once said to her, 'We pride ourselves on being a gossip-free service station. Loose lips sink ships, Miss Beechcroft.' He'd said it after she'd tried to drag him into a conversation about a certain checkout girl who had a 'thing' for him and kept putting ten dollars' worth of fuel in her car each time, hoping she would get Amos at the bowser, and all of town knew. Suddenly Miss Beechcroft realised the other brother, the one with the scar, had been the one tangled up with the now-deceased mayor's daughter all those years back. And the mayor had been so vindictive after the explosion too. She'd picked the wrong person to tell. Miss Beechcroft reached for her purse and paid Amos for the fuel.

Amos grimaced as he took the money to the till. Culvert people sure were weird. Dead and alive, he thought. Councillor-Mayor Jones had been horrible to Amos's family, but still he found a moment to send up a silent farewell to the man who must've struggled so much to like himself, and took that out on other people. Elsie would now have to face not only that her father was gone, but that Sarah Jones was on death's door too. Could it mean Elsie coming home? A big star like her? After all this time? To *Culvert*?

Amos went out the back. He slumped down at the table with Tara and his reunited family.

'Councillor-Mayor Jones fell off his perch,' Amos said. 'Just then. Miss Beechcroft said that she was at the IGA ... Anyway, she said he's died.'

Gwinnie set down the potato salad. 'At the IGA?'

Amos shook his head. 'No. At the council offices.'

'Oh, that's awful news.'

The Smith family looked at each other. Memories of the man came to them. The way he'd rolled in so many times to hound them.

'Heart attack?' Zac asked.

Amos pulled a 'don't know' face.

'More than likely,' Elvis said, 'given his physical, er, situation.'

'Poor Sarah, and Simon and Elsie,' Gwinnie said.

'Do you reckon?' Tara asked plainly. 'I reckon he's been driving them nuts for years, except for Elsie, who had the sense to stay as far away as possible. It might be a bit of relief for them. And besides, anyone who lets himself get that huge in life is clearly asking to leave the planet prematurely so he can float about weightlessly in the non-physical realm. Trust me, I know! I've been there! He'll be much nicer now he's just an energy.'

A slow smile spread over Elvis's face. 'You sure know how to pack a punch, Tara.'

'Well? I'm not saying there won't be pain for his poor family, and I'm not trying to say anything negative about that man either, but really, honestly, I think we'd all agree he's in a better place now.'

'Amen to that,' Zac said as he got up and went to the barbecue, taking the dish of meat from Elvis. In the void of silence all of them turned their thoughts to Elsie. Where was she? How would she take the news?

All Zac could wonder was, will she come home?

'So,' Tara said eventually, passing the plates out, 'looks like there might be room for me on council now.'

They all looked at her, surprised. 'You?' they chorused.

'Whyever not?' she responded brightly. 'I've got some big, big plans, and to be on council will only help them along further. Positive projects. Make-a-difference-to-the-town-and-*the-world* kind of projects.'

She looked to each one of them and narrowed her eyes, her pretty lips held in a wry grin. 'How are you going with your fuel experiments these days, by the way? Any progress?' She paused as the Smith family's minds ticked over.

Amos stooped to light the barbecue from a cylinder. It wasn't the usual regimented shape of gas bottles held in cages at service stations.

'Oh, those old ex-poo-riments?' Amos said with faux-vagueness as he tapped the side of the bottle with his index finger. He then theatrically swept his gaze to more gas bottles on the side of the house and pipes that disappeared under the lawn in the direction where Tara knew the roadhouse septic system lay. She noticed a new shed there with a solar panel on it.

'Funny you should mention those old experiments,' he said with a broad grin.

She was back to the family she knew were her tribe: Gwinnie in a pinny with her hair bunched up on top of her head, smiling with love at her; Zac looking at her with a new kind of openness, his barbecue tongs at the ready; Elvis beaming at her as if his daughter had at last come home; and then Amos, who had lit the barbecue and was now coming towards her to top up her drink, smiling at the answer to all their prayers. Amos, the boy who had held strong for her.

Tara reached for a newspaper clipping in her bag. She spread the article from *The Land* newspaper onto the table. 'I have some people who are keen to talk to you about partnership and improving their invention.'

The Smiths clustered around, taking in the pictures of the tractor that looked like it was wearing a silver radiator on its roof, with air-hose tubing that ran down the back. They began reading about the men who had designed a system that returned tractor exhaust to the soil.

Gwinnie read a section of the article aloud. 'People think of exhaust fumes as toxic, and while they are to humans, they aren't to plants. If you think about it, oil is really just composted organic matter.' She looked excitedly at Tara. 'But why use oil from ancient plants, when you can ...'

'Use human methane!' they all chorused.

'This system, plus ours, is the answer!' said Elvis.

'Yes!' Amos was beaming. 'If we can merge their technology with ours, we will have even more punch with our earth-friendly farming and another chance!'

'The inventors are just waiting for your call,' Tara said.

Elvis cast his head to the sky as if giving thanks, a grin from ear to ear.

'Now you'll have council on side, you'd better get that shed cranking again,' Tara said to him.

'Thank you, Tara,' Elvis said as if he could breathe properly for the first time in years.

'Now we're cooking with gas,' Tara said, laughing. She paused again and looked from the bottles to the meat on the barbecue. 'Does that mean tonight's meal will be cooked with pure natural methane gas produced courtesy of the Smith family and their passing trade?'

'Yup,' said Zac, snapping the tongs and holding up a sausage.

'Food cooked from our family's very own septic,' Amos added proudly.

'Just don't tell anyone on council, when you're on council,' Elvis said.

'At least I have a bottom to sit on council. Not like the last poor bugger.' Tara grinned. And the family all fell about laughing. As they did, Tara thought how incredibly funny it was to be eating a barbecue using gas created by the very same family serving up the dinner. The perfect cycle. The poo-fect cycle, she corrected herself in her head. It sure was good to be home in Culvert and now she at last knew she and the Smiths were about to become 'fart-most'.

'And for dessert,' Gwinnie proudly announced, 'we're cooking crepes!'

Yes, Tara thought again, she had come home to her tribe.

Fifty-two

The first thing Tara noticed when she stepped into the Grassmore homestead was how much the house was weighted down with the energy of depression and death. Tara shook the feeling off her and visualised protective energies about her.

Zelda Rogerson, the community nurse, was walking ahead of Tara down the hallway. Zelda'd taken up residence to care for the bedridden, cancer-riddled Sarah Jones, but all the locals knew the real reason she was there. It was because her husband, Cuthbertson, had kicked her out of their house following his discovery of Constable Gilbert in his marital bed the previous week. He had resigned as Deputy Mayor, now had the house on the market and was moving to Rington. Nathanial had moved in with the hairdresser from Snip and Clip, twenty years his senior, and was refusing to speak to Zelda.

Tara knew Zelda was now puzzling as to who she was, when she had stood brightly at Grassmore's front door, asking for Mrs Jones. Maybe Zelda suspected she was another of the banker professionals coming for an assessment of the farm estate? Zelda cleared her throat and showed Tara the door into what had been the dining room she and Elsie had cleaned years before. The stairs must've been too much for the frail Mrs Jones, as the room had been converted into a bedroom. A morphine drip stood beside the bed, its stainless-steel stand out of place against the faded plush curtains and antique sideboard. Tara, who was not afraid of death as she didn't believe in it from a spiritual standpoint, stepped inside and said cheerfully, 'Hello, Mrs Jones.'

Physically Sarah was unrecognisable, but Tara saw she was unchanged within. The woman's mindset of anger, bitterness, tension, jealousy and resistance to anything remotely spiritual had manifested into a body starved of life-force. Mrs Jones looked up with the eyes of someone haunted. 'Do I know you?'

'No,' said Tara truthfully — Mrs Jones would never take the time to truly *know* her. 'But I have met you before a few times.'

The woman frowned. She was not yet sixty and here she was a recent widow and a shell of a human. Cancer was eating her away.

Tara felt a wave of compassion. 'I'm Tara Green.'

Sarah tipped her head to one side, her face blank.

'From the abattoir house,' Tara added.

Sarah Jones's eyes widened and her dry mouth with the crusted lips gasped and rasped like Darth Vader. 'No!'

She couldn't match the well-dressed, beautiful, curvaceous healthy woman before her with her memories.

'Yes.' Tara fell short of doing a twirl for her.

'What are you doing here?'

The question had a barb. Sarah Jones thought Tara had come to gloat.

'I came to say how sorry I was that your husband passed over, and see if I could help you,' Tara said.

'Help me?' Sarah shifted uncomfortably. All her life she'd spent worrying about the size of her backside. Exercising it, wearing underpants that reduced it, gazing at it in the mirror, not liking it. Now all she wished for was more padding. She was on her bones and pressure sores were oozing into the incontinence nappies Zelda now made her wear to save her taking her for an afternoon trip to the toilet.

'Yes,' said Tara gently, moving closer. 'I've set up a business in town. I do healing work. Houses and humans.'

Sarah snorted through her nose. 'It's a little too late for that,' she said bitterly. She lifted a frail bony hand and waved it weakly about. 'I don't have any money to pay you.'

'I'm not asking for money, Mrs Jones. I just want to make amends for the past. Elsie and me. Running away like that. I was very young. I was very desperate. I'm sorry.'

The mention of her daughter's name froze Sarah Jones. 'Eleanor? You've heard from her?'

'No. We lost touch. After … after she left the cattle station for her music career.'

Sarah's gaze slid to the blankets hiding her bony feet in their large corduroy crimson slippers. She was always so cold. 'She sent an apology, via her manager, for her own father's funeral.' Sarah's mouth twisted in anger and upset.

'Does she know you're sick?'

One shrug of an angled shoulder. 'Sick? Dying you mean. They've given me two months more.'

Tara held her tongue. She wanted to say: 'Our bodies are all dying from our birthday until our deathday, but our energy lives on forever, that's why it's important to live life from a place of love, free of judgement of self and others, always.' But Tara knew that Sarah Jones was not up for hearing that. She was one of the most closed-off women energetically she'd ever met and she knew Elsie, unless something drastic in life woke her up, would take on the same patterning as her mother.

Tara knew it was basic physics that lighter-frequency energies could push denser ones upwards to match them, so a bright, sparky person could shift the weight of a negative one. All Tara had to do was watch the meeting between herself and Mrs Jones from outside and stay in touch with her inner spirit, and Sarah Jones would come along with her. Like a sour, aloof horse, she would eventually choose to amble over. Sarah Jones shifted her body and her inner self a little. She began to talk.

'We ... I ... send her emails from time to time. Sometimes her manager's people answer, sometimes they don't. Always she's working. Same as Simon. He married a girl from Victoria. Moved down there to her farm. Wants nothing of us and this place. Both my children always too busy.' Her eyes slid to a trashy magazine that lay beneath a dirty plate. The headlines loomed large. *EJ to Tour Down Under. Lock Up Your Husbands!* Zelda had got a lot of enjoyment out of bringing that one, just to watch her face. A face that gave away nothing, which was amusing in itself to Zelda, who was not brave enough to face her own misery.

'Maybe you'd have more luck?' It was the first time Tara heard Sarah's voice soften a bit. Like she was reaching for some help. 'It would be nice if she'd come to my funeral.'

'I'll try,' Tara said. 'In the meantime, you're not dead yet. With respect, you've still got living to do, Mrs Jones. Let's freshen up this room. It won't take me a sec.'

'Please, no.'

'It's no trouble. Then I'll leave you be. But I'll be back tomorrow. And the next day. And the next. We'll soon have you feeling better, even enjoying moments.'

Tara moved over to the stereo, pulled out a cheerful-looking jazz CD and put it on. She drew open the curtains and, for the first time in weeks, sunlight poured into the tired old Grassmore dining room.

'Just pretend I'm Elsie come home, Mrs Jones. Let's just pretend.'

As sunlight glowed over her on the bed, tears slid down the bones of Sarah Jones's face and she understood, finally, that there really were kind people in the world. It was time for her to stop being so unkind to people, and especially to herself.

Fifty-three

Tara stood right at the spot where the councillor-mayor's bodily fluids had seeped from out of him after his death. 'First things first. This carpet has *got* to go.'

Tammie gave a wry smile.

'But it's brand new,' Christine said. She didn't remember Tara from school days, having been quite a few years ahead, but she'd heard from the town gossips that at one stage Tara was a total heffalump and her mum was worse and had to be lifted by a crane out of the house when she had carked it. That story didn't seem to match the woman she saw now, their new councillor and emergency acting mayor. Tara was definitely curvy but not fat. She was extremely attractive and also so dynamic.

'Oh, come on, Christine,' Tammie said with a snigger. 'We all tried to talk Kelvin out of the carpet. Remember? You called it pornstar purple and got down to dry-hump it.'

Tara looked at both women with amusement. They clearly weren't standing on ceremony in front of the mayor's replacement. Tara admired them for it.

'That was just for a bit of a laugh,' Tammie explained to Tara.

Everyone knew Christine had taunted poor Kelvin Jones for years, right from when she'd come as a work experience girl in Year Ten from Culvert High. In fact everyone had egged her on, because they all found him so pompous and liked to see his face turn red. All that dimpled flesh and wobbling breast that she had on show for him at the photocopier, at the printer, at the pot plants dribbling water suggestively out of the spout of the thin nozzle of the watering can with her hip cocked up.

'If only he'd had a sense of humour,' Christine sighed.

Tara grinned at Christine. 'We're going to need a good sense of humour if we're to hatch the plans we now have for Culvert.'

'What plans are those?' Christine asked, trying to catch up to Tara, who was now walking purposefully throughout the offices. Christine began taking notes as fast as she could, as Tara fired off dozens of suggestions to alter things. She knew change was a scary thing for the women in her company so when she was done with her office audit, she spun around. She could see the women were summing her up. They wore suspicious expressions as if trying to suss out what the catch would be with her. She understood why they were hesitant with her. After working with so many overwhelmed women in her feng shui business, Tara knew so many had lost their inner compass of self-love in this crazy modern, highly masculine world. Adding to that was the media that only undermined their trust in other women. Tara resolved to set them straight.

She could also feel the whole town reeling from the shock that Tara had been elected to council and as acting mayor. Everyone of course liked her. She was like a dose of sunshine after a long winter. She was like a shower of rain after the dusty dry. But a *woman*? As *mayor*? Leading *council*? In *Culvert*? Even the ones who voted for her had felt a shiver. It was as if the gods had orchestrated the entire thing, taking hold of people's senses at the emergency ballot box. Which of course they had. Tara knew that. She was tapped into the power of the greater good and was doing this for love not money, so she knew all would be well.

'Just for the record, my friends,' she said, beaming a smile at them, 'I'm not just here to redecorate. I'm here to help breathe life into this little town. If you hadn't noticed, Culvert is dying like a fly.'

She buzzed a bit and waved her hands around like zizzing wings for comic effect. The council girls chuckled.

'We're at the mercy of all those big-wig bureaucrats, those fuel giants, the agricultural monopolies, right through from the supermarkets to the seed companies: it's crushing us. I need you, my dear girls, to open your minds. Open your hearts and see this town as the place to be. *The* centre of the world. *The* hub of change. It's up to us to be the inspiration for the town. For the sake of not only ourselves, but our children and our children's children. What this council and the people of Culvert can achieve is beyond the scope of human thought at this time! And we are the people to do it. You and me, united. And do you know where it starts?'

Tammie and Christine shook their heads, though Tara's passion and the fire in her words had done their work.

'It all starts with the Culvert Waste-Treatment Plant.'

Tammie's and Christine's energy flopped for a moment and they groaned within.

'The shit pits?' Christine asked, frowning. So much for a new broom. Here was another mayor banging on about the same thing as the last one.

Tara grabbed Christine's arms and swung her about. 'Yes! But I'm not talking about the former mayor's expensive obsessions. I'm talking about poo power, delivered back to the people.'

Christine looked at Tammie, wondering how she should act from this point. She'd never been in the company of someone like Tara before, a woman who seemed to not follow any of the rules on how a woman should be.

'Poo power? For the people?' Tammie looked sceptical.

'Yes. Imagine if all of Culvert's council vehicles ran on the town sewage. We could get to work for a quarter of the cost. The Smiths have the technology to adapt your engine and fuel your vehicles with pure natural methane gas. Cheaper trips between here and Rington to see ... what's his name? Your fella? Gavin?'

Christine nodded.

Tammie narrowed her eyes. 'You're not talking about using the Smiths' shed to make poo fuel? Are you? Surely not?'

Tara stood before Tammie and pulled in all her positive energy. 'It's not poo by the time it becomes fuel. It's a similar gas to the ancient stuff they pipe out of the earth to put in cars and cook with now.'

'Really?' Tammie asked.

Tara nodded. 'What's the one thing your husband grizzles about the most on the farm, Tammie?'

'Not enough fellatio.'

Tammie whacked Christine on the arm. 'Shut up.'

'Besides that,' Tara said, smirking.

'The fuel bills.' Tammie grimaced, folding her arms.

'Imagine this. Your husband, what's his name? Phillip? Phillip ordering a tanker of cheap methane gas delivered to the farm tanks. Then imagine the tractor the Smiths have modified for him, which he can fuel at a quarter of the cost. Not only that: using the machinery the Smiths have developed, he directly sows grain into the soils when the perennial grasses are dormant. No need for going round the paddock several times for ploughing or harrowing. That's another huge saving. Plus you are building up your soils by putting the tractor exhaust back in using another innovative invention we've just heard of. And making the farm more efficient. And any organic waste the farm produces can be sent back to the biofuel plant so you earn carbon-recycling credits. The farm works more efficiently, benefiting the environment *and* your bank account. You could cut your hours here on council, job-share with another mum and spend more time with your children.'

Tammie began to picture it, then hauled on the brakes. 'That sounds awfully like a money-making venture for the Smiths.'

Tara paused patiently. 'No. The Smiths are one of the few families around not motivated by money. They want to form a co-operative so all the townspeople are shareholders. They want to supply jobs to the Culvert families so we stop this drain of talent to the cities. And they want to share the technology with the next rural town and the next so those big cities stop draining us. So we quite literally get our power back.'

Tammie's mind ticked over. She could see it working. She was so tired of her husband going broke on the farm and having to work long hours herself to pay bills, mostly for chemicals, superphosphate and diesel. She'd never understood the need for sprays near her precious kids. Nor could she understand the way the land seemed so dry on her husband's farm when the Smiths' seemed so green and abundant. She sure would like to see Phillip achieve the same thing. She had been steeling herself for the day her kids left school and, like the other children, were forced to leave for Rington or the cities where work could be found. She liked this mad idea. 'Yes, it could work, but …'

Tara felt it coming.

'… I'm not sure Phillip'd be convinced.'

'There is one way I know you could convince him … or at least encourage him,' Christine said suggestively, jamming her tongue into her cheek.

Tara laughed. Tammie rolled her eyes.

'You forget, Tammie, you are a powerhouse yourself. We all are if we let ourselves be,' Tara said. 'I bet you'd do anything to better the place for your kids. Well, this is it. This is the answer for us all. We are the innovators. How many governments are looking for answers to carbon emissions? Which brings me to my next project to submit to council. The site of the old abattoir house. Now you know there is a new garden in place. That's a framework for what I want to build there.'

'So it's not Jamie Durie?' Christine asked, not bothering to hide her disappointment.

'No. I have a business plan to submit to council and I intend to start building next year. It'll be the Cleanagain Energy Hub. It's where the engineers will roll the Smiths' and global company

Cleanagain's technology out to the community and then hopefully the rest of regional Australia. It'll be a centre that can advise other councils how to convert their waste plants and refuse sites and how to establish a fuel co-operative.

'It'll be a gathering space too. As you know, the gardens are ready to go. We'll need the school on board — the kids can attend an education program there, growing fruit and vegetables. I've even got plans with the Smiths to run a pilot program inventing gym equipment that will generate power for the novelty of it, but also to teach them awareness. Imagine the Culvert kids coming in each day, gardening, growing food, getting on the running machines and exercise bikes to create power that goes back into the grid. Then feed 'em a good brekky or lunch and then back they go to school. Crazy idea? I think not. Culvert will be the first town with zero obesity in its kids and zero power costs for the facility. We'll need the Elderly Care Centre to organise daily trips to the gardens too, so the old folks can walk a dog or keep some chooks, plus eat the food grown there, even jump on the gym equipment if they feel inclined. So what do you say?'

The women shook their heads, smiles lighting their faces.

'It sounds amazing. You are amazing,' Tammie said.

'It's not me being amazing. It's ...' How could Tara explain her way of living? Living in the moment. Living with gratitude. Living with the universal forces of love, kindness and joy within every cell of her body. 'It's all of us who are amazing. This town has the potential to be amazing. You just need to *believe* it.' She linked arms with both women.

'We need the numbers stacked so we get the vote through. Tell me, girls, who on council will need a little TLC to get this new vision for Culvert over the line? Which crusty old bastards will block this? We need to hatch a plan.'

The women, refreshed by Tara's vigour and inspired by her mere presence, practically waltzed with her into the tea room. After they'd made their drinks they moved into the delicious sunshine that was blasting the back of the offices.

Sitting on a chair they'd taken from the mayor's old chambers, Tara sipped on her tea.

'Make a note please, Christine, to knock this wall out and replace it with glass. We need some light in the building. It's been angled all the wrong way. And some outdoor beanbags and chairs. We can have our team sessions out here some days. And for godsakes get onto one of the Nicholson boys to drag out that awful chainsaw sculpture from the front. The energetics of a dead tree stump are not a good thing. Trust me. We'll replace it with a fountain and an ornamental food garden. Get onto Sylvia. She can supply us with what we need.'

'But the budget —' Tammie began.

'Ah … the budget,' said Tara, wondering where she started with them on the notion of universal abundance. 'We'll cross that bridge.' Even she had no idea where the money would come from. Once they were teamed with Cleanagain in the States, though, she knew in her heart there would be plenty. As she went to sip her tea, the phone clipped to Christine's pocket rang.

'Culvert Council, Christine speaking.' Her brow furrowed. 'Uh-huh. Uh-huh. Oh. Oh,' she said softly.

She hung up and looked at Tara and Tammie.

'That was Zelda. Sarah Jones died early this morning.'

Fifty-four

Elsie Jones pressed her back to the emergency-exit door in the laneway, asking the security guard to give her a moment of privacy. He swept his palm over a sideways slick of black hair, his round face expressing disapproval, but when he got a spoiled-diva glare from Elsie, he grimaced a smile and slipped inside the building.

Suddenly alone, Elsie felt the relief of solitude and near silence, save for the scream of the Nashville night-city on the other side of the building. She barely believed she'd made it through her gig. She was in a severe drug come-down and Jacinta was still fuming at her after finding her that morning, coked out in her hotel room like that. She wanted to hide herself away in the shadows, even for just one smoke. Sweat evaporated from her sheened skin, and the thrumming energy of the audience encore applause still zinged in her system. Elsie was just lighting her cigarette when from the shadows a tubby young girl on the bud of womanhood approached in the backstreet gloom. She was wearing an EJ world-tour T-shirt, black cowgirl hat and silver skinny jeans, too tight for her hammy legs. Elsie slumped her shoulders a little and slid her gaze to the pavement, avoiding eye contact. A dreaded member of the general public. How on earth had she got back here? She drew deeply on her cigarette as the girl began sprouting at her.

'One day I'm going to be famous,' she said breathlessly.

Elsie took another glance at her and knew that she wouldn't.

'And a great singer,' the girl said. 'Just like you.'

It was all EJ could do to stop herself rolling her eyes. She'd heard it that many times from that many girls over the past few years. They always seemed to track her down, no matter how much security Jacinta put in their way, just to be near 'someone famous'. She was about to go back inside, but there was something about the girl that held Elsie at the backstage door in the cold, still wearing her barely-there denim shorts and bustier singing costume. In that bitter Nashville night air something drew her towards the toxic energy of the girl. Like attracts like, Elsie thought, and so she lingered.

'You're a legend, EJ,' the girl said, digging into her pockets. 'You have changed my life. I wanted to thank you.'

She opened her hand; two tablets lay on her palm. Two innocent little orbs of chemicals.

'There's this guy at school,' the girl said, her dark over-made-up eyes looking tentatively at her. 'He gave me somethin' for us. He likes you and I think he might like me. He said if I got to meet ya … he'd … y'know. He and I are friends with you on Facebook.'

EJ looked blankly at her. You and several million others.

The girl soldiered on. 'Wanna share? I heard you do this stuff.' She pulled out a can of beer from the pocket of her coat and fizzed the top, washing one of the tabs down.

Elsie stubbed out her cigarette under the toe of her boot, her mouth twitching from side to side. How would the girl have heard she was using? Just little pick-me-ups now and then. To cope. How did the public find out this shit?

As she looked at the tablets, Elsie felt the world slow a little. She held herself still, her in-breath held captive in the cage of her ribs. After all the miles, all the men, all the loneliness, she realised she had no one else to spend tonight with. Elsie no longer cared about the plastic-fantastic A-list parties, about the scheduled world-tour mega concerts, about managing hair and wardrobe for her cowgirl-chic-but-a-dash-of-boho image. About the avalanche of media requests for photo shoots, even if many were for dodgy male get-your-rocks-off publications. About endless mundane radio and television promotions for the new album.

She sighed tiredly and reached out, taking the other tablet from the girl, and dry-swallowed it. She turned and knocked on the security door to get back in, but no one answered. She kicked the door with her thousand-dollar boots and swore.

Suddenly the girl's face turned pale and she was dropping into her arms, her lips turning blue in a nightmare scene. Taking the full weight of the kid's body, EJ screamed for help and kicked again at the door. Her own tears fell on the girl's foundation-laden cheeks — it was as if the girl hadn't wanted the world to touch her skin or see her clearly.

'God!' Elsie begged as she slumped to the ground with her. 'Don't die.' With horror she felt the girl's heavy body ease into unconsciousness … then she felt death take her last breath. She wished she had asked her name. She wished she had never seen her. She wished she was somewhere else, on her own, safe. She wished she didn't feel so sick. She tried to stand, pushing the body away, the world swirling. The fire door at last opened and she tumbled inside and then collapsed.

In that weightless space devoid of physical and emotional pain Elsie drifted. She reached out her fingertips, but she had none. She was just all air and rainbow light and lightness. She smiled, but when she did, it wasn't her body that did, it was her entire being. She could feel her father and mother with her. Her mother? She smiled, though, and said hello to them. But the words did not come as words. They came as intention. As a communicated feeling.

'Elsie,' she heard her parents' voices.

'What are you doing here?' she asked — if she had left her body, they must have left theirs. She realised, weirdly, there was no sadness in this knowing. Just a feeling of completeness and peace.

'You must go back,' Sarah Jones said.

But Elsie didn't want to go back. She wanted to drift.

'You must go and use your gifts,' her father said. 'You must go and help others. You've got to heal from this and inspire others to heal. To heal the earth.'

She smiled again at her mum and dad and turned her focus back to earth, which seemed so distant now. Elsie could only just see her body; it was now in a hospital bed. Jacinta was there, talking aggressively at a nurse, arguing they didn't have to wait for parental consent to turn off the machine as both her parents were dead. Jacinta was saying she was custodian of her affairs now.

Elsie wanted to tell Jacinta that she was causing great pain to herself and to others and that it wasn't necessary. Maybe she should go back? But back to all that heaviness and loneliness? She heard Sarah again, though not as an instrument of judgement and control. This time she saw her mother as the pure essence of love.

'If you decide to return, your life will change, I promise you,' her mother said, again not in words but in some kind of energetic force. 'You won't be lonely. You will be whole and happy. It's another chance.' Then Kelvin's presence was there again too. A feeling. One that was also pure love.

'I didn't learn in my lifetime. But you will. You will be healthy, loved and fulfilled if you go back, I assure you. So return. There are people there, calling you.' Her father's words drifted as unspoken intentions. 'It's up to you to go back and reshape the family. Heal the land. Help others heal from their addictions. It's your job to sing life into the soil. To sing love into the world. Go back.'

Elsie felt the intense love of her mother and father radiating outwards and yet enveloping her. She seemed to absorb the love that was her parents and with it, she hovered again, looking back at her body. She felt more love flow. This time it wasn't from the spirit plane. It came from the direction of earth. Then she saw them.

The Smiths at their table in Culvert: Gwinnie was crying over the news on the television that Elsie was about to be taken off life support; Elvis was comforting her. Elsie saw them and felt an intense rush of love and a complete knowledge that they needed her. They were her tribe. Her earth people. She must go to them.

But where was Zac? She looked, but he was nowhere to be seen. She searched for him from her bird's-eye view of the world. Scanning Culvert, looking for the boy she now knew she loved more than anyone. Instead she found Tara with Amos beside her, sitting in the middle of the most beautiful garden, praying under the moonlight in utter stillness. She heard Tara's voice begging her back. Saying she needed her. There was earth work to be done. The red-haired girl, surrounded by an emerald-green aura, was calling her home.

'Tara,' Elsie said.

Fifty-five

Tara entered the Dolls' House from the front door, calling out a greeting to Mr Queen, who she felt still floated in the ethers. His cats, a ginger tabby and a black fluffy moggy, trotted to greet her, their bells tinkling. She picked each up and cuddled them, but despite their presence, the house felt empty. Then she realised it wasn't the house that was empty, but her. She felt tired. And alone. Drained. Since finding out about Sarah Jones's death, Elsie had been constantly on her mind. Where was she? Had she been told? Would her brother, Simon, call her? Tonight she vowed to Google her music company to track her down. It was time.

Sadly, she thought of Amos, but even after months of being back in Culvert and Zac's constant stirrings and blatant encouragement, they hadn't made any progress. He was always lovely to her, but had never made a single move. Maybe she ought to be happy with their friendship? Although her body ached for him, there had never seemed the right moment for even a kiss or a touch. Perhaps, after the passing of years and what had happened on Goldsborough, there now only room for friendship? Anyway, the momentum of their energy project was so great they now seemed more like business colleagues. All of them had been working around the clock on the Cleanagain co-op and the town rejuvenation project. There was a buzz between the two of them, but she noted there was a buzz between all of them, such was the speed and excitement with which everything was unfolding. But if it was time to find Elsie, it was also time for her to truly find Amos.

She heard a knock on the door behind her. Already she knew it was Amos. She could *feel* him. She had conjured him up. It was time. A smile travelled to her face before she'd even turned to open the door.

'You heard about Elsie's mum?'

Tara nodded. He delivered her a quick sympathy hug.

A moment later he was in her kitchen, standing barefoot in blue jeans and wearing a *MythBusters* T-shirt that had tiny holes in it from welding flashes. The T-shirt revealed just how muscled this inventor farm boy's arms were as he reached down to pat Mr Queen's cats, who were brushing themselves against his legs happily.

'So?' he began, leaning back against the bench. 'How was your day in at council?'

'Oh, the staff are fantastic. Now. And funny too.' Tara busied herself with the kettle. She felt flustered. Almost annoyed. She knew she could manifest almost anything. The man standing here in her kitchen was proof of that. So *now* what?

'And?'

'And they are still all really excited about what we're proposing. We've got it past the old sticks in the mud, but it should all unfold officially by the next meeting, which is at the end of the month. Christine and Tammie are onto it.'

'Yes!' Amos said, pumping the air. 'Oh, Tara! You good, good thing! You are *amazing*!'

'Not amazing enough though, apparently,' Tara said, her green eyes darting to him. She turned to him and leaned against the opposite bench as the kettle gurgled and clicked off behind her.

'What do you mean?'

Tara set down the cup she was holding. She shrugged. She too was in bare feet and a floral dress of autumn colours clung to her curvaceous body in all the right places.

'What's the matter?'

'You, Amos. You're the matter.'

'Me?' He put a hand to his chest, his eyes wide.

'You don't seem to … I don't know … be interested.'

'Interested? In what?'

'In me!'

'In you? Oh, Tara, of course I am! You are fascinating. I could write an entire thesis …'

'No, not like that. I mean … like, you know. *That.*'

'Oh. Like *that*!' He looked at her, then laughed.

'Please don't laugh.'

'I'm not.'

'Not what?'

'Laughing. Don't you get it? I *am* interested in you like that. More than you could ever know. But I was looking for the *cues.*'

'The cues?'

'Yes. The cues women give to say they are interested in a man. I'm that hopeless, as you know, with women. When you came back, I decided to research the topic so I didn't muck things up. And so far I have calculated zero cues from you.'

'But I'm not a *woman*,' Tara said. Then she laughed.

'You're not?' Amusement glimmered in Amos's eyes too.

'I mean I'm not like *other* women. At all. I'm a … a … person.'

'Yes. I can see that.'

'I mean my upbringing, which I pretty much did myself, and my philosophies.' Tara struggled for words. 'They mean I sit outside the social boundaries of most women. If that makes sense.'

Amos nodded. 'Perfect sense.'

Tara inclined her head and frowned. 'So what are the cues you're looking for?'

'Oh, it's silly really,' he said. 'Things like flicking hair, reaching out to touch me on the arm, watching my mouth.'

'Are you for real? Watching your mouth? What? In case you dribble?'

Amos pulled a face. 'The research is inaccurate and it's all based on non-scientific observations. Dreadful. I Googled it for ages, each site more hopeless and contrived than the last.'

'Oh for godsakes, Amos, that's ridiculous.'

'I know.'

There was a pause between them.

'Do you want a cue?'

Amos nodded. 'Yes. Desperately.'

Tara looked at him, a twinkle in her eye. She flicked her hair back over her shoulder as if she was in a shampoo commercial. She walked over and swiped her palm down his shoulder, then delivered a mockingly smouldering gaze at his mouth.

'Oh, Tara, stop taking the piss out of me. Just shut up and kiss me.'

'OK,' she said.

A smile danced across his handsome face before they came together in an embrace, their hearts forming one rhythm, their breath melding as one. Amos looked into her eyes, leaning closer and closer.

'I've waited for so long,' he almost whispered.

'Same,' Tara said. 'You and your stupid cues.'

'You and your non-woman mannerisms.'

And then they kissed. At last. The kiss ignited a thousand years of longing. A thousand stars twinkling in a night sky. It was the kiss that set the future blazing on ahead with possibility. They felt their souls meld and fuse. In that moment the world came into balance. Gently, slowly at first, then with the gathering frenzy of a flooding river, Amos began to peel her clothing away.

Later that night, in Tara's big cloud-like bed upstairs, they slept together naked, limbs entwined, breath in sync, bodies satisfied and hearts filled to overflowing with love. But as the moon slid on by outside, Tara woke with a jolt and sat up.

'Elsie,' she breathed.

She stared at the night sky outside the big arched window, then turned to shake Amos awake. 'I know now,' she said, her eyes turning back to the glow of the moon.

'What?' Amos mumbled sleepily, propping himself up on one elbow. 'What do you know?'

'It's not going to work. The universe won't allow it to work unless we are *all* back in balance.'

'Tara, what are you talking about? Are you sleep-talking?'

Over time Amos would become used to Tara's night-time revelations and spoken epiphanies. He would come to see them as normal, making notes on what she said during her episodes of insight, but on this, his first night with her, she was scaring him a little. He reached out and pulled her face around to his. Her eyes were wide, as if she was awake but not seeing him. She smiled gently.

'Zac. Elsie. Their hearts are broken. Their spirits shattered. Elsie is leaving us.'

'What?'

'Yes,' Tara said as if in a half-waking daze. 'But no.' She shook her head and her rich hair tumbled over her shoulders, her skin lit softly by a white moon that now only just peeked from behind a cloud. 'Their soul journey is one. Their scarring is one. I have to go get her. I have to go find her and bring her back.'

'To America? But you've only just ...'

Before he finished his sentence, Tara was already getting up, dragging on her dressing gown.

'What are you doing?'

'Going to the garden.'

'To do what?'

At the doorway Tara glanced back at him, her eyes glinting with some kind of ancient wisdom and knowing. 'To call her back.'

Getting up, Amos went to the large attic window. Below in the moonlight he watched Tara tread barefoot across the grass, settling herself cross-legged under a woollen blanket in the middle of one of the curving lawns. Should he go to her? Was she really leaving again? Now they were together, he didn't want to lose her. Not for a second. Especially not to the United States on some mad mission to find Elsie, who was in a world of her own now. He gathered up a quilt from the bed and went out to join her. He knew he wanted her home, forever.

Zac couldn't sleep. He turned over. Maybe the cricket was on the radio, broadcast from India. If it was, he could do a little more on the Nicholsons' Jeep and listen to the match. What was the point of lying in bed with his mind revving? He got up, dragged on his jeans and padded out to the workshop. He flicked on the light and sleepily began to set parts out on the bench. He turned the radio on at the wall.

'Bloody oath, Dad,' Zac grumbled. His father always moved it off the ABC onto the Rington local station just so he could get his country-music fix. Zac twirled the dial, and suddenly through the static he could hear her voice. He recognised it instantly and turned up the song. She was singing about learning to love the skin you're living in. In his years on Haiti, Zac had managed to avoid most of the celebrity news on Elsie and had hardly even heard much of her music. Now, though, here she was. She was amazing.

Zac touched his finger to the scar on his face and thought of the frail, fearful girl so terrified of her own inner beauty and of being rejected because of a mole on her face. She was here, in his memory. So real. She was the first girl he had kissed. She was the first girl he had loved and he knew, at this moment, she would be the last. All those signs Tara banged on about. This was one. This was the moment when he would go to her and track her down so that he no longer lived in this limbo. Even if she rejected him and even if he was thrown out on his arse by her minders, at least he would've finished the chapter he'd been stuck on for years and years.

The song faded out and the announcer's voice came on. 'Ah, EJ, EJ, EJ, such a great, great song.' The announcer sighed. 'Already sadly a classic, folks. It was her last song. It's been confirmed by her management that our Aussie country-rock goddess EJ is in a coma in a Nashville hospital after a drug overdose. The doctors are waiting for her family to approve turning off the life-support system. Guess the little angel from Culvert, New South Wales, has left the building.' Elvis's 'Love Me Tender' sighed from the speakers and Zac's vision began to blur.

Fifty-six

'Tara? I'm not Tara? Who's Tara? It's *me*, Jacinta.'

Elsie looked about the room for faces of people she loved. People she had seen from that other realm. Zac. Tara. Amos. Gwinnie. Elvis. But all she could see now was the tight gaunt face of Jacinta.

'Oh. Not Tara. Hello,' Elsie said simply, still feeling the all-enveloping love of the other side.

'Hello,' Jacinta said, scrunching her face, confused. 'Shall I get a doctor? Are you sure you're alive? I mean awake?' She was not good at this sort of thing.

Elsie didn't seem to hear her.

'That rehab ranch Charity went to,' Elsie said with a rasping throat.

Jacinta tilted her head. WTF? The girl had been *dead*, for Chrissakes! Dead! They had turned off the machines, taken out the tubes. She'd just lain there. Like Sleeping fucking Beauty, Jacinta thought. And here she was awake, *talking* to her. It was lucky she hadn't yet sent out EJ's obituary to the media, nor called in her team to get the music artists lined up for the tribute album.

'The ranch? Yes?' Jacinta said, her mind spinning.

'Did it sort her out?'

'What?' Jacinta asked, trying to drag her mind back to EJ. The *alive* EJ.

'Rehab? Did it work for her?'

'Kinda. Some things about Charity will never be sorted, but if you're asking if it got her off the pills and booze, yes. It did.'

Elsie fingered the waffle hospital coverlet. 'Could you book me in, please?'

Jacinta cast her a smile that held no warmth. 'Sure.'

'Oh, and Jacinta.'

'Yes, honey?'

'Could you also tear up my contract, please? Sell everything, take your cut. I'm done.'

Jacinta stiffened, then turned on her motherly persona. 'Now, my dear,' she soothed, 'I know you've had a close call, but there's no need to give up your —'

Elsie held up her hand. She had an aura of calm about her. She could still feel the light of life swirling around her body.

'Crikey.' She giggled, looking wondrously at her upheld hand. 'I've woken up feeling like I'm Jesus!' While Jacinta looked at her as if she was totally crazy, Elsie held her wonder. It is true, she thought incredulously, we are all pieces of God! *We are all the children of God.* Except now she knew God wasn't a man with a long beard in a white gown, nor was he any of the other gods humans had conceived outside themselves. And he certainly wasn't a He with a capital H. God was simple Love with a capital L. It filled her now.

'Are you high still?' Jacinta asked, her gold chains jangling on her wrist as she tossed her hair back over her Yves Saint Laurent scarf-covered shoulder.

'I have never been more high in my life, nor more grounded,' Elsie said. 'Jacinta, I'm grateful for what you've done. When I was dead, because believe you me, I know I was dead, I saw how you are a part of my journey and my learning. I saw you kick me and swear at me when I was unconscious. I saw you arguing to turn off the life-support machines. You even called me a bitch. And I know you were withholding the news about my father and my mother dying until you'd seen me do the gig.'

Jacinta opened her mouth, her expression one of horror, though Elsie's voice was light. It held no trace of accusation or blame.

'Let me finish,' Elsie said. 'But out there, wherever I was, I saw clearly that I need to take a new direction. I was told. Shown. And that direction is away from what I'm doing now. Away from you.'

Jacinta's mouth screwed from side to side. She could tell Elsie was somehow utterly altered. There would be no bribing or coercing her now. Plus there was one question screaming in her mind: *How?* How did Elsie know these things? She had been clinically *dead*!

'I get it,' Jacinta said, trying to pull some composure in around herself. 'But you'll have to pay me my dues. For the rest of your life in royalties. It's all there in black and white.'

'I'm sure it is, Jacinta. But now I know it's not all about money and fame. Now I know I truly have a gift to give the world and I'm going to do it.'

Elsie extended her arms up. She felt weak physically, but inside her there was a torrent of strength like the base of a waterfall catching rainbows and casting beams of extraordinary light.

'Now give me a goodbye hug,' Elsie said.

Like a plastic doll that only bent in the middle, Jacinta hinged herself over and put her arms around Elsie.

She felt like steel under Elsie's hands.

'I'm sorry,' Elsie said. 'And I'm grateful for the lessons. And I hope you can heal yourself from this point on.'

'What are you?' Jacinta asked, pulling away. 'Some kinda born-again Christian?'

Elsie smiled. 'No. I haven't got a religious bone in my body. But what I do know now is I am lucky enough to have my body, my breath and above all my spirit and soul back where they should be, and I intend to use that to help this planet and others heal. And at the same time have a damn good time. A good time that doesn't need drugs or drink or money.'

'Good luck with that,' Jacinta said coldly. She was already backing out of the room, reaching for her phone, getting her lawyers all lined up to cash in as much as she could on EJ's legacy. Her next call would be to arrange sponsorship of another talent show, this time in South America. There would be some young talented beauties down there she could manufacture for the world. Elsie watched her go.

Poor Jacinta, Elsie thought, sending her on her way with love.

Ten days later a blue sky brushstroked with fine white clouds greeted Elsie as she stepped out on the large porch, cup of tea in hand. It was her seventh morning at the Tennessee recovery ranch on the outskirts of Nashville and she could barely contemplate just how beautiful it was here. She sat down on the swing seat that was nestled in a sunny corner of the eggshell-blue homestead. Trump, the Border Collie, tiptoed up the steps to her, wagging his tail and smiling a doggie smile at her, asking for a pat. Elsie looked out over the swathe of green pastures that rolled down towards a river and took a moment to remember Marbles.

She sipped on her tea and smiled. It was so peaceful. *She* was so peaceful. From the moment Elsie dumped her bag on the bed at the ranch that first day, she knew she'd never touch drugs again. She had been altered completely by her near-death experience and could now see her addiction. It was an addiction to her utterly negative view of herself, and to being a vulnerable little girl with an emotionally unavailable father and mother. The drugs weren't important to her now. Nor was the lifestyle she'd been living. It was time to follow her true calling, which was still of course music, but also the land. And it was time to forgive herself. To forgive her parents. To seek forgiveness from those she'd hurt. To buy some time to work out how she was going to achieve the next chapter of her life.

The recurring dreams came in varying forms, but all pointed her towards Grassmore: images of her mum and dad, standing in long wavering pastures. She hugged her knees to her chest, resting her feet on the floral cushion of the porch swing. She thought of the girl who'd given her that last pill, who had died in her arms. Jacinta might have kept that part of the awful night out of the papers, but Elsie would never forget it. Her lawyers were figuring out a way to get money to the girl's family anonymously — not because it would heal their grief, but because Elsie wanted less money in her own life, and it was one of the many ways she would achieve that.

She thought of all the young people on drugs: the ones who died; the ones who only ever half lived. The people shut away in houses addicted to food or television, like Tara's mum. People addicted to gambling and pornography and the suffering of others, like Dwaine. She thought of the poverty in the world. The slums. The misery. The child abuse. It was such a dark world if you looked at it that way, but Elsie had been shown another way. It was now up to her to live that way, thereby inspiring others. She thought of the magical moment she'd had yesterday evening on Cherokee, a thickset sage-like ranch horse, as she rode silently through the river, following Lee, the ranch rehab mentor. She had looked up and seen an eagle soaring above her. As the sun touched her face, Elsie vowed to live well, gratefully, mindfully and in love. Love with a capital L.

Now on the porch, with the day unfolding, she could see how her music *had* given something to people — she had just been too hard on herself to see it. And now she knew she had so much more to give. She looked skywards and felt excitement on her skin. She was ready to truly embrace her gifts and make a positive difference to the planet.

As she thought this, Lee stepped out on the porch, his big cowboy hat jammed down on his head.

'Better pack your bag,' he said through the veil of his downturned moustache.

'But I'm not out till next week.'

Lee shrugged. 'Had a phone call from a lady says you're goin' today.'

'If it's Jacinta, tell her I'm not going. No way. I'm never going back.'

Lee stooped to stroke the ear of the dog. 'Suit yourself. You leave when you're ready. Don't let no one push you round no more.' He extended the toe of his boot and pushed the swing so it rocked Elsie back and forth. He winked at her. 'You're doin' good, soldier. Group Therapy's on at eight. See you in there.'

He stepped off the porch and Trump fell in behind his Cuban heels, on their way to the barn. As he did, Elsie remembered her mother's advice on the other side that she would be healed. She looked at the drift of clouds shaped like wisped wings of angels and knew from her inner core her life was healed.

Elsie was just sitting down to lunch with the rehab group in the communal kitchen, enjoying the banter and companionship, when she heard a car drive to the front of the house, music trailing in with it. It was her own voice. Her hit song of ten years earlier.

'*I got nothin' to do, all day to do it. Could save the world, I'll get round to it,*' the old Elsie sang from the car radio.

She set down her knife and fork and pushed back her chair. She looked out the window over the sink.

In the drive, in a rust-bucket blue convertible with a silver grinning grill, sat two tall men in cowboy hats and a pretty woman with long wavy flame-red-brown hair. All of them were smiling. They cut the engine. The song cut off too, and Elsie watched in amazement as the men got out, each a mirror of the other. Broad shoulders, tapered waists. Country boys, from the looks of their clothes. Different clothes but identical bodies. One of them lifted his hat and revealed what looked like scarring on one side of his face. Zac! Elsie let out a cry, tears emerging suddenly in her eyes. She flew from the kitchen, tore down the steps and ran to them, squealing with joy.

'Whaaaaat?!' she screamed, leaping first at Tara and swirling her around in a hug. Then she swamped both boys in a wild embrace. 'What? What? *Whaaaaat?!*' They all held hands in a circle and jumped up and down together like primary-school kids, grinning at each other like idiots. Laughing hysterically. On the porch, Lee and the rehab guests watched with amusement and emotion.

'What are you doing here?' she half screamed.

Tara looked at Elsie with a big smile. 'Picking you up. Taking you on a road trip. It's time to get the Poo Crew back together.'

Fifty-seven

From where Elsie sat in the back of the convertible, she could see Amos's and Tara's heads jammed into cowboy hats as Amos drove. The wind was whipping the ends of Tara's hair; under her hat she also wore an Audrey Hepburn-esque scarf and big sunnies. She turned around and smiled at Elsie. Elsie smiled back. Then they screamed at each other and laughed, the sound captured by the fast-moving air, their voices hurled out to the desert that whizzed by.

'Where are we going again?' Elsie asked.

Zac leaned closer so she could hear him over the roar of the old Yank-tank. 'Arizona. Travelling time twenty-four hours and forty-one minutes. Give or take.'

'I know we're going to Arizona. But *where* in Arizona?'

'Friends of mine,' Zac said. 'Met them in India, then later in Haiti.'

'It's all part of our global Poo Crew plan!' Tara shouted back over her shoulder.

Elsie looked out to the landscape rushing past, to the flat red desert rising up to what looked like Road Runner rocks. She couldn't believe it. Back in the boot were her bag and her acoustic guitar from all those years ago at the cleanskin camp, she was wearing her leather cuff again on her wrist, and she was travelling with Zac, Tara and Amos. When she thought about it, they were people she now hardly knew. And yet now she could feel she knew them better than anyone. It felt so right. She had come home to her family. Her tribe.

As the miles passed, she sat and listened to all of their plans. The changes they were preparing in Culvert. Amos and Elvis's breakthrough in the technology of converting gas to efficient energy in engines teamed with putting the exhaust fumes of tractors back into the soil. Of Zac's amazing travels that took him to countries like India, Borneo and Thailand and eventually Port-au-Prince in Haiti, all working on biomethane energy systems for Cleanagain. The more they talked, the more excited Elsie became. This was what she'd been shown on the other side. This was her dharma. She smiled up to the sky and sent up her thanks to the larger part of herself that she now knew existed in spirit form on some other plane than this earthly realm.

A few miles on, they had talked so much they had barely registered how far they had travelled.

'We're almost outta gas,' Amos said in a comical American drawl.

'Are you referring to the car or global supplies?' Zac chipped in.

'Ha, ha,' Amos said. Tara turned and rolled her eyes at Elsie, smiling, both girls elated they were back with the bantering twins.

They were not far out of a tiny New Mexico town so soon they were pulling into a gas station, Amos getting out, opening the passenger door for Tara and taking her by the hand. He drew her to him, delivering a passionate series of kisses to her lips, his arm scooped lovingly around her waist. Elsie watched, warmed by the sight, and smiled. Next thing, Zac was opening her door and taking her hand, only he was shy and reserved. He didn't kiss her. He did smile kindly at her. Elsie thanked him and stood watching him unhitch the pump and begin to fill the car. He was beyond gorgeous, she concluded. She was in love. Still. After all this time. This time she *knew*.

As the boys busied themselves with checking the oil and tyres on the old rig, Tara looped her arm in Elsie's, leading her to a shady spot under some trees. She sat Elsie down at a picnic table, arms still looped.

'You OK?' Tara asked. 'Being kidnapped for a random road trip like this?' The roadhouse was the kind of place you expected tumble weed to blow through to the sound of eerie whistling. Elsie squinted to look at the horizon.

'I am. The last trip I took was a bigger headspin than this,' Elsie said. If there was one person in the world she could debrief with about her otherworldly near-death experience, it was Tara. In fact, Elsie now felt totally on the same wavelength as her old friend. And she knew Tara knew it. She was looking at her now, her beautiful heart-shaped face, hair tumbling around it, eyes burning green with life and vibrancy.

'I got to know your mum a bit,' Tara said gently, 'when she was dying.' Elsie flicked her a grateful glance. 'She said, "Tell Elsie I'm sorry." Sorry that she wasn't the best mother.'

'She said that?'

'Yes,' Tara said.

'She called me Elsie?'

'Yup.' Tears came to Elsie's eyes as Tara sat in silence, remembering the last time she'd visited Sarah Jones at Grassmore. It had been a dull, still sort of day. Tara put on Elsie's CD so it gently played in the background. The unconscious Sarah Jones must have been absorbing the beautiful voice of her daughter as a soft smile arrived on her gaunt face and stayed there. Tara had placed a white summer rose on Sarah Jones's sunken chest and stroked her hair gently, promising her she would find her daughter and bring her home.

'It's time to let go, Mrs Jones.' Then she had watched the swirl of a rainbow outside the window that fell through a tiny break in the misty clouds. Tara had washed Sarah's high paper-skin forehead lovingly with warm lavender water and painted her lips with her favourite colour lipstick and arranged her hair before she had left. The next morning she had died.

Tara rested her head on Elsie's shoulder. 'Your mum was so proud of you when she left, you know?'

Elsie looked at Tara earnestly and nodded, emotion twisting her sad face. 'I know. Now I know. She wasn't the best mother, but she sure gave me the best lessons.' They smiled at each other, knowing there were so many miles and minutes and moments to catch up on together, but for now Tara had a more pressing issue.

Tara looked over to the twins and turned back to grin at Elsie. 'What do you think? Pretty gorgeous, eh?'

'They are divine.'

'They are.'

'You and Amos?' Elsie asked.

'Wonderful,' Tara said. 'Best mates on all levels.'

Elsie thought of the awful time she'd created for them all back in their long-lost youth. It was as if she was thinking about a totally different person. She couldn't believe she had been that type of person. Now she knew she had changed, utterly. It was time to make amends.

'Can you forgive me?' she asked.

Tara turned to her, her generous big green eyes filled with emotion, and said, 'Yes, of course. We were young and dumb. Both of us were.'

Elsie let out a sigh of relief. 'Thank you.'

'I know you never actually slept with him. He told me that and I believe him.'

Elsie nodded. 'It's true. He stopped. Said he loved you too much. I was jealous of that, but I cared about you too so I knew he was right. Plus at that time, I couldn't even love myself, let alone commit to anyone, so poor Zac got the raw deal.'

Tara waved it away. 'It's the past. You've got a whole new future headed your way if you want it.' She elbowed Elsie and nodded towards Zac, who was walking over with some drink bottles in his hands.

Elsie looked at Tara and giggled, hugging her friend again. 'Thank you,' she whispered, 'for coming to get me.'

'My pleasure,' Tara said, knowing Elsie meant not just coming for her on the ranch, but also when she was lost in the drift. 'You're my friend for more than this lifetime. I think we both know that by now.'

That night they stayed, travel weary but happy, at a roadside motel in Albuquerque. They had all stood at the check-in desk, Elsie a little behind the rest, wearing Tara's sunglasses and scarf as a rather pathetic and predictable celebrity disguise. It felt weird walking into a place like that after years of plush five-star hotels. She was overjoyed to see the fraying carpet, the Dr Pepper vending machine on the blink and the plastic pot plant with cigarette holes burned through several of its leaves.

'This place OK?' whispered Tara.

'Perfect,' Elsie whispered back. 'Love it.'

The comforting-as-apple-pie woman at the desk didn't seem to notice EJ the famous singer, and Elsie was glad. She didn't want the bubble to burst. She had enjoyed the day of just being her 'new self'.

'Two doubles, please,' Amos said.

Zac glanced nervously in Elsie's direction.

'Certainly,' said the woman. 'Licence plate number here and names here.' She placed the two room registration forms in front of them and made Xs on the pages.

Tara turned and winked at Elsie.

'You don't want two singles?' Zac whispered to Elsie. 'Or a separate room?'

Elsie bit her lip and quickly looked at Zac. She dragged her glasses down. 'The double will do nicely, thanks.'

Zac smiled back and took up the pen in his large strong hands. Amos waggled his eyebrows up and down, and Tara slapped him on the arm. 'Juvenile,' she said.

On the form Elsie felt a buzz when she saw Zac write *Zac and Elsie Smith* before picking up the key.

'Smith. Jones,' he said as they made their way out to the car. 'It's all interchangeable. I was protecting your identity.'

'Were you now?' Elsie grinned. 'So it wasn't a marriage proposal?'

'It certainly was not,' Zac said. 'I've got to woo you and win you back first.'

As Elsie reached for her bag from the boot of the car, the fading sunlight caught her smile. 'I have a feeling it's me who needs to win you back.'

Zac took her bag from her and carried it over to the door of the motel. 'You already have,' he said.

They looked to the number 69 on the door, then their eyes caught each other with amusement: teenagers again.

Tara, passing them with Amos, pointed to the door. 'It's a sign,' she said, grinning as she inserted the key in the next room and turned it with a smile and a wink. 'Definitely a sign.'

Inside, though, when Zac drew Elsie down on the bed, there was no unveiling of clothes. No moans of passion. The couple just simply held each other and let the tears of relief spill from their eyes. They cried for the wasted years. The miscommunication. Their youthful ignorance. The lonely times. And the long journey back to each other. When they were done crying, Zac and Elsie looked into each other's eyes, each stroking the other's hair. Elsie trailed her fingers over Zac's scars; Zac drifted his finger over the mark above her lip.

'I love you,' he said.

'I love you too,' Elsie replied. They kissed gently and soon both of them were sound asleep, wrapped in each other's arms, their spirits soaring together at last beyond the twinkling blanket of night sky.

The next morning the four set off and by sunset were having dinner in Phoenix's St Francis restaurant beside the glowing heat of a wood-fired oven. They were chowing down on spicy pork chile verde and prime steak with Mike Schnelle, the Arizona CEO of global energy company Cleanagain. The fit middle-aged Mike had greeted Zac like a long-lost son, embracing him and slapping him on his back.

'Zac, my boy!' he said before turning to the others. 'How y'all doing?' He wore a crisp blue shirt, jeans and pointed cowboy boots and had an air of worldly confidence about him.

Zac had introduced them and explained to Elsie that he had met Mike during his stint with the company in India, then had kept in touch, working for Mike in Haiti.

Mike sipped a glass of water as he beamed at Zac. 'I can spot brilliance when I see it. Zac has more than just mental intelligence, but practicality also. I said to Zac, if he ever made it home to Australia and thought he could make methane production work there for Cleanagain, to give me a call. Next thing, I'm Skyping this lovely lady Tara, who I believe is now a councillor and mayor. And we are about to enter a joint venture with you guys in a little town called Culvert.' He chinked his glass with Tara. 'But it gets better! Next thing, Zac is on the phone to me, saying he's in America on his way to me to consolidate the deal. But not only that: he's bringing a friend. Who turns out to be you! *The* EJ, who he casually mentions happened to be his childhood sweetheart.'

Zac looked to Elsie, embarrassed, but Elsie smiled at him, overjoyed he thought of her that way.

'I'm sorry, but I'm no longer *the* EJ,' she said candidly. 'I'm simple Elsie, Zac's childhood sweetheart.'

Mike looked quizzically at her.

'I'm having a break from big-time music and I've joined this crew. So here I am, at your service, Mr Schnelle. I've got so much I want to bring to the project, and it's not just finances I'm thinking of. I want to bolster the agricultural component of the project and focus my energies on carbon sequestration of the gas we're selling into soils by educating people about the importance of grasslands.'

She laced her fingers into Zac's under the table and Mike Schnelle raised his eyebrows in approval. To have a big-name celebrity backing a project like this was one thing, but to have someone like EJ who actually knew her stuff on carbon plant function and soils could move them forwards in leaps and bounds with the media. The twins and Tara could tell he was impressed. And so were they. They had all wondered if Elsie's life journey would have left her too scarred, too far removed from them, but now they could see she was absolutely on the same path.

'I understand,' Mike said. 'You're not the only celeb we have on board to help move this technology on when the time is right. If we are to get the concept mainstream, we're going to need backing from people like you. There're some huge mindset mountains to move, but I can see Australians coming with us on this. With the energy and environmental crisis we face, it's too crucial for them not to. It's great to have you on the team, Elsie Jones.'

As the dessert order came round, Tara and Elsie pondered over cheesecake in a jar or chocolate stout cake, leaning their heads together as they viewed the menu. Elsie was glowing from within, pulling the occasional 'can you believe it?' face at Tara. They listened as Zac and Mike explained that Cleanagain had signed a deal with the Pima County Council in Arizona to build a large-scale biogas upgrading facility, and tomorrow they would all have a tour of it to give them ideas for the Culvert venture. Mike explained it would produce biomethane for sale.

'It'll not only offset the use of conventional fossil fuel,' Mike said, 'but it will also eliminate having to flare the waste product, which is common practice here in Arizona.'

'Flare?' Elsie asked.

'All organic waste, including human waste, creates a gas at the refuse sites and currently we simply light it and burn it into the atmosphere. Not good for the ozone layer or company profits.'

Zac smiled at Elsie as Amos chipped in. 'Wastewater-treatment plants across the world are searching for innovative ways to convert their tips and sewage plants into resource recovery centres ... exactly like we were aiming for at home. Except we missed a little with Culvert Council.'

'We may have missed the first time,' Tara corrected, 'but we're not going to miss again. Cleanagain are going to do what they are already doing in Europe, North America and Asia. They already have sixteen hundred anaerobic digestion plants worldwide and they not only use human waste in those systems, but also agricultural waste and organic waste from households and industry. Culvert is the ideal place to start small. Then we can roll it out from there.'

'Genius,' Elsie said. 'Or should I say geniuses. All of you.'

Later, Mike Schnelle put his napkin down, waved for the bill, then stood. 'You young'uns stay on. I wanna get back to tuck my kids into bed. I'll see you at the plant at, let's say, nine-thirty for our tour.'

They could see he was delighted he now had a partnership with Zac's vibrant group of young Australians. They were smart and enthusiastic and they would make it happen, he knew it. Mike said his goodbyes, then Zac, Amos, Tara and Elsie sat around the table, absorbing how amazing it was that they were all here together. At last. The restaurant was emptying, the red-bricked, gold-lit room was becoming quieter. The candles flickered, burning low. The waiters were beginning to set up for the following evening with fresh tablecloths, glasses and cutlery.

'I think we've done it,' Tara said.

Amos reached for her hand. 'I do believe we have. At least we're on our way.'

Zac picked up his glass, reaching his other hand for Elsie's. 'To the Poo Crew,' he said, raising his glass. The rest of them joined hands.

'To the Poo Crew!' they all echoed.

Fifty-eight

Twelve months later

Elsie looked out across the Grassmore paddocks and set her hands on her hips. Like the land around her, her body and spirit were strong and healthy now. Her mind was clear and her heart was bursting with love, gratitude and passion — not just for the beautiful man treading electric fence posts into long grasses for the next grazing move, but for the way her life was now rich with purpose. She was back, grounded on the increasingly healthy soil of Grassmore. The sun was skimming up over the plains. It would be a perfect day under one of her and Zac's blue-jean skies, she thought. Just right for the big launch later this morning of the new Culvert Co-operative and the partnership with Mike Schnelle's Cleanagain Energy.

She pulled on her work gloves and ran out the top strand of white fence tape behind Zac, feeling the life of the land beneath her work boots as the spool turned with a clickety-clack. Beside her, their new red-and-tan working dog, Excuses, who they'd bought as a started dog, raised himself from the nest he'd made in the dewy grasses and fell in behind her heels. At eighteen months he was still really a pup, but these easy-move stock jobs were good for him. No excuses for not bringing him along. His name was a fun reminder to Elsie and Zac to make no excuses about anything in life now. No matter what.

Behind the gate the sheep had mobbed themselves and were bleating in chorus. The animals now knew that when Zac and Elsie appeared, fresh grassland aplenty would open up for them. Zac smiled at her, a bundle of tread-ins under his arms, the sun catching the smooth and in places puckered skin of his burns, though Elsie only saw the life in his eyes and his beautiful soul radiating out to her.

When she'd first arrived back in Australia with the others, still a little weak and feeble of body, she was nevertheless strong in her certainty that her life would change. She was now fearless in creating an entirely new life from the place of her altered perspective.

The financial wealth she continued to amass through her celebrity, her music and the sale of her near-death story was now all channelled into establishing the Culvert Co-operative with the community, headed by the Smiths and Tara. Music royalties along with Cleanagain had funded the rolling out of a pilot natural-gas project in Culvert at the old sewage plant. Her songs paid for the conversion of commercial tractors that ran on the renewable fuel that was generated at the state-of-the-art sewage and gas-generation plant. The council too had chipped in, using money they had at last received from the state government. Elsie, Zac, Tara, Amos, Gwinnie and Elvis, on a roll, had even established a line of direct-seeding implements. The seeders were not only reinvigorating Grassmore by direct-drill cropping, backed by time-controlled grazing, but were now being quietly sold to other interested farmers at really good prices. Better than the machinery giants who cornered the market with big marketing budgets and blokey advertising.

The Grassmore ballroom had been revamped and Elsie had already hosted her first round of inspiring agricultural and new-science speakers, ones she had idolised at school and ones she studied now. She was beside herself with excitement that Allan Savory was due to visit the next month. Rangeland scientist Dr Fred Provenza, who she met so briefly all those years ago on Goldsborough, was booked for the following year. Even Gordon Fairweather was scheduled to come and speak about training young people into agriculture, along with Joel Salatin from Polyface Farms. The list went on and on as more speakers said yes to the beautiful musician who had gone bush and 'found herself'. She even had a concert planned, like a big B&S ball, but one with top-name artists and a message to impart about soils and sewage, getting high on living in the now, and not escaping with drugs. The email list grew and grew as more and more people wanted to travel to Culvert to discover for themselves what was going on out there.

Also, for Elsie, beneath the big western-plains sky the weighty crush of fame had dissipated. No one paid celebrity much heed at the IGA or the pub or in the shearing shed, so it wasn't long before Elsie was simply one of the locals again. She knew fame was merely an illusion created by people who craved it. People like Jacinta.

As she attached an insulator to the fence and turned to get the solar battery, she thanked the stars that a clever lawyer friend of Elvis's had found a loophole in Jacinta's dodgy Tamworth-to-Nashville competition contracts, so now, creatively and financially, Elsie was as free as a bird.

She looked again to the grasses beneath her feet and scuffed at them to reveal the damp soil below. That's real, she thought. That was what she needed. The soil. Glancing up at Zac, she felt a melody drift to her and words forming above her like rain clouds lit by sunlight. She knew she would soon be ready to create music again. How could she not with a man like Zac by her side?

This time, though, the music would be under her own label, and she would sing and perform for the greater good, and foster young musicians' careers too. She wouldn't be using her gift of music any more just to feed her frail and hungry-for-love ego created by a lonely childhood. She looked back to the homestead a small distance away, sending love from her heart to her brother, Simon, who had all but given her his share of Grassmore, so happy was he to have his own life and a second chance at family down in Victoria. She now knew her parents, though flawed, had loved her, and with that knowledge she could let all else go. She, along with her friends, had a planet to save. And today, they would take their vision to the world. It was all so exciting it felt like a dream. But as Elsie had learned from dying then coming back, life was a dream. Death had felt more real to her. It meant that she could play out her days on earth with no fear or guilt. No fear of death or failure or judgement. She now knew at the end of the line there was only love.

'It's almost time to change,' Elsie said as Zac opened the gate and watched the sheep happily amble into the newly set-up grazing strip.

'I think we both already have changed,' Zac said, laughing.

She took off her gloves and slipped her hand into Zac's, smiling up at him. 'Ha, ha. Very funny. But you're not wrong!' He bent to kiss her and she felt butterflies of joy flutter in her heart.

'Let's do it,' he said. 'Let's show the world.'

Fifty-nine

The morning sun turned the new Culvert sewage-plant walls to gold — though after this particular day, it was no longer going to be called a sewage plant. It would officially become the Culvert Cleanagain Energy Co-op Resource Centre. The first of the journalists were arriving, enjoying fresh coffees out of Sylvia's Silverspoon Café marquee and stuffing themselves on CWA cream-filled sponges available for a gold-coin donation. More helicopters hovered, setting down in one of the Smiths' paddocks; this one was slashed, and now had a windsock and a runway marked with white rubber tyres. Elsie and Zac stood beside Tara and Amos, watching it all unfolding, knowing by the end of the day their positive news stories would be taken back to the cities where the rest of Australia and the world was about to be inspired.

The Smiths, along with Mike Schnelle and his Cleanagain colleagues, welcomed the visiting politicians and media at the new gas-generation plant. The visitors looked around in wonder. Tara had fenged the design at the plant, so instead of a cold industrial feel, the place had high windows, colourful pipes and artfully designed steel. The visitors craned their necks, looking up and around the series of tanks and sheds. It was a pretty poo plant, Tara decided as she followed their gaze. It was also a miracle. Yet another miracle of the Poo Prophecy. A miracle they had made.

'The way it works is simple,' Amos said, looking like a country-boy model in a royal-blue drill shirt and new jeans. 'The waste comes in from the sewage ponds into the reaction tanks, which during winter can be solar warmed if required to keep all that lovely bacterial digestion going. The fermentation process begins, producing biogas. The gas crosses a column of water and comes to rest at the top of a tank. It can then be piped to cylinders or tankers, depending on where it is required.

'A population as small as Culvert is somewhat limited by outputs, which is why we're topping up the system with organic waste from the tip next door and any agricultural bio-waste from local industry. We are then diverting all our fuel back to farmers for food production, but if our population grows, which it will given the new industry here, we have the capacity to transfer the technology to cars driven by the general public. But that's not all. The filtered water that comes out of the biodigester is rich in nutrients and can support many forms of plant and animal life. We are in the process of setting up a fishery and free-range poultry enterprise in the next phase of construction. This will create more jobs and more local food produced without chemicals.' Amos paused and roamed his intense brown eyes over the crowd. 'Imagine the potential of harvesting the volumes of such resources in cities like Hong Kong, Beijing, London or New York.' The good-looking young man, who spoke with such clarity and intelligence, began to open the minds of his audience. 'Imagine.'

And as Elsie and Tara stood beside him smiling at them all, the media pack's sometimes judgemental hearts melted too. What gorgeous girls. Everyone knew Elsie's story, and to see her looking so happy, natural and down to earth in her Dogger boots, jeans and checked cowgirl shirt gave them heart. She was so *accessible*. And so *normal*. And this project sounded so exciting, for everyone.

Not long after the plant tour, Elsie and Tara had loaded the two Culvert school buses with the visiting journalists and politicians, and the twins had driven them the short distance to the Cleanagain Energy Community Hub, the site of Tara's old abattoir house. Entering via a wide gate, visitors were treated to a garden of Eden, where fruit and vegetables grew in boxes amid trellised flowers and ornamental trees. School children from Culvert Primary greeted the guests with a gift of a strawberry or a snow pea served on napkins saying *Today's food, Tomorrow's fuel*. Under the verandah of the modest but beautiful building made from recycled wood and steel, the elderly from the nursing home offered the visitors cups of tea. It was Tara who this time led the group inside the foyer, where Elvis presented a computerised display of the engines he and the twins had designed.

'Using this cheap plentiful resource and this new technology, we are now able to convert methane gas to power in agricultural machinery with significantly more efficiency than that of traditional engines powered by fossil fuel. At Culvert, our plan is to roll out the fuel to the farmers first. If we can enhance our food sector, and the people in it who produce our food, then we stabilise our entire society. Our next step will be altering the local cropping and grazing systems, using animals, grass and manure to sequester the gas emissions back into the soil as carbon. It's a win, win, win.'

The media took grabs of Elvis on their television cameras as he talked about the monetary savings, the environmental savings and also the social answers to rural decline and pollution around the world. He even answered their questions about his earlier 'unapproved' experiments and the explosion, but this time the interviewers' slant was aimed at a hero-to-a-cause everyone had finally come to support. Then they turned their cameras to Mike Schnelle, who outlined the business models the company were operating with success in other countries.

With smooth efficiency as the media were ushered again to the bus bound for Grassmore, the team from council, headed by Tammie and Christine, answered further questions, with Christine enjoying the attention she was getting from some of the men in her extremely low-cut top.

At the homestead Amos pointed out a home-sewage prototype unit that was piped to the kitchen and fuelled the gas stove. On the farm he showed them the gas bowser that fuelled the tractors. Just inside the gate of the northern paddock, the cameras panned over the modified tractor and its pristine engine and exhaust system that put emissions back into the soil. Then Amos hauled his handsome farm-boy body up into the cab and fired the tractor up, giving it a few impressive revs and turns, showing the visitors how to direct-drill oats into the pastures to kick-start the microbes in the soil back to health. Elsie then pointed out the happy sheep, all of whom were camped now in long grasses, chewing and relaxed, doing their bit for the environment by manuring onto pasture and using their hooves to compress leaf litter back into the soil for the microbes to feed on.

'It's a perfect closed cycle,' Elsie said. 'It's Mother Nature's way.'

By twelve-thirty pm, the journalists and politicians were corralled onto the Grassmore lawn, where Gwinnie had prepared a spread of sandwiches on a large trestle table under one of the giant sleepy trees. There the farm dogs, Arnie and Excuses, charmed them with their dog-smiles.

Zac clapped his hands together. 'Folks, we're almost done for the day. The buses will be leaving in ten minutes to take you back to the gas plant, where your varying modes of transport await you. But for now, the toilets are that way …' He indicated the outdoor toilet on the side verandah of the house. 'We would appreciate your generous donation to our Culvert power supply. Thank you so very much.'

He grinned as he said it and a rumble of amusement passed through the crowd; they began to clap. The applause spread and soon Zac reached for Elsie's hand, Elsie reached for Tara's, Tara reached for Amos's, and Gwinnie and Elvis reached for each other and then Zac's hand.

'We did it,' Tara said, tears in her eyes.

'We did it,' Elvis said, and they folded into one another in a big hug as the applause continued, rising up and rippling out into the clear wide plains sky.

Sixty

That evening in the Grassmore kitchen Tara laid out trays of hot home-cooked pizza on the giant old wooden table, while Elsie set out glasses and a big jug of water with fresh lemon and mint floating in it. Sunlight spilled into the house from recently added bi-fold doors, outside which Gwinnie and Elvis stood embracing each other on the deck overlooking the garden. They were smiling softly and Elvis was humming to Gwinnie, rocking her in a slow dance.

Elsie glanced at them. 'Do you reckon we'll all still be in love like that in years to come?' she asked, pausing wistfully.

Tara smiled. 'That'll be entirely up to each individual us. You get what you give. You reap what you sow.'

'You poo what you eat. You use what you poo.'

Tara laughed and whacked Elsie on the arm. 'Don't be silly.'

'Me? Silly? You're the silly one. You're the poo-joke queen.' They smiled at each other, the distance of miles and years falling away.

'Ah, poo jokes. It's so good to be home,' Elsie said.

'It sure is.' They hugged each other and each felt the love that transcended time and place. They knew that this was it. This was how their life would be from now on, with Zac and Amos. They had at last found each other again.

'Speaking of poo,' Elsie said, smiling warmly at Tara, 'where are those boys?'

And on cue, in they tramped, holding aloft two bottles of champagne.

'Don't get too excited,' Amos said. 'It's non-alcoholic from the IGA.'

'The pub's run out of the real stuff,' Zac added. 'It seems everyone in Culvert is celebrating tonight.'

'Suits me just fine,' Elsie said with a grin, gathering up some glasses from the kitchen dresser.

'C'mon,' Amos said, grabbing Tara's hand and dragging her over to the lounge. 'It must be news time! Let's see what the world will see!'

'Mum! Dad! Get in here, or get a room,' called Zac out the doors. 'News time.'

As they flicked on the first of the nightly news programs and Tara popped the cork off the faux-champagne, they were met with the image of Chunky Nicholson standing outside the Energy Co-op, grinning at the cameras like a nitwit.

'Coming up in the program,' said the newsreader with the dome of blonde hair, 'a good news, or should I say good poos, story on the future of renewable energy.'

'What they've done here is amazing,' Chunky said emphatically. 'It's the best thing coulda happened to this town. Who'da thought our Culvert crap could change the world?' The footage flicked to Miss Beechcroft standing with her flushed cheeks, blinking behind her glasses outside the Cleanagain Energy Community Hub, while children from the primary school waved madly at the camera in the background.

'I taught Elsie Jones to play guitar in the first place, so it's nice to know my teaching skills have come to some good purpose. It's EJ's music funds and the know-how of the Smiths and Mayor Tara that have got this whole thing rolling. They're a credit to the town.'

Then Nathanial Rogerson flashed up, his red hair and freckled face full screen. 'It's amazing it's people's shit we're talking about here. Hard to believe. Why didn't we use our crap ponds like this before now? Later I'll be doin' my bit to help supply a bit of fuel.' He grinned a crooked grin, then bit down into a pie and roughly began to chew like a dog.

Zac shook his head. 'That's all so base and basic. What are they thinking putting him on, saying that?'

'Shush shush,' Elsie said. 'It's just a way of getting the viewers in. I know how they package these things for the everyday Joe Blow … Just you wait.'

And there on the screen came Tara outside the council offices, her hair falling over her shoulders prettily, her green eyes clear. She wore a tailored white shirt, jeans and green flats. She looked utterly serene, even though they all knew she had faced a wall of journalists armed with all kinds of recording devices. A close-up shot showed just how naturally beautiful she was; and her voice was steady, her speech intelligent, and just right.

'It's a technology for the people, so it's not up for sale to any corporation. This technology, teamed with the agricultural practices showcased here, sets a platform for the recovery of all regional Australia. Over time it will mean better food supplies for everyone and carbon sequestered into soils via grasslands. It means no more corporate coal and gas mining and destruction of land, waterways and the atmosphere.'

The footage flicked to Grassmore, of the paddocks and the tractor, the healthy sheep. A journalist voiceover said, 'For every five rural councils that sign up for the project, the Culvert Co-operative has pledged to donate a sewage-conversion plant to a developing-nation rural village. The wait list is long — already ten regional councils have expressed interest in working with Culvert, with the larger neighbouring town of Rington starting their conversion as soon as next week.'

The media package flicked back to Tara talking. 'It's big companies, big bucks and power-hungry people who have caused constipation in both agriculture and the energy industries — pardon my pun. But no more ... It's time for the people to take back their power. And if it's poo power, then so be it. Culvert is the capital of the world in terms of change.'

Gathered around the television, they all let out a cheer and again hugged one another. Tara flicked to three more channels, all with lengthy good news reports. It was out. The project was under way. Change was happening and the Smiths and Tara and Elsie couldn't be happier.

Tara's mobile buzzed with the arrival of a text. It was Christine at the council offices manning the phones. 'Wow!' Tara said as she read it. 'Christine reckons the phones are ringing off the hooks, there're emails coming in from around the world, and the Facebook page for Cleanagain Energy has gone nuts. She also said the media team has it in hand, so we are to enjoy our night off. Apparently, we deserve it.'

With the realisation that they had achieved what they had set out to do, there was a lull in their energy and all six of them drifted out to watch the sun go down.

'What a day,' Elsie said.

'It hasn't ended quite yet,' Zac said.

Elsie looked at him enquiringly. Amos and Tara looked at each other and smiled while Elvis and Gwinnie reached for each other's hands.

'What?' Elsie asked, through narrowed eyes. 'What are you lot up to?'

'There's one last thing.'

Zac took her by the hand and led her out across the new back deck and onto the lawn. The rest of them followed a short distance away. Beside the house were two trees they'd planted in her mother's and father's memories. At first Elsie thought he was leading her to that; instead Zac led her out the garden gate towards the old stables. There, standing in the house paddock, draped in gilded light from the dipping sun, was a white pony. An old, old pony, judging by the deep sway of his back and the high rise of his wither.

'Jasper?' whispered Elsie in disbelief.

Zac nodded.

'How? How did you ...?' Her voice trailed off, weighted by too much emotion.

'I tracked him down. Pony club is a small pond. He's yours again, Else. He's ours. For our kids to sit on and pat.'

Zac opened the gate for her and let her pass.

Tears welled in her eyes as softly, gently Elsie walked towards Jasper. The little pony nodded his head and flicked his ears forwards, taking a few steps towards her. He whickered gently. She put her arms around the pony's neck and buried her face in his long old-man shaggy white coat. She breathed in his baked-bread smell. She felt joy overtake her.

She turned to see Zac, Amos, Tara, Gwinnie and Elvis looking at her with love.

'Thank you, thank you, *thank you*,' she said.

Later that night, the universe did what the universe does. It created the strangest, most synergistic moment under the stars, as it does every minute of every day.

As the twins lay with the loves of their lives, the stars aligned once again, and there, in the black space of creation, the lives of more twins were sparked. Within Tara manifested two girls, within Elsie two boys, and though they didn't know it for a matter of weeks, the girls would find the biggest adventure of their lives was about to begin and their greatest lessons were yet to come. In nine months' time, motherhood would be waiting for them to take them on an even wilder, more challenging and joyful journey. Right there in Culvert.

Acknowledgements

Thank yous can be more challenging to write than an actual entire novel because so many beautiful people help me along this path. From the beautiful 'standing people' — the trees that my books are printed on — right to the end point in the process, my readers. I write for you. To inspire you. To challenge you. To show you we can all create 'planet yum' — a gently farmed earth we are proud of and healthy in! So thank YOU for picking up this book! I hope it brings you joy and your own inner road map of where you want to travel in life! I am utterly grateful you help me realise my dreams!

Thanks also to Kevin McCloud from *Grand Designs*. His TV program gave me the inspiration to write an entire subplot on the potential of human methane as an energy source! Thanks to all of the people who are actually exploring this path for humanity. (I just explored it in my head! It's fictional so apologies to the actual scientists and mechanical engineers who create this technology for real! Bring it on!)

Thanks to my HarperCollins writing tribe — legends, each and every one of you. There are so many of you to name individually we would need more trees to print it. You are so aligned with my vision. I am grateful every day for your dedication to beautiful books and to helping me on my journey.

Thanks to my RT Company tribe — my literary agent Margaret Connolly and Heidi Latham and your family members who support you when you are supporting me!

Thanks to my money tribe — Michael, Kellie and the ACCRU team. You've helped a sole parent sleep at night!

Thanks to my Loane family tribe — Ian (Eee-arn-eee), Doug (Daggis), Jamie (Jay-babe-alay), Claire (Wooksamunga). Without your crazy inventions in Pop Collin's farm shed, I never would've dreamed up Zac and Amos. Thanks also to all my blood clan who inspire me to meet the challenges and shatter the old paradigms with my passion and self-belief.

Thanks to my friendship tribe, who keep it all going for me — particularly Jackie and Luella, but you know who the rest of you are! All the child minders, sick poodle sitters, shuttle runners to school, text buddies, wood deliverers, floor moppers, ute fixers, inner-spirit coaches, the list goes on and on. I am blessed I am so loved …

Thanks to my Tassie Wolfe pack — the Wolfe Brothers band and Steve White Management … you rock. Thanks particularly to Nick Wolfe for writing a song with me for this novel and sharing your cleanskin shots! And to the rest of the guys, thanks for entertaining my wildest dreams of having our song mixed in Nashville! Cool.

To my creature-teachers, my animal tribe. You teach me each and every day to live in the moment, to be grateful for small things, to doze in the sunshine or leap happily about, depending on the mood that takes you.

And lastly and not leastly, thanks to my heart tribe — my kids, Rosie and Charlie. You inspire me each and every day. You give me the gift of seeing life again with fresh, vibrant, grateful eyes and I love you more than words can express!

Poo Power to the People!

Love,

Rachael ⚡

र.

Further Reading

You may like to Google these good people and their work ...

People power
Author Gregg Braden
It's Cool to be Conscious by Harry O'Brien
Dying to be Me by Anita Moorjani
Women Who Run with the Wolves by Clarissa Pinkola Estés
Diamond Feng Shui by Marie Diamond with Paul R Scheele
You Can Heal Your Life by Louise Hay
Excuses Begone! by Dr Wayne Dyer

Primary production power
The Biggest Estate on Earth by Bill Gammage
Joel Salatin, Polyface Farms
Colin Seis, Stipa Native Grasses Association

Poo power
Haiti biofuel projects
Arizona biofuel projects
Kevin McCloud's Man Made Home
Exhaust Fertiliser System, www.exhaustfertiliser.com.au

Many other sources were used for *Cleanskin Cowgirls*, but the network above will give you a big slice of inspiration.

Download a Free Song

Music makes my day and keeps me not just surviving but thriving, so it was only a matter of time until a country song escaped from the pages of my book for you to enjoy!

How did that happen? A few years back the Wolfe Brothers band and I kept bumping into each other at local shows and ute-judging comps. Because creative country artists with international careers are thin on the ground in our island state of Tasmania, it was natural that we would gravitate together and then hook up to blend words and music from our grassroots perspectives.

Nick is a natural poet and a top blokey kinda guy, so it was a joy to pen this song with him and then to weave it through the narrative of my novel. His homemade moonshine helped in the process too!

Not long afterwards, life began imitating art, and like my character Elsie, the Wolfe Brothers were soon headed to Nashville, where this song was mixed! A dream come true for me. I hope it inspires you to have a 'lazy day' despite the demands of daily life. Enjoy 'Nothin' to Do, All Day to Do It' …

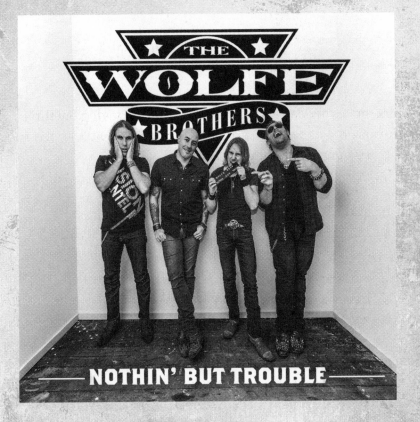
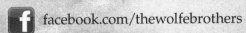

INCLUDES
BONUS
SHORT STORY!

Rachael
Treasure
The Farmer's Wife

'True grit, wit and warmth' *Australian Women's Weekly*

After ten years being married to larrikin Charlie Lewis and living on her beloved property, Waters Meeting, Rebecca is confronted by a wife's biggest fear, a mother's worst nightmare and a farm business that's struggling to stay afloat. Can Rebecca draw on the inner strength and optimism she had as a young jillaroo to save the things she loves the most? Or will this down-to-earth cowgirl finally accept that happily ever after isn't always what it's cracked up to be?

This uplifting, insightful and enchanting tale reveals the truth behind the Cinderella stories and shows that the rollercoaster of life doesn't stop just because you say 'I do'.

Look out for ...

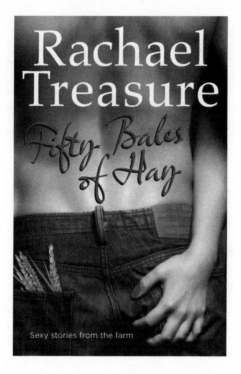

Come have a roll in the hay with Australia's leading rural fiction author, Rachael Treasure, in her romping, rollicking first-ever collection of Agricultural Erotica. Guaranteed to get your tractor revving, *Fifty Bales of Hay* is an honest and imaginative exploration of everyday men and women getting down and dirty on the land.

From the dairy shed to the Royal Agricultural Show pavilion, Treasure's cheeky satirical humour and wicked imagination offer up a dozen fun-filled, and sometimes poignant, tales of dust and lust.

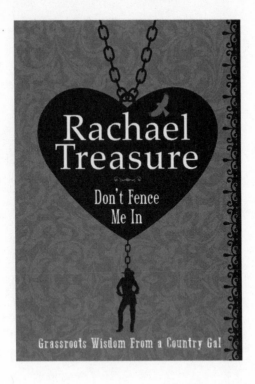
In this gorgeous collection of feel-good stories, sayings and life lessons, bestselling author Rachael Treasure serves up a dose of pure positivity with a side of down-to-earth cowgirl wisdom.

Accompanied by charming illustrations, these bite-sized morsels of home-grown advice will brighten the most monotonous day and leave you feeling inspired and at peace with the world.

Get in touch with nature, appreciate the little things, be mindful of your surroundings and learn to love your life with this witty anthology of optimistic thinking.